Also by Linda Broday

Bachelors of Battle Creek
Texas Mail Order Bride
Twice a Texas Bride
Forever His Texas Bride

Men of Legend
To Love a Texas Ranger
The Heart of a Texas Cowboy
To Marry a Texas Outlaw

Texas Heroes
Knight on the Texas Plains
The Cowboy Who Came Calling
To Catch a Texas Star

Outlaw Mail Order Brides
The Outlaw's Mail Order Bride
Saving the Mail Order Bride
The Mail Order Bride's Secret
Once Upon a Mail Order Bride

Lone Star Legends
A Cowboy of Legend

Texas Redemption
Christmas in a Cowboy's Arms anthology
Longing for a Cowboy Christmas anthology

a
COWBOY
CHRISTMAS
LEGEND

LINDA
BRODAY

sourcebooks
casablanca

Dear Reader,

I'm a sucker for Christmas stories and the affirming message of hope and love they bring. They've always been a bit magical to me, and often these stories center around miracles.

Sam Legend, son of famed Sam Sr., certainly needs one. He's taken a bit of a wrong turn and separated himself from friends and family. But then who's to ever say that a misstep is a wrong turn? Often those take us to exactly the place we need to be, as Sam finds out.

Cheyenne Ronan is the perfect woman for him, and she has a secret or two. Life seemed destined to make her a spinster, never letting her know love or have a family of her own. But Sam changed that for her, and she discovers another life waiting that is full of exciting and wonderful possibility.

Then, of course, I love writing about children, so I added Aaron and Ellen, two scared kids needing security and love. After all, the holiday is mainly for little children.

I'm really having fun writing about this new generation of Legends. They have just as much heart as their famous dads. If you didn't read book one, it was about Gracie Legend and her adventures in finding love. Writing about the offspring keeps the Legend family and the Lone Star Ranch alive in readers' minds.

I hope this Christmas season brings each of you an abundance of joy and happiness. I'll be thinking of you and praying for good things to come your way. Maybe even a miracle or two.

So, settle back and enjoy Sam and Cheyenne. I'd love to hear from you. You can contact me through my website: lindabroday.com.

Merry Christmas and Happy Reading,
Linda Broday

One

SAM LEGEND STARTLED FROM A DEEP SLEEP TO THE WHISPER of a sound. Or was it a mere dream?

Was someone outside? Or had he imagined everything? Hard telling.

He lay still and listened a moment but heard nothing more. Finally, he rubbed sleep from his eyes and sat up, reaching for his pocket watch. He fumbled around until he located the matches and struck one. The hands showed a little after midnight. He reached for the blanket on his bed and pulled it over the pair of faded red long johns, then grabbed the Colt from under his pillow. He didn't bother with boots and skirted the fire on the floor in the middle of the room.

Still listening to every sound, he slowly pulled back the flap of his wickiup. Cold November air rushed in, drawing a shiver. The abode of sticks and grass proved little protection against the elements on the best of days, and during winter in the high plains of the Panhandle, it was downright piss-poor.

He quickly scanned left, then right, and saw no flicker of movement. Maybe some animal had caused the noise. From the top of the rocky escarpment where he'd made his home, he stared across the dark expanse of the barren landscape, watching far-off streaks of lightning.

Silence, his constant companion, skulked against his skin like a thief looking to steal a man's peace. But Sam had always been unsocial, so solitude provided a perfect setting. Yet unending days of aloneness created fear that he might become completely uncivilized like some mad dog and try to bite everyone he ran across. A year ago, his adopted brother called him "prickly" and his little sister used the word "crabby." They should see him now. They'd probably run.

Maybe that was why he was dreaming of three-legged dogs licking cactus thorns.

Some folks had told him he leaned toward the mountain man look, with dark hair flowing wild to his shoulders, an unkempt mustache, and long beard. Fair to say, he didn't resemble a single one of his famous Legend family, owners of the largest ranch in North Texas.

That suited him fine. He didn't have to explain to anyone why he'd become a recluse.

A whine drew his focus, accompanied by a familiar nudge on his hand. Sam glanced down at the gray-and-silver dog that had wandered up last year and decided this was her home. Shadow and he were a perfect match, since neither liked most people. The dog most definitely had a great deal of wolf blood in her.

"Hey there." Sam patted the sleek head, meeting the intelligent gray eyes glancing up at him. "We're quite a pair. I see you're not missing a leg like the dog in my dream. Bet you have more smarts than to lick a damn cactus."

Shadow whined and nuzzled his hand. Then she pulled back and pricked her ears at some noise that escaped Sam.

"What is it, girl? What'cha hearing?"

With a soft huff, the wolf dog turned to go back inside, telling him everything he needed to know.

Sam seemed to have lost what sense he had, standing out there in faded red long johns, freezing his rear off. He glanced at the small shed that housed a cold forge and sighed. He'd have to keep it going strong throughout the next day to complete the Christmas knife orders. Sam loved plying the bladesmith trade, and the creative opportunities it afforded fulfilled something deep inside that was hard to explain. The fun part was turning his imagination loose and seeing what he could design. His knives had begun to gain recognition for both craftsmanship and quality, which meant he had to talk to more and more people.

Dammit! He couldn't have one without the other, and he needed the income to live on.

Finding all this reflection bothersome, Sam slipped inside and lowered the flap. Stoking the fire, he crawled back beneath the covers.

The soft crackle and pop of the fire lulled him to sleep in no time.

A sudden burst of air rushed into the crude abode. A fleeting image crossed his vision.

Was this just another crazy dream?

Or was it more of the danger that existed far outside of town?

He started to throw back the covers when a figure ran across the room and leaped on him. "Where is he?" the person growled. "What did you do with the man living here? Kill him?"

Shadow lunged at the intruder, teeth bared. The voice, belonging to a woman, spoke gently to the dog. "I have no quarrel with you, *Taklishim*. Quiet." The obedient animal lay down.

Sam struggled to get his bearings. The pressure at his throat had to be a sharp blade. That much was clear. He swallowed very slowly and glanced up, moving nothing but his eyes.

Long hair hung over her shoulders; the ends of a few strands brushed his cheek like the whisper of silk. She seemed tall. Slender.

The firelight revealed strong facial features, though not the color of her shadowed eyes, and led him to believe she was probably pretty. The woman sitting on his chest had curves in all the right places. Even though Sam hadn't been to town in a blue moon, or been with a woman longer than that, he recognized that softness.

"Who the hell are you, lady, and what are you doing here?"

"I ask the questions." She pressed the blade against his windpipe and growled. "What happened to the man living here? It's a simple request."

"He died."

"Liar!"

Anger swept over him. "You got some damn nerve!"

For the first time, her glance wavered, and the sharp edges of her face cast a softer shadow. "When did he pass?"

"About four months ago."

"You'd say anything to save your hairy neck."

"Come daylight, I'll take you to his grave."

She snorted. "Name one reason why I should believe you."

"Because it's the truth?" Sam eyed the woman with fire in her eyes. He wondered who she was. Tarak had been pretty old. Maybe a great-granddaughter?

When he caught her casting a curious glance around the room, he grabbed her arms and flipped her onto her back. He held her arms above her head, the knife still in her hand. Her chest heaved with seething anger. Though she wore some kind of long duster, her deerskin dress indicated a Native. Comanche? Apache? Both had occupied this area until forced onto reservations. Maybe she'd walked off one.

"My turn now. Who are you?"

Her eyes, glistening pools of black in the dim light, stared silently up. Rage tightened every inch of her supple body. If she got free, she'd probably plunge that blade into his heart faster than he could spit. Her glare promised that.

She remained stubbornly mute. Finally, she grated out, "One you should fear."

Maybe he should, but his gut wasn't screaming that loud a warning. At least not yet.

"Was Tarak your grandfather?"

"No. A friend."

"Lady, this is twice tonight I've had my sleep interrupted. I'm tired and I have a full day of work looking at me come daylight." He got off and pulled her up, taking the knife from her. Looking around, he tugged her toward the large trunk in the corner, three paces from the bed. He found a long strip of rawhide. He lowered her to the pile of furs and lashed her to the trunk, not too tightly though, lest he mar her skin. "That should hold you 'til first light and we can sort all this out." He tucked a warm blanket around her.

"My pinto. I need…" She sighed. "Looks like rain."

That a woman in her predicament would think about her horse surprised him a little. But then he recalled how gently she'd spoken to Shadow. She liked animals.

"Where is the horse? I'll get it out of the weather."

"She's north about a hundred yards out, tied to a mesquite." A moment later she muttered, "Thanks."

"Don't mention it." He wasn't about to let a horse stand the rest of the night freezing to death. He pulled on his britches and boots and went out into the wind that had kicked up, cussing a blue streak that he'd forgotten his coat.

The horse was right where the woman said. Sam lost no time getting the animal into the warmth of a small lean-to with his Appaloosa named Rio. He removed the saddle before rushing back inside his grass-and-twig house.

The woman's sharp glance held a question.

"I put your pinto with my horse." Sam removed his boots.

"Thank you, *kuruk*."

Sam paused midway of yanking off his britches. "What did you call me?"

"*Kuruk*. That means bear in Apache. When I was on top of you,

I wasn't sure if you were man or beast. Why do you want all that hair? You must be lazy."

She appeared to form an instant opinion about everything.

Sam grunted. "Makes it harder for you to slit my throat. I'm surprised you even found my skin."

"Hmph! *Muy loco.*"

The Spanish words for crazy he understood. Sam crawled back in his bed and tugged the covers around his chin. "Try not to snore."

He'd just gotten comfortable when a teary voice spoke. "How did Tarak die?"

"Old age most likely." The old man had been almost a hundred.

"I should've been here."

Why did it matter so much?

Questions about her kept circling, keeping him awake. Then when the rain started, he finally put the blanket over his head.

But nothing could blot out the driven, determined lady who'd reminded him he wasn't near dead yet.

Two

THE RAIN HAD STOPPED BY FIRST LIGHT. SAM ROSE AND DREW on his clothes, then threw more wood on the fire. After getting coffee boiling, he studied the sleeping woman that he could now see.

The mass of russet hair and white skin came as a shock. Despite the deerskin dress she wore, she was no more Native American than he was. That discovery raised even more questions. She'd asked about Tarak, the man the wickiup belonged to until he had passed. The old Apache had been a friend ever since Sam had arrived about a year ago, and taught him everything about how to be a good bladesmith. If she was so worried about Tarak, why had it taken so long to check on him? And where had she come from?

Shadow looked up from the side of the bed she slept on and stretched, letting out a soft whine, then padded to the flap hanging across the doorway and went out.

Suddenly the woman's eyes fluttered, then opened. The startling green shocked him as much as the russet hair had.

She glared, not speaking, though clearly furious. If anyone had a reason to be pissed off, it would be him, not her. He still felt the sharp blade of the knife against his throat.

"Coffee's on." He moved closer, keeping a wary eye.

"I don't bite," she snapped.

"Lady, nothing would surprise me. Not sure you're civilized."

"And you are? I won't hurt you, for God's sake. I can't say the same about you. You look more bear than human. Probably have rabies." She tried to lift a hand to her face but was stopped by the rope. "When you get through gawking, do you mind untying me?"

"You're a regular Miss Ray of Sunshine." Sam grunted and knelt to remove the bindings. "You have a name?"

"Cheyenne. All right?"

"Last name."

"Ronan." She rubbed her freed wrists and stood. "My father is—"

"Bert Ronan," he finished. "He sold me this land after I promised to let Tarak stay on it. Why didn't you tell me your name last night?"

"I didn't trust you. I had to find out who you were first."

"I've never seen you before at Bert's." He rolled up the rawhide strip. So this was the daughter he'd heard about but never met. "Why didn't you know Tarak died?"

She stared with sullen eyes and pushed back her hair. "I've been away, teaching English to the Apache under the government assimilation program." She sighed and looked away, blinking hard. "You said you'd take me to Tarak's grave."

"Hold on a minute, will you? Let the sun finish coming up first, for God's sake." He couldn't think very well with her anger slapping him in the face. He coiled the rope and tossed it in a corner. "A man has to have his coffee. Want some?"

She glanced at the fire on the floor in the center of the small room. "No, thanks."

"Suit yourself." He filled the pot with water, added coffee, and set it on the glowing embers at the side, instead of directly on the flames. "Might as well sit." He lowered to one of the rugs around the fire. "You're not a prisoner."

Arms crossed, she spat, "Aren't I? You tied me up."

"Lady, you can leave anytime you like. I'm not stopping you."

The wolf-dog ambled in and lay down next to Sam, giving Cheyenne a baleful look.

"I'll just sit a minute to warm. It's cold out." She lowered herself to a colorful rug opposite him.

"Why aren't you still there teaching?" He ran a hand across Shadow's fur, watching Ronan's daughter.

"A long story."

He could believe that, with her ease at using a knife.

Cheyenne seemed at home with the simple accommodations, which showed she'd spent a lot of time here with Tarak. They sat in silence. Sam reached for a short block of wood and started whittling. When the coffee had boiled, he took it off the fire to let the grounds settle and picked the wood back up.

"What are you making?" she asked, glancing at his project.

"Don't know yet. I'm waiting for the wood to tell me. Mostly, it's a way to pass time." When the grounds had settled, he filled a tin cup. "Are you sure you don't want some?"

"I might take a little if it's no bother," she said quietly.

Sam handed her what he'd poured, then reached for a second tin cup and blew the dust out of it. He stifled a chuckle. Cheyenne was working hard to be mad but seemed to find his manners baffling. The devil in him liked to keep her guessing. She took a sip and made a face.

"I should've warned you it was strong. That's the only way I like it."

"Would you have a smidgen of sugar?" she asked.

"Nope." He poured himself some coffee. "Why choose midnight to come calling?"

"Wanted to catch you off guard. I'd been hiding and watching all yesterday. It scared me when I didn't see Tarak, and you look mean. Catching you with your guard down seemed the best strategy."

He snorted. "So your first thought was that I killed him?"

"Of course. With the godforsaken town of Tascosa within a stone's throw, it made perfect sense to me. Killers and cutthroats are about all that live there."

"Your argument might make sense if I lived on the outskirts of town. I'm a little over fifteen miles north," he pointed out, taking a sip from his cup. "You couldn't have asked your parents what happened to Tarak. Oh no, that was too easy."

She gave him the kind of smile she probably reserved for two-year-olds. "My father's hired man said they left for Adobe Walls ten days ago to visit my father's friend Billy Dixon, so I've yet to see them."

Sam tried to keep an impassive expression as she took another small sip of the strong brew and made a face, shaking her head. "Look, I'm sorry about tying you up. I was afraid of what else you'd do."

Her green eyes swung to him. Clearly, she hadn't expected an apology. "I'm sorry too for...you know...the knife and everything. I wouldn't really have cut you."

"That's small comfort now." He studied her clothing, adorned with hundreds of tiny beads. "It's none of my business, but why are you wearing a deerskin dress that belongs to the Native people?"

"Number one, the dress was a gift from a dear friend. Number two, it's comfortable. Fits much better than any of my other clothes."

All this talking had exhausted Sam. He'd already said more in the last ten minutes than he'd said all month. "The rain last night created quagmires. Best wait a couple of hours to go to Tarak's grave." Sam slid his coat on, grabbed his coffee, and went outside in the weak sunlight.

A noise warned him of Cheyenne's presence. He didn't acknowledge her.

"Did Tarak suffer?" she asked softly.

"Went in his sleep." Sam stared into the horizon and softened his tone. "I woke one morning to find him dead."

"That's good. He suffered enough while he lived."

Shadow sauntered over and nudged Sam's hand. "I was half-asleep last night. Who was he again to you?"

"A very dear friend. Tarak taught me to ride and rope. He gave me the knife you took—stole—last night." She gave him a look of reproach. If she thought to shame him, she was barking up the wrong tree.

Damn, he didn't like all this talking before breakfast. Or during. Or after. He drained his cup, set it down, and walked off.

"Hey, where are you going?"

"Gotta feed the horses."

"I can help."

"No, thank you. I need the quiet."

She stood and placed her hands on her hips. "Are you saying I talk too much?"

When she started to follow, he turned, pointing. "Stay."

"Hey, you never told me your name!"

Sam kept walking, praying she'd gotten the message.

Three

IT WAS HARD TO STAY FURIOUS AT HER HOST, EVEN THOUGH SHE did her best. After a breakfast of roasted rabbit that the stubborn man killed, Cheyenne finally found herself at Tarak's grave.

She took an oilskin from her saddlebag and spread it on the wet ground and knelt on it, drawing her duster closer to block out the chilly wind. A lump filled her throat at the sight of the mound of dirt. Tears welled up at the cherished memories crowding her mind. Separated from his people, Tarak was the grandson of a respected chief and one of the best bladesmiths she'd ever seen.

Thank goodness the grouchy man who'd brought her had left. She didn't want him seeing her tears. This alone time with her dearest friend was special.

Cheyenne brushed dirt and mud from the stone marker the bear-looking man had set. Tarak's chiseled name and dates revealed obvious caring, so she had to believe Tarak had possibly been a friend to him as well.

"I stayed away too long, my friend. Should've come home sooner." She ought to have done so many things. Taking him back to his tribe ranked at the top of that list. But he'd always seemed so frail, and maybe he couldn't have made the journey.

What was that Apache prayer he'd taught her?

Oh yes. *Looking behind I am filled with gratitude. Looking forward I am filled with vision. Looking upwards I am filled with strength. Looking within I discover peace.*

"Peace be with you, Tarak."

The dog wandered up and lay down beside her. The uncouth

hairy man had called the female dog Shadow, and it fit. Cheyenne ran her hands across the lovely silver-and-gray fur. "You're a pretty girl. I don't know how you put up with your master, though."

Shadow yawned and released a half moan–half word.

"My sentiments exactly." She glanced at Tarak's peaceful resting spot under the only real tree that must grow away from the winding Canadian River that ran south of here. The owner of the property now had her a little baffled. He pretended to share no sentiment for anyone, but he'd cared deeply for the old Apache. Actions didn't lie.

And despite her brazen assault in the middle of the night, he'd also cared for her comfort. Else, why give her a blanket and tuck it around her to shield against the cold? Also, why had he left the rope so slack around her hands and feet? Had she not been so cold and tired, she could've easily gotten loose.

Memories of last night swirled. The dim light of the fire had revealed confusion, then fury in his dark eyes. He'd examined her with such a sharp, calculating gaze, both then and this morning, that had warned her not to test him further. Turn the other cheek? Not a chance. Something said he would give back in equal measure whatever he got.

Another memory swept that one away. This one of his large body and muscular arms. He'd lifted her as if she'd been a child and had been on top her before she could blink.

His deep, husky voice she'd remember to her dying day. And how it vibrated against her skin. That hadn't belonged on a bear of a man, a recluse. It was more suited to nobility.

What on earth had she been thinking? If he'd wanted to hurt her, he could have. She needed her head examined.

Her thoughts scattered to the four winds, and disquiet filled her.

After everything she'd been through, she needed time spent in meditation to get her bearings. The worst part was having to leave the scared children with no one to protect them against those with little regard for them as humans. And now Christmas was upon them. All her plans had vanished. She'd cried all the way back home only to find her parents gone.

And Tarak dead.

The administrator would surely make good on his promise to bar her from teaching again, to drive her from the children she longed to protect. Even though she strongly disagreed with the program's motives, she could be of service to the Apache. Getting fired...well, that made it impossible now to carry out her plans.

The sudden hammering of steel drew her curiosity. It had to be the *kuruk*. Who else could it be? She got to her feet and folded the oilskin. Shadow scampered in the lead. They rounded the wickiup to see the small shed where a forge glowed red-hot. The man wore a leather apron, striking a piece of slender steel, flattening it. She'd watched Tarak make knives, so the process was familiar.

"You're a bladesmith. Did Tarak teach you?" she asked.

Maybe he hadn't heard her. She kept standing, determined to wait him out.

Finally banging the steel into the shape he wanted, he thrust it back into the flames of the forge and wiped sweat from his forehead. "I already knew a little about making knives, but Tarak turned me from a mediocre bladesmith to a sought-after craftsman. He was the best."

"I agree. Would you mind if I see some of your finished ones?"

He jerked a nod. "There's a box under my bed of what I plan to sell soon."

"Where do you go?"

"Amarillo mostly. Sometimes Fort Worth or other places that meet my price."

Cheyenne turned to go inside but swung back at the flap. "Do you have a name?"

For a moment she thought he'd ignore her again. Then he spoke. "Sam."

"Is that all?" Why no last name?

He took the red-hot steel out and held it up to check for straightness. "Legend," he finally said in a low voice.

Legend? The name jolted her.

Everyone in Texas had heard about the Legend family. They were the only ones she knew to carry the name. Their million-and-a-half-acre ranch, the Lone Star, was known far and wide. She tried to remember what her father once said. Stoker Legend was the old man and he had three sons. One was named Sam as best she could recollect. The Sam here might be his son? Her father and Houston Legend were acquaintances, and her mother often spoke of their wives—Sierra, Lara, and Josie—as fine ladies all. Sierra would be Sam's mother if she recalled.

The Legend family had wealth, fame, and more importantly... land. Lots of it.

What on earth had happened for Sam to leave all that for a hovel on the prairie?

"Okay. Nice to meet you, Sam." She pushed the wickiup's flap aside and went in.

Full of questions, she knelt and retrieved the heavy wooden box from underneath the bed. Opening the lid, she let out a soft cry. The sharp steel blades reflected the light from an oil lamp. Each knife represented the loving work of an artist. The handles were as unique as the knives—some made from deer antler, bone, embossed leather, and stone. He should make quite a handsome return on these. And just in time for Christmas.

That put her to thinking. She'd become quite skillful at weaving beautiful baskets and knew they sold well in places like Fort Worth. Maybe after she got to know Sam better, she might ask to go along. Let him simmer down from this meeting, though. She had to go slow and lure him into her web. But what with?

Cheyenne slid the knives back under the bed and glanced around. The only furniture was the bed that sat against the back. The campfire in the middle of the room had to serve for cooking and heat. He lived as simply as any Native. The trunk probably held his clothing.

What could she give him to get on his good side? All men seemed to like pies. Her mother had put up a bunch of fruit— peaches, berries, and rhubarb in fall canning, so their root cellar was well stocked.

Yes, she'd make Sam a pie. Maybe that would soften him up enough to ask for a ride when he went to sell his knives.

Before she hurried out, she glanced around. For Christmas, he could use a good quilt or maybe a warm scarf. It'd have to be a very long one though to go around all that bushy hair. Imagining the sight brought laughter, and before she knew it, she couldn't stop.

The flap suddenly parted and Sam stepped inside. "What's so all-fired funny?"

She wiped her eyes. "Nothing. Not a thing."

He scowled, then went to the large trunk and removed a box. Retracing his steps, he handed it to her. "Tarak's belongings." His voice was curiously soft. "They're yours."

Cheyenne took the box, thickness setting in her throat. "You don't know what this means."

"I think I do."

"Don't you want to keep anything?"

"What I want is in here." Sam tapped his heart. "I wish—" His voice trailed off.

"I know." She wanted to lay a hand on his arm in comfort but stopped short. "I, too, wish I could talk to him one more time."

Sam straightened, clearing his throat. "Come, I'll see you home."

A clear hint she'd worn out her welcome if she ever heard one. "No, I can manage. I got here by myself, and I can get home the same way."

They walked out into the sunshine. She was surprised to see her pinto saddled and tied to a mesquite. The message was unmistakable that she needed to hurry along. "I see you got Lady ready for me. Thank you. I've had a lovely time."

Sam stood, his dark, brooding eyes staring a hole through her, his hair and long beard ruffling in the breeze. He braced his legs apart as if expecting a blow.

The lovely visit she spoke of was anything but and almost started her laughing again. She put Tarak's meager belongings into a saddlebag and turned. "I'll have my knife back."

Without a word, he disappeared into the house and came back with it. "Sorry. I forgot."

She placed the weapon in the saddlebag with the other things and mounted up. "You take care, Sam Legend. Maybe I'll see you again soon."

"Next time you come back, you might leave that knife at home." A smile teased the corners of his mouth. Before she could get a good look, it vanished.

"Who knows? Maybe you'll cut some of that hair."

"Don't count on it."

"Oh, I won't." She tugged the reins to the left, turned, and galloped from his homestead.

Cheyenne was almost home before she remembered the strange recluse's words: "the next time you came back," not *if* she came back. A sudden laugh bubbled up and spilled over. Maybe Sam hadn't been as tired of her as he'd seemed.

It almost sounded like an invitation.

Four

BLESSED SILENCE AT LAST. SAM BENT OVER HIS WORK, SHAPING, molding the hot steel into the shape of the Bowie knife he wanted. He got his metal from old leaf springs and plow blades. Sometimes he was lucky to find wagon springs. All of those were made of high carbon steel and produced the strongest blades.

Engrossed in his work, he blocked out noises. But something had suddenly gotten into Shadow. The fool dog barked her head off, and each time she started up, Sam's heart gave a funny little leap, expecting to see Cheyenne come riding back.

He kept heating and stretching the piece of steel, getting the tang the right length for the handle to fit onto, trying to keep his mind on his craft. He'd never had a focus problem before she burst in last night and sat on his chest. He couldn't forget that womanly figure—and all that softness that came with it.

His frown deepened. Looks like he should've recalled the knife blade she'd held to his throat. Now that would make better sense. Only the knife had barely gotten a glance.

With a snort, he held up the hot steel with a pair of stout tongs and let out a loud curse. He had a big flaw where the two layers of steel had separated. Hell and be damned! That hadn't happened in a while. Disgusted, he flung it back in the coals to reheat, praying he could get the weld to take. If not, he'd have to start over, and he was already behind. His plan was to take the knives to Amarillo in two weeks.

If he didn't get the money by then, he'd be late with gifts for his parents and seventeen-year-old sister, Marisol, in addition to all the nieces and nephews living on the Lone Star. His older adopted brother, Hector, had gotten married last year and had his own spread.

But the bulk of the gifts would be for kids in the orphanage in Medicine Springs that had recently burned to the ground. Those kids had lost everything—clothes, shoes, toys. The need was great, so he'd ramped up production.

He'd hire a freighter to deliver everything. The Lone Star was no place Sam wanted to be. Not in a million years.

Especially not at Christmas, when his family would expect so much more.

His father and uncles, not to mention Grandpa Stoker, shook their heads. To a man they thought he'd lost his mind, moving way up here in the panhandle by himself. They couldn't understand why he had to put distance between them.

Couldn't understand why he'd rejected his part of the land and cattle.

Maybe he was the adopted one instead of Hector, who'd fallen right in line and become a cattleman.

Nor did Sam wish to follow in his father's footsteps. Sam Sr. had been a top-rate Texas Ranger, then moved right into a sheriff's job in Lost Point, Texas. This made his father's twenty-third year there. His father excelled in everything he'd ever done. How could Sam compete with that? How could he ever measure up to a bona fide legend?

His stomach twisted at the thought. The cool breeze blew through the brush, creating a lonesome sound. He closed his eyes, and a pretty face swam before him, her eyes as blue as a robin's egg.

"I love you, Sam. I'm so happy to be your wife." Then she'd kissed him.

That day, everything had seemed just about perfect, his life set. Two months later, he had lain her in the cold ground, his heart shattering into a million pieces.

Gone were their plans. Their bright future. Their life as a newly married couple.

"Peace will come if you look," Tarak had told him. "You must find a way to put your past behind you or it will swallow you whole." He'd lapsed into silence for a few minutes, then added, "Someday you will smile and laugh again. This I know."

The old man had been able to read a piece of steel like some people did books, but he hadn't known squat about Sam's future.

He scanned the cold, dreary landscape and saw nothing but emptiness.

That afternoon, Shadow suddenly raised and barked. Sam glanced up. Damn! All this company was getting on his nerves. Someone had apparently opened the floodgate.

Bert Ronan, his neighbor, pulled to a stop and dismounted. "Got a minute?"

"Sure. How was the trip to Adobe Walls?"

"I enjoyed seeing my old friend Billy Dixon and reliving the glory days. A nice break for the missus too, but we couldn't wait to get home." Bert took off his hat and beat it against the side of his trousers. "I have a good hired man, but he's been acting kinda strange. Guess he has a lot on his mind. Some fellows rode up a few days before we left, and from the gestures, they seemed to be having words. Mitchell hasn't been the same since."

Sam laid down his hammer. "Sometimes folks don't see eye to eye. I wouldn't worry too much."

"I know." Bert's red hair sticking from his hat fired brilliant in the sunlight. The stocky cattleman stood several inches shorter than Sam and was built solid. He'd worked as an agent on the Cherokee Indian Reservation, leaving his job after becoming sickened by the horrible practices and shameful treatment the government had expected him to implement and carry out. The kindly neighbor had been a good friend to Sam. Bert put his hat back on and reached to pet the dog.

"Is that a new Stetson, Bert?"

"Yep. Cora insisted, said it would be an early Christmas gift."

"It's real nice. Looks good on you."

"I'll tell her." Bert paused. "Look, Sam, I'm sorry about Cheyenne coming over and raising a ruckus over Tarak. I never wrote her with the news of his passing. Figured I'd tell her when she came home for Christmas, only I didn't count on her getting fired and us being out of town."

She'd gotten fired? The news settled over Sam. Due to her penchant for using knives, it didn't shock him too much.

"It's fine, Bert. I lived through it. Don't fret about it."

The stocky neighbor let out a heavy sigh. "Cheyenne can be a little headstrong at times, but she has a good, caring heart."

"We got it all worked out." In a manner of speaking. Silence spun between them like fragile glass. "She sure talks a lot."

"That's for sure." Bert laughed. "It wouldn't have been so bad if we'd have been able to give her a brother or sister. I guess she tries to make up for that."

Still, that seemed no good reason to chatter like a magpie.

"Reckon so."

"Well, I need to get back. Just wanted to apologize for Cheyenne's late-night call. She told me all about it. I'm surprised you didn't fill her with lead." Bert chuckled and reached for his reins. "Well, I can see you're busy and you don't need anyone blabbering your ear off, especially when you hate talking. Cora said to invite you to Thanksgiving dinner on Thursday and also to celebrate Cheyenne's homecoming." Bert mounted up. "Hope you come. Twelve noon."

A sit-down dinner with fancy plates, napkins, and four kinds of silverware. Dammit!

Sam gave him a curt nod. "Look forward to it."

Shadow looked up at him and let out a sharp bark as though scolding him, then lay down and put her paws over her eyes. Even the dog knew he had no business trying to act all civilized. Well, no way in hell was he going to shave! The entire bunch of Ronans might as well forget that.

A few moments later as he watched his neighbor gallop away, he wondered why the heck he'd accepted. The last place he needed to be was at a table with Cheyenne Ronan.

And if she got an inkling of what he'd done, she'd blame him as everyone else had. As he blamed himself. He had to bury the past and forget—somehow.

He'd chosen this spot of land for the remote location. Only now it was getting very crowded.

Five

THAT AFTERNOON, CHEYENNE DECIDED FOR SURE TO MAKE baskets. She'd have to gather the willow right away in order for it to dry enough to weave. Excited with her plan, she saddled her little pinto and rode to the Canadian River, part of which crossed their property. She should be safe enough on their own land. Though Sam's place was visible, she stayed clear—for now. He hated visitors with a passion.

It surprised her that he'd agreed to come to Thanksgiving dinner, but she was glad he'd accepted the invitation. Clearly, he spent too much time alone. The dinner conversation should be interesting, since he didn't talk much.

The breeze was chilly, normal for November. She pulled her long duster closer.

Willow grew in abundance along the banks of the river, so she chose a large one and dismounted. Like 90 percent of the trees, the willow lost its leaves in winter. She strode forward with her knife, and as she worked to collect the thin limbs, her thoughts drifted to a few of her former students. She prayed Joseph would stay out of the new teacher's way and sweet little Lenna would resist the urge to sing in her native tongue. Guyan, Kuruk, Cocheta, and all the others—forbidden to use their own names, made to forget their language, their culture, their identity. And it wasn't just happening to the Apache. Children of every Indian Nation were taken from their homes, snatched from their parents, and put in white government schools. It was a cruel, heartless practice and one she'd done her best to change.

Cheyenne's mind was on all the atrocities she'd witnessed when she heard someone come up behind her. A horse snorted.

"Well, well. What do you reckon this one is doing so far from the reservation?"

The man's lazy drawl shot alarm through her. She turned, clutching the knife tighter, and saw it was not one but three strangers. She knew their kind, could see meanness in their eyes. Although parts of the country had become more law abiding, it still had a ways to go. Being away so long, she'd forgotten how close they were to the rough town of Tascosa.

"Hell, she's got red hair. She's nothing but a stinking white woman." This came from a pimply faced young man with a cigarette dangling from his mouth.

"Don't make no difference to me. Let's get her."

They moved closer, gawking. Grinning. Thinking things they had no right.

Cheyenne held her knife in front of her. "Step back! I keep my blade real sharp just for the likes of you."

"Whoo-ee! She's sure got sass. I like feisty women." The man grinned like a jackass.

"Lady, why are you dressed like that? That's what we wanna know." The speaker scratched his head with a dirty fingernail.

She took a calming breath. "My question is why you came onto my property, threatening me with whatever it is you think you intend to do." She raised the long knife and gave a sharp order. "Leave!"

They hesitated for the barest of seconds before they crept closer, splitting up, with one going left, one right, and one up the middle. She couldn't cover them all. Up to now, she'd been calm but perturbed. Now, fear started the long crawl up her throat. She was too far from the house. And they'd be on her before she reached her horse. Screaming might alert Sam, but she couldn't bank on that.

Despite the disadvantages, she kept flashing the knife. When the cigarette smoker came too close, she sliced through his thin coat sleeve, drawing blood. He leaped back with a surprised cry, but that didn't take the grin off his face. It just made his eyes glitter with excitement.

"What did I tell you? This blade is mighty sharp." She switched the knife from left hand to right, her eyes darting between the trio.

"Reckon we'll take our chances."

"We like the wild ones best. I'm gonna kiss you. Yes, I am."

"I have something to say about that." She lunged and caught the grinning jackass's belly through his open coat. He grabbed for her but missed as she leaped back.

"Dammit!" The man held his stomach, the grin gone. "You're gonna pay!"

"What's wrong? Am I ruining your fun?"

"Come on, let's go," urged the third man.

"Nope, I'm gonna teach this uppity white girl a thing or two." Cigarette smoker wiped his mouth with a bloody hand and tried again to latch hold of the knife.

She leaped back, evading him.

All of a sudden, the trio rushed her and wrenched the knife away. One grabbed her arms and held them behind her back while another kissed her and the third grabbed at her clothes. She twisted and kicked, trying to get away. She even attempted to bite one, but his coat padded his arm.

The men jumped at a sudden gunshot.

"Let the lady go." The deep voice sounded familiar.

Cheyenne raised her eyes. Sam Legend stood several yards away, a rifle in one hand and Shadow's raised ruff in the other. She'd never been so glad to see anyone.

Her attackers turned. "Now, I think you're butting into our business, mister," said the smoker. "Ain't polite."

"I didn't stutter, and whatever you got going on here *is* my business. Make a choice—a bullet or the dog." Teeth bared, Shadow strained to get to the trio. "Me, I'd rather take the bullet. This dog will tear you limb from limb. Leaves a god-awful mess."

"There's three of us," replied the cocky attacker. "Only one of you."

"And the dog." Sam sighed. "You're clearly too dumb to understand and wastin' my time. Get him, Shadow!"

The wolf-dog sprang onto the speaker. She clamped down on the man's arm with her sharp teeth and pulled him to the ground amid horrible screams. "Get it off! Call it off! I'm dying!"

Cheyenne shook free of the men and ran behind Sam, grateful for his large body blocking her from trouble. Her knees shook so hard, she clutched him to keep from falling.

"If you don't want me to unleash this rifle on you, get the hell out of here," Sam told the other two.

"We was just funning, mister. Didn't mean no harm."

"Ma'am, we're awful sorry." The men leaped onto their horses and galloped off.

"Shadow, enough!" The dog turned his prey loose and returned to Sam's side, eyes glued on Cheyenne's attacker.

The man staggered to his feet, blood coming from his arm, face, and throat. He held his arm against his belly.

"I ever see you around here again, the wolf gets another go at you. Got that?" Sam's voice held a sharp edge.

Thankfulness ran through Cheyenne that he wasn't speaking to her. Sam Legend could sure put the fear of God in a man and make him see the error of his ways.

The bloody attacker stood as though unsure what to do. Probably too scared to move.

Sam waved the rifle. "Now, apologize to the lady and get out of here."

"I'm real s-sorry, ma'am." The man wiped his nose with his sleeve. "I won't bother you no more."

"I've learned a lesson too," Cheyenne told him quietly.

Nodding, the man cradled his arm, got on his sorry-looking mount, and rode off.

Trembling, Cheyenne threw her arms around Sam's neck. "Thank you."

"Well, you damn near got yourself killed."

Anger rising, she stepped away from him. "I'm not stupid. I *was* paying attention. They snuck up on me is all."

"I apologize." He inhaled a deep breath, glancing at the pile of cut willow. "I heard voices, and they didn't sound friendly. Glad I came to see what was going on." Sam's gaze came back to her. "Did they hurt you?"

"No." She glanced down at her dress where the leather was torn.

His attention shifted to the tear, and something dark crossed his eyes.

"I can fix the dress," she hurried to assure him. "It's fine. Really."

"You're shaking." He helped her to the trunk of the willow tree and lowered her. Sam removed a kerchief from inside his coat. He must've seen her look of surprise. "It's clean."

"I believe you." All the same, it did seem farfetched, given his appearance.

He knelt on the riverbank to wet it, then came back. "It'll help to wet your face."

"Thanks." Cheyenne wiped her eyes and applied the coolness to her forehead and cheeks. His caring said a lot about the recluse. Sam Legend had a kind heart.

"I never saw a woman with your kind of fight. You did some damage before I got here." His eyes held admiration, though she didn't think it was warranted. Fighting them had changed nothing.

"Not enough to matter. They still kept coming." She drew in a shaky breath. She'd probably see their faces in a few nightmares.

"Far be it from me to argue with a lady." He picked up her knife and handed it to her, then bent to collect the willow she'd dropped.

Cheyenne helped him, glad to have a distraction—not for her, for Sam. The way he'd looked at her dress, she wouldn't put it past him to take out after the men, and who knew what would happen.

From the deep anger in his eyes, someone would die. Maybe him, and she couldn't bear to think about one more person dying.

She tried to force a chuckle, but a weird sound came out. "You've probably had your fill of Ronans for one day. First me, then my father, now this."

"It has been a hell of a day. Did you bring something to tie the willow to your horse?"

"Look in my right saddlebag."

"What are you going to do with it?"

She smiled. "I'm going to weave baskets. I can use some Christmas money. The school administrator refused to pay me for the last month I worked." She picked up the last of the limbs. "I worry for those children, but he threatened to shoot me if I went back."

"Stay away."

"I'm not crazy. There are plenty more places in need of a kind teacher."

Sam took her willow limbs and lashed them to the others, then gave her a hand up.

"Thanks again."

He lifted his rifle from the riverbank grass. "First, I'll see you home."

"There's really no need, and I hate to take more of your time." He apparently stayed extra busy trying to avoid people, but she didn't mention that.

"In case those jackasses might still be around."

The wisdom of the extra prodding changed her mind. "Then I'd best accept the escort graciously."

He cut off a few more limbs with quick slices of his knife. "Ready?"

"Whenever you are."

With his arms full of the extra willow, he and Shadow walked beside her horse. She didn't dare try to strike up a conversation during the short distance, and even though the silence began to get to her, she kept quiet. Thirty minutes later, it was a relief to see her parents' house come into view.

"Let's take these around to where I live." She pointed the way.

"You have your own place?"

"Yes. My father built it for my twentieth birthday, and I love having my own little space."

They went around the main house, past a two-man bunkhouse for the hired help, to a small, whitewashed dwelling, curtains at each window, and a white picket fence around it. Though it only consisted of three rooms, she found it more than adequate.

Cheyenne dismounted before he could help. "This is home. I'll leave the willow outside and only dry a few limbs at a time."

"Show me where to put them."

When she did, he made quick work of stacking them next to the house.

Her father came out. "Thought I heard voices. Hi, Sam."

"Bert." Sam finished neatly stacking the willow.

She felt a need to explain and told her father about the attackers. "I couldn't fight them off, and if Sam hadn't come along, I don't know what might've happened."

Bert held out a hand for Sam to shake. "Thank you, my friend. I'm in your debt."

"I was nearby and happy to change the odds." Sam glanced around as though looking for an escape route. If he hadn't been so pitiful, Cheyenne would've laughed. "I need to go," he murmured.

"Want me to get a horse for you?" Bert asked. "I'll come by to fetch him later."

"No, thanks. I don't mind walking."

Before either could reply, he set off toward his place with Shadow bounding ahead.

"Daughter, you need to be more careful and watch how far you wander. It's not safe."

Guilt rose that she'd worried her father. She rested a palm against the side of his face. Her heart swelled with love. "I know and I'm sorry. I know how lucky I was to have escaped those men's clutches. From now on, I'll be more careful."

Cheyenne turned back to Sam Legend's tall figure. If he'd cut off some of that hair and trim his beard, he'd probably be a nice-looking man. She sighed.

There seemed as much chance of that as her acting like a proper lady.

Six

THE NEXT THREE DAYS PASSED UNEVENTFULLY, WITH HIS WORK and thoughts of Cheyenne occupying the hours. Then Sam rose on Thanksgiving morning, heavy dread sitting in his stomach, wishing he hadn't given his word to go to the Ronans for a sit-down dinner. Hell! They'd expect him to talk.

Shadow yawned and stretched on her side of the bed.

"You better be glad you're a dog. Don't suppose you'd trade places?"

The wolf-dog released a series of yips, yawns, and sharp barks, trying her best to speak. Sam took it that either she wanted no part of Thanksgiving dinner either or was calling him a crazy fool for accepting an invitation where he had no business.

Well, he'd best hunt for something to wear in a little while. He glanced down at his faded red long johns. A bath was in order. That meant heading down to the river. The water would be freezing. He'd probably take his death of cold. But this was a matter he had no choice in, so he might as well get ready and do it.

For a moment, Sam thought he heard Tarak's deep chuckle. The old Apache would be laughing. His friend had possessed an odd sense of humor. Damn, Sam missed that. And the days of working silently at his side, both creating something beautiful out of steel.

He made coffee and took it outside to drink while he checked the weather. It was a cold but clear day. Maybe it would warm up some in a couple of hours.

Thoughts drifted from one subject to another while he sipped. Peaceful and lazy. But the second cup seemed to call thoughts of Cheyenne. They swarmed around his head like pestering bees looking for a lost hive.

She was pretty, if a man liked skinny women. Sam preferred a little more meat on a woman's bones.

Another thought filled his head, and he swallowed hard. She wouldn't have gotten much food at the government school, and suspected she probably gave most of what she had to her students, sacrificing her health. He'd known people who willingly sacrificed for others, but never a fighter like Cheyenne.

Her ordeal with the attackers shot into his head like an iron ball from a cannon. He'd ridden into Tascosa looking for them two nights ago but hadn't found them. Just as well, or Sam would either be in jail or six feet under.

He ended up pouring his coffee out, his thirst ruined.

Two hours later, he hauled water from the river and bathed, then slipped into his only clean shirt, vest, and trousers. He combed his hair and tied it back with a leather strip, then inspected his beard in a small piece of broken mirror. Dammit! Looked like some wild derelict. Someone would probably shoot his ass. Getting out his knife, he went to work trimming the beard up a tad to keep it from looking quite so bushy.

Sam had his reasons for growing his hair long—the main one being he didn't care squat about his appearance.

Guilt had stopped him in his tracks, and his heart hadn't yet found a way to beat right again. Time hadn't stood still quite long enough for that. Sliding the knife into the scabbard at his waist, he buckled on his gun belt and grabbed his beat-up Stetson, then saddled Rio.

Shadow tried to follow, but he told her to go home. Thankfully, she minded.

Ten minutes to noon, he stood on the Ronans' porch,

spit-shined and still cussing. Cora answered the door. "Come in, Sam. You're right on time."

Sam removed his hat and stepped inside. Cora always had sparkling eyes and a smile on her chubby face. The woman appeared to love life and clearly spent a lot of time cooking and eating. Speaking of food, luscious smells drifted from the kitchen. His mouth watered for roasted turkey.

Cheyenne came from the other room. "I'll take your coat and hat, Sam."

He stared. This was the first time he'd seen her in a dress like the majority of women wore. The deep purple made her russet hair appear more lustrous and rich. The fitted bodice cradled her breasts like a glove, and heat climbed up the back of his neck. He looked away before she caught him gawking.

Why had he thought her too thin? She didn't seem that way now. Maybe it was the dress.

"Thank you." Sam removed his coat and ran a finger around his shirt collar to loosen it.

Her hands full with his coat and hat, Cheyenne smiled. "Father's in the parlor, itching for someone to talk to. Go on in. I'm told you know the way." She dropped her voice to a whisper. "He'll be disappointed if you simply sit and stare."

"I think I'll manage." Sam started to sweat despite the cold day.

"I see." Her eyes twinkled. "I'm happy you came. Enjoy your chat with Father, and we'll call you to eat in a few minutes."

Sam had been there many times over the year since he'd bought his property from Bert, so he went on to the parlor. The fire in the hearth cast a welcoming glow.

"Come on in, Sam." Bert lowered the newspaper. "Have a seat."

Sam chose a straight-back chair. "Any news?"

"They're just about ready to open a three-story public school over in Amarillo, and the population of the town has grown to fourteen hundred and some odd. That place is blooming like a weed. But for every person it gains, it's another Tascosa loses."

"Might not be a bad thing for the place to dry up. It's nothing but a haven for the lawless." Sam sighed. "However, talk in the saloons in Tascosa is that the Bowery district in Amarillo is taking over the crime situation."

"The paper says they had a big ruckus over there a month ago, and three people ended up shot. A sad state of affairs." Bert folded the lifeline to the outside world. "I don't know why they can't get the criminal element corralled. No man wants to move his family near something like that."

"Nope." Sam took a moment to digest the information. Last time he was in Tascosa, he'd noticed all the people moving out. "Bert, you realize if Tascosa folds, we'll have a lot farther to travel for supplies."

"It'll be a damn shame, but that's the way it's looking."

They lapsed into silence, the fire's pop and snap filling the void.

At last, Bert cleared his throat, leaned forward, and rested a hand on Sam's knee. "Son, I don't know what you've been through or what happened to drive you way off up here, but it had to be something powerful bad. If you ever want to talk, I can make a good listener. I care about you just like you were my own."

The unexpected turn in the conversation, and Bert's kind voice, had Sam blinking hard.

Before he could utter a word, a lanky hired man entered, his hair slicked down. Mitchell was the only name Sam had heard and didn't know if it was a first name or last. It was hard to figure his age, but he seemed older, although his light-brown hair didn't show any gray. Sam liked the honesty in his face and the grip of his shake. It also said a lot about a man when he looked you straight in the eye.

"Mitchell, good to see you." Sam stood and shook his hand.

"Nice to see you, Sam." Mitchell stood by the fire, warming his hands. The threadbare jacket he wore wouldn't offer much protection from the elements.

The men talked about the weather, then Cheyenne appeared in the doorway. "Dinner is served, gentlemen."

Sam's stomach bucked like a wild bronc as he offered her his arm, praying this would all be over soon.

Seven

Sam pulled out Cheyenne's chair and held it. A glance revealed the still-somber expression he'd worn since arriving, and she wanted to tell him this wasn't a funeral. He'd live through it. "Thank you, Sam. I'm so happy we could save you from your own cooking for one meal."

"Yes, ma'am. I appreciate that." Sam took the seat beside her.

She was quick to notice he'd taken some pains with his appearance. She'd caught a soap fragrance on him first thing at the door. He looked less like a bear with his hair pulled back and clean clothes. At times, the wild impression he gave off worked to his advantage. Her attackers had certainly wasted no time in letting her go when they'd seen him.

Part of it most certainly had been the steel in his voice. Whenever he took a mind to open his mouth, he had a commanding way of speaking and could shoot fear through a person with that deep voice of his.

Again, she wondered what had happened for him to break ties with his family and move so far away from the ranch. It had to have been something big or he'd have stayed on the land that had been in the Legend family for three generations. And why had he taken up the bladesmith profession? That was really odd. Lots of mystery surrounded the younger Sam Legend.

Mitchell took a seat on the opposite side of the table.

"Let's bow our heads." Bert offered a short prayer.

Cheyenne peeked at Sam through her lowered lashes. Even if he wasn't a praying man, his bowed head and closed eyes showed respect. But then, she hadn't expected anything different. She'd already seen that he'd been raised with manners and regard for others.

When the blessing ended, her father carved the golden-brown turkey and put a large portion on the plates she passed him. "What kind of knife are you working on right now, Sam?"

"Bowie. That's my biggest seller." He took the plate filled with turkey she handed him.

"Take as much as you want, Sam," Cora insisted. "You men have big appetites, and there's plenty."

Sam thanked her and said he'd eat what he had first. Cheyenne noticed hesitance not only in conversation but in each movement, as though afraid he would make a mistake.

"What weapon did you have the most fun making?" Bert finished filling the plates and sat down, tucking his napkin in the collar of his shirt.

"A Mexican officer's sword. The blade was straight with a deep double fuller the entire length, which made it extremely light and easy to swing. It had great balance. I etched a lion's head on the guard and wrapped a snake around the inside of the hilt." Sam stopped as though aware he'd gotten carried away and used up all his allotted words at once.

It appeared that passion was the secret in getting Sam to open up.

Mitchell buttered a slice of hot bread. "Explain what the fuller is."

"It's a deep groove running the length of the blade. Sometimes a bladesmith adds just one and other times two. I think they add a lot to the beauty of the steel. And it makes the weapon lighter."

"I wish I could've seen it." Mitchell had yet to take a bite, so engrossed he'd been.

"Your sword sounds just lovely, Sam." Cheyenne dipped out some spiced yams. "What did you do with it?"

Sam put a large spoonful of dressing next to his helping of turkey. "Sold it." He gave her a flicker of a grin. "I just wanted to see if I could do it."

"I'm curious. How long does it take you to make a regular hunting knife?" Bert reached for the giblet gravy.

"Generally, two to five days from start to finish for the normal ones. The long sword took three weeks."

"We all like to stretch our boundaries from time to time." Bert's words were quiet. "Just to prove something to ourselves. I wish I'd learned a trade in my younger days. I envy you, Sam."

"You served an important purpose during your time as an Indian agent." Sam met Bert's gaze. "You offered kindness, respect, and comfort to downtrodden people in need. Don't ever sell yourself short. You did a thankless job to the best of your ability and eased their suffering for a while."

"Well said, Sam." Cheyenne felt like clapping. She was proud of her father, and for others to see it too filled her with warmth.

Cora glanced at her over the rim of her water glass. "I asked the woman who helped with your birth if I could name you after her. Your birth was quite difficult, and if it hadn't been for her extraordinary efforts, you probably would've died. I'll never forget her and the time spent in Oklahoma Territory." Tears filled Cora's eyes. "Or when I held you in my arms for the first time."

"I'm sure I loved you from that first moment, Mother. And I can't imagine having a different name." Cheyenne noticed Sam's glass was empty and rose to refill it. The conversation had shifted to Tarak's last Thanksgiving with them and the turkey the old friend had provided. "I've been meaning to ask, Father…who did the chisel work on Tarak's stone?"

"Actually, Sam did that. It's nice, isn't it?"

"I think it's exceptional. Thank you, Sam. You're a man of many talents." Cheyenne brushed his arm when she took her seat.

Sam reached for his glass and knocked his knife into the floor.

"Sorry." He bent over to pick it up at the same time she did, and they bumped heads. "Sorry again. I'm not used to eating anywhere but over a campfire, and usually with my fingers." He tried to smile, but only one side of his mouth quirked up for a brief moment.

In reaching for the knife, her hand closed around his. "You're fine. Don't fret over this dinner. Pretend you're sitting over a low fire inside your wickiup."

After a moment's hesitation, Sam gave her a nod. She thought he might've given her hand a slight squeeze. But then again, she probably imagined that.

"The turkey is excellent, Mrs. Ronan. It's been quite a while since I've had anything this tasty," Sam said.

"I certainly agree," Mitchell added.

Cora gave them a warm smile. "You're both welcome. I love to cook."

"Yes, ma'am." Sam gave her wide smile.

"Before you leave, Sam, I want to show you the willow basket I made." Cheyenne hoped the craftsmanship measured up. "I think it turned out well, but I want your opinion."

"I'm sure it's fine. I don't know anything about basket weaving."

"But you do have an eye for quality, and I respect your judgment. I want to sell them where I can get top dollar. I have plans for that money." She cast him a side glance, praying he took the hint.

Bert laid down his fork. "Maybe Sam will let you ride along when he goes to sell his knives. How about it, Sam?"

Leave it to her father. He must've read her mind.

Sam met her hopeful gaze with a frown. The poor thing seemed at a loss on what to say. "I don't know, Bert. I plan to be gone for a week or more, depending on how long it takes to empty my boxes. I'll sleep in the loft at the livery but—"

"Lodging is no problem," she cut in. "I have acquaintances in Amarillo and Fort Worth that I can stay with. And I promise not to wear your ear off talking." The ensuing silence wasn't a good sign.

"But think about it. You don't have to decide today. I still have to make the baskets. It's just that it's too dangerous for me to go by myself, and that's the only reason Father suggests we go together." She paused for several heartbeats. "However, the last thing I want to do is put you on the spot."

"Let me think about it."

The conversation turned to the growth of Amarillo, the two additional rail lines that had come in, and how bad the winter might be. Cheyenne was quick with a word or question here or there when she had something to contribute, but mostly she just listened.

"Bert, I assume you were here in '87 when all the cattle died." Sam reached for more turkey, this time without urging, a sign he was relaxing.

With a smile, Cheyenne rose and went to the kitchen, returning with both a pumpkin and pecan pie, along with small plates.

"Yep, that sure was a bad winter." Her father pushed back his plate. "I'll never forget the sight of all those cattle carcasses as long as I live. The Big Die-Up they called it, and that's exactly what it was. I lost ninety percent of my herd, and I'm still fighting to recover. That's the main reason I sold that parcel to you. I needed the infusion of cash to keep from going under."

"I heard about that." Mitchell leaned back in his chair. "I hope this is a milder winter."

"The Lone Star escaped the worst part of that '87 blizzard. Being farther east saved us, but we still lost a fourth of our herds."

After asking each their preference, Cora placed a piece of pie on each dessert plate and passed them around the table.

"Ma'am, I can't tell you the last time I had pie." Sam wore a big smile that showed his white teeth. "I'm pretty sure it was the last time I went home. Mama makes a peach pie that melts in your mouth."

"She must be an excellent cook. Coffee, Sam?" Cheyenne held out the pot.

"Always."

She filled his cup. "Will you be going home for Christmas?"

Although it would probably do him good, she didn't want him to leave for selfish reasons. He was the first man to interest her in a long while, and she wasn't exactly sure what drew her. He looked like some grumpy old mountain man, for pity's sake, and he had the personality of a porcupine. Maybe it was the fact that he seemed so alone, so sad. She wanted to put a smile back on his face. Or maybe he drew her because they'd shared Tarak.

Whatever it was, she couldn't turn her back on him.

Sam studied his cup with dainty blue flowers around the rim. It looked rather odd in his large hand. "I don't plan to. I'll stay here with my dog." He took a bite of pumpkin pie. "The orphanage in Medicine Springs recently burned down, and my father and uncles want help rebuilding it, but they have plenty of hands without me."

Why had he added that last part? Cheyenne wondered. A guilty conscience? Something he was struggling to reconcile?

"Oh, those poor children!" Cora exclaimed. "They probably lost everything."

"Yes, ma'am, they did. I'll help out with part of my knife money."

"I can contribute." Cheyenne's thoughts whirled. Her basket money could come in handy. They probably needed blankets and clothes. She'd halfway thought about sending a shipment of toys to the children at the Indian school, but she knew they'd probably not get them. The administrator was full of spite.

"How about you, Mitchell? Any Christmas plans?" Sam asked.

"I'll leave for a few days. Got a wife and two kids I'm anxious to see."

This was the first Cheyenne had heard about Mitchell being married. But then she hadn't been home long enough to even ask her father. She liked the quiet ranch hand and felt easy in his company. And now that she knew he had a wife and kids, she'd make something for him to take to them.

Once they'd consumed the dessert, she went over to her little house for the willow basket she'd dyed a pretty blue and brought it back to Sam.

"This is great work." He glanced up, his dark eyes alive with approval. "What are these two shiny triangles interwoven into each side?"

"Thin pieces of pressed metal. It was easy to punch holes for the willow to go through." She was silent a moment. "You really like the basket?"

"Absolutely. I'll buy one for my mother."

"Do you think she'd want one?"

"I certainly do." He ran a finger across the tight weave. "The shiny metal gives the basket a little extra appeal."

"I'm glad. I want to incorporate other things into the weave. Maybe thin stones or tree bark. Whatever I can find in nature. I want them all to be different."

"You're very talented and have a good eye for detail." He paused, piercing her with his gaze. "I don't mind having you tag along when I go to Amarillo."

Real happiness bubbled up for the first time since she'd been back. Sam didn't know what he'd given her.

Eight

THAT AFTERNOON, SAM SAT BY THE WARM GLOW OF HIS FIRE, his belly full of turkey and all the fixings. Cora had sent two pieces back of both the pecan and pumpkin pies, along with a good portion of turkey. Time spent with Cheyenne and her folks hadn't been half-bad, and the food was good.

Shadow lay down beside him and rested her muzzle on his leg.

On the way home, he'd mulled something over. He could forge some pieces of thin steel for Cheyenne to use on her baskets. Wouldn't take any time, and that would certainly fetch more money.

He and the dog dozed off. Dark fell before he knew it. He took the leather strip loose from his hair and shook it wild. He grabbed his sheepskin coat and headed out for some fresh air.

His breath fogged as he walked along the bluff where he lived. Night creatures scurried ahead of him, startled by his footsteps, and in the distance, a coyote howled.

Shadow trotted to his side and fell into step with him. Thoughts turned to his work and the Bowie knife he was making. A little more hammering to stretch the blade out, then he'd quench it. That would temper and harden the steel to make it strong.

Other thoughts—memories mostly—tried to crowd in, and he quickly pushed them away.

Some things pained a man too much.

A low growl suddenly rumbled in Shadow's throat, and the ruff on her neck rose.

"Who's there?" Sam pulled his gun. "Show yourself or I'll shoot."

A tall figure stole from the darkness. The Spanish curses meant it could only be one man.

"Uncle Luke? That you?"

Soft laughter accompanied the man into the rocky clearing. He led a dark horse. "*Hola*, Sam Jr." A long duster holding back the cold wind from his body, the former outlaw grinned. "Your futile attempts to hide did not stop me from finding you."

Sam stared, wondering if rudeness might send his uncle away. "More's the pity," he ground out in his driest tone. "Out here I'm only Sam. Nothing with it. Remember that."

"*Dios mío.*" The visitor released a sigh. "I will try. Do you have coffee?"

Sam shifted away from the stare that saw too much. "Might as well come in." With luck, Luke wouldn't stay long.

His half Spanish uncle tied his horse's reins to the forging shed door and followed Sam into the wickiup. Luke dropped onto the rugs in front of the fire. "I had heard you were living like a mountain man."

Sam filled the coffeepot with water he'd hauled from the river. "Why are you here?"

"I was riding by?"

"Not hardly. Try again." In the silence, Sam threw some coffee into the pot and set it on the open flame.

"Your *mamá* worries," Luke said low. "She gets no sleep. Losing weight. The whole family thinks you've lost your mind."

Thoughts of his mother made Sam wince. He knew everything Luke said to be true, but he could do nothing about it at the present.

Luke waved an arm around the wickiup. "This is not you, nephew. You've thrown away your family, your home, your education, your birthright. And for what? For this?" He muttered something in Spanish under his breath. "You look like some wild animal."

"It's my life, and if I want to live it like this, I will." Sam dropped onto the rugs beside his uncle. "If I'm not mistaken, you pretty much did the same thing when you plied the trade of an outlaw. Grandpa begged you to come join the family, but you were a stubborn cuss."

"Our circumstances are not the same, *mijo*. I was an outcast to start with. I had to be sure they really wanted me for the man I was and not to try to change me." Luke stared into the flames, his voice quiet. "I used to trail your father, a Texas Ranger then, from a distance, watching over him, making sure he stayed safe and able to go home when he wanted."

"It's a good thing you did, or he'd have died when the rustlers hung him."

"*Si*. Your father was as good as dead when I rode up and saw him hanging from that oak tree. Even after I cut him down, I was not sure he was breathing."

Sam couldn't imagine such a horrifying sight. "It took time for Dad to heal mentally, and the family gave him that. Why not me?"

"You've had over a year, Sam," Luke said softly. "Beth died, and flogging yourself won't bring her back."

"It was my damned fault! If it wasn't for me, she would still be alive. Doolin wanted me. Why take her?" Sam buried his hands in his hair. "Because I wasn't there, that's why. I left my wife to face her killer scared and alone."

There was the bald, unvarnished truth that he had to live with every single day.

Nine

MESQUITE WOOD IN THE FIRE FELL WITH A LOUD POP, breaking the silence in the wickiup while the night breeze fought against the side of the makeshift dwelling, trying to find a way inside.

Luke shifted and laid a hand on Sam's shoulder. "Stop, *mijo*. That wasn't the way it was. Quit making yourself out to be a coward. You had no reason to think the woman you loved was in danger. And when you found out she'd been taken, you tried to save her."

Not hard enough. Doolin had tricked him and escaped into the wind.

There on the floor of the gaily decorated parlor, next to a glittering Christmas tree, laid the woman he loved. Sam shook away the memories before they could take root.

"I gambled and lost, and Beth died as a result." Sam stared into the flames, the past searing into him. "I dream of her sometimes, and she's always begging me to save her. Until I have some sense that she forgives me, I'll go on blaming myself, and there's nothing you or anyone else can say that will change that."

"You are probably right." Luke lay back and propped himself on an elbow, stretching his long legs. The silver conchos running down the sides of his black trousers reflected the firelight. "Do you know why I waited so long to join the family and accept the land, the money my father kept for me?"

"No, why?" Sam had never heard a lot about those early days with Luke.

"I didn't want what I had become, the bad things I'd done, to touch my father and brothers. I did not want them to be ashamed of me and have to lie to protect me. I had a big price on my head, and if lawmen knew Stoker Legend was my father, they'd have staked out the Lone Star, cut off supplies until Stoker gave them what they wanted. This is my truth, *mi sobrino*."

Shadow poked her snout through the flap of the door and wandered in, lying down next to Luke.

"The worst thing is for them to be ashamed of me, Uncle. Just about everyone in Texas knows Grandpa in one way or another, and my father made a name for himself catching criminals. I left Beth to die alone. I might as well have pulled the trigger myself. I don't belong in the family. So here I am." Sam rose for tin cups and filled them, handing one to Luke.

"You were trying to save her."

"Well, I didn't!"

They sipped on coffee and stared into the fire. Sam appreciated Luke trying to help, but there was nothing short of bringing his wife out of the grave that would ease his conscience.

⌒

Luke ended up staying for two days, and Sam found the company nice. Their talks helped him consider his situation from a little different angle. Maybe it was Luke's easy way of saying things and the fact that he didn't judge that got Sam thinking maybe he still had something left to give.

He showed his uncle a few tricks about bladesmithing and made a dozen or so of the thin pieces of steel for Cheyenne's baskets.

She rode up out of the blue, and Luke helped her down from her pinto. Sam introduced them.

"My parents had to suddenly leave, so I brought the extra food before it spoils. Looks like it'll come in handy with your uncle being here." She unhooked a basket from the pommel and handed it to him. "There's quite a bit of turkey and other things. Even a whole pecan pie."

Sam took the offering. "Look, you have to quit bringing me food. I can manage."

Cheyenne captured her bottom lip with her teeth. "I know, but taking this off my hands will do me a favor."

"Why your parents' sudden trip? Bad news?"

"My mother's twin sister is near death in East Texas. They've always been very close." Cheyenne's eyes filled with tears. "The doctor gives my aunt no hope. And right here at Christmas."

"I'm sorry." Sam put an arm around her shoulders. From the corner of his eye, he noticed Luke's rapt attention. His uncle would be sure to have something to say. Hell! "If I can do anything to help, let me know. You have Mitchell, but if you need something he can't do, I'm only five miles away."

"I appreciate your kindness." She drew herself up and pulled away. "I'll try to handle everything myself, but it's a comfort knowing you're nearby." She glanced at Luke. "How long are you staying?"

Luke gave her a warm smile. "I will leave tomorrow, Miss Cheyenne. I have business in Amarillo, then head home to my wife and kids."

"What kind of business are you in?"

"My wife and I have a bride service for men and women living in the shadows." Luke ran his hands along her pinto's long neck. "When I can, I like to see to the marriages myself."

"That's interesting. I have to say you don't look the type for that kind of work."

Sam grinned, eyeing his tall, lean uncle in traditional Spanish dress. "I see what you mean, Miss Cheyenne. But I happen to know he and his wife, Josie, have made somewhere around forty or fifty bride matches."

Luke shrugged and rolled his eyes. "*Dios mío*, someone had to help the poor outlaws and fallen women. However, this one in the town of Amarillo is our last."

"And whatever will you do then?" Cheyenne asked.

Deep pride replaced the humor in Luke's eyes. "I will become a cattleman like my father."

It had taken Luke years of reconciliation to get to this point and Sam knew how much it meant to his uncle to become more like the man who'd fathered him.

Their conversations during Luke's stay circled around in Sam's head and how similar their reasons were for putting space between them and their family. Neither had wanted to bring shame to the Legend name.

"I just remembered something." Cheyenne swung back to her horse and reached into her saddlebag, pulling out several lengths of yaupon holly with its bright red berries. "I brought this to add cheer." She strode to his wickiup and attached the holly over the entrance and stood back. "There. I like it."

Sam didn't have the heart to tell her he had no need of the Christmas reminder. She didn't know the depth of his pain and despair, and he'd keep it that way.

"I made some thin steel pieces for your baskets, Cheyenne." Sam handed her what he'd made. "I forged several shapes so they're not all alike."

The sun's bright rays dancing in her hair made each reddish-gold strand appear on fire. Sam didn't think he'd ever seen a prettier sight. He met her sparkling green eyes and warmth flooded over him.

She rested a hand on his arm. "These are so nice. Thank you, Sam. They're just what I need. They'll add special touches to my baskets. I daresay no one will have any like mine this Christmas. Well, I need to be going." She stepped over to shake Luke's hand. "It's been a pleasure meeting you."

"Likewise." Luke kissed her cheek. "Thanks for looking after my nephew."

Peals of laughter rang out. "I'm afraid I have no desire to tackle that."

Sam gave her a hand up into the saddle. "Thanks for the food."

With a nod and a touch of her heel to the pony's side, she rode off waving.

"You did not tell me of this young woman." Luke's voice was soft, searching.

"Nothing to tell. She's my neighbor's daughter." Sam tied his leather apron on, then busied himself at the forge.

"Nothing, huh? I think she is quite something, *mijo*. And I believe you think so too."

Heat inched up the back of Sam's neck. He squirmed under those twinkling dark eyes and his uncle's teasing smile. He quickly turned to thrust a piece of raw steel into the flames. Talking about Cheyenne wasn't going to get his work done.

Dark clouds drifted in, and it started snowing big fat flakes before dark. He and Luke dove into their supper, then turned in.

Sam lay awake in the dark, thinking about what Luke had said. His uncle had read a lot into Cheyenne's short visit. Maybe in another lifetime, he could love again.

Not this one.

A man didn't have to have feelings for a pretty woman to see the fight inside her. To admire her toughness, her spunk, her boldness.

Beth had been just the opposite, afraid of everything. Still, he'd loved her with his heart and soul. The fact that she must've been frozen stiff with fear in her last moments made his guilt a hundred times worse. She was waiting on him to rescue her, and he'd never come.

His deep, frustrated sigh brought Shadow's head up, her gray eyes staring. He patted the faithful companion, and she lay back down.

The night turned into a very long one, and the snow-covered morning didn't come too soon. After breakfast, Luke saddled his gelding. Sam pulled out a knife he especially liked and offered it to Luke. A big smile formed on his uncle's face.

"Exquisite work, Sam. I'll treasure this."

They stood beside the horse, their boots crunching in the white powder with each movement.

"I pray I did not wear out my welcome, *mijo*." Luke clasped Sam's hand and pulled him into a short hug.

"Never." Sam glanced away, hesitating a moment. "Tell Mother I'm fine and not to worry. I'll see her soon."

"And your father?"

"He knows I'm doing the best I can." Sam paused and frowned. "On second thought, give both the same message."

Luke nodded and swung into the saddle with ease. Waving, he spurred the horse into a trot, kicking up the snow with each stride. Sam was sorry to see his uncle go. He also liked his uncle Houston, but he had a special connection to Luke. Sam lit his forge and went back inside for another cup of coffee while it heated.

Now that he'd gotten rid of his visitor, he could work undisturbed.

Ten

THAT DAY HE SWUNG THE HAMMER WITH A GREATER INTENSITY, trying to pound the memories out of his head. At times, tears streamed down his face. He didn't mind the cold, the falling snow, or an empty stomach. Demons and despair drove him.

Shadow whined and lay under a tarp, watching him with sad gray eyes.

The knife Sam worked on was something new, something he felt driven to make. He let his heart lead, let whatever embellishments come from that creative place where spontaneity reigned supreme. He'd twisted the steel before welding to give the blade a swirled pattern that was beautiful to behold by the time he'd pounded it out. Next he plunged the red-hot steel into boiling oil to add hardness and strength.

Although he ran out of daylight before he got the edge ground on, he was satisfied with his work. Under the light, the blade was one of the best he'd ever made.

Sam ate the last of the food Cheyenne had delivered and slept without dreaming.

The next day it snowed more, but Sam was right back at it in the cold forging shed. Using the stone wheel powered by the foot crank, he put a razor-sharp edge on the swirled blade. He reached into a box for a piece of deer antler he'd cut into various lengths and began carving, shaping the bone into a comfortable handle. Grinding away the rough edges, he admired his handiwork.

An unseen force took hold, and before he realized what he was doing, he'd etched his father's initials into it with the word Legend underneath.

&

He worked the next seven days straight as though possessed and had five new knives to show for it, along with aching muscles from wielding the hammer day after day from morning to night. But it was time to take a break. Down to the last of the coffee, he saddled his Appaloosa and rode toward town in the first sunshine in days.

As he passed the Ronans', he spied Cheyenne attempting to chop wood. She was having a difficult time lifting the long ax high enough. It puzzled him why Mitchell wasn't doing that.

"Whoa." Sam pulled up on the reins, stopping. He dismounted. "Looks like you could use a hand."

She shaded her eyes with an arm. "I'll eventually get it. I'm not used to this long ax, and I can't find the shorter one."

"Where's Mitchell? Isn't this his job?"

"Mitchell's disappeared, and I don't know where he went or when he'll be back."

"When did he leave?"

"He was gone this morning when I got up. I never heard his horse. The funny thing is, he left all his belongings. Looked like there had been a scuffle in the bunkhouse. The table and a chair were turned over and some blood on the floor. Not a lot, mind you, but more than what would come from a nosebleed. I don't know what to think. I was going to come tell you after I finished this, but here you are."

Most likely Mitchell had gotten drunk or was with a woman. Still, there was the matter of the blood. That was concerning.

Sam removed his coat and took the ax from her. "I'll get this chopped and take a look around. I'm going into town and will check with the doc."

A hesitant smile curved her lips. "I appreciate it. Our wood supply has dwindled with the cold weather the last few weeks. I want to make sure I don't run out."

It wasn't like Bert to let it get low, but then he and Cora had left in a hurry. He'd relied on Mitchell to keep the ranch running. Sam would get some answers when he found him.

He set a thick piece of mesquite upright on the chopping stump and swung the ax, splitting it in half.

"I haven't seen much of you, Sam. Don't you freeze, working outside in snowy weather?" Cheyenne asked.

"Nope. I don't feel the cold when I'm creating."

"If you don't mind me saying, you don't seem to take very good care of yourself."

Long strands of russet hair slipped from the hood she wore, and her eyes held the bright glitter of green stones. The chill had put two becoming pink spots in her cheeks, and for a moment, Sam wished he were a painter instead of bladesmith and could capture her likeness in a portrait.

"As you can see, I'm alive and well." He chopped another piece of wood in half and reached for another.

"You sound like my father." She picked up the logs he'd chopped and stacked them.

Sam chuckled. "I think our skin is thicker than women's."

"I suppose." She released a long sigh. "But I've learned I can never make another person do as I wish. Especially not a wild man like you. I've seen pictures of the earliest man in history books and sometimes wonder if you posed for them."

Rubbing his bearded jaw, Sam squinted at her like she'd spoken in gibberish.

"They were probably just as standoffish," she added.

He frowned. "Is that a complaint or a compliment?"

"Stop it, Sam Legend! I'm just saying you could be more sociable. There's nothing wrong with being friendly and smiling once in a while."

"I do when I have a reason and it's necessary." He swung the ax. Seeing the fine fit she was in, he growled, "I don't believe in waste."

"I'm going in the house and leave you to your silence. If you take a notion, come in for coffee when you finish. Real coffee, not that sludge you make that walks to the cup."

"Now you're griping about my coffee? Is there anything you *do* like?"

She tilted her head, and the sunlight tangled in her reddish-brown curls. "You have a good dog. Even Shadow is more sociable than you are."

"My dog, huh? At least we agree on something." He watched the sway of her hips as she walked away. She was flat in a horn-tossing mood, and besides that, she could talk the legs right off a chair.

People might call him a bastard and an inhospitable recluse, but he lived as he saw fit.

However, with the mystery of Mitchell's disappearance and having to do all the work, she had reason to be snippy.

He finished up the wood, then went to the bunkhouse. Cheyenne had righted the table and chair, but the blood had soaked into the plank floor in several places. The largest circle was two inches in diameter. Like she said, not a lot, but more than for a normal split lip or bloody nose. Definitely a fight of some sort that ended with him leaving with them, whether forced or of his own volition.

Sam checked through Mitchell's belongings and found a letter from a woman, but with no envelope or anything to indicate who sent it, he had no name for her. She spoke of missing him and concern that he hadn't written. Had to be from his wife. But Mitchell wouldn't be the first man to keep a woman on the side. That was possible.

Whoever she was, she ended the letter saying she looked forward to seeing him at Christmas. Folding it, Sam put it back.

Next, he searched around the bunkhouse and other outbuildings. Nothing.

Long strides carried him to the Ronans' back door. A tap on the glass, and she let him in. He removed his hat. "Did you see the letter in Mitchell's stuff?" he asked.

Cheyenne pursed her lips and shook her head. "I didn't want to pry too much. I started to read it, but it made me feel strange, so I didn't. What did it say?"

"It had no name, but I assume his wife sent it, and it sounded like they were going to see each other for Christmas, just like Mitchell said at Thanksgiving. He might've gone home early." He hung his hat on a hook by the door. "But there's the blood issue and the fact that I don't think he would've left without telling you."

"Absolutely not. He's a very respectful man. He would've told me." She poured coffee and handed it to him. "I'm very worried."

"Like I mentioned earlier, I'll see what I can find out in town." Hopefully, Doc Tyler would know something.

"If we just knew where he went and if he's all right."

"Don't borrow trouble. There could be a logical explanation for all this." Although Sam couldn't imagine what that might be. At least it was winter, and Cheyenne could probably handle most of the work herself. He'd drop by of course to check on her.

It was the neighborly thing to do. And if nothing else, he intended to be a caring neighbor.

Eleven

"No, I'm afraid no one matching that description has been by here." Doc Tyler's eyes were bloodshot. "Excuse me. I've had a slew of gunshot wounds to treat and haven't slept more than a wink in two days, so I'm not the best right now. Between delivering babies and men trying their darndest to kill each other, I stay busy."

"I can imagine."

Tyler, a short, middle-aged man with a receding hairline, cleaned the lenses of his glasses and put them on. "Good luck finding your friend."

"Thank you for your time." Sam stuck his hat back on. "I'll look around town before I head out."

The clerk at the mercantile provided no help either, so Sam had the man grind his coffee beans and left with the sack. None of the six saloons were open yet, nor were the numerous houses of ill repute. With nowhere else to check, he climbed back on Rio and trotted from town.

Cheyenne was out with the herd on her pinto, so he rode out and gave her the news.

"I'm out of ideas." He pulled his hat lower to shield his eyes against the sun. "Maybe he'll show back up on his own accord. The only thing left is to wait. I could go back into town tonight I suppose and check the saloons and…other places." He glanced away.

"You mean whorehouses?"

"Yep."

"You think Mitchell would frequent those women?" she asked, her voice quiet.

Her green eyes seemed to search his thoughts. Sam was glad she couldn't.

He shrugged. "He's a lonely man."

"By all accounts, so are you, Sam." She seemed to catch herself, and her cheeks colored. "Sorry, that's none of my business."

"No, ma'am." He tugged right on Rio's reins. "I'm not that far if you need help."

"I should be able to handle things. Thanks for filling my wood pile."

Sam rode off, wondering if Cheyenne wasn't touched in the head a bit. He'd never met another like her, that's for sure. But she sure was pretty.

❧

Night fell, and Sam was in the wickiup when Shadow started raising old Billy hell outside.

A man yelled, "Hello, the house. Come get your dog."

Sam burst through the flap, pistol drawn. He recognized the caller right away and released an oath. "What do you want, Cap?" He didn't bother calling Shadow off yet. Let the man know he hadn't been invited.

"Just a favor, Sam. Hopefully, you'll be in a mood to accept." The Texas Ranger wore his hat pulled low, and his gray, droopy mustache kind of reflected Sam's mood.

"Quiet, Shadow!" Sam ordered sharply.

"Mind if I climb out of the saddle? I've been riding since Noah built the ark."

"That long, huh?"

Cap chuckled in that low voice of his. "Damn sure feels like it. Could you have possibly gotten any farther from civilization?"

It seemed pretty odd for the man to gripe about the distance when Sam hadn't sent for him. "Get down and stretch your legs. Maybe I can rustle up a bit of coffee."

The way company kept popping up, you'd think he had a damn welcome sign hanging out on a mesquite or something. What did a man have to do to be alone?

Cap eyed Shadow. "Will your dog bite?"

"Only if you look at her wrong. I've found her to be an excellent judge of character." Sam held the flap. "Might as well come on in since you got this far."

He knew he was being downright rude, but he really didn't want to see any company, most of all this one. Cap would be sure to bring up a past Sam was trying desperately to bury.

The Texas Ranger was one of the best, and he'd learned a lot from their time riding together and nights of sharing a campfire. The man had an uncommon penchant for meddling in things he had no business in. Cap entered and glanced around, then lowered himself to the rug. Shadow edged in too, sniffing at the stranger. Trust wouldn't come easy. That was one of the main things Sam liked about her.

Murmuring low words, Cap extended his left arm, palm up, to show he wasn't a threat. Shadow turned her nose up at his hand, then lay across the doorway, still protecting.

Cap shifted his attention to Sam. "I didn't recognize you. Almost pulled my gun. Been a while and, from the looks of you, you've taken to being a wild cuss."

"I know you didn't come just to compliment my youthful appearance." Sam dipped water into the pot.

"Nope. Damn sure didn't." Cap reached for a piece of wood from Sam's stack and laid it on the fire. "I think it must be true what they say about nothing but a fence separating the Panhandle from the North Pole. Hell, I think it moved even closer."

Sam snorted and set the pot on the hot coals. "Cap, you always did like to bellyache." He sat across from the old friend. "But you're the best in the business at hauling in the worst of the worst."

"I do enjoy my job." Cap scrubbed his face with his hands. "I'll get right to it before you throw me out. I already feel it's an iffy proposition." He let a moment's silence pass. "Here's the deal. We have a counterfeit ring operating out of Tascosa, and the boys and me can't make any headway. Mouths are locked up tighter than a virgin's chastity belt."

Undeniable interest sparked in Sam. He'd derived a certain pleasure out of catching criminals, but that didn't mean he wanted to—or could—return to that life.

He threw back his head in laughter. "What the hell would you know about a chastity belt? Or even better—a virgin? The only women you hang around with are pert'near ready to cash in their chips."

Cap swelled up and shook his finger. "I'll have you know I'm a walking encyclopedia. A man don't get to be my age without acquiring a whole lot of information. Both useful and not."

"An encyclopedia, huh?" Sam grinned in spite of himself. "So that morning you were chased buck naked from that house by a jealous husband, clutching your clothes, boots, and more importantly, your gun—that was part of the *acquired information* you're talking about?"

"You're damn right. Now, you got me off the subject." Cap jerked his hat off and whipped it against Sam's arm. When they settled, he got serious. "This group in Tascosa is printing ones and fives. They're flooding all these small towns with 'em. And they're good—almost fooled the experts."

An itch started to develop. Sam wanted to scratch it. Damn! But he was done with law work. Didn't mean he couldn't listen, though.

Sam whistled. "I see the urgency. This'll ruin everyone in this part of Texas."

If they got saddled with phony money, they'd have to eat the loss. With the average wage less than three dollars a week and some not even a dollar, no one could afford losing one cent.

"You bet'cha. And the governor is throwing a hissy. Then I happened to remember you'd plopped yourself down up here." Cap grinned.

"You might as well stop looking at me." Irritation rose that Cap had put him in this position. "I'd like to help. I really would. But I'm making these knives. So, no. Respectfully, I'll pass."

Cap sighed. "Look, what happened to Beth shocked us all, and we understand why you had to take a leave. But, son, it's time to come back. The past is like reaching for a hot pan over a flame. The pain is a whole lot less if you just turn it loose. The longer you hold on, the more severe the burn."

Hot anger rushed through Sam. "Looking at me, do *you* think I belong in your ranks?"

Cap nodded. "I do. There comes a day when you have to stop flaying yourself with that razor whip. Beth is dead, and she's not coming back." The ranger gazed into the fire for several long seconds. "Nothing you or any of us could've done would've saved her."

Sam shook his head. "If I hadn't chased after Doolin, I would've been there to stop the bullet. After dogging him for so long, I should've been wise to his tricks. I should've known he'd leave his brother behind to finish the job."

"Quit being so damn hardheaded! It was pitch-black and heavy clouds. When Doolin burst from that barn on his horse with guns blazing, you couldn't see well enough to know who the woman on the back was. Anyone would've thought it was Beth."

"Not anyone. Me. I thought he was making a getaway with my wife because he knew you and other rangers were coming."

"That seemed logical, given what you knew." Cap met Sam's eyes. His voice grew soft. "No one blames you."

"I blame myself for not letting Doolin ride on and busting into the house. I could've saved her. My mistake cost her life."

"So you say." Cap's words cracked like a whip.

"So I know!" Sam snapped.

The fire burned low and wind whistled around the stovepipe sticking through the ceiling.

"We can argue this till doomsday." Cap took a bottle from his pocket and uncorked it, offering it to Sam. "That second woman puzzles me to this day. Beats me where she came from. There was only supposed to be Beth in that house. So, when you saw the woman on the back with Doolin, you thought it was your wife. Hell, I would've thought the same."

Sam grunted, took a swallow of hooch, and passed it back. He'd been over this a hundred times and always came back to the same conclusion. He'd messed up, and the woman he loved and meant to spend the rest of his life with rested beneath the cold, hard ground, blaming him.

"A leader has a tough chore. Not getting the right information fast enough can lead to things going bad. I made mistakes that night too. I didn't get your message because my new recruit lost it." Cap took a gulp from the bottle, stoppered it, and put it away. He laced his hands behind his head. "By the time we got there, it was too damn late."

"Still doesn't change anything. I messed up. If I'd only busted into the house."

"Then Doolin's accomplices would've killed you in a hail of bullets."

Sam shrugged. "Would've been a damn sight better than this."

"I've had it. Sit here 'til you moss over. What do I care? Go ahead and drown in self-pity and guilt." Cap's eyes blazed. "And you call yourself a Legend? You don't know the first thing about what it takes to be one, sonny boy." Cap got to his feet. "Keep the coffee. If you do happen to find their red blood running through your veins, I'm in room 10 at that butt-ugly yellow hotel in Tascosa."

He disappeared through the flap, leaving Sam alone, wrestling with his ghosts.

Twelve

SAM WOKE THE NEXT MORNING WITH WHISKEY BREATH AND thoughts of Cap in his head. The cold words that carried the weight of a ball peen hammer had etched into his brain.

And you call yourself a Legend? You don't know the first thing about what it takes to be one, sonny boy.

He released a string of curse words. The pain went so deep, it took his breath. The worst part was Cap had spoken the truth. His family's kind of bravery, mental toughness, and determination had escaped him. When everything came down to it, he'd cracked like a rotten melon sitting in the sun.

After drinking coffee, he saddled Rio and went for a ride, the Appaloosa kicking up the snow. Maybe the fresh air would help this torment. He didn't know how far he rode trying to outrun Cap's words, but it was a good distance. Yet in the end, he hadn't ridden far enough.

Then all at once his head cleared and the anger left. Out of everyone, Cap had been the only person to get down to the core of the situation, the only one to say what everyone else wanted to but didn't. Sam was tired of everyone treating him like he was going to break. Well, Cap didn't. That tough ranger had let the hide go with the tallow and in no uncertain terms. Exactly what he'd needed.

Nothing but the sheer, unvarnished truth that scalded his insides.

Sam turned and circled back around the Ronan place to see if Mitchell had returned. It startled him to find Cheyenne outside in the snow, in the middle of some sort of strange ritual. Wearing leather leggings and the Apache dress, she bent, stretched, and strained to reach the sky. Then she twirled on her toes and leaped, pulling one arm across her chest like she was shooting an arrow from a bow. Was this something she'd done on a reservation or at the school?

If so, it was new.

Cheyenne bent over and stuck her bottom in the air, and he struggled to draw air into his lungs. The sight stirred all manner of stimulating images.

The loose deerskin dress probably made it easier, but even so, with each movement, the dress pulled tight across her breasts, waist, hips. A dark leather jacket lay near on the white powder. Working like that could definitely make a person overheated.

His breath fogging in the cold air, Sam rested an arm on the pommel and watched the graceful arm gestures, pirouettes, and balancing on one booted foot.

She resembled some kind of snow princess.

Not that he knew what those looked like. When he was busy forging, one would have to bite him on the butt for him to notice her.

When Cheyenne saw him, she froze, unsure what to do. Then she quickly recovered and stretched out a hand. "Hi, Sam. Come join me."

He dismounted and strode to her. "What are you doing? I've never seen anything like this."

The exertion had brought a nice pink bloom to Cheyenne's cheeks. "They're called calisthenics. I've been hearing a great deal about the importance of keeping the mind and body attuned and sharp. I saw these simple movements in the *Journal of Health*, which led me to make them part of my day." She laughed. "I feel alive. Healthy."

She certainly wore a pretty glow, no mistaking that.

"It looked rather"—what was the word he was searching for?— "complicated, I suppose, with all the bending and turning on one toe."

"Not really. None is too strenuous, and the exercise keeps me trim. I like to keep myself in good physical shape as much as I can. What do you think?"

Spit hung in his throat. What did he think of her body? "Well, your body looks fine to me. That is, it's well…uh, you know… nice."

Cheyenne laughed. "I was asking what you thought of the exercises. Are you for or against? Most men are of the opinion that it's nothing women should be allowed to do." She rolled her eyes. "Like we'll break or something, for pity's sake."

"I think you should do whatever makes you happy. Don't worry about anyone else. You have to do what's best for you."

"Well put, Sam." Her light laugh reminded him of the bells on a sleigh. "Now, I'm having to eat my own words. Sorry for criticizing your lifestyle earlier." A moment passed. "Hey, would you care for something to drink?"

"Coffee would hit the spot."

"I hope you don't mind that we go to my little cottage. I prefer the coziness to the big house."

"Lead the way."

She scooped up her coat, and they went inside. The tiny kitchen carried the scents of Christmas. Oranges with cloves sticking out of them hung everywhere, and fragrant juniper branches hung over the doors and stood in corners. Made him think he was in a faraway forest.

"Have a seat while I get the coffee on." She dropped her jacket on a chair and put water in the pot.

"It smells good in here." He laid his hat on the table, taking in the small combined sitting room and kitchen area. Through an open doorway, he noticed a bed covered with a colorful quilt. Her place was a lot bigger and fancier than his wickiup.

Cheyenne moved a gingerbread cake aside that she'd decorated with some red berries. "I love Christmas and tend to get a little carried away. I hope I can persuade you to take half of this ginger-bread cake home with you. I don't know why I made it. I guess I'm missing Mama."

"Cold weather makes my mother bake. She'll fire up the stove and get out her pans." A wave of homesickness washed over him for a moment. "Have you heard from your parents?"

"No, but it takes a letter a while to get here, and they may not write until there's news."

"My mother loves to decorate too and starts at Thanksgiving, filling the house with sweet-smelling things." He glanced around the tidy place and went to the small bookcase. A few titles were some he liked—*Around the World in Eighty Days*, *A Tale of Two Cities*, and *Great Expectations*. Then there was the usual fare by Jane Austen and Charlotte Brontë that appealed more to women.

She glanced at him. "Are you a reader, Sam?"

"I like to on occasion, but I don't have a lot of time for that."

"I think books are wonderful for lifting sagging spirits and taking you to places you'd never get to explore." She set the pot on the flame. "Care to sit at the table? We can have a slice of this cake with our coffee."

A few steps took him to the small kitchen area. He sat down with her. Why was he there? He knew she'd ask. Even if he was about to be flogged, he couldn't have said.

They chatted about any number of topics, and he found her interest widespread. Her sharp mind fascinated him and the fact she liked learning of things she knew little about.

"What brings you, Sam?" she asked gently, as though she'd read his mind.

"Hell if I know." He raked through his hair with his fingers. "I was out riding, and before I realized, I was here."

"What's wrong?"

Maybe it was the gentle sound of her voice, or it could've been the way she held his gaze. Whatever it was, he found himself talking. "I had a visitor last night who wants my help with a... problem. Before he left, he said some things about me that burrowed under my skin, and I can't let them go."

She absently drew circles on the tablecloth with a finger. "Were they hard truths?"

"Yep." He glanced out the curtained window at the bare trees—bare just like his life.

"I see. Sometimes we get no relief until we face whatever it is. But examining ourselves is the hardest thing we can possibly do. It's too painful to see this side of ourselves that we've fed. It's like some wild animal we've kept caged and then..." Her voice broke. "Then when we release it, the thing claws at our throat."

Cheyenne seemed to have forgotten him. Her soft words sprang from some unnamed source that spoke of her own struggle. Suddenly, she jerked. "I'm sorry. I didn't mean to ramble."

"You weren't. Actually, you might've helped."

"Then I'm glad."

She served the coffee, and they talked more about everything and nothing. Sam had never felt more at ease. He had a night of soul-searching ahead, but for the moment, he was happy for the reprieve.

"Sometimes I get so lonely, even when my parents are here. They're a stone's throw away, but they might as well be hundreds of miles." Cheyenne ran a finger around the rim of her cup. She seemed in a strange mood, and he could see no reason for it. She glanced up. Dark secrets had lodged in her green eyes. "Would you hold me for a moment, Sam Legend?"

The question startled him. He didn't know what to say, and the silence was loud in his ears.

"I'm sorry." She jerked to her feet and stood at the window. "I shouldn't have asked that."

Whatever was going on with her, Sam couldn't deny her comfort.

Before he could stop, he moved behind her and slipped his hands around her small waist. "Turn around."

Cheyenne swiveled and buried her face in his chest. "We don't have to talk. Just let me feel you."

Her heart thudded against him as though she were running. He folded his arms around her and inhaled the fragrant scent of oranges and gingerbread that lingered on her. It was hard not to notice how perfectly her body fit against his, how delicate she seemed. One might think her weak by her dainty face and hands, but oh, how they'd be wrong.

Sam didn't know what had prompted her sudden need, but he hoped he could give her whatever she sought.

After several long moments, she pulled away. "Thank you. Ever since that day by the river, I've had a few moments of anxiety. Were those men's wishes greater or more important than mine?"

"No. I'm sorry that happened and that you're struggling with the incident."

"I'll be fine. Things just crash down on me at odd moments." She pushed back her russet hair and released a sigh. "Would you like more coffee?"

Sam shook his head. "I have to be going. I should be making knives instead of riding all over the countryside."

"I'm glad you came." Cheyenne handed him his hat. "I wish you well in sorting out those hard truths. Stop feeding the guilt—if you can."

Maybe it was time to let the past go. It wasn't doing him any good holding on to it.

"I will try. Someday I may succeed."

She stretched to kiss his cheek. "Thank you for being a friend."

With a nod, Sam went out to Rio and swung up into the saddle. A friend? Well, he guessed a man could never have too many. Waving, he trotted off toward home.

That afternoon as he worked, he thought about his distinguished family who'd made a name for themselves by standing up against those seeking to destroy them. His grandfather had fought rustlers, landgrabbers, and thieves. Uncle Houston's bride had been gunned down at the altar, then a year later he had married a woman sight unseen for no other reason than to give her poor baby a name. His father, the senior Sam, hunted down the men who'd hung him and left him for dead. Uncle Luke, an outlaw son, worked hard to be worthy of carrying the Legend name.

Not one among them ever gave up in achieving their goal. Each had gotten the job done.

Except Sam. Beth's killers were still out there running free.

It was time to rectify that if possible. One day he might run into them, and he'd get his chance. At the least, he could bring in others just as evil, and that had to count for something.

Come night, Sam saddled his horse and rode into Tascosa. Music, yelling, gunshots burst through the doors of each saloon. Taking the alley in case the ugly yellow hotel was being watched, Sam kept to the shadows and climbed a back staircase.

Within a few minutes, he tapped on the door of room 10.

Cap opened it and stepped back, motioning him inside. "Can't say I'm surprised."

"Thought about what you said. Tell me about this counterfeiting ring."

The ranger dumped some clothes out of a chair. "Have a seat. My maid didn't show up."

"Yeah, mine didn't either." Sam sat down. "Maybe yours is looking for a chastity belt."

"Ha! That's probably it. Want a drink?" Cap waved a bottle.

"I never mix business with pleasure. Let's get this over with first." Sam glanced around the room that was bare except for the bed, a washstand, and the chair he was sitting in. Cap dropped on the end of the bed.

"Like I already told you, we don't know a lot about this criminal enterprise. I think they're operating out of the Hitching Post Saloon. They keep a back room locked and guarded at all times. I've seen them carting boxes in and out but can't get close enough to even get a sniff at the contents."

"Do you have any names? Anything to go on?"

"How about Doolin?"

Shock rippled through Sam. It took a moment to form words. "Are you sure?"

"Right now, just a hunch." Cap reached into his pocket for a match stem and stuck it in his mouth. "I saw Tom Doolin entering the Hitching Post yesterday. Before I could arrest the sorry piece of scum, I lost him. You know, if there's anything illegal going on close to where he's spied, he's involved."

"Seems a likely bet." Sam agreed. If he could catch Doolin, he'd kill the bastard. That might make Beth's death sit a bit easier in his mind.

"Go over what you know about the piece of shit, Sam. You followed him on and off for about a year, trying to get him for that string of bank robberies."

"Never caught him. He has two brothers—Deek and Ford. Mother's dead. Father's name is Lem. Years ago, Lem served time for holding up a stagecoach and killing the driver. The family homestead is south of here at Abernathy, but I never saw anyone working the land. I think Deek is the one responsible for pulling the trigger and killing Beth, but I can't prove it. He'd jump off a bridge if his brother Tom told him to do it."

"Sounds like they're all a sorry mess. Do you know Tom's family by sight?"

"Only Ford, and Tom, of course."

They probably all shared prominent features—a high forehead, crooked nose, and trademark thick, wavy hair.

Cap grunted. "Good old Tom. If we don't catch him with this fake money ring, we'll get him for killing Beth. I'm sure that will take a load off your shoulders." He was silent a moment, then winced. "Say, I'm sorry for those things I said."

"Don't be. You were right, and that was what I needed to hear. So, how do you want to proceed?" Sam had his own ideas, but he respected Cap too much not to listen to his plan. "I guess I'll have to shave."

"No. I want you just like you are. No one will ever suspect you're a Texas Ranger. That's the beauty of this whole thing. You'll be able to slip in and out of their midst, and they'll say things, do things, and not give you another thought. To them, you're just another bum down on his luck. That makes you invisible."

Sam grinned. "My boyish good looks must be growing on you, Cap. Everybody else wants to know when I'll be shaving."

"Don't mistake necessity for thinking all that mop on your head looks good." Cap scowled. "I can only imagine what your family says about you. They probably sit around the supper table drawing straws to see who gets to shoot you first."

"I see your point. But back to our investigation. I'll go into the Hitching Post and watch. If I see an opening, I'll get inside the locked room."

"Or you could strike up a conversation with one of the Doolins. See what they let slip."

Sam mulled that over. "Sooner or later, someone will mess up. Secrets leak out because people can't keep their mouths shut for long." It was usually an ego thing. Men with big ones had to try to impress others. Never failed.

"I'm adjourning this meeting. Pleasure coming up." Cap reached for the bottle and poured portions into two coffee cups, handing Sam one.

The hooch burned like fire all the way down, but Sam didn't care. It would soon smooth out, and he'd even start to forgive himself—a little anyway.

"Sam, what you need is to find yourself a good woman." Cap's droopy mustache twitched with his grin. "There's a lot of 'em around in case you haven't noticed."

"I'm not dead. My neighbor has a daughter." Now why the hell had he said that?

Cap pounced like a cat on a bug. "Whooee! You're keeping a secret, Sammy boy! What gives?"

"Nothing. Absolutely nothing." But Sam had trouble forgetting certain things. Especially the way she'd fit in his arms, the soft curves, and the fresh scent of her that had drifted around his head. "This way, if it doesn't work out, you won't be forced to pour rotgut down me until I either puke or grow horns." He lifted the cup to his mouth. "What about you, Cap? When are you going to pick one and settle down?"

"Funny you should ask. I was pondering that same question before you showed up at my door. The problem is, I cain't pick just one. I like 'em all. If I could combine them into one woman, she'd be perfect. Yes, sir. Mighty perfect. As it is, they all got something wrong with 'em."

"You must not know a blooming thing. You're supposed to overlook a few faults. What's their few when your own minus column is as long as from here to the Mississippi?"

Cap scowled. "I think you're getting a little too big for your britches, boy."

"What's the matter? Does your own medicine taste a bit on the sour side?"

The old ranger wagged his finger back and forth. "Just you never mind. Better put your energy to work on this job in front of us."

They lapsed into silence, and Sam thought about these ne'er-do-wells that had set up a criminal enterprise under his very nose. In between keeping an eye on Cheyenne, he was going to catch them. And if Tom Doolin was in fact involved…ah, that would make the job all the sweeter.

Regardless, he was coming, and he had fire in his blood.

He was a Legend, from a family known for resolute courage, determination, and sheer guts. And it was high time to start acting like one.

Thirteen

CHEYENNE SAT NEXT TO THE FIRE IN HER LITTLE HOUSE THAT night, listening to the wind howling like a banshee outside. She clutched a small blanket, her heart breaking.

Why? She was so empty inside. A failure.

She rocked back and forth, tears spilling down her face. There was no fixing this.

That was her hard truth. There was no fixing what she'd done.

Sam's arms had been so strong and comforting around her, the solid planes of his body hard against hers, but the solace hadn't lasted.

How long had it been since she'd given a promise only to break it? How long since she'd felt whole? She closed her eyes and let the happier part of the memories sweep her along. There had been some good times amid the horrible danger.

The wind beat against her door, and a crack like a rifle shot sounded.

Cheyenne dove to the floor, the blanket falling beside her. She drew it to her, sobbing and trembling. Soldiers. She had to hide. She had no gun. No place to run. Her heart pounded.

The sound came again. Then she realized it had only been a shutter banging somewhere.

Still shaking, she pulled her chair closer to the fire and sat down. Her thoughts drifted to the year she'd just spent in New Mexico Territory at the government school in Santa Fe and on the reservation.

The conversation she'd had with her mother shortly after

Thanksgiving before her parents left for East Texas played in her mind.

"Your father and I planned to have a whole houseful of children, but you ended up being the only one." Her mother's voice had held sadness. "I miss having little ones. On the reservation, I had my fill of holding them, loving them, protecting them."

"Me too. I loved my work in the New Mexico Territory on the Apache reservation—at first." Cheyenne had met her mother's eyes. "I have a confession."

"What's that, dear?"

"I wasn't a teacher for long."

The secret should've made her mother at least blink, but she didn't seem very surprised.

Cora reached for her hand. "I knew you were keeping a secret but had faith you'd talk in your own time. Something has troubled you deeply."

"I wasn't there a month before I saw how they treated those poor children. They were punished for the smallest of infractions—whipped, put in isolation, made to stand at attention for hours in the heat and the cold, saluting the flag. Small children, too young to understand what they'd done wrong. Bigger ones who became confused and bitter."

"It's a shame and a disgrace! That's why your father resigned from his post as the Indian agent on the Cherokee reservation. The higher-ups wanted him to do things that went against his conscience."

"Some things are worth standing up to."

"Especially when the white men in government decided they knew what was best for the Cherokees instead of trusting them to manage their own lives and make their own decisions. Your father realized that even though he was a fair and decent man, the Native people really didn't need or want him to save them."

Cheyenne nodded. "I started to understand this while I was with the Apache."

"So, what have you been doing for over a year if not teaching?" her mother had asked.

"I joined a group of brave Native women already working to lead as many Apaches as they could to safety in Mexico. Then we started smuggling children out of the school and taking them to their parents we'd already moved."

Cora had sucked in a quick breath. "That was so dangerous! You could've been killed."

Cheyenne shivered and huddled in the chair in her little house. Yes, she could have died, had come close numerous times. Then there were two incidents when… Memories washed over her, and she couldn't suppress the remnant of fear. Who would've ever dreamed she could go that far? Not even her. As she sat quietly in her little home far removed from that now, she didn't seem capable of such a raging, sweeping storm inside.

More of the conversation with her mother drifted around.

"We couldn't let the danger stop us, Mama. My conscience wouldn't let me quit. Since Geronimo had led the army on such a long, frustrating chase, the government was harsher on the Apaches, the last holdouts. I could see the Native women felt duty-bound to save as many of their people as they could, and I wanted to stand beside them in solidarity."

"You're your father's daughter. He taught you to listen to your heart and do what's right."

"You both did, Mama. You both instilled in me this strong moral compass to guide my steps."

The north wind battered against the house, banging the shutter again. Cheyenne shivered, remembering how she'd made hot tea for them and how proud her mother had been that she'd joined the Native population in making a difference to so many.

Make no mistake. She'd been terrified. In the desert away from the fort, no rules existed. People could meet with death out there at any given moment with no one the wiser.

The fire crackled, the log falling and spewing ashes.

Secrets had to stay locked up. She could never breathe a word about what had transpired.

Her mother had asked what happened to send her home, or if she'd gotten tired and quit.

"I'd still be there except the Apaches decided it had become too dangerous and called a halt," Cheyenne had answered.

"Do you think you'll go back when and if they resume?"

"I really don't know if they'd want me, Mama." She'd tried to force a laugh. "Never say never, I guess."

They'd talked about a Christmas tree and how far her father would have to go to find anything more than scrub brush. Cimarron in New Mexico Territory was discussed as a possibility.

Now, it made no difference. There was no one to celebrate the holiday with.

She'd never felt so lonely. There was nothing to look forward to. She glanced at the oranges hanging with the cloves stuck into the rind. It didn't matter. Nothing mattered.

Her mother would be sorely disappointed in her, but what was the use? Maybe she could invite Sam over and they could share a meal. He was alone too, yet his solitude seemed self-imposed. Or at least that was the impression she'd gotten.

His wickiup had to be downright frigid with little to block out the north wind. But a strong man to snuggle up to when it was freezing might not be too bad. Delicious tingles waltzed up her spine.

When he had his hair tied back with a strip of leather and she could see his eyes, Sam was quite handsome. She wondered what he'd look like without the beard. Hmmm.

Who was really to know? She didn't think he'd shave anytime soon and quench her burning curiosity. Nope. She tugged her blanket higher and tucked it around her body, her thoughts turning to what he was wrestling with. Whatever it was, it had to be a doozy for him to trade all that land, comfortable house, and caring family for the desolation of the Panhandle.

Maybe he'd confide in her one of these days.

But if his secrets went as deep as hers, she held no hope.

Shame and guilt surrounding hard truths kept them buried deep down where no light could reach. And that's right where hers were going to stay.

She only hoped she could learn to live with them and time would dull the sharp torment.

❧

Sam left Cap, wandered into the Hitching Post, and sat at a dark table in the corner where he had a good view. He panned the room and paused at the armed guard in front of a door. A combination of dim lighting and the brim of the man's hat made it impossible to see his face.

Sam considered getting up and wandering over that way but nixed the idea, not wanting to draw attention to himself. Tonight, he'd just watch.

Over the past year, he had come into town no more than a handful of times, never staying long. The card table held no interest, and he took the whiskey home. If Heck Raines happened to come in, Sam usually talked to him for a bit. Heck was an old bladesmith from way back and had more knowledge about forging steel than anyone he knew besides Tarak.

A customer in a fancy suit got rowdy at the long bar, drawing his attention. From what Sam could hear, he was looking for Lem. No last name, but his ears perked up. What were the chances the man wanted to meet up with Lem Doolin? There must be other Lems.

The bartender leaned forward. "If I say I don't know him, I do not know the man!"

"I say you're a liar!"

The loud talk and music ceased. Tension grew so thick you could taste it.

The barkeep whipped a pistol out from under the bar. "Mister, if you don't head for the door right now, you're a dead man."

"Whatever you say." The well-dressed patron tossed back a drink and raised his hands. "Tell Lem that Nate Seymour has a delivery for him." He sauntered out onto the street.

Sam committed the name to memory. The man was worth checking out. He pushed back his chair to get up when Heck Raines shuffled in, leaning heavily on the hickory cane he always carried.

He saw Sam and joined him, dropping heavily into a chair that probably groaned a little under his large frame. One day his cane was going to snap in half. The sixty-year-old was the largest, tallest man Sam had ever seen.

"Thought I might find you here, Legend." He settled in the chair and folded his hands over his large belly.

"Wanted some fresh air, and my horse needed riding. Any particular reason you're looking for me?"

Heck leaned closer. "A fellow stopped by my place today with a drawing of a part that appears to go to a printing press of some kind and asked me to make it. He got real nervous when I asked what he'd be printing and sidestepped the question, never answering. I was just trying to make conversation like I always do, but he wasn't a bit friendly."

"That's odd. What did you tell him?"

"I said I would, only now I'm having second thoughts. I think there's something shady going on."

The piano player sat down and began to pound out a jaunty "Jingle Bells." One or two drunk patrons with silver tinsel around their necks linked arms and bellowed, "Fa la la la la la la la la! 'Tis the season to be jolly!"

The piano player finally threw up his hands and stormed out.

Sam shook his head at the interruption and leaned closer to Heck. "Did he give a name?"

If the visitor he'd spoken of had nothing to hide, he'd have said what he wanted the part for.

Heck signaled the barkeep for two beers. "Pope, but I think it's made up. He studied the ground for almost a minute before he gave it, and he had this funny voice. Wonder why he acted so strange."

"I don't know, Heck." In Sam's experience, it was usually a man with something to hide, someone breaking the law. "Say, have you heard of Nate Seymour?"

The portly man thought a minute. "I might've seen such a man yesterday. He dressed real fancy like. Can't recall where I saw him." Heck stared off a second, then he snapped his fingers. "Outside the undertaker. He was buying a coffin."

A coffin? That put a new wrinkle in things.

"How do you know that was Seymour?"

"Heard the undertaker call him that."

"Did he say who had died?" Sam asked.

The same drunks whooped it up across the room, raising the roof with their off-key singing and celebrating. They'd had a little too much pre-Christmas liquid cheer.

Heck glanced their way before answering. "Nope. He just loaded it in his wagon, then drove out of town. It was a rough-hewn wooden one. Never saw him before that. Why?"

"He's back. He just got into an argument with the barkeep before you came in."

"You don't say. Did he mention who'd died?"

"No. He was asking for Lem. No last name. Almost took a bullet for his trouble." Sam still thought the man meant Lem Doolin.

The scowling barkeep brought their beers, and the conversation turned to knife-making.

"I don't have much left to do in being ready to sell what I've made. I think I'll make quite a bit from them."

"Sam, your knives are something special. Everything you make is top-notch."

"Thank you, Heck. That's a real compliment coming from you. You and Tarak taught me how to pay attention to detail and take my time."

"You were a good pupil and grabbed hold of everything like it was fixin' to get away."

A stranger entered and strode to the guarded door, had a few words with the guard, and entered. Sam observed everything. A few minutes later, the same man emerged with two large boxes and left. The fellow didn't seem to strain carrying them, so they must not've been real heavy, but not light either.

"Heck, do you ever wonder what that man's guarding over there?"

"Only one thing makes sense—money. I don't figure there's much else around here to keep locked up. But money from what? That's the question. It's certainly not from this place. They hardly make enough to keep the doors open."

"I think you're probably right." Fake money was more like it. Sam noticed Heck didn't look so good. His friend was wincing and fisted a hand over his heart. "Are you okay? Do you need to see the doc?"

"Aw, I got a bad ticker, and it acts up from time to time. No need to get excited. It'll straighten out."

"I sure hope so." Sam glanced around. With only a handful of tables occupied and no one standing at the bar, it looked to be a slow night. Even the singing drunks got up and wandered out. Two rough-looking men pushed inside, went straight to the guarded door, and entered.

"Curiosity can get a man killed," Heck muttered thickly.

"How long did you say you've lived around here?" Sam asked, changing the subject.

"Born nearby. Pa worked for Goodnight. There were thirteen of us kids."

"Good Lord! A lot of hungry mouths to feed."

"Last I heard only five are living counting me and they're all off in California or Nevada. Who the hell knows?" Heck coughed and lifted his beer. "Why I never married. I didn't want kids."

"Nothing wrong with that. Lots don't." He and Beth had never got around to a serious discussion about starting a family. She'd been enough for him.

The guarded door opened again, and the two men who'd entered lugged boxes out and left the saloon. Sam watched through narrowed eyes.

He pushed back his chair and tossed some bills on the table. "I need to head home."

"Me too." Heck struggled to his feet and propped himself on his cane.

They walked out into the night, and Sam pulled his coat around him, striding to his Appaloosa. Heck went the opposite way. Sam stared up and down the street, hoping to spy the two men, but they were nowhere in sight.

Dammit!

A couple singing Christmas hymns came down the street, arm in arm, her in red satin and fur and he in a suit and thick overcoat. He recognized Mickey and Frenchie McCormick, the husband and wife who always seemed to be in the paper for some outlandish situation. Both excellent shots, they'd arrived in the early days of Tascosa from Mobeetie. Mickey opened a livery, and Frenchie began plying her trade at the gambling tables. The pair appeared to live life their way with no apologizing.

They stopped. "Nice horse, mister," Mickey said. "Are you wanting to sell him?"

Sam smiled, untying the reins. "Afraid not. Sorry."

"Well, he's a beauty."

"This is a cold night to be out for a stroll, isn't it?" Sam asked.

Frenchie laughed, staring into her husband's eyes. "Mickey calls me his good luck charm. We won a few pots down the street and on our way home."

"A good luck charm is true, darlin', and my plans for you don't involve any cards." He gave her a long kiss. "Evening, mister. And Merry Christmas!"

Sam wished them every happiness, but he doubted they heard him, wrapped up in each other the way they were. He swung up into the saddle, his thoughts on Cheyenne's warm body for some reason. He knew she had no interest in him other than as a friend, but he found himself wishing that maybe somewhere in the future, there might be more. He liked holding her. The feel of her pressing against him. The scent of oranges and gingerbread dancing around had managed to work themselves into his head.

Under the curtain of night, he rode, wondering how kissing her would feel.

Not just a peck on the lips. A real kiss like the one Mickey gave Frenchie, that came straight from the heart. He realized how deeply he'd missed that. Still, until he got rid of his shaggy hair and beard, he doubted Cheyenne would have any part of him. Except to try to slice his damn throat.

He barked a laugh. The lady wasn't interested in him in any romantic sort of way, which was just as well. This new direction his life had taken called for no distractions.

An irony hit him. Now that he was beginning to feel the stirrings to take his place as a Legend, he couldn't clean himself up or it would ruin the investigation.

Hate burned in his chest every minute of every day for Tom Doolin and his brothers, and he wouldn't be satisfied to simply catch them. No, he wanted to make them beg for their lives—just like they made Beth. And he wanted that so bad he could taste it.

And if they had a part in making this phony money, even better.

Fourteen

A FAINT SNIFFLING, THEN SHADOW RUSHING OVER THE TOP OF him to get outside awakened Sam the next morning. Dammit, if he had another visitor, he was moving!

He rose and pulled a blanket around his faded red long johns, walking barefoot to the flap and pushing through. "Who's there?"

Shadow gave a sharp bark, came to his side, and whined.

In the pale light of the early dawn, Sam noticed a skinny kid several feet away sniffling, couldn't have been no more than six. Looked to be a boy in a thin coat. Even from where Sam stood, he could see the bluish lips.

Shadow ran back to the kid and licked his hand, giving a sharp bark.

"Hey there, want to come inside and get warm?" Sam asked.

The kid stared with large eyes but didn't move.

"I won't hurt you." Sam waved. "Come on inside by the fire. You look cold."

The words came barely louder than a whisper. "Do you have anything to eat?"

"Come in and I'll find you something." Sam wasn't sure what, though. He kept little on hand for a child.

The boy slowly came closer, and Sam held the flap aside for him. His teeth chattering, the youngster went straight to the fire and held his hands over the flickering flames.

Sam transferred his blanket to the kid's slender shoulders. "What's your name?"

"Aaron."

"Hi, Aaron. I'm Sam. Do you have a last name?"

A shrug was the only answer he got. "Okay, where do you live?"

"Don't got no home. A wagon." The kid pointed at the flap.

"Where's your mother and father?"

Aaron pointed silently at the flap. They were getting nowhere. Sam knelt in front of him. "When did you last eat?"

"A long, long time ago. We didn't get no fire. Or food."

Sam scrounged around in his boxes and found some jerky. "Gnaw on this while I get some clothes on."

The way the boy snatched it and started chewing told of his hunger. Sam watched him while he threw on some clothes and his boots. He didn't have a clue what to do with the kid. Surely, Aaron hadn't wandered too far. His parents must've been traveling, and maybe their wagon broke down.

"Do you have any brothers or sisters?" Sam handed him a cup of water, all he had to drink that was suitable for a child.

"Yep." The boy held his forehead in his hands, apparently thinking, and finally held up one finger.

Alrighty. Sam felt like he was playing a guessing game and the kid was winning. Aaron scooted closer to the fire. Wherever his family was, they must be just as cold and hungry. Let Aaron get warm, and they'd ride out to find his kin. He just prayed the kid knew the way.

Aaron held his head in his hands, then scrunched up his face. "Mama's real bad sick."

"Okay." Sam had better find her fast. It sounded like his mother's life depended on it.

"Mama said hurry."

"I'm trying." Sam buckled on his gun belt for good measure, since he didn't know what he'd be running into.

Why hadn't the boy mentioned his father? And why not send him for help instead of a kid?

Full of questions, he pulled a handkerchief from his pocket and wiped the boy's runny nose. Tenderness stirred in his heart. Either the hunger in Aaron's empty belly had been too powerful, or else he'd needed help for his mother. Whichever one, it had sent him out into the cold. How many others were in the same shape where he'd come from?

Surely a woman hadn't brought her kids out by herself. How far had she come?

The boy needed something more than jerky. Sam riffled through another box but found nothing but some soda crackers.

"Here, stuff these in your coat pocket for later." Sam would shoot some game and cook it when he found the wagon.

Aaron glanced up at him and chewed his jerky. Hope filled the kid's eyes. Maybe he thought Sam had all the answers, and if so, he'd be sadly mistaken.

"Can you tell me how far you walked? Did it seem a long way?"

The boy shrugged. "It was real cold. And dark. I got tired."

None of that told Sam much. The sun was just coming up, so it would've been dark the entire way. And all kids got tired, even after a short distance. "Keep thinking of things you noticed. Any houses or barns?"

"Didn't see any."

"Don't worry, we'll figure it out. I'm going to saddle my horse. You stay in by the fire. I won't be long."

"We gotta hurry, mister."

"I know. Just rest here by the fire." He grabbed the rifle and went out.

Once he'd saddled Rio, Sam wrapped the kid in the blanket and took off north in the direction of the small pointing finger. Shadow ran point, racing ahead of them.

Snowdrifts remained in places where the sun hadn't gotten, but the rocky ground was clear for the most part. The bitter cold was compounded by the gray sky and the threat of more snow. He looked for footprints but saw none. Figured.

They rode across the barren landscape, seeing nothing. It would've been hard for the kid to walk more than a mile or two.

Sam stopped. "Aaron, are you sure this is right?"

The boy looked around and began to sob. "I don't know. I saw a windmill and then had to climb over a fence. I fell."

Could be the Ronans'. Or the gigantic XIT Ranch that ran down the western part of the Texas Panhandle and extended south 185 miles. Finding the boy's family would be like searching for a peanut in this vast land.

"I'm sorry, Aaron. Try not to worry. I'm going to find your family."

Life was hard enough for adults, but for kids it was so much worse. Sam scanned the landscape, looking for anything out of place. All he knew to do was to make a circle and expand outward. It seemed a miracle that Aaron had found the wickiup.

Sam tugged on the reins, and they turned west. They encountered a fence almost right away, but there was no windmill in sight, so Sam swung south until about even with the Ronan place. Smoke rose from the stovepipe on the roof above the kitchen. He pulled to a halt by the back door and dismounted, reaching for Aaron.

Shadow crowded close to the boy as though sensing his need to cling to something.

Cheyenne heard them and opened the door. "Sam, come in. Who do you have there?"

"This is Aaron, and he appeared at my place this morning, starving and cold. No last name. Says his family is in a wagon and his mama is real sick."

Concern lined her face. Her eyes met his, and her cheeks deepened to a pretty shade of pink. "Come in for a moment and get warm. We'll discuss what to do."

Sam and Aaron stepped inside. Shadow followed. The boy's gaze went to the stove, probably lured by the smell of breakfast cooking. "So, you haven't seen any travelers broke down?" Sam asked.

"No, and he doesn't look familiar." She bent and laid a hand on Aaron's shoulder. "My name is Cheyenne. I'm happy to meet you. You're just in time to eat this delicious breakfast. I made far too much for just me."

"I won't eat much, ma'am," Aaron murmured. "I promise."

Quick tears filled her eyes, and she had to look away for a moment. "You can eat to your heart's content. Take off your coat and sit at the table while I make you a plate."

"Thanks, Cheyenne." Sam removed Aaron's coat and laid it on an empty chair. "Is it okay if the boy stays? I need to keep riding and try to find his family, and he doesn't remember the direction he came." Sam glanced down at Aaron's blue lips. "He's frozen clear through."

"Yes, of course. He'll wind up sick himself. The poor darling. I suggest you ride east. I chased after a stray cow over there this morning and thought I glimpsed something through the fog but figured I was just imagining things. Maybe that's them." She filled a plate with eggs, sausage, and a biscuit and set it in front of Aaron. "Where were you headed, young man?"

"To my daddy for Christmas."

"Where is he?" Sam asked.

Aaron laid down his fork and slid his hand inside Sam's. "I don't know."

Something squeezed in his chest. Little boys needed love, food, and protection from the cold world. This one was brave to have struck out on his own at such a young age, and Sam ached for him.

"That's okay. Your mama will know." Sam released his hold. "Go ahead and eat."

"I ain't had eggs an' sausage in a long time," the boy whispered.

"Then, I hope you get your fill." Sam's gaze followed Cheyenne's slender figure to the stove, admiring her split riding skirt and blue shirt that hugged her form.

She returned with another plate of food and a cup of coffee for

Sam. "You might as well eat. You don't know how long you'll be out there."

"I can't tarry. It's urgent that I find them." He grabbed a biscuit and stuffed a piece of sausage in it, then hurried with the coffee.

"Do you know how many there are of his family?"

"A mother and one sibling according to Aaron."

Aaron nodded. "Mama and sissy."

"Are you the oldest?" Cheyenne asked.

"Yep. I'm big." He held up eight fingers.

"Every bit of it," Sam assured him. "Take your time and chew each bite. We don't want you to get a bellyache."

Cheyenne left the room and came back with her arms overloaded with blankets. "You'll need these, Sam. Who knows what you'll find. And take the wagon. You'll need something to haul them back in."

For some reason, his thoughts went back to the day he caught her doing calisthenics in the snow, and heat flooded over him. Damn it. He had to keep his mind off that. This was no time to be thinking about such things.

Aaron patted his arm. "I'll go with you."

"It's way too cold, son. I'd like you to stay here. All right?" Lord knew Aaron wouldn't be much help anyway. His nose hadn't stopped running, and he was so weak, he could barely walk. The kid wasn't in the best of health.

Cheyenne laid a hand on top of his head. "I'd like you to keep me company, Aaron. You can help me string popcorn and cranberries to decorate the house with. Doesn't that sound like fun?"

"I ain't ever done that before, ma'am."

"It's easy and lots of fun. You'll see."

Sam nodded his thanks to her and turned back to Aaron, resting his hand on the boy's shoulder. "I'll bring your mama and sister back real soon."

"Promise?"

"Cross my heart."

Tears filled Aaron's brown eyes, and his bottom lip quivered. "You gotta hurry and find Mama. She might die, and..." His voice dropped to a whisper. "I need her."

"I will." Sam took the last drop of coffee and reached for his sheepskin coat. He pulled on a pair of leather gloves, grabbed his hat, and went out to hitch the wagon.

Cheyenne brought out the load of blankets and quilts. "Sam, I pray you're not too late. Dear God, I don't know what that boy in there would do."

"I don't know either. Wouldn't be much of a Christmas."

Soon after, Sam drove away from the house with Shadow riding next to him on the seat, the wagon bumping over the uneven ground. He glanced up at the cloudy sky and pulled his collar around his neck. He prayed they found Aaron's kin soon—alive. Just as he thought that, it began spitting sleet in his face, and the wind gusted fit to beat all.

It was slow going in the wagon, encountering a gully he had to go around. Ice collected on Sam's beard and clothes, and it appeared he might come up empty-handed.

In the back of his mind pounded the fact that Aaron's mother might not live out the day.

Keeping in mind that Aaron had walked this, and Cheyenne might've seen something that morning, he confined his search to less than a mile.

As he drove the wagon down an incline, he spied it.

Sam blinked back the stinging sleet and stared. The wagon listed to the side with a broken wheel. The mother had driven it as far as she could.

He drove the last few yards and pulled the brake, jumping down. "Hello! Can anyone hear me?"

Shadow scampered from the wagon, sniffing around.

A small child about four or five, a girl by the dress, poked her head over the wagon tailgate.

"Hey, are you Aaron's sister?"

The girl nodded.

"I'm Sam and I've come to get you." He glanced beyond her to the huddled lump under a few blankets. Must be the mother. She hadn't stirred at the sound of his voice, and fear set in that she'd died.

He climbed in and knelt over her and moved the blankets from her face. "Ma'am, I'm Sam. Can you hear me?"

No reply came.

Removing one glove, he touched her forehead and found her burning with fever. She moaned. She was alive. Thank God! It seemed odd how a person could have a high fever in such icy surroundings, but he knew it to be true.

She wasn't going to last long if he didn't hurry.

The girl watched him silently, eyes large in her face. Blue lips, a runny nose, and a cough gave him an idea of her shape. The mother had tried to keep her daughter warm though and had put layers of clothes on her. Though he couldn't see them, he assumed she wore thick stockings. It appeared remnants of tears had frozen to her lashes.

His heart lurched as he lifted her and put her little body inside his coat, pulling it around her. "I'll have you warm in a minute, sweetheart. Let's move you first, then I'll get your mama. I'll take you to Aaron." He held her close against him until he felt her shaking start to ease.

"Aaron's dead," she said in a dull voice, sniffling.

"No, honey. He's alive. You'll see him soon."

She didn't protest being moved. Sam unfolded the blankets and made a bed for the woman, then he carried her over and tucked the mound of blankets tightly around her and the girl.

The mother stirred, and her feverish eyes sought his. "Aaron?" Her voice was so weak Sam could barely hear her.

"He's being cared for, ma'am. I left him where it was warm."

"I sent him…help." She erupted into a coughing spell that lasted several minutes, then lay weak and shuddering.

"Aaron found me, ma'am. He's a smart boy. Mind telling me your name?"

"Loretta but I go by…Retta. My…daughter…Ellen."

"I'm Sam Legend, and I live around five miles northwest."

Retta shook her head. "Husband…" Her tongue worked in her mouth. "Trying to find him."

"Yes, ma'am. I'll do my best to help you. But first we've got to get you to a doctor."

Retta nodded and fell back asleep.

Sam knew two things: she could die before they reached a doctor, and she was in the family way. He didn't know how far along, but there was no hiding the protruding stomach.

Hell! Their problem had just multiplied.

A wall of sleet continued to pepper Sam's face. He glanced up at the dark-gray sky, vowing to not stop until he got the family to food and a blazing fire.

Fifteen

THE JOURNEY BACK WITH THE TWO TOOK SAM LONGER THAN expected. He had to keep stopping to find a smoother road around perilous rocks and gullies, then once to see to Loretta, but they finally made it, and he was more than relieved to pull next to the Ronans' ranch house.

Cheyenne and Aaron ran out, the door slamming.

"Mama!" Aaron cried, trying to crawl up into the wagon.

Ellen's head popped out from the blankets. "Aaron!"

Sam lifted the girl out and the two siblings hugged as though they'd been separated for a hundred years. Shadow danced around them like a kid herself.

"I have a bed ready for the mother inside and some bone broth warming." Cheyenne leaned over the side of the wagon to look. "How is she?"

"Barely clinging to life. I wasn't sure we'd make it here in time." He removed the tailgate and grabbed the blankets to gently pull Retta down to where he could lift her out.

Cheyenne led the way, holding the door and getting the children inside. She directed him to the room, and he laid the woman down, covering her. Heat from the fireplace in the parlor kept the room warm, and that was a blessing.

"Her name is Loretta but she goes by Retta. She woke up briefly after I transferred her to my wagon but not since. Mumbled that she's trying to find her husband."

"I'm so glad you found her. Poor thing. I wonder how long they'd been out there."

"I don't know, but when I first arrived, I thought she'd died."

For a long moment, he held Cheyenne's gaze, wanting to take away some of the worry from her eyes. But he didn't know what to say that might help and finally turned toward the wide-eyed children talking in whispers in the doorway. They had to know on some level how gravely ill their mother was.

"I'll leave Retta in your care and get the girl something to eat. She's half-starved."

"I put a plate for her in the warming oven, Sam. Soon as you can, go for the doctor," Cheyenne threw over her shoulder. She raised the quilts at the foot of the bed and tucked a heated brick next to Retta's feet. While she'd waited, she'd had time to prepare and seemed to have thought of everything.

Including a room containing an extra bed for the children, so they could be close to their mother.

"It'll only take a moment to get Ellen situated. Aaron will sit with her." Sam herded the children into the kitchen and removed a plate of eggs, sausage, and a biscuit from the warmer. He set it in front of her, along with a glass of milk.

Aaron grabbed a napkin and stuck it in the neck of his sister's dress. "It's good, Ellen. And the nice lady gave me a piece of gingerbread cake. Bet she'll give you some too."

"Yes, she will." In fact, Sam cut a piece and set it next to the girl's plate. "I have to go fetch the doctor now. If you need anything, ask Miss Cheyenne."

"We will," Aaron promised. "I'll look after Ellen." He paused a moment. "Will you leave your dog, Mr. Sam? I like dogs."

"Yes, I'll leave her. Her name is Shadow."

"She's pretty."

"I think so too." Sam bundled up and drove the wagon around to the barn and unhitched the team. Then he led Rio out and galloped for town.

The trip was bone-chilling, but he made it in record time and found Dr. Tyler in his office. He looked dead beat, and Sam wondered if the man ever got any decent rest. "I spent the night pulling a bullet out of a patient, but I'll come with you. I may have to have some coffee when I get there though."

"That's a deal."

The doctor climbed into his buggy and followed Sam to the Ronans'.

While Doc Tyler examined Retta, Sam took care of their horses then waited in the parlor with the kids. They were quiet and kept staring toward the room where their mother lay. Every so often, Aaron tiptoed to the door.

"When this storm passes, I'll go back and fetch your belongings from the wagon. You probably packed some toys." And Sam had noticed a few gaily wrapped Christmas gifts.

"We brought Daddy some presents," Ellen said. "I cain't wait to see him."

"I'm sure he'll be happy to see you too. Did you ever hear where he lives or works?"

Aaron lifted his head and stopped picking at his sleeve. "Nope."

"Well, I'm sure your mama knows. We'll wait for her to wake up."

"Is she gonna die?" Ellen asked.

Sam wasn't sure how to answer. He wasn't about to start lying to little kids. "The doctor is going to do everything in his power to make sure she doesn't."

Just then, Cheyenne bustled from the bedroom and hurried to the kitchen.

"Wait here, and I'll try to find out something about your mother," Sam told the children. He followed the creak of the pump and found Cheyenne filling a pan with water. "Those kids out there are desperate for anything about their mother."

She set the pan of water on the stove. "Retta has pneumonia, and it's very bad." She turned to face him. "We're going to form a tent over her with a blanket and get her to breathe steam from this pan. The doctor thinks it might help. I'm not sure anything can." She released a worried sigh. "Sam, I'm afraid for her."

He put an arm around her, and she placed her forehead on his shoulder. "We just have to do everything we can, then leave the rest to a higher power."

"I know. Doc says the baby is still alive but barely. Retta is in and out of consciousness, but she keeps a protective hand on her stomach. The doctor guesses she's probably five months along and could lose it. We need a miracle."

Yes, they did. Sam gazed out the window at the gray day that reflected their spirits. "We should probably consider what'll happen to Aaron and Ellen if their mother doesn't pull through." Sam rubbed her back, enjoying the feel of her.

"I suppose they'll have to go to an orphanage if we can't find any next of kin."

Sam set his jaw. "We can't. Not right here at Christmas."

Nothing got kids more excited than Christmas, and orphanages were notorious for never having any funds. The day would likely be sad, lonely, and bleak. He wasn't going to let that happen. No matter what he had to do.

Cheyenne glanced up at him. "What else can we do?"

"Maybe their father will turn up alive." Sam wasn't sure how they'd even find him without a name to start with.

"I hope you're right. Anything's possible." She pushed back her hair. "I have to make a mustard plaster for Doc Tyler. When this water heats, will you bring it into the bedroom?"

"Sure. I think I'll make some coffee. Tyler can probably use some, and so can I." Sam met her steady green gaze. "We're going to get through this."

"Yes, we are."

Her smile showed a perfect row of white teeth. He wondered if she ever let her mind drift to that day in her little kitchen when he'd held her in his arms, the smells of Christmas drifting around them. He hadn't been able to forget the feel of her next to him.

"I feel sorry for those kids out there, half scared out of their wits in a strange house with people they've never seen before." Sam glanced toward the parlor door.

"Me too." She touched his arm for a moment, and the warmth penetrated his sleeve. She disappeared into a little room off the kitchen and emerged with some salves, clean cloths, and various other items. "Sam, if you hadn't gone out trying to find Retta, she would've died before nightfall."

"Don't dwell on what might've been. Focus on what is. For now, we're doing the best we can."

Cheyenne nodded, tears filling her eyes. Sam wiped away an escaping teardrop with a fingertip. "Try not to worry. Even the darkest night has a dawn."

With a nod, she turned and went back to the bedroom. Sam hunted around for coffee and put some on.

"Did you find out about Mama?" Aaron asked from the doorway, a protective arm around his little sister.

"Yes, I did. Come sit at the table."

When they did, he was as honest as he could be without scaring them more. "Your mother has pneumonia. She's very sick, but the doctor is hopeful she'll be back on her feet soon."

Relief washed across Aaron's face. "Oh good. I think so too." He hugged Ellen.

It was odd how the barest of news could sometimes send a person's spirits soaring. And even though Aaron and Ellen didn't fully understand, they seemed satisfied. He made them some hot chocolate and cut two more slices of gingerbread cake.

The next morning, he went back to Retta's wagon for their belongings. The children were smiling and happy to have their things. Aaron placed the wrapped packages in the parlor, then dug around in a carpetbag for something.

Sam watched, curious to see what he was looking for.

"Here it is." The boy pulled out a locket on a silver chain. He brought it to Sam and opened it. "See? Mama and Daddy."

The picture wasn't the best quality. The man, his face shadowed by his hat, had moved slightly as the photographer snapped it, but Sam could sense the love between the couple. Wide smiles on Aaron's and Ellen's faces said it all. "That's real nice. What are you going to do with it?"

"My mama needs it. She always feels better when she looks at this."

Aaron took it into the bedroom with Ellen following. Sam watched him open Retta's hand and lay it on her palm. Cheyenne glanced at Sam, and her luminous green eyes held tears.

"Now, she can get all better," Aaron announced. "She has us."

Ellen patted the quilt covering her mother. "Here we are, Mama. Don't go to heaven."

Cheyenne moved to Sam, sniffling. "I think that's the sweetest thing I've ever seen. How can she not get well after that?"

"Yes, indeed."

"Sam, will you consider staying here for a while? I need help."

That might've been the first time Cheyenne had ever used those words. He'd never known a more independent woman. But with running the ranch, cooking, and taking care of Retta and the kids, it was a little bit much, even for a strong, capable woman like her.

He searched her pretty face, finding worry and tiredness lodged in her gaze. "I'll be glad to take some of it off your shoulders. I'll get a few things and move into the bunkhouse. I'll take the cattle off your hands and help with the kids and cooking." And he could still go to his place to work some during the day. He'd reserve the nighttime for his ranger work. At least for now.

This fight to save Loretta was going to take them all.

Sixteen

CHEYENNE INHALED HER FIRST DEEP BREATH SINCE SAM HAD brought Retta and the children in from the cold. She hated to admit needing help but didn't find it as bad as she'd dreaded the asking. "You don't know how much I appreciate you lending a hand. And this is probably your busiest time of the entire year."

"Nothing else is important when a life is on the line." His voice was quiet, stirring something deep inside her. "I can put a stew on to cook. I saw some venison hanging in your father's smokehouse. That with cornbread will make a filling supper. That is, if it's all right with you."

"I could hug you, Sam. It's perfect." She realized what she'd said and felt heat rising. "I mean, I'm happy you…uh…offered yourself." She'd better leave it at that or dig a deeper hole.

He chuckled. "I'd best get busy. I got a lot to do."

She watched him walk away, admiring his nicely formed backside. He had such a confident stride on those long legs. A girl could get used to having him around. The more she saw of his actions and strong convictions, the more drawn she was to him. Again, she wondered what had brought him to move so far away from family.

One day she might be bold enough to ask.

Cheyenne went to heat up the brick she kept at Retta's feet. Maybe this might be the day the woman woke up—at least for a while.

Optimism swirled around her. Yes, Retta had them, and they had each other. She'd start thinking about what to do for Aaron and Ellen for Christmas. They seemed to be far from the home they knew, so she'd make this the best Christmas she could.

Sam got the stew cooking, then went to get a few things from the wickiup. From his place, he could see Heck Raines's small house in the distance. Strange, he couldn't see smoke rising from the chimney. He leaned forward, focusing harder, but still couldn't make it out.

Something urged him to ride over that way.

He grabbed his rifle and stuck it in the scabbard on Rio. Ten minutes later, he approached his friend's three-room house in need of repair and found it eerily quiet. Sam dismounted and looked inside the forging shed. No sign of his friend. A bloodhound lifted his head and trotted off the porch to welcome him.

"Heck, are you home, old buddy?"

No answer came.

The dog yawned and stretched, nudging Sam's hand. Ignoring the hound, Sam opened the door and stepped over the threshold, stopping cold at the sight.

Heck slumped in his chair, his head lolling on his wide chest. A fist rested over his heart. After examining his old friend's body and finding no apparent cause of death, Sam had to assume he'd had a heart attack.

He sat on the sofa and put his head in his hands. The stubborn old coot. If he'd seen the doctor, he might still be alive.

A sheet of paper was wedged between Heck and the arm of the chair. Sam pulled it free. It was a drawing of a piece of equipment. Must be the part Heck was making for some kind of printing press. The one he'd told Sam about in the Hitching Post Saloon.

At the bottom of the page, Heck had written, *Pope* with the name *Doolin* next to that, with a question mark and circled.

Dammit! Sam had never wanted to hit anything so bad. He'd lost another good friend.

He folded the drawing and stuck it in his pocket. Getting Heck on a horse or mule would be out of the question, but he had to get him into town somehow.

Thankfully, Sam found a wagon and Heck's team in the barn. He hitched up the wagon, drove it next to the porch, and went inside. The hound began to bark. Glad he'd worn his gun, Sam slid it out and peered through a crack in the door.

One horse and rider.

The man wore a beat-up old hat that shaded his face. He stopped next to Sam's Rio and dismounted. Sam stepped out, the gun leveled on the visitor. "Hold it right there, mister."

"Sam? Want to put that gun away?"

He recognized Cap's gravelly voice and stepped out. "What are you doing here?"

"Thought I recognized your horse." Cap pushed back his hat. "I could ask you the same thing."

"Heck Raines was my friend." Sam put his gun away. "I couldn't see smoke rising from the chimney and got concerned, so I rode over. Found Heck dead inside. No cause of death but he had heart trouble. Your turn."

"I found a note under my door this morning, asking me to ride out. Raines knew I was a Texas Ranger and said he had some information that I'd be interested in."

"Come on in. I feel like a big buck sporting a large rack of antlers out here."

Cap snorted. "A rack of something. That's for sure. Just don't know what."

The door scraped against the floor as they went inside. Cap inspected Heck's body. "A bad heart, you say?"

"Yeah. He complained of it the last time I saw him. He looked bad. And he was having trouble walking." Sam stuck his hands in his pockets, trying not to think about never seeing Heck again. "I think I know what he wanted to talk to you about."

"Spill it."

"The last time I saw Heck in the Hitching Post, he told me about a man hiring him to make this." Sam handed Cap the crumpled drawing he'd found in the cushion. "He had a bad feeling about the whole thing."

Cap grunted and looked up. "Seems he might've thought some, or all, of the Doolins were eyeball deep in something shady. Most likely this counterfeiting."

"Maybe. This part definitely goes to a printing press. It's a piece that feeds the paper onto the inked typeset is my guess. I don't know what they're called, but I've seen them."

"That would be my guess as well, Sammy boy."

"All we have to do is find the one calling himself Pope. I wonder how hard it would be for me to offer to make the part for them. If I succeed, I'd be on the inside. Privy to conversations…and maybe plans."

"Whoo-ee, that's using your noggin! But more than a mite dangerous."

"Yeah. All I have to do is figure out who to make the offer to without winding up at the undertaker."

"No problem." Cap patted Sam's cheek. "Who wouldn't trust this face? Downright lovable."

Every time the old ranger's droopy mustache twitched like it was doing now, Sam got a feeling his life was about to get a whole lot more difficult.

"One thing we have to do is try to find out where the Doolins are living. That'll help a whole bunch. Any idea, Cap?"

"The only place they've been seen is the Hitching Post saloon. Maybe they're staying in the back."

"Maybe." Sam folded the drawing and stuck it in a pocket. "Let's get Heck into the wagon out there. Once I get him on the floor where he's easier to lift, you grab one end and I'll take the other."

"This reminds me of the time I burst into a hotel room and encountered Miss Bertha." Cap pushed back his hat. "Now, that was something. Did I ever tell you about her?"

"I don't recall. But then, I have a way of turning a deaf ear when you start on one of your long-winded stories." Taking a deep breath, Sam stood in front of Heck and transferred his body from the chair to the floor.

"Are you saying my stories are boring, Sam? Is that what you're saying?" Cap picked up Heck's legs. "You're fixin' to hurt my feelings, son."

"I'm saying they're endless, and I get tired of the constant drone. What's wrong with silence?" Doing his best to block the sorrow, Sam slid his arms around Heck's chest, and they moved toward the open door. It was no easy task, given the heavy weight.

"Silence, huh? That would drive me plumb batty." Cap's face reddened under the load.

"It'd be hard to drive you that way…seeing as how you're… already there." Huffing and puffing, Sam made it outside. Then with him on one side and Cap the other, they managed to get Heck's enormous frame into the wagon bed.

Both men collapsed on the porch. The muscles in Sam's arms were quivering. He loved Heck like a brother, but he sure was an armful.

"What are we going to do with the dog?" Cap asked.

"You tell me. Any ideas?"

"There's a family living outside Tascosa with about fifteen kids. I'll see if they want him. I'll tell them his name is Outlaw." His grin fading, Cap glanced at Sam. "I'm sorry about your friend. You shared some good times with him I expect, not to mention a common interest in the knife business."

"Thanks. Yep, we did."

Cap rose. "Do you know if he had family?"

"He came from a large family of thirteen kids. Only five…make that four now…might still be alive. If so, they're off someplace in California or Nevada. They didn't keep in touch. He never married, and his folks died a long time ago."

"Too bad. Guess it'll be up to the sheriff to deal with." Cap gazed at the house for a moment, his thoughts twisting in the wind. "Since it's not healthy for us to be seen together, I'll gather the dog and ride on ahead."

Sam nodded, gazing at the forging shed. "I'll be along."

After Cap left, he wandered over to look at Heck's tools. He could almost hear the man telling him to take what he wanted. After all, few others around had need of them. He stuffed the raw steel in his saddlebags as well as a handful of finished Bowie knives. The rest could wait until he came back.

He started to turn away, when a piece of metal on the ground, half covered with dirt, caught his attention. He picked it up, turning it over in his hand. Pulling Heck's paper from his pocket, the comparison revealed they were both the same, only the one on the ground wasn't finished.

Had Heck found out what it went to and why Pope wanted it so bad? Maybe someone came upon Heck by surprise, and he'd dropped it in the dirt and tried to cover it.

But there was no sign he'd been murdered. Sam stared at the piece of unfinished work. He could probably have it in workable condition in a day or two.

His thoughts turned to how to find Pope. Mickey McCormick could probably help, with him owning a livery and seeing a lot of people. That sounded like an excellent place to start.

❧

The town still seemed sleepy, the street almost deserted, when Sam rode in. He went straight to the doc's office.

Dr. Tyler looked the body over. "It appears a heart attack, but it could've been anything."

"Thanks, Doc." Sam drove to the undertakers and paid for a coffin and burial. He gave the man one of Heck's knives and asked him to put it inside the coffin with the body, then left.

Despite not knowing who to trust, Sam's next stop was Sheriff Jim Winslow's small adobe office where he filed a vague report and answered a few questions, claiming he didn't know anything. For all he knew, Winslow could be up to his neck in cahoots with the counterfeiters. To be safe, Sam gave his name as Sam Fletcher and signed the report.

Outside the sheriff's office, Sam eyed his friend's horse team. Selling them should bring enough to give Heck a right good send-off. Probably better than this town had seen. He tied Rio to the back of the wagon and drove down to the livery.

Mickey McCormick came from a small room. "Did you decide to sell your Appaloosa?"

"Not hardly, but I am needing to find a buyer for this team and wagon. The owner died and I'm settling his affairs."

"I think I might know someone looking for good mounts." McCormick ran a hand down the horses' legs and lifted the hooves to check them. Then he inspected the teeth. "They're both in excellent shape. Should easily fetch at least a hundred and seventy dollars. I'll take the wagon. I'm always looking to buy those."

A moment of silence followed while Sam mulled that over. At last, he stuck out his hand and they shook. "Anything you get above that for the horses is yours, plus the price of doing business. You can have the wagon for sixty dollars."

"You got a deal. I might have your money by closing time if you want to stop by."

"Let's wait until tomorrow. This weather isn't the best."

McCormick nodded and led the horse to the corral next to the livery.

"Mind if I ask you something, McCormick?"

"Whatever it is, I didn't do it," the livery owner said with a grin.

"I'm sure you see all kinds of people coming through here." Sam took a match stem from his pocket and stuck it in his mouth. "Would you know of anyone named Pope?"

"I can't say as I do offhand."

"Okay, thanks." Sam started to turn away.

"Wait. Come to think of it…the name sounds familiar."

Sam moved the match stem from one side of his mouth to the other, waiting.

"A fellow boarded his horse here about a week ago, calling himself Pope and several other names. Can't recall much about him, but he rode a solid black gelding with a white star on its forehead. One of the nicest pieces of horseflesh I've seen." McCormick grinned. "I can forget faces, but I never forget a horse."

"Has he left town?"

"Rode out late last night or early this morning." Mickey rested a hand on the corral. "He slid the money he owed under the door. I never saw him before, but he hung around the Hitching Post a lot. Kept to himself. Downright unfriendly. Why are you asking?"

"I was going to offer my services. Heard he might be looking for a smithy. Guess I'm too late."

"Maybe not. Let me see what I can find out."

Was Mickey in on this scheme? Sam hoped not. Mickey seemed one of the good ones.

"I'll be back tomorrow. Hopefully, you'll have some good news."

"Say, what's your name anyway?"

"Sam. Sam Fletcher." If anyone in town discovered his real name, his goose would be cooked to a fine fare-thee-well. Dammit, he could almost hear Cap laughing.

Seventeen

DOC TYLER'S BUGGY FADED INTO THE DISTANCE, AND THE FIRE crackled in the quiet. Cheyenne bathed Retta's forehead with a cool washcloth, praying for relief from the fever. Twice, the doctor and Cheyenne had put Loretta under a blanket tent with a steaming kettle of water. Then they made a mustard poultice and put it on her chest. She didn't seem to struggle as hard to breathe. Yet each moment, each heartbeat measured what seemed her remaining time on earth.

Doc seemed very concerned about the baby and had listened to Retta's belly for a long while, then only said the babe's heartbeat was weak. His quiet voice and grim expression had relayed his thoughts.

Aaron tapped her arm. "Can Mama hear me?"

Cheyenne wasn't really sure how to answer. Sometimes unconscious people could hear voices. Anyway, it wouldn't hurt to try. "Yes, I think she can. Go ahead. Lean over the bed and try." She wondered what the little boy had to say. It seemed important to him.

He leaned as far as he could and patted the quilt covering Retta. He spoke barely above a whisper. "Mama, it's me. Aaron. I love you and Ellen does too. Please don't die. We want you to get well so we can be a fam'ly again. Daddy's still gone so we don't have anybody an' we're scared. We don't wanna be orphans 'cause nobody will like us." Aaron glanced around as though thinking what to say next. "I'm watching after Ellen just like you told me. She's real sad like me. I told her to smile, but she ain't got any left. Me either." Aaron crawled up on the bed and kissed his mother's pale cheek.

Then Retta's eyes fluttered and opened. She lifted a hand and touched her son's face. For a second, she knew and responded.

"She did hear me. She did." Aaron wiped away a tear.

"I'm so glad, honey." Cheyenne helped him down, unable to speak for the lump clogging her throat. She thought of the Apache students at the school and how they'd clung to her. All children, no matter the color of their skin, hurt the same.

From the window, she could see the sun trying to come out. Maybe their luck was turning. Feeling encouraged, she swung her attention back to Retta and dribbled water into her mouth, moistening her cracked lips.

Her thoughts shifted to her mother, and she wondered how her aunt was faring. Thank goodness her mother had gone. It might be the last time she saw her twin sister. They had been inseparable for most of their lives. Cheyenne couldn't imagine a closeness like that. She would dearly miss Aunt Betty and the good times the two of them had shared.

Aaron scooted off the second bed where he and Ellen were playing with Shadow and went to the window to look out. "I wish Mr. Sam would come back."

"He'll be here soon, I'm sure."

"I guess." Aaron sighed. "He might get lost though."

"Not a chance, honey. He must know his way all over this land."

"I wish my daddy wasn't lost. We need him bad."

Cheyenne got to her feet and knelt in front of him, putting her arms around his small frame. "I know you do, and I'd give anything in this world to find him for you. All we can do is pray that God will show him the way to you."

He clung to her, crying. "I pray and pray, but everything's still the same."

"I know it looks like that now, but one day things will change, and you'll be able to laugh again."

"I hope so."

The kitchen door opened, and footsteps sounded on the wooden floor. Then Sam was standing in the doorway. "Where is everyone?"

Aaron's eyes grew round. "He's back."

"Yes, he is." Cheyenne stood, feeling as happy as the children looked. "We were just talking about you."

"I hope it was good. I apologize for being late. Had something to take care of." His voice came from the deepness of his throat and emerged a bit raspy as he came on in.

He wore a solemn expression, and that drew Cheyenne's concern. Something had happened.

"I was afraid you couldn't find your way back." Aaron put his arms around Sam's waist. Then Ellen had to do the same.

"But here I am. Not lost or anything." He ruffled the kids' hair. "I need to check on the stew."

"I stirred it a bit earlier and it looked so good." Cheyenne pulled the kids off him. "Retta's sleeping, so I can help make the cornbread."

He gave her a strange glance but shrugged and turned. She told the children to play and followed.

"I made coffee a little bit ago. It might need warming. I didn't know what time you'd be back." She tied her apron around her slim waist. "What's wrong? I can tell something is."

The lines of his face looked as though cut from stone, and he seemed unusually quiet. "I couldn't see smoke coming from a friend's chimney and found him dead of a heart attack." Sam let out a long breath. "Heck Raines was a damn good bladesman, and I'm gonna miss him."

"I'm sorry. He used to stop by here sometimes and talk to my father. I always liked him. How long had he been dead?"

"Must've died late yesterday by the looks of it. I knew he had a heart problem, but he didn't want to go to the doctor."

"Poor guy. What's going to happen to all his property?"

"The house and land are up to the sheriff to handle, I suppose." Sam lapsed into silence for a moment. "Heck had gotten himself caught up in a business deal that underneath the surface appeared to be criminal. The last time I saw him, he told me about it and seemed scared."

"Do you think that had anything to do with him dying?"

"Can't be sure. A healthy dose of fright can hurry someone to the grave. These are the kind of men that fill nightmares."

Though the heat in the kitchen cast a warm glow, a chill invaded Cheyenne. She thought she'd outrun evil, but it seemed to be alive and well even here in the Texas Panhandle—evil like what had found her one moonless night in the New Mexico desert, and no one had heard her screams.

An infant's weak cries…

The cruel hands that bit into her arms…

Then silence and blood dripping from the knife…

Cheyenne's mouth went dry as she desperately shook the memories from her head and stilled her trembles. "Anything else, Sam?" she asked.

"Just be careful in town. I heard there's some fake money being passed."

"I never go alone to that place, so you don't have to worry." She'd learned the hard way that bad things could find her when no one was around. She pulled her shawl closer and forced a smile. "What are your plans for tomorrow?"

"There's Heck's burial of course, and I have some things to do at his place, then I'll come back and keep Aaron and Ellen busy."

She handed him one of her father's larger cups. "I'm glad you offered to stay here, Sam. But I won't hold you to it."

"You don't want me?" He met her gaze, his dark eyes studying her.

"I—of course I do, but only if this is what you want and it fits with your life."

Several heartbeats passed before he spoke. "Anytime I offer to do something, it means that I want to, not that I feel obligated."

His quiet words rang true, and she stuck her hands in her apron pockets.

He wants to be here.

A flash of happiness sizzled inside, and she looked away to keep him from reading her face.

"I had a thought." Sam took a sip of coffee and reached for a bowl to stir the cornbread in. "What do you think about teaching Aaron to make some of your Christmas baskets? The boy's smart, and I can take them when I sell my knives."

"What an excellent idea, and it'll give him something to do. Ellen can also work on one herself. I've been so busy with Retta, I haven't had time to think. We were going to go sell your knives and my baskets."

"Understandable. You have a lot going on."

"Guess that's out of the question now. Speaking of selling things…I hope you brought your knives." She met his dark eyes. "I wouldn't want anyone to steal them."

"Of course. And I put away my tools, so they won't tempt passersby. Weather permitting, I'll probably go back some during the day to work at my forge."

Cheyenne nodded, her thoughts on the nights with Sam after the children went to bed. They could talk and share pieces of their lives.

But she could never let him know her secret. No one must know what she'd done out on the desert one night under a dark sky. She glanced down at her shaking hands. She'd carry that to her grave.

∾

That night after supper, Cheyenne sat with Sam and the children in the parlor by a warm fire. Retta had endured the day and all the movements her treatments called for. She now slept in a nearby room, comfortable and warm. Cheyenne had bathed her in cool water and was able to get her fever down a little.

Retta had roused briefly, asking about her baby. After Cheyenne assured her the babe was alive, the woman had gone back to sleep. She prayed the babe would keep fighting to live. They desperately needed a miracle.

Except for a few things, they looked like a family, relaxing after a trying day.

Shadow stretched out in front of the parlor fireplace, occasionally raising her head to look around when someone moved.

Aaron brought a tattered copy of Grimm's fairy tales to Sam that had been in their belongings in the wagon. "Would you read to us?"

Sam seemed a bit shocked that he'd ask. Cheyenne didn't think he saw himself as a kid person, but she thought having that hair and beard made him look lovable. The children must've thought so too, because neither were one bit afraid of him. Not one iota.

"I'd be happy to." He moved to the settee between Aaron and Ellen and read "Hansel and Gretel" then "Cinderella" and "Rapunzel."

By then, Ellen was rubbing her eyes. Sam put the book away and she climbed into his lap. "I get real scared sometimes," she said, her voice very quiet.

"What of?" he asked.

"I don't know. Just stuff. I miss my daddy."

The little sob in Ellen's voice pierced Cheyenne's heart. She could feel her sad longing.

"I wish I could snap my fingers and make him appear." Sam folded his arms around her. With a sad sigh, she laid her head on his chest. "I'm really sorry."

The girl twisted a button on his shirt. "Will you be my daddy?"

In the dim light of the lamp, Cheyenne didn't miss the jolt that ran through Sam. She wondered how he'd answer. It was a tough question and the child needed comforting.

Aaron thrust his hands in his hair and groaned. "What a dumb thing to ask, Ellen."

"Honey, you already have a daddy. I can't take his place," Sam answered, his voice gentle.

"But I don't have one. He's gone far, far away."

Sam kissed the top of her head. "I think he'll come back, and everything will be just the way it was."

"Nope. He ain't coming back. I don't think he wants me or Aaron anymore." Tears trickled down her face.

Aaron scooted next to Sam and awkwardly tried to put his arm around Ellen. Cheyenne's heart melted.

"Ellen, we're still a fam'ly, even if he don't come back," Aaron said. "I'll take care of you an' Mama an' we'll be okay. We just gotta stick together is all."

"Your brother's right." Sam's words came out husky. He cleared his throat before adding, "Wherever he is, your father still loves you. The main thing is to keep hope in your heart that he'll return. He could be sick or had an accident and is working hard to get back to you. Never give up."

Cheyenne knelt in front of Sam and lightly rubbed each of the kids' legs. "I know your father loves you more than anything on earth. But until he comes through the door, maybe Mr. Sam won't mind filling in a little." She met Sam's warm gaze, wondering what he thought of all this. He seemed to truly want to ease the children's sadness at a time of year that should be the happiest.

"I will be here for as long as you need me." He kissed the top of Ellen's head again.

The girl nodded. "Okay. But don't ever go away."

"Now, who would like some popcorn?" Cheyenne stood, blinking hard, her smile a little wobbly. Listening to Sam's attempt to quiet the children's fears had touched her deep inside. He'd seemed to know exactly what to say that would bring Ellen and Aaron some peace.

Later, after the children had gone to bed and it was just Cheyenne and Sam, she rocked in her mama's rocker that sat beside his chair. "Thank you for soothing the kids. They're really scared right now with their mother so ill and not sure what to think about their father's absence. I wonder where he could be."

"Hard telling." He glanced at her over the rim of his cup with those dark eyes that always spoke louder than words.

"We have to try to find him." She looked at the gaily wrapped gifts beside the fireplace and wanted to cry. "Somehow."

He reached for her hand. "As soon as we get a name, I'll set to work."

"Thank you. You always make me feel better."

"Glad I can." He squeezed her fingers. "I wasn't sure how to answer Ellen tonight."

"You did a great job. A lot better than I would've. They're hurting and so alone." Cheyenne tugged her hand from him and stood. "I'll check on Retta once more, then go to bed. Will you be okay in the bunkhouse?"

"I'll be fine. It's perfect for my and Shadow's needs."

She started from the room and turned. "Sam, I—" Cheyenne caught her bottom lip between her teeth. "Do you think you could hold me again? Just for a moment? These damnable nights are filled with too many memories."

Sam got to his feet. He opened his arms and she walked into them.

With the soft crack and snap of the fire around them, she laid her head on his chest and closed her eyes. If she tried real hard, she could almost imagine a life with this man working so hard to be a recluse and bound and determined not to need anyone.

But the truth lay in his raspy breath and the whisper of his heart.

This strong man with steel inside needed someone to hold him too.

Eighteen

DAWN ARRIVED WITH A WHISPER AND A SIGH. SAM LET Shadow out and dressed, pulling back his hair with a strip of leather. Easing into the kitchen door, he found the Ronan house quiet. He hadn't slept that well, unaccustomed to a strange place with its various sounds and smells.

Thank goodness for his memory. It didn't take him long to locate the coffee, and soon he had the pot sitting on the cookstove. Shadow padded to the door and whined. Sam let her out. The December air rushed in around him, bringing shivers and made him glad for the sturdy walls, even if they did close in around him too much. His wickiup wouldn't be able to hold the heat.

A rustle of fabric alerted him. He turned to see Cheyenne standing in the doorway. His breath caught at the sight of her looking all sleepy eyed, wearing a rumpled dress that told him she'd slept in it. Her russet hair was arranged in a long braid down her back.

To him, there was no prettier sight than a woman just after she'd gotten out of bed. In daylight, Beth had been all prim and proper, but in bed, she became a wild woman. Her hair, drowsy smile, and throaty voice reflected that come morning. For that and a million other reasons, it had taken a long time to get past life without his beautiful wife.

Pushing the memories aside, he offered Cheyenne a smile. "Hope I didn't wake you. I tried to be quiet."

"It's time to get up." She smothered a yawn. "I had to check on Retta again anyway."

Sam pulled out a chair for her. "I take it she had a rough night."

Cheyenne sat down with a heavy sigh. "She had a hard time breathing. I'm worried. I had high hopes when she opened her eyes and touched Aaron's face yesterday, but now, I don't know."

"Will the doctor come back out today?"

"Sometime this morning."

"Good. You know, sometimes life is taking two steps forward and one back. Maybe this is nothing more than Retta getting her bearings and gaining strength for another try. I wouldn't fret too much."

Despite the optimism he spouted, he wasn't so sure. Maybe she'd just wanted to see her son's face one last time.

"I hope you're right." Cheyenne rolled her shoulders, rubbing her neck. "I miss my calisthenics. I've gotten so tight."

"Maybe I can help." Sam stepped behind her. "Close your eyes and relax."

He moved her braid aside and began to slowly massage the knotted muscles along her neck and shoulders.

"Mmmm. That feels so good," she murmured. "Where did you learn to do this?"

"Just something I picked up." Actually, Beth had taught him, and he'd loved touching her. Also being touched in return. He expected pain to stab his heart at remembering their special times, but the memory failed to deliver the sting. Maybe he'd become numb to it.

"Well, you can keep this up all day and get no complaints from me, buster."

"Can't. I got cows to feed and water, a friend to bury, and a bunch of other things." He'd wanted to run back out to Heck's place but didn't know if he could fit that in.

"I'm sorry, Sam." She half turned and laid a hand on his arm. "I wish I could be there for the service, and you wouldn't have to go alone. Do you think anyone else will attend the burial?"

"I'll be surprised if they do."

"How sad."

Yes, it was. A man could spend his whole life in one place and not have but one or two good friends to bid him farewell.

Despite the list he couldn't possibly complete, Sam would, however, find Cap and tell him what he'd learned at the livery. He'd tried yesterday, but the ranger was nowhere to be found. He might've ridden over to Amarillo to a less conspicuous telegraph office.

Cheyenne rolled her shoulders. "You're a busy man. Used to be you'd hammer and shape steel all day."

"I will again when all this dies down. A man has to switch things up now and again." He massaged a few more minutes, then gave her shoulder a pat. "That's all for now."

"That made all the difference." She raised her head and smiled. "You're pretty handy to have around."

"A compliment?" He chuckled and moved the coffee off the flame. "Not so long ago, you wanted to slit my throat."

"That was before I knew you had magic hands. I hope you don't hold a grudge."

Her green eyes still wore that sleepy look, and he nearly dropped one of the coffee cups. "Who me? Our surprise introduction is already forgotten."

Several heartbeats passed as he poured coffee and set hers on the table.

"You look real nice this morning, Sam," she said softly. "I think you're a handsome man beneath all that hair you're hiding under." She was silent a moment before going on. "What *are* you hiding from, I wonder."

Sam kept his eyes lowered to his mug and took a drink. Two little faces in the doorway saved him from a reply. "Good morning. You're up early," he said.

"We heard voices an' wondered if our daddy came," Aaron answered.

Ellen's face fell. "But it ain't."

"Not yet, but maybe soon." Cheyenne rose with a smile. "How about some milk or hot chocolate?"

Before Sam finished his first cup of coffee, both children were in a better mood and took his teasing well. He made breakfast while Cheyenne took care of Retta's needs, then with a full belly, he put on his hat, coat, and gloves and went to feed the cattle.

Two hours later, he pulled up at McCormick's livery. Mickey came out grinning. "Good news, I sold both horses and for more than you asked."

"Excellent. Like I said, you can keep any over."

"Come on in and we'll settle up."

Sam followed him inside and took an envelope from Mickey. "Thanks."

"Folks are always looking for good horses. Just a matter of getting the word out." Mickey lowered his voice. "About the smithy job, go to the Hitching Post and ask for Deek Doolin."

A jolt went through Sam. He kept his expression blank. "I owe you, Mickey."

"I'm sure you can use the money right here at Christmas." The livery man chuckled. "I'm still trying to figure out if you're as hard up as you look. I see you in town always alone, hair and beard shaggy, never with a woman, and I wonder why that is. Pardon me, but you look like some derelict."

"I guess I'm just one of those men who can't seem to get ahead." Sam held up the envelope. "This will make a difference, and maybe Deek Doolin will hire me."

"Good luck, Sam Fletcher."

They shook hands, and Sam led Rio down the street. The saloon was locked up, but a man stood in front holding a shotgun. "Mister, I was told to come down here and ask for Deek Doolin about a job."

"Can't you see it's closed?"

Sam shrugged. "All I know is what I was told. Don't blame me if you get an ass-chewing." He turned toward his horse.

"Hold on," the man called. "Wait here." He went inside and came out a minute later with Deek Doolin.

"You're a smithy?" Deek asked.

Prickles ran up Sam's spine as he glared at the sorry piece of shit. The urge to grab him around the neck and choke the life from him was stronger than anything he'd ever known. But it wasn't time for that yet. He observed the man through narrowed eyes. "Mickey said you might have a job."

Deek gave him a dark scowl and stepped closer. "You look familiar. Have we met?"

"Doubt it. I've been over in New Mexico. Name's Sam Fletcher." Sam's nerves stretched like a rubber band. A bit more, and he'd snap. Deek had been the brother Tom left behind with Beth when he'd galloped out of that dark barn. Unless Tom had killed her before he hightailed it, Deek was the one to pull the trigger. Sam forced a half smile. "What are you needing?"

"A machine part, and everyone who works for me will call me mister." Deek pulled out a drawing just like the one Heck had stuffed in the side of his chair. "We're in a bit of hurry. How long do you think it might take?"

"Probably a couple of days."

"You think or you know?" Deek snapped.

Red flashed in front of Sam's eyes. "I'll get you the damn part as soon as I can. That'll have to be good enough."

Deek rested a palm on the handle of his .45. "I don't think I like your tone."

Sam clenched his fist and took two deep breaths, wanting to tell Deek where he could put the things he didn't like. He had to keep calm until he could arrest this bunch. "You'll get your part." He took a step toward his horse.

"Aren't you forgetting something, Fletcher?"

"I don't think so. I have the drawing."

"You'll call me *Mister* Doolin."

If Sam wasn't mad enough before, he was livid now, and it took everything in him not to drive a fist into Deek and bust into this saloon for the others. He silently counted to ten and pasted on a fake smile. "I hope you have a good day, Mr. Doolin, sir."

The guard in front of the door laughed. Sam shot him a look that could kill and mounted his horse. He rode out of town a ways in case he was followed and doubled back, slipping into the alley behind the yellow hotel. He tapped on Cap's door.

The ranger opened it a crack. "Who's there?"

"Sam."

The door opened wider, and Cap grabbed his coat and pulled him inside. "Where have you been?"

Sam straightened his coat and glared. "I've been here. The bigger question is where the hell did you disappear to? I came by yesterday and couldn't find you."

"I've been doing some scouting around and rode back out to your friend's house."

"And?"

"I don't think he was honest with you." Cap held out a Mason jar. "I found this full of money buried behind his house. And guess what?"

"Just tell me, for God's sake! I didn't come here to play games."

"You're in a piss-poor mood. Your family oughta send you to charm school. But you'd probably flunk out. I don't know why I even try to work with you." Cap shook his head then met Sam's gaze. "The fives and ones stuffed inside the jar are counterfeit."

"You sure about that?" Sam's head was spinning. When? How?

"Positive. The dirt was fresh, indicating he'd just buried the jar."

Everyone, with the exception of bankers, buried money in their yard. Didn't mean they were criminals.

"Heck could've seen the bills and taken them maybe as proof of the crime. Or maybe as insurance, thinking they wouldn't kill him as long as he held that over them." Sam knew one thing, and that was the fact that he counted Heck as a good friend. The man was as honest as the day was long. He'd bet all the money in the Denver mint on that. Another thought crossed Sam's mind. Maybe Heck had thought he could get the fake money safely to lawmen or rangers and help put the Doolins behind bars.

"He did slip that note under your door to come out here," Sam pointed out. "Not something a criminal would do."

"Maybe." Cap smoothed his droopy mustache. "Guess we'll never know."

"It appears we have a mystery, Sherlock." Sam shed his coat and gloves. "It's my turn now. I just came from a meeting with Deek Doolin." He paused a moment to let that sink in.

Cap looked like someone had slapped him. "Here in Tascosa?"

"Yep. And he hired me to make that part to a printing press."

The ranger's eyes widened. "You're on the inside, Sam!"

"Yeah, as long as I remember one thing."

"What's that?"

"Get ready. I have to call him *Mr. Doolin*." That still stuck in Sam's craw. Hell!

"I don't know about you, but I'd rather take a bullet. After all the crimes he's committed and people killed, he deserves no respect. Not one iota. Nor any of his skunk-eating family." Cap stuck a thumb in his worn gun belt. "What are you going to do?"

"Whatever the job calls for. I'll call him Yankee Doodle if he wants me to. We're going to get these bastards. That I can promise you." Sam had to play this right. He couldn't let the Doolins escape justice again.

"I take it he didn't recognize you, so that's good."

"He picked up on something familiar, though. Looked at me funny and asked if we'd met. I'm glad I haven't cut my hair yet."

"Ain't that the damn truth? I wish we could take the Doolins down now. Dammit! But we need to find out for sure who all is involved in this counterfeiting mess." Cap paused, listening to a noise outside the room. When the footsteps faded, he asked, "Where are you going from here?"

"Heck's funeral. It's going to be quick and private. I hate burying people I like."

"Yeah, we probably should've buried him on his property. Can't help that now."

"Nope. It's early in the day, when most of the riffraff is sleeping, so that'll help."

"Maybe, but you know they have spies everywhere. I'd go with you, but we can't afford to be seen together." Cap was silent a moment, listening to more sounds in the hall. "Do you think you'll have that part done by the time they want it?"

"Pretty sure I can, but I'll have to drop some other things. I can use what Heck had already started, and that'll get me further along." He'd have to get started today. Going back out to Heck's place would have to wait. "I'm wondering what to do with the money I got from the sale of Heck's horses and wagon. Any ideas?"

"An orphanage always appreciates a hefty donation, especially with Christmas coming. Or give it to some widow woman who has a bunch of kids. Heck would probably like that."

"For sure." The man had had a big heart. For now, Sam'd stick the money aside in case any relative of Heck's showed up. "When I get time, I'll take a wagon back for his forge and tools. Heck said the only thing his brothers were interested in was selling patented medicines and conning people out of their money. What I can't use of his, I'll give to someone else." Sam put his coat back on. "Guess I need to get over to the churchyard." He'd be glad to get it over with. He reached for the doorknob and turned. "What about Heck's dog? Did you find him a home?"

"Do you remember that family with a bunch of kids I was

telling you about? Well, they took him. The man is a hunter, so he'll use the hound a lot, and Outlaw looked happy."

"That's real good. Thanks, Cap."

The undertaker had already arrived at the small cemetery next to the church, and a preacher showed up right behind Sam. He took the preacher aside and gave him twenty dollars. "Just say a few words over him. Nothing long."

"Did he have a favorite Scripture?"

"Beats me." Sam had never heard Heck mention anything besides knife-making.

A woman in black entered the little cemetery and made her way to them.

Wondering who she was, Sam tipped his hat. "Ma'am, thank you for paying respects."

She raised her veil, and he was surprised to see Frenchie McCormick's beautiful features. Her eyes held tears. "Heck was an old friend of mine. Wouldn't be right not to pay my respects."

"I'm sure he'll appreciate you coming."

"Yes, he probably will."

The preacher stepped to the head of the roughly hewn coffin and opened a Bible. He read a passage and asked for God's mercy on Heck's soul, then offered a prayer.

Frenchie rested a hand on the coffin and muttered quietly, then left with the preacher.

Sam helped the undertaker lower Heck into the ground and stood silently as the man filled the hole. He glanced up at the sky at the weak sun that had popped out, breathed the crisp air, and listened to the sound of the dirt hitting the top of the coffin.

Again, he vowed that if anyone helped send Heck to eternity, he'd find justice for his friend. Somehow. Someway.

His heart heavy and missing his friend, he rode for home. He stopped at the Ronan house to check on the situation there, and Cheyenne had already started the children on the baskets. She'd baked another cake, and the entire house smelled of the wonderful fragrance of Christmas.

For a moment, he stood watching her, seeing how capable she was and how much she adored the children. There were none of those earlier flighty tendencies. Just quiet strength.

"Those baskets look real good," he told the kids. He took some of Ellen's apart and helped her straighten it out, but it was excellent for a first try.

Aaron glanced up. "This is fun, but can I go with you?"

"I'm just going to do a little work, and I won't be able to bring you back if you decide you don't want to be there."

"I know. Can I go?"

Sam looked over the boy's head at Cheyenne, and she nodded. "Sure. Get your coat and gloves." When the boy ran into the bedroom, Sam turned his attention back to her. "I shouldn't be gone too long. I just have a little work to do."

"Take all the time you need. I have things under control here. Retta opened her eyes for a while. I think when she gets stronger, she'll want out of that bed. Dr. Tyler seemed encouraged when he came out. It's funny how quickly things can change."

"That's great news." He told her Frenchie McCormick came to Heck's burial. "She said they were old friends. Who knows? Maybe Heck was an old suitor or something."

"Stranger things have happened." She stood there smiling, her pretty hair flaming in the flickering light of the fireplace.

Sam lifted a silky strand and rubbed it between his thumb and forefinger, and for a moment, it seemed they were alone in the world. Cheyenne Ronan pulled him to her like a strong magnet, and he couldn't take his eyes from her moist, pink mouth.

He bent his head and brushed a kiss across her enticing lips.

The moment their lips touched, a jolt of pleasure washed over him. Then awareness that she clutched his vest.

Sliding a gentle hand under her jaw, he deepened the kiss,

knowing this was one of those moments that was defined by a before and after. Something would change. Either for the better or worse.

He released her, his voice raspy. "I should be sorry for doing that. But I'm not."

Cheyenne placed a hand to her throat. "Me either. Sometimes I have such a need to be touched—to be reminded I'm alive. That I'm a woman. Today was one of those. Please keep an eye out for trouble." She turned and left the room.

"I'll be fine."

It was only one kiss. It didn't mean anything.

A voice came inside his head: "Liar."

Nineteen

HER THOUGHTS DRIFTING TO SAM'S KISS AND HER OWN surprising reaction to his lips on hers, Cheyenne set the supper table. She was ready to slide the cornbread in the oven when she heard riders. Her heart leaped. It must be Sam and Aaron. But a quick glance out the window revealed three grim-faced strangers.

Something about the hardness in their faces made the hair on her neck rise. She took a rifle from the cabinet where her father kept it. "I want you to go in with your mother, Ellen. Don't come out until I call for you."

"Okay." The girl's eyes widened, and she hurried into the bedroom, closing the door.

Cheyenne jerked the lever of the rifle down and up to ratchet a bullet into the chamber before going to the door. The riders were dismounting. "Get back on your horses and state your business from there."

The man growled something but followed her instructions. "Looking for Sam Fletcher."

"I'm afraid you've come to the wrong place. This is the Ronan spread."

The men muttered something between them.

"We think he might've come here, ma'am," one said. "Could be he works for your father."

"I'm afraid you're mistaken. I know no one by the name of Fletcher. Now, I'll have to ask you to leave."

The shorter man in the middle tipped his hat. "Our apologies, ma'am. You have a good evening now, you hear?"

She stepped back inside and watched them leave through the window. They dawdled and stopped to chat among themselves before riding off toward Tascosa. Who was Sam Fletcher, and why had they thought he lived here? Was it her Sam? Had he taken an alias? Possibly.

Cheyenne put the rifle away and let Ellen come out.

"Who were those men?" the girl asked, staring up with her big brown eyes.

"No one, dear. They were looking for someone and thought he lived here. Your brother and Mr. Sam should be back very soon. Are you hungry?"

Ellen brushed her hair out of eyes, clinging to a little rag doll. "A little. I wish Aaron would hurry."

The lengthening shadows outside said it'd soon be dark. "They'll be here before you can blink."

"My daddy left and didn't come back. Maybe they won't either."

The sadness in the sweet girl's words brought an ache to Cheyenne's heart. She knelt. "Honey, I'm sorry for what happened to you, and your daddy being gone so long, but please don't think that everyone who leaves will never come back. They will. Mr. Sam has work to do here."

"Okay." Ellen put her arms around Cheyenne's neck in a hug. When they broke apart, the girl wore a smile. "I can count to five. Wanna hear?"

"I sure do." Cheyenne stood, amazed how quickly the girl went from sorrow to smiles.

Ellen counted without messing up, and Cheyenne praised her.

A few minutes later came the sound of a horse. Cheyenne looked out. "Here they are." She glanced at her reflection in the hall mirror and smoothed some loose hair, then adjusted the white collar of her emerald-green dress, the color adding to the Christmas spirit tugging at her.

"Oh boy! Aaron!" When Ellen's brother came into the kitchen, she hugged him.

He made a face and tried to push her away. "Stop, Ellen."

"I missed you."

"Well, I wasn't gone forever."

Cheyenne hid a grin as she helped the boy with his coat. "Where's Sam?"

"Taking care of Rio. I'm starving."

"It's ready, but we'll wait for Sam. Why don't you go tell your mother hello if she's awake? I know she'll love seeing you," she suggested softly. She had some bone broth ready to serve Retta if she was awake.

After several more treatments under a blanket tent with the steam, the mother did seem to breathe much easier, and she'd been awake longer today. Maybe Retta would sit with them a little after supper. She had to get her strength back. Her children needed her.

Aaron and Ellen went in to see their mother, and the voices said Retta was awake. Cheyenne poured the broth into a bowl and carried a tray into the bedroom.

"And I got to go with Mr. Sam to watch him work." Aaron leaned on the bed. "He makes knives, and they're real sharp too."

Ellen crowded close to her brother. "I got to make a basket today out of sticks."

"That's nice," Retta said weakly. "I hope you're being good."

"They really are well behaved." Cheyenne set the tray on the dresser. "I brought some broth. Do you think you can sip some?"

"A bit maybe."

"I'll help you sit up." She used the sheet and pulled Retta up to the headboard, then stuffed a mountain of pillows underneath where she was half sitting. The mother managed about half of the soup and took several sips of hot tea that would help with the fever. "That's very good, Retta. Keep this up, and you'll soon be back on your feet."

The kitchen door opened. Sam must be finished. Cheyenne

took the tray, lying Retta back down. She gathered the children and went to greet the man whose kiss had ignited a firestorm inside her.

Had he thought about it at all as he'd gone through the day?

He was dipping the stew into bowls and turned when he heard them. "I hope I didn't keep you waiting long."

His deep voice brushed her like a soft wind, and his dark eyes met hers. She turned all quivery inside. The collarless shirt lay open at his throat, allowing her a view of the hollow of his wide neck, and his rolled sleeves revealed corded muscles. The leather strip that pulled back his hair had tamed the wild look. Everything about him seemed large.

Sam Legend was all man, and she was extremely aware of that.

Cheyenne inhaled a deep breath and set her tray down. "Not at all. I was just feeding Retta. Do you think you might carry her into the parlor after supper so she can sit awhile with us? After a long nap and breathing steam under the blanket, she seems much improved."

"Sure. She must be anxious to spend some time out of bed."

"I think she is." She helped him carry the bowls of stew to the table, then poured milk for the children. "Sam, I need a private word after we finish."

"Anything wrong?" His well-shaped mouth curved in a frown.

"I'm not sure. I'll let you decide."

The children took over the conversation and kept up until they emptied their bowls, then ran off to play.

Sam rose. "Tell me what happened."

"We had visitors today." Cheyenne pushed back her chair and faced him. "Three hard-looking men. They were looking for Sam Fletcher."

He winced. "What else?"

"Of course, I told them no one of that name lived here, then they asked if he worked for us. I had a feeling they might've become trouble if I hadn't been holding a rifle on them. I had to ask them to leave, and even then, they were a bit reluctant to ride off." She touched his arm. "I have to ask. Are you Sam Fletcher?"

Twenty

THE CLOCK IN THE HALL OFF THE KITCHEN TICKED LOUDLY. Sam rubbed the back of his neck. "I'll answer that if you tell me about the demons you're running from and why you ask me to hold you."

"I can't." She released a low sob, her eyes swimming in unshed tears. "Please don't ask that of me."

Her whispered plea held fear. Sam wanted to pull her close and wrap his arms around her, tell her that ghosts couldn't hurt her. Whatever she'd done or whatever was done to her was something so horrific she couldn't bear to speak of it.

"We both hold secrets, it appears. When we first met, you told me you taught English at the Indian school. How long?"

Cheyenne's green eyes met his. "For only a few months."

Yet she was there a year. Doing what?

Something that brought out painful memories at night. Memories she needed help to push back behind a locked door. He knew a little something about that.

Sam cupped her jaw. "I'll respect your secret. Yes, I'm Sam Fletcher when I'm in town. I'm doing something very dangerous, and it's best you don't know. Don't trust those men. I'll make sure they don't come back."

"Thank you." She stepped back and wiped the weariness from her eyes. "Please be careful, Sam. I couldn't bear it if anything happened to you."

"It won't. Now, you go sit with your patient. I'll clean up the kitchen."

"I can't do that. Retta is fine for now." She put her hands on her hips. "We'll both do it and get through in record time." Cheyenne filled the kettle with water and put it on the stove to heat.

"You drive a hard bargain, lady." He was glad she was smiling again. He couldn't look at her without remembering the feel of her lips. Kissing her hadn't been in his mind, but when he'd seen her standing in the parlor, the lamplight playing in her hair, wild horses couldn't have stopped him. No, he wasn't one bit sorry.

Funny she hadn't mentioned it. But then they'd had other things to talk about and children with big ears within hearing distance.

His mind whirling with the uninvited visitors, along with everything else, he enjoyed working beside her, rubbing elbows while the scents of the kitchen danced merrily around them. "I think the venison stew was a hit." He carried a stack of dishes from the table. "We have plenty left for another meal. I'll make some fry bread to go with it."

For a moment it struck him that they were acting like an old married couple, and it felt oddly comforting in a strange sort of way. He wasn't sure what that meant, except that he liked being with her. And kissing her.

Only now, he'd put her and the others in danger—just like he'd done with Beth.

Dammit to hell! He wanted to hit something.

"I haven't had any fry bread lately, Sam. That will be wonderful."

The silence between them grew, and he didn't know what to say to fill it. Sometimes it was best to enjoy the quiet.

Only he sensed she had something to say. They were about finished when she spoke. "Sam, I don't know why you feel driven to be involved in whatever it is going on in town. Is this about the phony money being passed?"

He hesitated a moment, then decided to be honest. "Yes."

"Why does it have to involve you? What part are you playing?"

"It's best if you don't know. I'm trying to protect you."

"I haven't asked you to." She set her jaw. "I need to know where danger lies. I need the truth, so I can be ready when more strangers show up at my door."

Sam winced. She was right. Despite his promise to make sure certain unwanted visitors wouldn't ride this way again, he couldn't guarantee that. The past had shown he couldn't guarantee one thing where the Doolins were concerned.

Full of regret for making her worry more, he pinched the bridge of his nose and took a deep breath. "I'm forging a part for them—something that goes to a printing press. You should probably know...I'm a Texas Ranger working with the man over me to clean up this mess."

"You've been a Texas Ranger the whole time you've been here?" Her voice was tight.

"I quit and moved to the Panhandle to escape. Cap paid me a visit five days ago, and I took this job. I don't know for how long, but I'll complete what he's asking me to do." Then he'd see the direction he wanted his life to go.

"What are you running from, Sam?" she asked softly. "Escaping what exactly?"

He folded the dish towel and laid it on the sideboard. "I'd rather not talk about that."

"Fair enough."

Aaron appeared in the doorway. "Are y'all finished?"

"Yes, we are." Cheyenne went to the boy, rubbing the top of his head. "I suppose you want someone to read a story."

Aaron grinned. "How did you know?"

"I'm a good guesser. Is your mother awake?"

"Yep."

"Good. Sam, will you carry her into the parlor?"

"I'd be happy to."

A short time later, they were all in the parlor with Retta

surrounded by pillows in Bert's easy chair. Cheyenne's father would be glad they made use of his chair. Sam read to the children and Retta dozed, then Cheyenne made hot chocolate for the kids and chamomile tea for their mother. Sam accepted the last bit of coffee left from supper and took in the scene. Warmth filled his heart. The relief on the children's faces to see their mother feeling better added to the feeling of thankfulness.

And if the Doolins weren't close enough to spit on, Sam would've enjoyed it far more. Tomorrow he'd move back to his place. It was the only way to keep Cheyenne safe. He was not going to have a repeat of Beth's tragedy. No way in hell would he let that happen.

They sat around sipping from their cups and talking. Sam took advantage of Loretta's lucidness. "Miss Retta, I'd like to hear more about your husband if you're up to it. What's his name, for starters?"

Retta weakly pushed back a strand of hair. "Jared. Jared Mitchell."

Shock ran through Sam, and his gaze flew to Cheyenne. She looked just as stunned. Of all the names, he never expected Mitchell's.

"He'd gotten a job with Bert Ronan," Retta continued. "Why do you look taken aback?"

Cheyenne leaned forward. "Bert Ronan is my father, and this is his home you're in. I'm his daughter. I'm sorry we never got around to sharing our full names."

Now it was Retta's turn to be shaken. "Then where is Jared? Can you get him for me?"

"I wish we could, Miss Retta. I don't know how to tell you this. I guess it's best just straight out. Your husband has disappeared." Sam tried to soften the blow with a smile. "He was living in the bunkhouse here until about a week ago."

"Disappeared? How?"

"Retta, there appeared to have been a scuffle," Cheyenne said gently. "The table and a chair were turned over."

Sam was glad she hadn't mentioned the blood. Retta's face had gone white enough.

"You might as well know, I guess." Retta met Sam's gaze. "Jared spent time in prison and hasn't been released long. Somehow he heard of the need of a ranch hand to run things, so he came ahead to work. He wanted a fresh start. Jared's a good man. There's none better, but he got caught up in some worthless schemes with his friends."

That was interesting. Had he gotten in with the wrong crowd again in Tascosa? Sam would get Cap to find out. Had the first bunch of friends found and killed him? Or maybe a new group had coerced him into joining them or silenced him when he refused? Lots of possibilities.

"Thank you for being honest, ma'am. This puts a new perspective on his disappearance. I'll go see the sheriff. I think he needs to be looking for Jared."

"Yes, thank you."

Cheyenne helped Ellen crawl up beside her mother. "Retta, how did you and the kids find yourselves stuck in that broken-down wagon?"

"A long story." Retta licked her dry lips. "He was supposed to send for us, but I never heard from him. I wrote letters and didn't get a reply. Not a word. So I packed us up, and we came to find him. I wanted to surprise him for Christmas."

"So you were staying not far from here?" Sam asked.

"With my folks at their place near Abernathy. These children need their father."

"Is my daddy all right?" Ellen asked in a scared voice.

Retta drew her daughter close. "Yes, honey, your daddy is just fine. He'll be here soon." She said the defiant words as though a warning that they better not say different.

"I hope so." Ellen clung to her mother, and Aaron climbed up beside them.

Sam itched to ask what her husband went to prison for but wouldn't in front of the kids. They looked scared enough with all this talk about their father. Best to wait on that.

Thankfully, Cheyenne distracted the kids. She told about living with the Apaches and had a rapt audience. Aaron and Ellen asked lots of questions about the children there, what kind of food they ate, and could they read. They sat there enthralled and curious. Sam enjoyed learning a little about her life, so hearing her speak of her time in New Mexico Territory answered some of his questions.

Retta grew tired, and Sam carried her back to bed, then shortly after, the children joined her.

Finally, he was alone with Cheyenne. "I'm going to move back to my place tomorrow."

She sucked in a sharp breath. "No, please don't."

"It's probably the only way to keep you and the others safe."

"You plan to go back and forth?"

"For now."

"That will only add to the danger, not alleviate it. Your horse will be in plain sight. That Appaloosa is eye-catching. And what if they see you coming and going? Or Shadow."

"I thought about that, but I still think it's best to go back to my wickiup. I can put Rio in the barn while I'm here, and I can still keep doing everything I promised."

"Is it me that put the notion in your mind?"

"Absolutely not. I just don't want to put you in danger."

"I am already," she snapped. "There is no way to avoid it. At least with you here, you can send them on their way." When he frowned, she added, "You can still play the part of Sam Fletcher. I'll keep up the ruse."

As she'd pointed out, he'd already messed up. He should've

taken into account they'd check on him. His stomach twisted. He only had one other chance of fixing the problem.

But if he failed…

"Looks like you shot down all my arguments." He opened his arms. "Time for your nightly hug—if you want it."

"Most definitely." She came into his arms, and he closed them around her.

The feel of her soft body against him settled the jumpiness inside. He was glad he didn't have to leave.

Maybe one day he'd tell her about Beth and why he'd go through hell and fire and everything between to catch her killers.

Twenty-one

CHEYENNE HELPED SAM TURN DOWN THE WICKS IN THE parlor lamps, her mind on how safe she felt in his strong arms. Muscles formed by wielding a blacksmith hammer on the steel provided extra security.

"I have to run into town for a bit," he said quietly. "I'll be quiet when I come back."

She stood in front of him and grabbed his vest in both hands. "Please be careful and keep your gun loaded."

"I always do. I need to tell Cap about your visitors."

"Figured as much. I'll be up awhile giving Retta another steam treatment, and I put a mustard poultice on her earlier that I need to change."

"You're doing a fine job caring for her, Cheyenne. I'm sure you probably learned a lot living with the Apaches."

"I did." She sensed he was wanting to know more about that year, but this wasn't the time. Maybe not the place either for such discussion. The events were still raw. And the other had placed a stain upon her soul. "I won't be able to sleep until you get back."

"Then, I won't tarry. Keep the door locked. I'll knock." He grabbed his sheepskin coat and hat and went out into the cold night.

She turned the bolt and listened to the crunch of his boots as he went to the barn.

"Where is Mr. Sam going?" Ellen asked, surprising her from behind.

"He has something to do, but he won't be gone long. Why aren't you in bed, honey?"

"I ain't sleepy. Would you hold me in the rocker?" Ellen's quiet voice pleaded.

"Yes, I can." Cheyenne took her hand and led her into the dark parlor. She raised the wick a little higher in the lamps, then sat in the rocker, pulling Ellen onto her lap and holding her close. "When I was a little girl, my mother used to rock me just like this when I was needing some comfort."

"She did?"

"Especially when I was troubled and trying not to be scared." Cheyenne smoothed the girl's hair. "Tell me what's wrong."

"I'm scared for Mr. Sam. What if he dies?"

Cheyenne stopped the rocker and lifted Ellen's face. "Honey, Mr. Sam isn't going to die. Why do you think he might?"

"I heard him say he might leave and sleep in his house, and those mean old bad people will find him if he does." The girl twisted her finger in the fabric of her gown. "He needs us, and we need him."

"I think you're right, but he decided to sleep here with us. I swear. You don't have to worry."

"Okay." Ellen snuggled into Cheyenne's arms. "Would you tell me a Christmas story?"

"Do you have a favorite?"

"Mama told us one about baby Jesus. Do you know that one?"

"Yes, I do." So for the next half hour, Cheyenne told the child about Mary and Joseph and the journey to Bethlehem. Aaron crept in and sat at her feet, resting his head against her knees.

Tears filled Cheyenne's eyes. They needed their mother desperately, and Cheyenne was happy to give them comfort until Retta recovered.

Finally, Ellen's eyes grew heavy, and Cheyenne tucked the siblings back in bed, then turned her attention to Retta, who was awake.

"Thank you," Retta murmured weakly. "I feel so helpless."

"It's just for a little while. The rate you're going, you'll soon be up and around. I want to put you under the steam tent for a bit and change your mustard poultice."

"My baby? Is it...?"

"Your babe is fine. The doc seemed heartened his last visit. Your little one is a fighter it seems, just like its mama."

Relief filled Retta's thin face. "Glad."

Cheyenne bustled around, caring for the woman, but her thoughts were on Sam somewhere in the wicked town of Tascosa. It seemed a little strange that he'd come to mean so much to her in such a short time.

But she knew better than to rely on him too much. Like her, he harbored secrets. She'd seen the dark storm in his eyes and knew there were things he couldn't face.

Part of her also knew that if he ever found the strength, he'd leave. And that put dread in her heart.

❧

It was spitting snow as Sam rode silently into the alley behind the ugly yellow building and crept up to Cap's room. The man answered to the light tap and let him in.

The rumpled bed piqued Sam's curiosity. He lifted an eyebrow. "No maid again?"

Cap's droopy mustache twitched with his grin. He shut the open window. "Just missed her."

"I hope she ain't as homely as your others have been."

"Ha-ha! Who can see when the lamp's out?" Cap rolled a cigarette. "I had a notion you might be around this evening. What's up?"

"Two things." Sam told him about the visitors that showed up at the Ronans'. "I knew Deek was skittish and doesn't trust me, but I never thought he'd try to find out where I was staying. Maybe that was a little naive of me. In any event, I should be more careful.

Now I've put Cheyenne and the Mitchells in danger and came in to try to fix that."

"Yeah, those folks don't need that. But Doolin's yahoos didn't follow you, or they'd have known you weren't at the Ronan place. You aren't, are you?"

"I'm sleeping there."

"Aha! I figured you might have a maid too."

Sam threw up a hand. "Stop right there. It's not that. Cheyenne's parents were called away and I'm helping her out on the ranch. Then there's the Mitchell kids I try to keep busy. But no, the riders didn't follow me or else they'd have seen me leave for my place and come there. I was only at the Ronan place after the funeral long enough to pick up the boy."

"Still, you don't want them coming back."

"Right. Therefore, I'm going to pay Deek a visit when I leave here." Sam didn't exactly know how he was going to handle that, but he meant to set down some rules. "Another thing I wanted to talk about. Did you ever have any dealings with or hear of Jared Mitchell?"

Cap lit his cigarette. "No, I don't recall him, but that ain't saying anything. After twenty years of doing this, the names of criminals have all run together. Why?"

Sam dropped onto the end of the bed with a sigh. "He's the husband of the woman Cheyenne Ronan is caring for along with her kids. Mitchell was working as a ranch hand for Bert Ronan but disappeared about a week ago. Retta felt well enough to sit for a while this evening, and I finally got her husband's last name. She said he hasn't been out of prison long. Never got a chance to ask her what he served time for, but it started me thinking."

"That he fell in with the Doolins?"

"Yeah. Maybe he had some special skill they needed. Could be they asked him to join them. Or they might not've given him a choice. I'll try to find out something when I head over there."

"I'll be close if you need help." Cap grinned. "I can't let you have all the fun."

Fun? The ranger was loony.

They talked for several more minutes, then Sam left, thankful for his warm coat. The wind was whipping around and blowing snow. He pulled the warmth tighter and rode Rio to the front of the Hitching Post Saloon and went inside.

"Whiskey." He slapped two bits onto the bar and swept the room for Deek. He found him sitting in a dark corner with two of his cronies. Sam picked up the drink the bartender set in front of him and tossed it back, enjoying the burn that chased away the chill.

He wove through the dingy saloon and placed his palms on the table, leaning across from Deek. "I don't appreciate the riders you sent to poke around about me. Apparently neither did that Ronan woman to find them at her door. You can find someone else to make your part."

"Wait just a cotton-pickin' minute." When Deek tried to rise, Sam shoved him back down.

The other two men reached for their guns only to find Sam's leveled in their faces. "Don't try it," he growled.

"How do you know they paid the Ronan girl a visit?" Deek spat.

The saloon door opened and Cap entered, his hat pulled low above a heavy Mexican serape. Sam breathed a little easier.

"Do you think I'm as dumb as calf slobber? I followed them. Figured you'd send someone to turn the tables and I was right." Sam glanced at the locked door he'd seen previously and the guard unlocking it for a gentleman. Once it was open, the guard shoved the man inside. Seemed to him the man had balked at going in. Sam swung back to Deek. "I want the work, but I don't want to be killed for it."

"No one's gonna kill you, Fletcher. Settle down, dammit." Deek leaned back in his chair. "I had to make sure you were who you said. However, I might've misjudged you."

Sam got in the killer's face. "Leave me alone and stop this nonsense, and you'll have it this time tomorrow."

Deek's eyes widened with surprise. "Good."

"Just so we understand each other. The Ronan woman isn't to be hurt."

"You seem real protective of her, yet she doesn't know you. Why is that?"

"Damn right I'm protective. I'm looking out for her. She's been away for a year, and I owe her father." Sam slid his weapon back in the holster and rolled his shoulders. "Hey, give Mitchell a message?"

"Mitchell? How do you know Jared?" Deek narrowed his eyes.

That settled the question. Jared Mitchell was alive and well. And in the company of the Doolins—whether willing or not remained to be seen.

"Did a job with him before he went to prison. Heard he was in Tascosa now."

One of the other men at the table chuckled. "Yep, Fletcher's one of us."

"Your message?" Deek asked.

"Tell him Retta's sick but would do better if he came back to the Ronans." Sam straightened and strode past Cap, winking on the way out the door.

He was satisfied with the way things had gone, but he still had to be careful and stay out of sight while at the Ronans.

If anyone harmed Cheyenne, Loretta, or the kids in any way, there *would* be hell to pay.

Twenty-two

SURE ENOUGH, WHEN SAM RETURNED FROM TASCOSA AND tapped on the kitchen door, Cheyenne was right there to unlock it. The quickness indicated she must've been looking out the window and seen him ride up.

The pinched lines of her face eased into a ready smile. "No blood. That's good."

"Yep, a sign I'm not dead or leaking all over your floor." He wanted to pull her close and kiss the daylights out of her, but he simply transferred his beat-up Stetson to her head. It looked mighty fine sitting on her soft curls that cascaded down her back and over her shoulders.

She glanced up at him in surprise, her smile widening. "You seem in a good mood."

"I'm happy with the way things went, but I'm about frozen stiff." He glanced at the pot on the stove. "Don't suppose we have any coffee left."

"I'm sorry, we don't. It'll only take a minute to make some." She filled the pot from the pump at the sink, added the coffee, and set it on the fire that was already going to keep the kitchen warm. "Sit down. I'll keep you company while it boils."

Sam pulled out a chair opposite her. She still wore his hat, which made his heart do a funny little flip. Something it should definitely not be doing.

"Did you learn what you went into town for?" She propped an elbow on the table and rested her chin on her fist.

"Retta's husband is alive and well. He's working with—or

for—the counterfeiters. Not sure which yet. I didn't get to speak
to him." He reached for her hand and turned it over to study her
palm. It was a hand that belonged to a woman not afraid of work.
A scar marred the delicate skin of her wrist, and he wondered what
had happened.

"Will you tell her tomorrow? It would ease her mind."

"Not sure. I think she has a right to know, but I'll probably
wait until I find out if being there is his idea or the gang's. They
could've forced him. But I won't tell those kids. They'd be confused, and Ellen for sure would think he doesn't want them."

"I agree. We can't. I think Retta will be relieved he's alive."

He studied Cheyenne and saw the tired lines around her eyes.
"I don't think those riders will be back. Let's just say that tonight
we got some things cleared up."

"I do hope so. They looked dangerous."

"They're good at threatening women but find it harder when
it's a man." He released her hand and rose for a mug. "It's trying to
snow, so the cattle's water will be frozen by morning. I'll take care
of that and go to my place to work. Need to finish what I promised
to deliver."

"I'll be glad when you're done with whatever it is. Will you
make an arrest?"

"Depends on a few things. If we try too soon, they could run
and we'll never find them. I've chased Tom Doolin for a long while.
He's slippery. The whole bunch is. We have to be careful this time
and not let them get away. We also have to determine how far this
counterfeiting operation reaches and who all is involved. We have
to get them all." He stood at the sideboard, twirling his cup.

"How long have you been a Texas Ranger?"

"Three years. My father was one and is still a lawman. The
sheriff in Lost Point."

"I guess it's in the blood, just like working to help the Natives
is in mine." She was silent a moment. "You asked what I did for the

time I was in New Mexico Territory." Cheyenne looked up, meeting his stare. "I was fired from my teaching job at the government school in Santa Fe for helping kids escape back to their parents. After that, I joined a group leading Apache men, women, and children to safety across the border."

"Into Mexico?"

"Yes."

The admission startled him. No wonder she didn't want to talk about it. "That was dangerous. Brave. But you could've been imprisoned. Why take the risk?"

She shrugged. "Had you seen the cruelty you wouldn't ask that. There were things that made me sick to my stomach. They asked for my help, and I couldn't turn them down and live with my conscience."

"That explains why you attacked me while I was sleeping. I'm lucky you didn't slit my throat." He rose and pulled the pot off the stove to let the grinds settle to the bottom. It also explained the way she'd fought like a wildcat when those men cornered her at the river. She'd been forced to defend herself before. Probably many times.

"Why aren't you still there?" Sam searched her face. He saw a woman with deep convictions, and those led her to make life-altering choices. She wasn't willing to take the safe, easier route. She wasn't willing to turn her back on wrongdoing. Or turn a blind eye to pain.

It would've been easy to follow a safe path. That she chose the hard said volumes.

The clocked ticked. Dark shadows crossed her eyes, and she glanced down. "We stopped for a while."

That wasn't the truth. At least not all of it. He wondered at the real reason. It had something to do with why she needed to be held at night. Something had scared her so badly, she couldn't get past it. Yes, there was a lot more she wasn't telling. At least he knew part of what she'd done for that year. A person held things back, some all the rest of their lives. She might never reveal the whole of it.

Cheyenne stood and hung his hat on a hook beside the door. "I should check on Retta."

He followed her with his gaze as she left the room, then got to his feet to fill his cup with coffee and finish thawing.

A minute or two passed before she returned. "The patient is fine. Good night." But she didn't turn to go.

"Would you like me to hold you?" he asked softly.

"Do you mind? I'd like that very much." She walked to him.

As Sam took her in his arms and held her against him, he could feel the rapid beat of her heart as though someone were chasing her. "It's okay, pretty lady. I've got you."

For however long she wanted to stay next to him.

～

The following morning, Sam froze his rear off tromping through the light snow to break the ice for the cattle and feed them. After breakfast, he left to finish forging the part for Deek. Although Aaron begged to come, Sam refused. He couldn't be sure what Deek might do, and it was safer for the boy to stay with Cheyenne. But Shadow fell right in step with Rio and seemed anxious to get some exercise.

Sam passed the five-mile ride thinking about all he had to do before dark. He rounded a bend and pulled up when he spied smoke rising from the stovepipe of the wickiup. He left Rio tied behind the crude dwelling and crept to the front, his gun drawn.

A man came through the flap, the weak sun shining on the tin star pinned to his shirt. "About time you showed up, son."

"Dad." Sam put his gun away. "When did you get here?"

"Late last night. Made myself at home. You evidently stayed somewhere else."

They drank coffee while Sam told his dad about the Ronans, Cheyenne, and the Mitchells. "So I've been staying there most of the time. Why are you here?"

"Got a telegram from Cap McFarlan about the mess here and asking for my help." The senior Sam ran a hand through his dark hair that sported a few streaks of gray at his temples. His discerning dark eyes still had that knowing look, not in a judgmental way, but intuitive, as though he could sense things that troubled a man. "He knew I had some dealings with old man Doolin back in the day and put him away awhile for killing that stage driver."

Yeah, that excuse was as limp as wet newspaper. Cap didn't fool him. The old ranger had brought the senior Sam to watch out for his kid. Hell!

"What exactly does Cap want you to do?" Sam sipped on his coffee.

"Point Lem out for one thing. Cap doesn't know what he looks like, and I'm not sure you do either. I want to help pin down everyone involved in this scheme."

"A sure bet is the Doolins. Cap spotted Tom, and I met up with Deek. I can smell Ford and Daddy Lem, but they seem to be keeping out of sight. Still, as you pointed out, we don't know what they look like. And for certain they've enlisted some locals. How many is anyone's guess."

"Yep, they have to have some foot soldiers to distribute the fake bills in the surrounding towns." Shadow wandered in through the flap and Senior ran a hand over the thick fur. "Tell me about the death of a friend that Cap spoke of." His voice was quiet. "Cap said it affected you pretty bad."

The light shone on the deep scar around his dad's throat where the shirt fell away. He'd eventually killed the rustlers who'd tried to hang him, but it had taken months. Sam swallowed hard. His dad had come awfully close to dying. The pain his namesake must've endured sobered him.

Senior was a Legend through and through, and Sam wondered if he'd ever measure up.

"His name was Heck Raines, and he was a good friend and fellow bladesmith." Sam told about finding him dead, then backtracked to when Pope went out to Heck's place with a drawing, asking if he could make it. "I found the names Pope and Doolin on a paper stuck down between Heck and his chair. Not sure why. It sorta looked like Heck had his suspicions about who he was working for."

The senior Sam raised his eyes. "Who is this Pope?"

"That's just it. I don't know. Mickey McCormick said he left town. Heck thought it was a fake name, so I guess it could be anybody. I never saw him." Sam reached for the pot and poured the last in his dad's tin cup. "I told Deek Doolin last night I'd have his part ready by late today, so I came out to work on it. Hopefully, when I take it to Deek, I'll get a chance for a word with Jared Mitchell. I need to find out what part he's playing in all this and if he's there willingly or coerced."

"When we find out what he was in prison for, we'll know more about the Doolins. How far is it to Amarillo?"

"Forty miles give or take. Why?"

"Just wondering if they'd have any information on this ring. I'll ride back by there when I leave and have a chat with the sheriff." Senior finished his coffee and squeezed Sam's shoulder. "How are you doing, son? Your mother and I hope the memories are fading a bit. She's another reason I came. I'm to find out your state of mind."

"At times it seems like I buried Beth a lifetime ago. Others, just yesterday. I'm okay, though. I love making my knives and doing something few people can."

"I'm proud of you, you know that, don't you?" Those dark eyes so much like Sam's held the immeasurable love of a parent.

"Yep." Sam had never doubted that for a second.

"And we loved Beth like a daughter. The tragedy affected your mother and me deeply. So now we have a chance to get the bastards."

"No matter what Cap says, I have to hold myself back to keep from riding into town and emptying my .45 in them." Sam scooted over to the bed and pulled out his box of knives, selecting one in particular and holding it out. "I was going to give this to you for Christmas. But one thing Beth's death taught me is that I can't count on a future. Who knows how long I'll be alive? Or you."

Senior took the knife and slid it from the scabbard Sam had made. He inhaled a slow breath, examining the design the twisted piece of steel made, testing the sharpness of the blade, admiring the handle. Then he found the initials with the word Legend underneath and stared. Finally, he looked up, his expression solemn. "Son, this is a piece of art. Words don't exist for what I want to say."

"So you like it?"

"It's a beauty. You don't know how much I'll cherish this. You have a true gift, and I don't say that lightly. What you make is rare. It's like you put your heart and soul into each piece of steel."

"Me and steel connect in a way I never have with people. I know it sounds crazy, but it talks to me. I love the feel of it in my hands."

"It's not crazy at all. I understand that. It's called passion, and only a select few ever find that in their work. I can't wait to show this to your grandpa." Senior grinned. "He'll probably try to wheedle it out of me like he tends to do with anything he takes a shine to."

Sam laughed. "He's worse than a kid at times. We'll solve that." He selected a knife from the box with a blue stone inset into the dark grain of a rosewood handle. "Give him this."

Senior whistled. "Nice. I think your grandpa will be happy."

"I never got around to making a sheath for it."

"I'm sure he has one, so that won't matter one bit." Senior picked up the one Sam made him, turning it so the blade reflected the light. "I admit when you first started as a bladesmith, I thought it was just a hobby that wouldn't last. I was wrong for trying to limit your abilities. I see now what you were trying to tell your mother and me."

"It's all right."

"You should've seen Luke when he got back from here." Senior chuckled. "He went around, showing the knife to everyone—even showed it to a few steers, I was told."

Sam laughed. Yeah, he could see Luke doing that.

"I'm supposed to talk you into moving back home." Senior sighed. "But I see now that this is right where you need to be. This is where you're happiest."

"It's home now. And when I take a longing for family, I can come visit." Sam put another piece of wood on the fire. "Tell Mother I've cut the apron strings and am forging my own life. I'm better than I've been in a while." He rose. "I need to work for a while. You're welcome to watch, or maybe you want to ride into Tascosa."

"This will be a short visit, so I want to stay right here with you and see what it is you do."

For once, the sun shone bright in the crystal blue sky. The hours passed in the quiet company of his father—just Sam and his steel.

Creating.

Honing.

Polishing.

The process reminded him a lot of life. What you started out with changed, both in thought and action. It was learning as a man went. And then for some reason, he started thinking about Cheyenne and their nightly ritual.

Twenty-three

CHEYENNE SPENT THE DAY CARING FOR LORETTA AND HELPING the kids with their baskets. Each time she heard a noise, she went to the window to look out. The hours dragged by. But a pleasurable part was sitting beside Retta's bed, talking.

"Didn't you say you were living in Abernathy?" Cheyenne asked.

"Yes, with my folks on their farm. They spoiled the kids rotten."

"I think all grandparents do that." Cheyenne laughed. "The reason I asked is that my grandma and grandpa lived there before they passed, and I used to visit them a lot. It's a nice place."

"Yes, it is, and I love my parents, but I didn't like them constantly talking bad about Jared. The kids didn't need that. Their daddy is a good man, and I wish my folks could see it. It's time for us to be on our own again."

"Everyone on this earth makes mistakes." Cheyenne had made plenty. She thought about telling Retta what Sam had found out and decided against it. They needed to know more first. "I can help you find a place to live around here so Jared can keep working for us."

She hoped so anyway. It all depended on his involvement with the counterfeiting.

Retta sighed and clenched her hands. "When Jared got out, Ford Doolin promised him a job, a house, a new life. We were so full of hope. But nothing ever materialized, and then my husband found this job. He wrote that your father was very kind to him."

Cheyenne patted her hand, committing the name Ford Doolin to memory so she could tell Sam. "I hope you don't think I'm prying, and if so, please forgive me. What did Jared go to prison for?"

A long silence filled the room. She was about to say it didn't matter when Retta spoke.

"Engraving plates." Retta hid her face. "I'm so embarrassed."

There it was, and Sam had probably guessed that already.

"Please don't be embarrassed. He served time paying for his mistake and put it behind him." She hoped for Retta and the kids' sake.

If only Sam and Cap could arrest these men soon. They were in so much danger.

That, she knew something about. The unbidden image of a man's face shrouded by the night. Dark rage pouring from him. The gunshot still reverberating in her head.

The deadly quiet afterward had been as terrifying as the noises.

The jostling of her arm drew her back to the present. "Miss Ann, can we have a cookie?" Ellen asked.

That the girl had shortened her name came as no surprise. Cheyenne's name was hard for a five-year-old to say. "Of course, sweetie. You and Aaron shall have two of our sugar cookies." Cheyenne turned to Retta. "How about some hot tea?"

"That sounds good. Thank you." Retta touched her daughter's face.

Cheyenne took the girl's hand and Aaron followed them to the kitchen. The children were at the table with milk and cookies, and Cheyenne glanced out the window at a lone rider. Looked to be the boy from town who sometimes delivered letters. He dismounted, and she opened the door before he could knock.

"A letter, ma'am." He handed her an envelope.

"Just a moment, young man." She went to the kitchen and got the tin container that held her mother's egg money and brought him back a nickel. "Thank you for bringing it out to me."

The boy, who looked about fourteen, grinned. "Yes, ma'am."

Her eyes flew to the sender and saw her father's name in the corner. She shut the door and went to the quiet of the parlor to open the envelope.

> *Dear Daughter,*
>
> *We hope this finds you well. Your Aunt Betty is clinging to life but it appears to be in vain. The doctors offer no hope, and I don't see how she can last much longer. Your mother and I are fine and spend our days doing what we can for Betty and trying to bolster Donald. I'm having to feed his animals for him and make sure the cattle are fed and watered. We probably won't be home for Christmas which pains us greatly.*
>
> *Your Loving Father*

Cheyenne folded the letter and sat in thought. Sadness filled her that her aunt wouldn't recover. She'd always loved her mother's twin. In fact, she'd thought of her as a second mother. She'd pen a reply at the first opportunity. Sam could take it to town. Stirring in the kitchen reminded her of the children and of Retta waiting on tea. She stuck the letter in her pocket and went about the rest of her day.

Shadows had lengthened by the time Sam rode in along with a visitor. Was this the Cap he'd spoken of?

Thank goodness Sam had made a huge pot of stew. She had it warming and had decided to go ahead and stir up the fry bread for Sam when he opened the kitchen door. The children ran hollering and launched themselves on him. Shadow barked and leaped up as well. With a kid clinging to each muscular forearm, he lifted them off the floor and swung them around. An older, dark-haired man behind stood watching it all, a bemused expression on his face.

Cheyenne stopped to watch, a lump in her throat. Sam glanced at her and rolled his eyes, but she knew he loved it.

"I'm glad you weren't gone a month," she managed dryly over the noise.

"Me too." Grinning, he flipped the kids over in a somersault and wild hoots of laughter filled the room. Finally, he called it quits, and they ran off to tell their mother he was home, as though she couldn't hear.

He drew the visitor forward. "This is my father, Sam Sr. He spent last night in the wickiup and surprised me this morning."

Oh my! His legendary father. She'd always been curious about this youngest Legend son, still bearing the scars of a lynching by rustlers.

"Welcome." Flustered, Cheyenne wiped her hands on her apron and took his outstretched palm. "I'm so happy to meet you and awfully sorry about all the racket. I'm Cheyenne Ronan." She took in the tall, lean man bearing a lot of Sam's features. But he was a little intimidating both in size and the sense of authority he projected. He wore confidence well.

Shadow padded off, following Aaron's and Ellen's voices.

"It's a pleasure," the senior Legend said. "I like to see where my son spends part of his time. He told me about the Mitchells. You're doing a fine thing taking them in."

"We couldn't leave Retta and those kids out where they were." She took his hat and coat. "I have an empty bunkhouse, and I hope you'll make use of it while you're here."

"Thank you. I appreciate that. Another night in the wickiup, and I'd be frozen solid."

"There's coffee on the stove. Make yourself at home."

Her thoughts flying a million different directions, she hurried to hang his hat and coat. Lingering a second in the doorway, she watched father and son quietly talking, so alike but different. Yet theirs was a deep bond that surpassed disagreements and possible hurt that Sam chose to live away from the family.

She smiled. These Legends were as fine as she'd always heard, and not in name only. The men who'd filled those stories were larger than life, and she had two under her roof.

Twenty-four

SAM FOLLOWED CHEYENNE TO THE OAK HALL TREE IN FRONT where she hung his father's coat and hat. She glanced up at him, noticing how the lamplight softened the chiseled angles of his face. "How nice of your father to visit. Is there any particular reason for him coming?"

"Cap telegraphed him. Thought Dad needed to come help with the trouble in town." Sam rubbed the back of his neck. "Frankly, I think Dad just needed an excuse to check up on me."

"How do you feel about that?" She'd learned since knowing him that he often hid what he really thought about his family and their penchant for dropping by unannounced. She'd seen it clearly with his uncle and now with his father, although he'd been truly glad to see each.

"It's nice I guess, and we can use his help. We had a good talk today while he watched me work. And he's only staying a couple of days, which is ideal."

She smiled and moved closer. "I missed you today." After several heartbeats, she asked, "Did you finish that part you had to make?"

"Yes. I'll be taking it into town tonight."

Dread and foreboding filled her. "I have a lot to tell you, some things I found out from Retta, if we can find a moment and a quiet spot after supper."

"I'll make sure of it." He brushed the barest of fingertips across her cheek. "Thank you for mixing the batter for the fry bread. You look tired. Sit and talk to my dad while I finish making supper."

Before she could move, Aaron came to the doorway. "Mama needs you. Hurry!"

She rushed into the bedroom and found Retta struggling to breathe. "Aaron, go tell Sam to put a kettle of water on."

Cheyenne dipped a cloth in the cool water in the washing pan and applied it to Retta's thin face. "There, don't panic. Try to relax. That's good." She kept bathing the mother's face and murmuring soothing words until she stopped fighting.

Minutes passed as she worked. Sam must've put more wood in the stove to get the water boiling faster because it didn't seem that long before he brought it to her.

"Thank you, Sam." She added some eucalyptus leaves to the pot.

Wasting no time, she threw a blanket over Retta's head and aimed the steam underneath. "Take deep breaths, Retta. Nice deep breaths. Inhale in. Breathe out slowly."

"Breathe, Mama. Breathe!" Ellen hollered.

"Don't die, Mama." Aaron stood at the foot of the bed, wringing his hands.

When the steam stopped coming, Cheyenne took the blanket off Retta's head. The color in her face had returned to normal. "That's much better." She smoothed back the mother's light brown hair. "I'll make you some tea to soothe your throat, then I'll bring some of the venison broth for supper."

"Just the tea for right now. Please."

"Only if you're sure."

Retta reached for Cheyenne's hand and squeezed. "You've been far too kind. I would've died several times over if not for you."

"I have a vested interest." Cheyenne smiled and turned to the kids. "Let's go eat supper."

"Is Mama gonna be all right?" Aaron asked quietly.

"Yes. I believe she will." Despite her calm assurance, she wasn't all that confident. She needed some echinacea root. Maybe tomorrow she could go out and look for some if it wasn't snowing. The children needed fresh air. She thought about her calisthenics regime and the fact that she hadn't gotten to indulge since Retta and the kids had come. She'd gotten stiff.

The fry bread was as delicious as she remembered and went well with the stew. The children left the table the second they finished.

"That was an excellent meal, Miss Cheyenne." Senior leaned back in his chair.

"Thank your son. He cooked the stew and the fry bread."

"I'm learning something new." Senior glanced at his son. "Your mother can stop worrying about you starving. She'll be happy you can cook."

"No choice if I wanted to eat," Sam answered. "What I cook is simple but filling." He rose to refill his and his dad's coffee. "No visitors today, Cheyenne?"

"Only the postman bringing a letter from my father. There is no hope of recovery for my aunt, which brings such sorrow. Even after she passes, they'll have to stay a bit for Uncle Donald. He'll be so lost."

Sam explained the situation to his dad, then asked her, "They never had any children?"

"No. That's why they doted on me. When I was younger, I practically spent every summer with them. Aunt Betty made me a lot of clothes and taught me to sew and cook. I'll miss her." Her voice choked with the memories.

"I'm sorry."

"I'll be fine. Death is so hard." Cheyenne pulled a lacy handkerchief from her pocket and blew her nose. "Father said to tell you the earliest they can be back is Christmas and thank you for taking care of things here."

"No thanks needed. Glad to help." He sat back down and crossed his legs.

Anxious lines deepened the crow's feet at the corners of his eyes, and she assumed his thoughts were on facing one or more Doolins later. Maybe it would all end tonight and Tascosa would be a safer place. She wondered if Sam Senior would go along. She hoped so.

"Let's take your dad to the bunkhouse and get him settled," she suggested. "Then I need to tell you something."

Senior smiled. "If you need some private time, I know when to disappear."

Cheyenne laid a light hand on his arm. "You need to hear what I have to say if you're going to be working with Sam and Cap. Besides, the bunkhouse is away from the children."

Bundled in her coat, she led them out to the small living quarters apart from the house. Sam lit the round, potbelly stove, and Cheyenne got blankets and a pillow from a trunk at the foot of the nearest bed. Then they sat at the four-chair table. Shadow followed them in and plopped down by the fire.

"Retta and I talked some today, and she told me more about her husband." Cheyenne related the conversation to the men about Ford Doolin serving time with Jared, including that Jared had gone to prison for making plates.

"That's interesting. He has to be making them again now." Sam rubbed his eyes. "But they're already printing ones and fives. Why would they need Jared Mitchell?"

Senior's brows narrowed in thought. "Maybe they're thinking of expanding to larger cities. In places like that, they could pass larger bills virtually undetected."

Sam released a long whistle. "Of course. Around here, they're limited to small bills, since the larger would draw attention. They're greedy and probably seeing all the profit they're missing. And with the printing press out of commission, they're in a bigger pickle."

Desperate men were ten times more dangerous. A chill went up Cheyenne's spine.

"Jared could be making a plate for tens or twenties. Or both." She prayed the man wasn't there as a willing participant. Retta and those kids needed a good man to provide for them, darn it! What would happen to them if he went back to prison?

"It's very possible that's what he's doing." Sam steepled his fingers and propped his chin on them. "This could be a lot bigger than we thought. I always assumed the Doolins were opportunists, taking what they could when they could and spending little time planning. But now I'm not sure. This seems too organized. The Doolins are not this smart, which means they've more than likely got mob ties."

Senior nodded. "I agree."

"But if their press is down, what's in the boxes?" Cheyenne asked.

"Probably what remains of their last print run." Sam crossed his legs at the ankles and placed his hands behind his head. "Even after they get the money printed, they have to dirty it up some to look real. Probably wash it to take out the stiffness and who knows what else?

"So, what's the plan?" Senior asked. "I'd like to ride into town with you, Sam, but I'll stay here if you want. This is yours and Cap's deal."

"Come with me. We need to take advantage of you being here and maybe move forward faster. No one knows you, so you can sit in the saloon, watching the door. If they move some boxes out, you can follow them. We need to know where they're taking them. I'll meet with Deek and give him this part, maybe ask if he needs me to put it on whatever it goes to. Hopefully, I can get in the back room. I need to see their setup."

"Sounds good." Senior removed his sheriff's badge. "This might make some men skittish."

Cheyenne laughed, wanting to tell him that his size was enough to make people downright leery. Her eyes locked with

Sam's, praying for a private moment before they left. She pictured him without his beard and imagined he'd be the spitting image of his dark-haired father. Memories of their kiss swept into her mind, and tingles danced up her spine.

But nothing had happened since. Maybe he hadn't liked kissing her. Or maybe he'd seen that as a mistake, even though he'd said he wasn't sorry for doing it. The kiss must not've meant that much to him.

The men scooted back their chairs and rose. Sam met her gaze. "We'll head into town. I want to get this over with."

"I'll walk out with you. It'll be nice and warm in here when you get back, Mr. Legend."

Senior pulled on a pair of black leather gloves. "I couldn't ask for better accommodations, Miss Cheyenne. It'll be like old times with Sam and me. Thank you for your hospitality."

Their boots crunched on the frozen ground as they walked to the barn. Since Sam had not unsaddled their horses when they'd rode in, they led them out of the warm shelter into the night. Both men wore their guns in low-slung holsters.

Both riding to dispense the Legend brand of justice.

How could she ever have thought Sam was just a hairy recluse with no interest in anything but making knives? That was only a small part of him.

"Since we shouldn't be seen together, I'll go ahead and ride in first." Senior stuck his boot in a stirrup and swung into the saddle.

"See you there, Dad." Sam turned to Cheyenne as his father trotted away. "Don't wait up. It may be late when we get back. I don't want to bother you."

If they made it back. There was no guarantee.

"You're no bother. I'll probably be up." She shivered.

Sam put an arm around her. "Go back in. It's too cold to stand out here."

"Just a few minutes." She raised her face and found him looking down at her, his expression dark, unreadable. "Sam, I'm scared. A thousand things could go wrong."

He drew her closer and put his mouth next to her temple. "Just because they can doesn't mean they will. I've learned to roll the dice and deal with what comes. There are three of us now, which is one more than we had. And we have right on our side."

"I'm glad your father's here." She put her arms around his waist, bulky with the heavy coat. "Sam, you're not sorry you kissed me, are you?"

"Not one iota. I've just had a lot going on."

She moved against him. "If you want to kiss me again, I won't mind."

"That so?"

His raspy voice feathered softly against her face and aroused deep yearning. Her time for romance was slipping away. Soon, she'd be considered a spinster and whispered about by folks when she went into town. She wanted love, complete with fireworks and breathless moments. Nights making love, sleeping in a warm bed with the man she loved, and days walking next to him.

Was that too much to ask?

She wanted to be someone's everything and know she made a difference in his life by being there. This couldn't be all there was to her. She couldn't die without knowing love.

Dear God, for however longer she had, she needed more than days of toil and caring for other people's children. She yearned for her own.

Sam put a finger under her chin and lifted her face. "I'm sorry you had to ask."

Ever so gently, he lowered his lips to hers and settled them firmly into a kiss that stole her breath. Her thoughts. Her sanity.

This was no light peck on the mouth. This was a deep, sizzling kiss that relayed exactly how he must feel at the moment.

Cheyenne put her arms around his neck and held on to keep

her balance. Fireworks went off behind her eyelids in brilliant rainbow colors, and she was quite sure her heart was going to race right out of her chest.

This kiss completely erased the first one from her mind. The moment his lips touched hers, heat swept the length of her body like a raging prairie fire, arousing a wanting so powerful it shook her. She swayed, her knees suddenly weak, while flutters whipped a froth against the inside her stomach.

She'd remember this moment for the rest of her life and the sensitive Texas Ranger with strong arms, a burning touch, and fiery kisses.

Twenty-five

Damn, how Cheyenne made Sam wish for another time and place!

The lantern in the barn cast flickering light around them while the wind banged a piece of tin. Sam slipped a hand inside her long duster and traced the curves of her tantalizing body. What he wouldn't give for just one night...

One slow, tender night of skin next to skin, a warm fire burning both inside and out. With her. His hands caressing her luscious body like they shaped the steel for his knives.

Hunger blazed inside him and awakened everything he thought had long died.

A little moan escaped from her.

Moving his hand back up to her waist, he broke the kiss and stared into the soft glow of Cheyenne's green eyes. "Lady, you don't know..." He inhaled a ragged breath. "Let's just say we have unfinished business."

"Sam, you make me wish for things I shouldn't."

He held her soft body against him, the wild beat of her heart giving way to emotion that seemed to match his. The fragrance of the cold night swirled around them. He placed his mouth at her ear. "You don't know how beautiful you are and how tempted I am to take you to my bed. To show you how a man should treat a fine lady. But this night doesn't belong to me. I have other obligations."

"I know." Cheyenne didn't move from the circle of his warm embrace. "I'm an unlucky woman when it comes to these things."

"When this is all over, we'll see where this leads."

"Don't make promises you can't keep. There are still so many things between us that stand in the way. We both have secrets." She pushed away. "You need to go. Your father—"

"You're right. Sleep well, pretty lady." He lifted Rio's reins. Untying the leather strip holding his hair back, he pressed it in Cheyenne's palm. "Keep this for me. Tonight, I need to be at my uncivilized best."

"Do you have the part you made?"

He patted a pocket. "Yep."

Her eyes held sparkling tears. She placed her fingers to her lips and blew him a kiss. "Stay safe, Sam Legend."

With a firm jerk of his head, he rode away, his thoughts whirling. He wasn't supposed to care for another woman, not supposed to feel like this. Somehow, she'd scaled the wall he'd built around his heart and snuck in.

This definitely complicated things.

The night air froze his face, but it would've been worse if not for his beard and the lingering warmth of Cheyenne's enticing body. He tugged the collar of his coat up higher and lowered his Stetson, already wishing he were back in front of the fire. At least the night was clear of moisture. The full moon hanging in the sky had a circle around it. Grandpa Stoker called it a winter halo.

By the time he'd ridden the ten miles into town, he couldn't feel his face. He snuck up the back stairs of the yellow hotel and tapped on Cap's room.

The ranger peeked through a crack in the door before he opened it. "You look like an icicle, Sammy boy."

"Feel like one too. Got a drink?"

"Do porcupines have sharp quills?" Cap blew into a glass to get the dust out and filled it about a fourth high, handing it to him.

Sam looked at it, lifting an eyebrow. "Aren't you being a mite stingy? I'm frozen."

Cap wagged a finger. "I'm recalling how I rode up to your house of sticks all frozen in the dead of night. You made me sit there while you decided whether or not to sic your wolf on me. And *then*, when you finally let me go inside, you offered coffee. Coffee. I had to furnish my own damn bottle. Let this be a lesson to you."

Sam tossed the whiskey back and grimaced. "Play the martyr all you want, but the truth stands."

"Hmph! You always want the last word." Cap stoppered the bottle. "Did you finish the part?"

"I did. By the way, my father's in town. Should be over at the Hitching Post." Sam narrowed his eyes. "Seems you sent him a telegram. Didn't consult me or anything."

"Sammy boy, we all got crosses to bear. Get a move on. I ain't gettin' any younger."

It was useless to try to shame his friend. Cap had few scruples. "I'll give Deek the part and Senior will be watching the guarded door, following anyone toting boxes." Sam tilted his head to one side and crooked an eyebrow at Cap. "What'll you be doing?"

Cap grinned. "I'll be guarding your butt so no one puts a hole in that baby-soft skin."

"If you're through insulting me, I suggest we get on with this."

The ranger presented an open palm. "After you, princess."

Shaking his head, Sam headed for the stairs. A door opened two rooms down, and a rough-looking hombre stepped out, eyeing them. The deep lines slashing his cheeks looked like ten miles of washed-out road.

"Nice night." Sam nodded, the hair on his neck rising. Unease spread through him as he took a little longer stride to the stairs.

When he turned, the man had disappeared.

"Where did he go, Cap?" Sam whispered.

"Beats me. Maybe he went back inside. We'd best be on our toes."

"Yep."

They left the hotel and hurried past the deafening noise of

several saloons until they came to the Hitching Post. It must've been drunk fight night. One man came flying out the batwing doors as they approached and another barreled after, trying to shoot him. Of course, all the shots missed, seeing as how the shooter could barely stand up.

Inside was no different. Drunks were swinging right and left. Two scantily clad painted women were standing on the long bar, busting whiskey bottles over anyone's head that came near.

Senior stood in a far corner away from the all-out brawl.

Cap grinned. "My kind of place."

"You're crazy." Sam sidestepped a burly fist. "I'll see if I can find any of the Doolins."

He left Cap slinging a drunk like the string on a top and made his way to the locked door. Finding the guard engaged in bloodying a man's nose, Sam tried the knob and found it unlocked. He quickly slid inside.

A quick scan revealed four men. One sat at a table, hunched over his work, a bulky headband around his head from which a pair of strange-looking glasses were attached. They appeared outfitted with magnifying lenses like those jewelers wore—or men involved in intricate, very small work. With the man staring down and no identifying features visible at the moment, Sam couldn't make him out. Had to be Jared Mitchell though.

A large press sat against the back of the small room that was littered with paper and the smell of ink.

Another man was busy filling a box with fake money. Sam couldn't tell the size of the bills from where he was. Not important at the moment. The other two, one quite a bit older, were deep in conversation with their backs to him. He didn't see Deek anywhere.

"Hey, what are you doing in here?" the man packing the box yelled, picking up a gun.

Sam lifted both hands. "There wasn't anyone at the door. I'm Fletcher, and I got the part Doolin wanted made."

The two in conversation broke apart. One was Tom Doolin. "Who is it, Ford?"

"Says his name is Fletcher."

Tom hurried toward them. The man with him had to be Daddy Lem, judging by the resemblance. Beth's face drifted in front of him, and the overpowering need to grab Tom and beat that sneer off his face washed over Sam in waves. He ground his back teeth together.

Not yet. Just a little longer. Patience.

"Ain't no one allowed in here but us." Tom stood nose to nose with Sam. "No one."

Sam shrugged and stepped back, glaring. "Makes me no never mind. Deek said you needed this part, but guess you don't after all." Whirling, he turned to the door.

"Wait." Tom clutched his arm. "Deek said you'd bring it tonight. You just startled us."

"The whole saloon's in a fight out there, and your guard was busy." Sam tugged the eight-inch metal part from inside his coat and handed it to Tom. "Should fit if the drawing was to the right measurements."

"Ford, finish packing that box," Tom ordered. "The man will be after it soon."

From the set of Ford's mouth, he didn't appreciate being ordered around like some lackey, but he returned to his task without a word.

The older man came over and took the part from Tom, inspecting it. "Looks good to me. I'll go put it on." He took the part to the printing press at the back.

"I'll wait if you want to try it out." Sam prayed they'd let him stay for a bit. He needed to see more. When Tom hesitated, he added, "If it's a hair off, I need to know so I can fix it."

Finally, Tom pointed to a chair. "Take a seat and don't touch nothing."

"You're the boss." Before he could sit, Tom narrowed his gaze. Ice slid down Sam's spine.

The old enemy stared and walked closer. "There's something familiar about you."

"We might've crossed paths." Sam forced himself to remain nonchalant, even though he shook inside. "I've done jobs all around Texas. Served a stretch in prison."

The man with the large magnifying glasses took them off, and it was Mitchell. A jolt raced through him. Jared gave him a curious look. Praying the man wouldn't give him away, Sam returned his stare, hoping for a word before he got ushered out.

"Yeah, maybe." Tom glanced at the older man at the back that had to be Lem.

"What'cha got going on here?" Sam asked casually, smoothing his beard.

"Nothing that concerns you."

Sam widened his stance and hooked his thumbs in his gun belt. "Just thought you might cut me in is all."

Twenty-six

"WE'RE REAL PARTICULAR ABOUT WHO WE LET IN ON OUR operation." Tom Doolin's gaze narrowed. "We got partners to answer to."

"I see. Well, I understand." Sam's gaze followed Tom to the printing press. Deciding it was worth the risk, he sauntered over to Mitchell and took a seat. He kept his voice real low. "Glad to see you're in one piece. Cheyenne didn't know what happened to you."

"Yeah. I didn't have much choice."

"Look, we may not have much time, but you should know your wife and kids are at the Ronan home. Your wife is very sick. Your son came to me hungry and cold, needing help for his mother. Their wagon had broken down, and they'd run out of food."

"I was supposed to send for them." He released a long sigh. "Guess Retta got tired of waiting. Will she be all right?"

"The doc is hopeful, if she doesn't have a setback. Your family needs you."

"The Doolins won't let me go until I finish this metal plate."

The light created a glare on the silver finish and made it hard for Sam to read the lettering, but it looked to be a ten-dollar bill. "How long until you finish the plate?"

"Probably a week."

"Stop talking and work," Tom Doolin snapped behind them.

Sam jerked, startled. He hadn't heard the felon's footsteps. How long had he stood there, and what had he overheard? He told himself to stay calm and forced a grin. "Mitchell and me were talking over old times. We did a job together once. I ain't seen him since we both got out."

"I don't give a damn. He's working for me, and I make the rules."

Razor-thin tension filled the space between them. Sam slowly rose to his six-foot-four height. Tom took a step back. "I don't appreciate you talking to my friend that way. I doubt you're even paying him."

Tom's face reddened. "I intend to give him something."

Yeah, a bullet most likely. Sam narrowed his gaze. "Is he free to leave?"

"When he finishes the job and not before."

"Sounds to me like you're keeping him locked up. No better than a slave."

The band of tension stretched even thinner. The sudden sound of the printing press broke the thick silence that held them bound.

"It works fine, boy!" yelled the older man.

Tom Doolin jerked out his gun and pointed it at Sam's chest. "You better leave while you still can."

Sam put up his hands in a peaceful sign. "Don't get your pants in a wad there. You haven't paid me for making that part. It'll be ten dollars."

Doolin hesitated, his eyes as hard and unyielding as stone. Ford walked over and handed Sam the money. "We always pay our debts, Tom. You know that."

"I hope you don't mind if I check it, considering what you're doing and all." Sam held the bill to the light and tested the texture. Satisfied it was genuine, he stuck it inside his coat. "A pleasure doing business."

With a nod to Jared, he sauntered from the room, whistling. He shouldn't have antagonized Tom, but seeing the way he treated Mitchell had burrowed under his skin. And if he didn't have reason enough before to despise Tom Doolin and his family, he sure did now.

The fighting had stopped, and the men were nursing split lips, black eyes, and bruises. Cap nodded at him but didn't approach. Neither did Sam's dad. But both looked at him curiously. He wove around the tables and left the saloon, waiting around the corner of the building. One by one, they both came out and joined him.

"Tom Doolin took the part and let me wait until an older man, I'm guessing Daddy Doolin, put it on and started the press up to make sure it worked." Sam paused while three men walked past. None of them looked into the dark space. "Jared Mitchell is engraving what looked to be a ten-dollar plate, and I got a quick word in to tell him about his wife. The Doolins are holding him against his will, as I figured."

"You did good, Sammy boy." Cap's grin had a split in it from the fight, and he was rubbing his jaw.

"I only got one piece to add," Senior said. "I recognized the guard that was supposed to be in front of the door as an ex-convict named Tony Moretti. He served ten years for stagecoach robbery. I was a Texas Ranger back then and took him down."

"And a right good thing," Cap muttered.

"Amen." Sam watched a black cat mosey by with a rat in its mouth. "Here's a juicy tidbit I picked up when I asked to join Tom's gang. He said they're very particular about who they let in and that they have partners they answer to."

Cap snorted. "Figured as much. But this means the ring goes far beyond this. Dammit!"

It was hard for Sam to make out his father's features where he stood with his hat pulled lower than usual, but he imagined Senior's eyes had hardened and the lines in his face sliced deeper. He'd seen it many times before when his dad had been faced with a ruthless outlaw. Senior, too, was probably remembering the way they'd found Beth.

That night, his father had arrived at the scene almost the same time that Sam rode back, and they'd gone into the house together.

Senior's hand never left Sam's shoulder as he cradled his wife's life-less body. Then after they'd taken her away, his dad had held him as he sobbed.

Yeah, Sam Senior would wear that kind of look.

"I'm going to have to get a message to the governor right away." Senior stared at the telegraph office across the street. "What are the chances the operator can keep a secret?"

"Who knows? We ain't sorted everyone out." Cap pulled the collar of his coat up higher. "There's some sympathizers for sure, even if they aren't directly involved. Maybe it's time to find out where loyalties lie."

Sleet began to fall, and Sam could've sworn the temperature dropped another twenty degrees.

"I don't have much choice," Senior answered. "It's forty miles to Amarillo, and in this weather, it'd be a brutal ride that I'd rather not make unless I have to." He pulled a watch from his pocket and opened the lid.

Sam struck a match and held it close. "A quarter past seven. The telegraph operator should still be awake—if he's not in one of these saloons. I vote we find him."

"Yep." Cap nodded. "We oughta feel him out at least. We sure need a reliable operator."

All three climbed the stairs to the residence above the office, hoping the overwhelming number of lawmen would convince the man of the wisdom of living on the right side of the law.

A plump woman opened the door, wiping her hands on an apron. She cast curious glances at them.

Sam stepped forward. "We hate to disturb you, ma'am, but could we have a moment with your husband?"

She smiled. "We were just about to relax for the evening. Would you come in?"

The senior Sam removed his hat. "Begging your pardon, ma'am, we'll only be a moment."

They stepped into the small space, removing their hats, their large bodies swallowing the room. The missus spoke low to her husband and went into the next room, closing the door.

A man rose from a chair. "I'm Duggan Flannery, can I help you?"

Cap pulled out his silver star and showed it. "I'm Texas Ranger McFarlan. Are you the telegraph operator?"

"I am. Is something wrong?" Flannery's complexion was so ruddy, it looked like he'd been standing too close to a fire.

"Depends," Senior replied. "First, are you sympathetic with the Doolins?"

Flannery snorted. "Hardly. They're up to their eyeballs in no good. They came into town and threatened me if I didn't do what they said. The telegrams they've sent to a man named Pope let me know I want no part of them. Is that what you're here about?"

Sam relaxed his tense posture. The man seemed trustworthy.

"We need your help." Senior stuck out his hand. "I'm Sam Legend, Sr., sheriff of Lost Point and my son here is also a Texas Ranger. I'm a special envoy to the governor, and I need to telegraph him tonight. It's very urgent. Would you be willing to open up for just a moment?"

"I'll go downstairs and meet you at the front door. We have to stop this bunch."

"Thank you, sir." Sam put on his hat and braced himself for the chilling wind.

They were soon inside the office and kept the shades down to keep from drawing attention.

In no time, Senior had sent his telegram. "We'll wait for a reply," he told Flannery. "Shouldn't take long."

While they waited, Mrs. Flannery brought coffee down. "I know you men can use this."

"Yes, ma'am. Thank you kindly," Cap said, reaching for a cup.

To kill time, the three of them discussed how the Doolins were transporting the money and not getting caught.

Senior stared in thought, the steam from his cup curling around his hand. "It has to be something very common that doesn't draw attention."

Sam nodded. "Like shipments of lumber or a conglomeration of items for a mercantile."

"I don't think they're in boxes." Cap sipped on his coffee. "Maybe they tie them in bundles and stick them in furniture or other things a freighter would haul."

"That's good, Cap." Sam poured himself a tad more coffee. In fact, that was damn good. They'd once found a load of smuggled goods stuffed inside a piano.

They'd finished the discussion when the telegraph machine began chattering. Flannery transcribed the message and handed it to Senior.

He read it silently and glanced up. "The governor is sending out statewide orders to all law enforcement. He wants this nipped in the bud, and he's called me to Austin to spearhead the roundup. Looks like I'll head out at first light."

Sam was glad they'd have one more night before their paths took them in different directions.

"Well, they'll have a Legend there to end this." Cap took the last swig from his cup and set it on Mrs. Flannery's tray. "And I'll have a good one here to get it started."

Sam pulled out a lot more money than the telegram called for and handed it to Flannery.

The man shook his head. "Nope. Your money's no good here. I'm happy to have a hand in bringing down the Doolins. A word of warning. Sheriff Winslow is in their pocket, so be careful."

"Thanks. We appreciate your help." Sam put the money away and they went out into the night.

They parted company and went to their horses. Sam stuck a foot in the stirrup when he heard a noise.

"Pssst, over here, Sam."

He swung his attention to the alley and zeroed in on the arm waving him over. Alarm shot through him. He slid his gun from the holster. Slowly, he moved toward either a friend…or a trap.

Twenty-seven

THE RASPY VOICE CAME AGAIN. "COME ON, SAM, HURRY!"

Needles of warning lay against Sam's spine like porcupine quills. He rushed to the side of the building and inched toward the dark corner, every nerve taut. Cold sweat formed on his forehead as tinny piano music and bawdy singing came from the saloon across the way.

Finally, he called out, "Who's there?"

Nothing but silence came.

"If you're playing games, I'm not in the mood. Better speak up."

"It's me. Mitchell. I don't have much time before they find out I'm gone."

That was all well and good, but Sam wasn't born yesterday. "Who's with you?"

"I'm alone."

"Better be." Sam gripped the gun and stepped around the corner of the building.

Jared Mitchell raised his hands to show he had no weapon. "I have to hurry."

"Aren't you taking a big chance?"

"I have to know about my wife. Please!" Worry lined Jared's face.

"She has pneumonia and malnutrition." Sam hesitated for a second. Jared might not know about the baby. Finally, he decided to go ahead. "Doc says the baby isn't doing so good."

"A baby?" A smile broke across the father's face. "I'm going to have another kid?"

"Appears that way." If the little thing made it, but Sam didn't tell him that. "Aaron and Ellen are missing you bad and scared. With their mother so sick and you gone, they've been out of their minds with worry."

"Nothing I can help. Maybe when I finish engraving this plate, they'll let me go, but they're not known for keeping their word."

No, that was for sure. More than likely, they'd put a bullet in Jared's head. A sure way to silence him.

"Is there any way you can escape?" Sam asked. "We could hide you out."

"Not a chance. The only way I could be here to catch you is by pleading to visit the outhouse. Otherwise, someone's with me all the time."

Footsteps crunched, and three men with rifles came around the building.

"Mitchell!" one yelled.

"Quick. Do you have a weapon?"

"They took it."

Sam removed his Colt and handed it to him. "I don't want to scare you, but I don't think they intend to let you go. Hide this, and at least you'll have a shot of making it."

"Mitchell, who's that with you? Answer me, dammit!" another man yelled.

"Thanks, Legend." Jared took the gun and put it under his coat. "The thought crossed my mind that I'll die here. Please tell Retta I love her."

"I will."

A dog ran out and tried to bite the men approaching. Seeing they were occupied, Sam asked, "Hey, do you happen to know where the Doolins are living?"

"A rundown house close to town, but I don't know where. They always blindfold me when we leave each night."

"Okay, thanks. Be careful, Jared."

Sam watched as the ranch hand melted into the shadows in the opposite direction from the three men sent to find him. He prayed for his safety. Then turning, he swung onto Rio and trotted toward a warm fire in the Ronans' bunkhouse.

His father was waiting at the edge of town. "I was about to turn back to look for you."

"Jared Mitchell caught me." As they headed toward a warm fire, Sam told him what Jared had said. "He's scared."

"He has a right to be. The Doolins have no conscience. You saw that firsthand."

Yes, he had. "I wish we didn't have to wait. I want to arrest them right now. Tonight. For Beth. What if they get wind of us and escape? Or they could've seen us at Flannery's telegraph office. I'd never forgive myself."

"I know, son. But we're just not ready yet. We have to get more men in place or it's all going to fall apart."

Sam stared at the man he deeply admired and knew he spoke the truth. The set of Senior's broad shoulders and straight spine told of his dedication to uphold the law and find justice for those needing some. His had been a life of service and striving to make the world a better place. Maybe one day, if Sam was lucky, one of his children would think the same about him.

But that was way down the road and depended on finding the right woman willing to put up with his kind of lifestyle. He knew he'd never be content with city life. That wasn't for him.

The Ronan house was dark when they rode in. They took their horses to the barn and went to bed.

Sometime before morning, Sam dreamed of Beth. They were sitting together in the shade of a tree, holding hands. A slight breeze lifted strands of her blond hair, and the scent of honeysuckle drifted around them.

Though she didn't speak with her mouth, her words sounded in his head.

I will always love you, Sam, but you have to go on and live your life. Don't let bitterness and regret close your heart. Find someone to make you happy, have a family.

"That's impossible. My heart, my arms, want you," he answered.

It is not to be, dearest. Her voice was sad. *Be careful of the Doolins. They will kill you, Sam.*

Her nearness, her scent whispered along the fringes of his mind. When he reached for her, she faded into nothing.

Gasping, he sat up on the side of the bunk. Shadow whined and rose from the rug to lick his hand. He buried his face in the soft fur and sobbed silently so as not to wake his father.

A little before dawn, the senior Sam climbed from the bed in his woolen long johns. His gaze found Sam sitting at the small table in his faded red underwear, a blanket around his shoulders. "Anything wrong, son?"

"I dreamed of Beth."

"I see." Senior stuck his legs in his pants and sat across from him. "I believe loved ones who've passed watch over us and give us messages." He pulled on his socks and boots. "I dream of my mother sometimes. I was nine or ten when she died. But sometimes I dream she's hugging me or stroking my hair. She always says how proud she is of the way I turned out. It's a comfort."

"Beth told me to go on with my life."

"That's something you have to do. As bad as you want to yank back time, you can't."

"Part of me knows that, but it doesn't help a lot." Sam rose and put more wood in the round potbelly stove. "Beth also warned me to be careful. She said the Doolins want me dead."

"No surprise there." Senior finished dressing. "If they knew who you are, your life wouldn't be worth fifteen cents. Promise not to give yourself away."

"I won't—at least until I arrest them. Then you can be sure I'll rub their noses in the fact that I fooled them. Damn, I hope it's soon." Sam reached for his trousers. "Tom and Deek are not getting away this time." He pulled on his shirt and tucked it in. "I'm glad we can trust Duggan Flannery. Send me a message when you get to Austin, and keep me abreast of what's going on."

"You don't even have to ask."

With his dad's arm around his shoulders, they went to the main house for coffee and a quick breakfast.

Cheyenne turned away from the stove. "I'm so relieved to see you. I was about to make a trip to the barn to see if your horses were there."

From her neat appearance, she must've been up for hours. She'd arranged her hair in a knot at the nape of her neck. Sam saw something on her ears. He moved closer to take the coffee she handed him and saw they were dangly pearl earrings.

"Nice pearls," he murmured, meeting her green gaze.

"Thanks. A gift from my mother." She handed Senior a full cup. "I hope you slept well."

"Like a log, Miss Cheyenne. Thank you for putting me up." He took a seat at the table with Sam.

"I'll have breakfast ready by the time you drink that." She slid biscuits into the oven. "How did last night go?"

Sam gave her the rundown, especially the talk with Jared Mitchell, with Senior filling in some parts. "Dad has to ride out as soon as he finishes eating. He has to get to Amarillo to catch the train for Austin at the governor's request."

Cheyenne turned the bacon. "I hate to see you go so soon, sir."

"I had planned to stay a few days with my son, but work got in the way. I'm sure I'll be back, and I'll bring his mother next time."

Sam grinned. "I'm still not sure how you got away without her."

"I snuck off when her back was turned," Senior joked.

Laughing, Cheyenne put the bacon on a plate. "How do you like your eggs, sir?"

"Sunny-side up, young lady." He helped himself to more coffee.

The easy way his dad had of fitting in warmed Sam's heart. There was nothing cold or off-putting about him. He'd miss the old man.

Before he knew it, breakfast was over, and Senior rode out. Sam came back inside, his hand on the small of Cheyenne's back, feeling like it belonged there.

They were greeted by Aaron and Ellen, still rubbing sleep from their eyes. "We thought you left us," Aaron said.

"Nope, not a chance." Sam ruffled the boy's hair.

"Have a seat, and I'll pour you some milk while I cook your eggs." Cheyenne reached for two glasses.

"Do you think Retta is awake?" Sam asked.

Aaron nodded. "Yep, she is. She said she's tired of laying."

"I can imagine. Maybe I can do something to fix that." Sam turned to Cheyenne, speaking low, "I'm going to tell her the news."

"That's good. I'll keep the children in here. If you'll move her to a chair, I'll be in to wash and dress her when you finish."

Sam went into the bedroom to find Retta struggling to sit up. "Here, let me help you. Would you like to sit in a chair in the parlor for a bit? I have news of your husband."

Retta's eyes lit up. "Yes, I would love to get out of this bed."

He carried the woman to a comfortable easy chair in the parlor in front of the fire and covered her with a blanket.

Sam stood with a hand on the mantel. "I saw your husband last night and spoke to him privately. He's concerned about you and said to tell you he loves you and the kids."

"Thank you, but where is he? Why can't he tell me this himself?"

"He's being held by the Doolins, and they're forcing him to engrave another plate."

She gasped. "I felt like he was in danger. What's going to happen, Sam?"

"Jared said he has about a week left to finish, and they promised to let him go." He prayed she'd be satisfied with that much and there'd be no need to say more.

"But? I hear a but in there." She reached for his hand. "Please tell me the rest. I have to know."

"Well, as with everything, plans sometimes don't go the way the person wants. The Doolins may decide he's seen too much. They risk a lot in letting him ride off."

"So they might kill him. Isn't that what you're hem-hawing about for?"

Her words were blunt, and it was clear she wanted it all. He pulled free and knelt in front of her. "It'll hopefully be a comfort to know I gave him my gun. Insurance in case he needs it to defend himself."

Retta began to cry softly, tears rolling down her cheeks. "When will people let us live in peace? That's all we want. Just to raise our kids and carve out a life in peace."

"I don't know, ma'am. It's not fair, but the past sometimes follows a man."

"He paid for his mistake. No, it's not fair." She wiped her eyes and offered Sam a smile. "Thank you for trying to help Jared and for being so kind to me and the children."

"It's no hardship." He stood. "Cheyenne said she'll be in shortly. She's getting Aaron and Ellen their breakfast. And I need to go see to the cattle. You have a good day, ma'am."

"You too."

Loretta's strength on his mind, he went out into the cool morning. He was in the pasture, putting out feed for the cattle when he saw him.

A rider, halfway out of the saddle, slowly came toward him, then stopped. The reins hung loosely to the ground. The horse took advantage of the lull to nibble at some bit of frozen vegetation.

Twenty-eight

SAM SWUNG ONTO RIO AND GALLOPED TO THE HURT RIDER. Blood. So much blood. He couldn't tell who the man was.

His heart hammering, he leaped off. "Mister, can you hear me?"

"Sammy boy," the man managed.

"Cap?"

Shit, the ranger!

Sam eased Cap from the horse and laid him down. His old friend had been shot high, but there was so much blood Sam couldn't tell if it was his neck or down by the collarbone. His shirt and long johns underneath were soaked in scarlet.

"Hang on. Don't you die on me, you old codger. We have a lot more trails to ride and the Doolins to round up." Sam loosened the collarless shirt Cap wore. "Do you know who shot you?"

"Ambush. Faces covered."

You could bet it was the Doolins or someone working for them. Despite how careful Cap was, someone had found out he was a Texas Ranger.

"I'm going to have to leave you here to get a wagon." Sam removed his heavy coat and put it over Cap. "I'll be back as soon as I can."

Cap's tongue worked in his mouth. "Sam, sorry I…said you aren't a Legend."

"Don't talk. Save your strength." Sam put his face next to Cap's. "Don't you dare die."

No answer came. Cap's eyes closed, and he was out. That might be a blessing. The good thing was the house was in plain sight. Sam jumped on Rio and galloped toward help as fast as he could.

Cheyenne was outside, sweeping off the back stoop. He went right past her and on to the barn. She ran, chasing him. He raced into the barn.

"What's wrong?" She gasped for breath as he pulled the wagon out.

"Someone shot Cap McFarlan. He's lying hurt in the pasture."

"He'll need blankets. I can get them by the time you hitch that wagon." She whirled and ran back to the house.

Sam's hands shook so badly, he could barely get the harnesses on the horses and the traces attached. He finally managed and was about to pull out when Cheyenne arrived with the blankets.

She threw them into the back. "I'm coming too. I told Retta and the kids."

"Thanks. I may need you."

There was no need for more talking. Sam set a fire under the horses, and they raced over the uneven ground at breakneck speed. He didn't allow himself to think about what-if. This was a time for confidence. He would get Cap to the house, and the ranger was going to live. Period.

In nothing flat, they pulled alongside Cap, and Sam jumped down. He knelt beside the still form. Cheyenne was on the opposite side.

"I'm back, you old cuss. You can wake up now." Sam waited, but no response came. "He's out. Okay, I'm going to have to throw him over my shoulder and put him in the bed."

"Let me turn the wagon around and back it close so you won't have so far to carry him," Cheyenne suggested.

"Do it."

While she situated the wagon, he kept talking. "Hey, do you remember that time we were chasing that little four-foot-tall bank robber and he crawled underneath that preacher's wife's wide skirts that stuck way out? We didn't know where the heck he disappeared to until the woman started jumping around, screaming that some animal was attacking her. And then when we had to dive into the Brazos River to escape all those angry bees?"

Cap didn't move or open his eyes. What Sam wouldn't give for him to start talking about some of the women he was fond of.

With the wagon in position, Cheyenne got down and came around. She spread a blanket on the bed and stood by until Sam laid Cap down on it then tucked the rest of the blankets around him.

"I'll ride back here with him," she said quietly.

Nodding, he tied Cap's horse to the back and got in and drove toward the house, trying to avoid the rougher areas. Finally, he pulled up next to the bunkhouse. Cheyenne crawled from the back and went to open the door.

Sam didn't know any other way to get Cap inside short of throwing him over his shoulder again, so that's what he did. Warmth from the stove hit him, and he was glad for it. He eased Cap onto the bunk Senior had slept on and removed the blankets and Sam's coat, then slipped Cap's bloody coat off.

Cheyenne brought a pail of water from the house and some cloths. "I'll go back and get whatever else we need. It's hard to know right now," she said in a quiet voice.

"Gotta get some of this blood washed off. It's even in his mustache." Sam unbuttoned the ranger's shirt and long johns and checked the wound, both front and backside. "Looks like the bullet's still in there. No exit wound. If you'll do this, I'll ride for the doctor."

It appeared to have missed the jugular vein, thank God. The entry was at the base of his neck by the collarbone.

"Hurry." She took the cloth from him and gently washed the wound.

Cap's eyes fluttered and opened. He seemed to recognize Sam. "Where am I?"

"The Ronans' bunkhouse. Looks like we'll be bunkmates for

a while." Sam bent over him. "I'm going for the doc and leaving you with this pretty lady. Cheyenne is an expert with a knife, so I expect you'd best not give her a hard time."

"I don't need no damn doctor."

"The hole in you says otherwise. So don't start with that crap." Sam threw on his coat, paying little attention to the blood that would have to be washed from the sheepskin lining. That would come later.

Saying he'd be right back, Sam went out and led the team and wagon to the barn. Quickly unhitching the horses and putting them in stalls, he mounted Rio. Town came into view in no time. Sam took the stairs to Doc Tyler's office two at a time.

The sawbones sat at his desk, writing something, and glanced up. "Has Mrs. Mitchell worsened?"

"She's doing good. No, it's a Texas Ranger who got himself shot. Bullet's still in there."

"Guess we'd best hurry then." Doc stood and put on his coat, then grabbed his bag.

As Sam was about to get on Rio, Flannery came from around the side of the doctor's office. "I have something for you."

Duggan Flannery handed him a yellow telegram and faded back out of sight.

That would have to be read later. Sam stuck it in his pocket and fell in behind Doc.

By the time they got back, Cheyenne had finished the cleanup and had blankets on Cap. Her gaze flew to Sam. "Oh, good. He just went out again. What do you need, Doctor?"

Tyler already had his coat off and was rolling up his sleeves. "Hot water, some whiskey if old Bert keeps any around, and some kind of a bowl."

"I'll be back." She closed the door behind her.

Tyler bent over Cap to look at the wound. "He's one lucky man. An inch higher, and he'd be dead. Looks like it nicked his collarbone and went into the soft tissue at the base of the neck, where it lodged. Once I get this bullet out, he should heal up just fine. Let's get him undressed."

Between the two of them, they removed Cap's clothes.

While waiting on Cheyenne, Tyler washed his hands and got the medical instruments he'd need from his bag, laying them on the bed. "You folks are sure having your share of problems," Tyler remarked.

"That we are. Cap McFarlan here talked some and said he was ambushed. Not sure where. That's all he said."

"If he's a Texas Ranger as you said, it had to be that Doolin mess that came in here."

"What do you know about them?" Sam asked.

"They're trash and need to be run out of town." Doc Tyler wiped his glasses and put them back on. "I've seen some bad ones come through here. Billy the Kid, Jesse Jenkins, and 'Squirrel Eye' Charlie Emory left a black mark on the town. Now, it's the Doolins. Not sure what they're doing, but you can bet it's some kind of dirty scheme."

Cap woke up wild-eyed. "Sam, what the hell? Sam?"

"Settle down." Sam patted his chest. "This is Doc Tyler, and he's going to get that bullet out."

"Dig, you mean? Nope." Cap tried to throw his covers off.

Sam held him down. "You're out of your head. Bushwhackers shot you, and the wound'll get infected if we don't get it seen to."

"No." The old friend swung his arms, catching Sam's jaw.

Pain throbbing in his face, Sam tried reason. "Let me put it this way. Either you stop fighting us, or I'll strap you to the damn bunk."

Doc Tyler removed a vial and a white cloth from his bag. "This will help."

"Hope something does." Sam threw himself on top of the ranger, anchoring Cap's arms.

Moistening the cloth with a bit of the vial's contents, Tyler handed it to Sam. "Hold this over his nose."

Sam followed his instructions, and in seconds, Cap went limp. "There."

"Hold it in place until I finish. Hopefully, this won't take long."

A noise sounded, and the door opened. Sam took the pail of hot water from Cheyenne, and she handed the doctor a half bottle of whiskey. "This is all we have."

"It'll do." Doc uncorked the bottle and poured it over his hands. Then he put his instruments into the tin bowl and poured whiskey over them.

"I'll be standing by if you need me." Cheyenne moved to the table.

With everything ready, Doc picked up a metal probe, inserting it into the hole to hopefully locate the bullet. "Ahh, there it is. Now to remove it." He pulled the probe out and replaced it with a finger. He worked for what seemed forever. "It doesn't want to come out."

Thank God Cap was unconscious, or he'd have been screaming bloody hell.

"Can I help, Doc?" Sam asked.

"Just keep holding the cloth on our patient's face. I'll get this in a minute." Doc reached for what appeared to be a pair of long tweezers. After about a minute, he pulled out the piece of metal and dropped it in the bowl. "Now, to clean the wound out good and sew it up."

Cap's eyelids moved. No telling what he was dreaming of. Probably some woman. Sam had never met anyone so woman crazy, but he was a true friend. He glanced at Cheyenne watching the doctor work. "How are Retta and the kids doing?"

"Retta has them busy making more baskets. It's a good way to occupy them. Sam, I need to sell my baskets so I can buy some Christmas gifts for Aaron and Ellen. Christmas is only five days away. Any suggestions?"

"I might be able to take them to Amarillo in a day or two. And we need a tree of sorts for them." He didn't know how that was going to happen either. The nearest trees were over a hundred miles away.

"I may have a solution. Some folks around here decorate tumbleweeds." She laughed. "The Panhandle has those in profusion. They can be eye-catching all prettied up."

"Then a tumbleweed it is. I'll find a nice big one at the first opportunity."

"Thanks, Sam."

Doc Tyler poured the rest of the whiskey into Cap's wound. "I'm sure glad he's not feeling this."

"It's safer for all our sakes." Sam agreed. "I once saw him whip three men and handcuff them with a bullet and two knife wounds in him. He's one of the toughest men I know."

"Sounds like it." Doc got out the catgut and a needle and went to work sewing. "Did I hear you talking about a place to sell baskets?"

"Yes," Cheyenne answered. "Do you know of someone?"

"There's a peddler that comes through town each week. He's always looking for pretty things to sell for Christmas, and he'll give you a fair price. You can trust him. The name's Felix. I'll send him out here. He's due on Tuesday."

"Thank you, Doctor. Yes, please ask him to come out. I'd also love to check his wares for gifts for those two children in the house."

Sam was glad for Cheyenne but disappointed he had no one similar to sell his knives to. Six of them were special orders from customers in Amarillo. He'd try to find a way to get them to those clients, but it didn't look promising.

"You can take the cloth off his face now," Doc told Sam, securing the bandage.

His old friend's mood on awakening was anyone's guess. Sam stood ready for anything.

Cap came around just as Doc finished washing the blood from his hands. "I've gotten you taken care of, Ranger," Tyler said, reaching for a towel. "You should be up and around by suppertime."

"It feels like you put some live coals in there." Cap groaned, touching the bandage.

"Quit your bellyaching." Sam snorted. "You're alive. A sight more than I thought your chances were when I saw you hanging off your saddle a couple of hours ago."

Doc Tyler reached for some laudanum in his bag and told Cap to open wide. As bad as he was hurting, no one had to tell Cap twice.

"That stuff is terrible." He made an awful face. "I'm a mite woozy. Do you think I might have some coffee?"

"Of course." Cheyenne picked up the tin bowl. "I was going to the house anyway. I'll make some fresh and be right back. Doctor, will you stay for coffee?"

The sawbones's eyes lit up. "I believe I might. I'm dreading the ride back in the cold."

"Then I'll bring the whole pot." She took a long stride.

"Wait, I'll go help. I'm sure the kids have a lot of questions." Sam held the door for her and closed it behind them. "I'm glad Cap got lucky. Between you and me, I didn't give much chance of him making it."

Cheyenne glanced up at him. "All that blood terrified me. At first, it was hard to tell where it was coming from. You saved him, Sam."

"I just did what had to be done."

"Who do you think shot him?"

Their boots crunched on the frozen ground, the sound reminding him how fragile life was. "I have a pretty good idea. The Doolins must've found out he's a ranger."

They went into the kitchen of the main house, and Aaron and Ellen peppered Sam with questions.

"Is that man really a Texas Ranger?" Aaron asked.

"Yes, he is."

"How did he get hurt?"

"Someone shot him."

"Who?"

"We don't know."

Ellen crowded in and tugged on his arm. "Is he gonna die?"

"Nope, he's going to pull through. Scoot back and let me get inside." They moved, and he shut the door. "I know you have a lot of questions, so let's sit down and get them all out."

Cheyenne put coffee on while Sam told the kids about Cap and assured them they could go see him when he felt a little better. Then she set to work on Sam's coat, washing the blood from the lining. He doubted she could get it all out.

Ellen propped her arms on the table. "Does Mr. Cap like kids?"

Good question. Sam had never heard him say. Regardless, he knew Cap well enough to know he'd never be mean to two little kids. Not even if they got on his nerves.

"I'm sure he does, honey," he assured her.

"Can he tell good stories?" Aaron asked. "I sure hope so."

The question had come from the blue and threw Sam for a minute, then he laughed. "Cap has more stories than you can imagine." Of course, most of them were for adults, but maybe the old ranger would just happen to have a few for the younger set. Besides, he was good at making them up at the bat of an eye.

Plenty good at other things too. Like having Sam's back and being a friend.

"I think I got it clean," Cheyenne announced, holding the coat up. "I'll put in front of the fire in the parlor to dry. You'll have to wear something else."

"My duster will work fine."

They talked with the kids some more, then Cheyenne wrapped a dish towel around the metal coffeepot. Sam got up. "I need to help Miss Cheyenne now. I'll be back in a little bit. Go sit with your mama for a while."

"Okay." Ellen skipped from the room with Aaron following slower.

Cap's eyes lit up when he saw the coffee. He sat up slowly. "I think I might live now—if I can have a shot of whiskey in this."

"Not a chance." Sam laughed. "Doc used every drop on the instruments and your wound."

"Shucks."

Cheyenne filled the cups and passed them around, then sat with Sam. While they drank coffee, the four of them talked about Christmas.

"The other day I saw some giant tumbleweeds out near where Heck lived." Doc Tyler rose and stood in front of the potbelly stove, sipping on the hot brew. "They'd piled up along a fence row something awful."

"Then that's where I'll start looking." Sam shifted, and the paper in his pocket rustled. He'd forgotten about the telegram. He unfolded the message.

Made it to Austin. Stop. Will have arrests soon.

When those were in place, Sam would round up the Doolins. He'd shave for such an occasion and cut his hair, so Beth's killers would have no question about who exactly was taking them to jail. Seeing the shock on their faces was the only Christmas gift he wanted.

Twenty-nine

SAM FOUND THAT SHARING THE BUNKHOUSE WITH CAP WAS an experience in itself. The man talked in his sleep. Then about midnight or so, he sat straight up in bed and told whoever was in the dream with him that he was under arrest. Thank God Sam had hidden his gun, or Cap probably would've shot him. Needless to say, he didn't get much sleep between the ranger and Shadow, clawing the door to go out, then barking her fool head off until Sam went out to check the perimeter. He'd found nothing amiss and put her back in.

Cap was wide-awake, sitting at the small table in his gray long johns before sunup. "Well, I guess you're finally seeing fit to wake up. Thought you'd sleep the blasted morning away."

Sam raised on an elbow. "It ain't even daylight yet. What are you doing awake?"

From the rug on the floor, Shadow stretched and yawned big.

"Thinking. And it was cold in here, so I put more wood on the fire."

Sam blinked hard, threw the cover back, and sat up. "Pondering over who shot you?"

"Yep. I was coming out of the back of the hotel to go over to that little café nearby. As soon as I stepped out, three hooded men started shooting. I dove behind the rain barrel and returned fire. I don't know if I hit anyone, but I sure as hell know they hit me." Cap touched his bandage, rolled his shoulder, and winced.

"How did you manage to get to the livery? That's what I'd like to know."

"I had gone after my horse before breakfast because I was going to ride out to look at some abandoned places, thinking the Doolins could be using one as storage. They have to be putting all that paper and ink somewhere."

"I agree, but go on."

"My horse was tied in back of the hotel, so I managed to get to it. My only thought was making it here before I died."

And he almost had died. Sam wiped his eyes to rid himself of the sight of Cap hanging off the side of the horse. "You didn't see any faces or hear anything that would identify your attackers?"

"Someone yelled, 'I got him!' But I didn't recognize the voice." Cap ran a hand over his stubble. "I suspect it was the same fellow you and I saw when we were leaving to meet Senior."

"You have some the best instincts of anyone, so it probably was. I had a bad feeling about that man myself. Get dressed, and we'll go get some coffee." Sam reached for his trousers and pulled them on. "Be on your best behavior, because there's two little kids over there itching to meet you."

"Does the sight of blood scare 'em?"

"Hell if I know."

"Well, the only shirt I have is what I wore. I guess I'll just put my coat on over my long johns. They're not as bad." Cap eyed him. "Speaking of that, I guess I'm gonna have to buy you a new pair. Those you're wearing look plum worn-out and if you take a notion to crawl up into the bed with that little filly I saw you looking at, she'll change her mind fast."

"These work fine, so save your money. Me and Cheyenne are not your problem."

Cap scratched his neck. "You need the help is all I'm saying."

It was time to get the subject on something else. "After breakfast, I'll ride into town and get your clothes. Might be a good idea to check you out of the hotel, but not me. I'll use Frenchie. I think she'll do it. And I'll have her say you died."

"Well, I darn sure feel like it. But won't this put Frenchie in danger?"

Yeah, come to think of it, it probably would. Her associating with a Texas Ranger would get the Doolins thinking she was in cahoots with Cap.

"I guess I'd best think of something else. Maybe Flannery at the telegraph office, since I have to go by there."

Cap shook his finger. "Don't you let that hotel clerk charge one more cent. I just settled up with him before I got shot."

"Good to know." Some clerks were bad about overcharging and sticking the money in their pocket.

"Hey, we also have to protect Miss Cheyenne and the Mitchells. They're in danger with me being here." Cap reached for his boots. "I'm gonna need some help getting these on, Sammy boy."

Shadow whined at the door, and Sam let her out, then helped Cap. By the time they made it to the house, Cheyenne was already making coffee.

She let them in. "Ranger, you're looking better. Glad you're up and about. I'm sorry about your shirt. I'd offer one of my father's, except you're so much larger than him."

"Appreciate the thought, Miss Cheyenne, but Sam's going into town after my belongings."

"Good." Her gaze shifted to Sam, and memories flooded him of their last kiss that could've stripped paint from an iron jenny. The blush rising to her cheeks said she remembered too. Or was she recalling his promise to see where their relationship led when this was over? Maybe a bit of both. He was serious about exploring the fire that rose between them at each opportunity.

Sam took Cap's coat and hung it with his duster on the hooks beside the door. "Coffee smells good. That'll fix what ails a man."

"I got a lot riding on that." Cap glanced around the kitchen, and Sam watched him land on a painting of dew-drenched morning glories trailing on a picket fence. "Do you paint, Miss Cheyenne?" Cap asked.

"My mother does. I do nothing but dabble. Mine look like something a six-year-old would paint." She sat down with them. "How about you, Ranger? Do your talents lie in canvas and paint when you're not hunting down wanted men?"

"You mean Cap?" Sam died laughing but tried to keep it down for those sleeping. "I can't wait to hear this."

The ranger shot him a heavy scowl. "For your information I've been known to wield a paintbrush. Fences, barns, windmills, you name it."

"I'm sure you do a very good job." Cheyenne glanced at Sam. "I heard a coyote last night. I hope it and its cousins didn't get one of the cows."

"I'll check the herd." He started to rise.

She laid a hand over his. "It can wait until you've had coffee. If they got one, rushing out into the cold won't change anything. By the way, the lining of your coat is dry."

"Good. How's Retta and the kids?" Sam asked. "She seemed to be improving when I spoke with her yesterday to tell her about her husband."

"Each sunrise brings added strength, and Doc says the baby's heartbeat is stronger and steadier. And with Ranger McFarlan able to move around and sit at this table with us, I'd say we have lots to be thankful for."

"Amen, Miss Cheyenne." Cap patted her hand. "I just hope I ain't bringing trouble."

"I heard a long time ago that it'll come whether or not we invite it. We'll deal with whatever comes. I've run up against men like these Doolins before."

The three of them sat talking while the coffee finished brewing. Sam had a hard time pulling his gaze from the woman across from him. It had been a long time since he'd thought of any woman but Beth, but he found Cheyenne occupying his thoughts more and more these days. He'd seen her heart and knew her kindness. Maybe some kind of future had her in it.

They were drinking coffee when Aaron and Ellen came in, Ellen rubbing sleep from her eyes. Both hung back a little, bitten by shyness, until Cheyenne urged them forward.

Sam introduced Cap, and the ranger started filling their heads with stories of mangy outlaws, rabid skunks, and cold winters where the wind froze a man's eyelids shut. They listened, wide-eyed, inching closer to Cheyenne.

At last, Sam caught Cap taking a breath and leaped in. "I'll go check the herd and take care of them and gather the eggs."

Cheyenne went to the door with him. "I hope you don't find any dead ones."

"Me too. I'd better take my rifle in case those coyotes did kill one and are still feeding off it."

She tilted her face up to him and took advantage of the children's rapt attention on Cap for a kiss. He held her close and settled his lips on hers for a brief moment.

"I meant what I said about us having unfinished business. As soon as we can, we'll talk."

Her large green eyes filled with shifting stars. She smiled and nodded. "I'll be here."

Sam thought about that as he went to saddle Rio and still found her on his mind all during the ride to the pasture. The need to find a quiet place to be alone gave him a lot to contemplate. He yearned to wrap her in his arms and whisper in her ear how she'd snuck past all his defenses. The hunger to run his hands over every inch of her enticing body filled every waking hour.

Fair to say, he wanted her, but she was like one of those pieces of steel he worked with. Too cold and it'd shatter when hammered. Too hot and it'd melt and turn to liquid.

The temperature for making love had to hang right there in the middle of the perfect zone.

Heat collected in his belly, the kind that hadn't been there for a long while.

The frosty morning fogged both his and Rio's breath as the Appaloosa's hooves crunched on the icy ground with each step. The air was what they both needed though—or at least Sam. He couldn't speak for the horse. The crisp freshness helped clear the cobwebs in his head and decide on the path forward. It called for a new strategy.

On two fronts.

After checking the herd and finding them in good shape, he put out feed and broke the ice on the creek water. The chickens were a little different matter. Something had gotten into the coop and killed two sitting hens. The prints belonged to a fox. The varmint hadn't bothered the eggs. Maybe all the late activity in the bunkhouse had disturbed the animal.

For now, he blocked the hole the fox had made and collected the eggs left behind. The rest could wait for later.

Inviting smells and the children's laughter came from the kitchen. Cap appeared to have gotten wound up to a fine pitch.

"The herd is okay, but a fox got into the henhouse." Sam handed Cheyenne the basket of eggs he'd gathered. "I think the little intruder got interrupted. Might've been Shadow. She was raising hell late last night about something."

"How bad is it?"

"The fox killed two of your layers. I left them up here by the door."

"Shoot! Well, I guess you know what we'll have for supper." She hid her irritation over losing the hens well, Sam thought, but it would mean they'd be short of eggs, and with a full house.

Aaron was watching them and overheard. "Yay, fried chicken! You hear that, Mr. Cap?"

"Well, ain't that something?" The ranger ran a hand over his eyes and that said his pain was worsening. It'd be a fight to get some laudanum down him, though.

Maybe Sam would bring him back some whiskey after he went

into town. If he could do it without being seen, that is. In a pinch, Frenchie or Mickey might get it for him. Regardless, he'd get Cap whatever he needed. That man was almost like a father in many ways.

～

Cheyenne loved having a full table with lots of laughter. She liked Cap very much and could see the deep bond and respect between him and Sam. They'd been through the fire together and probably numerous times if she could hazard a guess.

Her heart lurched when she met Sam's dark gaze that was like a soft caress. Unspoken promises lurked in the depths of his eyes. The thought of the unfinished business he'd spoken of made her pulse race.

No one kissed like Sam, and that was a fact. She ached for his lips on hers, his touch on her skin, and his deep voice against her face. Tingles of expectation curled against her spine.

They rose from the table. "Go see if your mama is ready for breakfast," she told the kids.

Sam helped her gather the plates. "Let me get Cap back to his bunk, then I'll wash these."

"Nope." She laid her palm on his chest. "I know you have a lot of things to do. I was thinking I might turn the dish washing over to Aaron and Ellen. I think they're both big enough, and it'll keep them busy for a bit."

"They might make a bigger mess than they prove to be a help, but I say let them try."

Cap pushed back his chair. "Thank you for the fine breakfast, Miss Cheyenne. I'll get out of your way."

"I'm glad you enjoyed it. The kids and I loved your company." She went to help him with his coat.

Sam pulled his on and waited for Cap to go out before he gave her a quick kiss. "I have a favor to ask if you have some free time in a bit, but let me see to Cap first. He's trying to outsmart me. No one hates taking medicine worse than him."

"He's in pain and needs it, so if I can help, just holler. I'm good at sweet-talking."

Sam growled. "Watch who you're doing that to, lady."

"No one but you, Sam. You're my one and only." She loved this teasing banter. It's something she'd never done but found fun.

"Remember that." He was about to pull her close when Ellen hurried in.

"My mama wants a sunny egg, Miss Ann."

Cheyenne laughed. "Sunny-side up?"

Ellen nodded. "And bacon. No coffee though." She handed Sam something that he stuck in his coat pocket so quickly, Cheyenne couldn't see.

He was definitely up to something.

"Coming right up." Cheyenne turned back to Sam. "About that favor…I'll be free after I feed Retta and get her and the kids dressed. Probably take an hour or so."

Aware that Ellen was listening and watching, she kept space between them.

"That would fit my schedule about right." Sam ruffled Ellen's hair, and she ran out of the kitchen. "I can repair the henhouse while you get ready. Do you think Retta's up to watching the kids?"

"Yes, she's getting stronger every day and spends a lot of time in a chair now and does simple tasks." Cheyenne inhaled the fresh scent of the air on him combined with saddle leather. "You're not going to give me any hints of what you want me to do?"

"Nope." A teasing smile curved his mouth.

"You're not playing nice."

"Tough." He went out the door, whistling, the happy sound sending her spirits soaring.

Thirty

CHEYENNE WAS ABOUT TO EXPLODE WITH ANTICIPATION WHEN she finally saw Sam through the window with their saddled horses. "We're taking a ride?"

"Yes, ma'am."

His wide grin set her heart pumping. He had something up his sleeve, and those promises were still sparkling in his eyes when he made a step with his hands and gave her a boost into the saddle.

Shadow whined, and he knelt in front of her. "Guard this place. Don't let anyone hurt Cap or the Mitchells."

The dog gave a sharp bark and went to sit on the porch, where she had a good view.

After the heaviness of the last few days, the sunshine was welcome on Cheyenne's face. She sat back and enjoyed the ride that appeared to be taking them to his wickiup.

Why would he be taking her there? She couldn't imagine what he'd need her for.

Maybe that was just a ruse to get her to come along, but he hadn't needed to go to those lengths. She'd willingly follow him anywhere.

They cut a direct path and reined up in front of the crude abode. The holly and red berries still above the door added a cheery welcome. She took in the bluff with its breathtaking view that seemed to extend forever.

"I've always loved this place. The sky appears to touch the earth."

"That's why I was drawn here. It stirs something deep in your soul." Sam dismounted, then reached for her waist and swung her down. "Let me go inside first and make sure no varmints have set up housekeeping in my absence."

"Gladly. I have no wish to encounter any wild critters." She glanced at Sam, with his unkept mane. He was plenty wild enough.

He was only gone a minute before he poked his head out. "It's clear."

Inside, she faced him. "Okay, you got me here. It's time to tell me why."

"I want you to cut my hair and help trim my beard."

Oh dear. This was big. She inhaled a sharp breath. "Only if you tell me why now, why on this day."

"I'm getting ready to round up the Doolins, and when I do, I want them to know exactly who I am. I want there to be no mistake. The arrest warrant will also cover the murder of my wife, Beth."

A wife? The news shook her. Why hadn't he mentioned this?

She searched his eyes, her voice soft. "You were married before?"

It really shouldn't surprise her, she guessed. Somewhere in the back of her mind, she must've suspected that. He'd had that maturity about him that came with marriage.

"We'd only been married a few short months but had made so many plans for our life together. I'm sorry I didn't tell you before." He let out a long breath. "It hurts to talk about her."

This was the secret he'd spoken of in her kitchen.

"You said she was murdered?"

"Yes."

No wonder he'd moved so far away from everyone and everything. It made sense now.

"How horrible. It's not my business, of course. We aren't beholden to each other." An awkward web of silence dropped between them for a long moment. Finally, she asked, "The Doolins killed her? Are you sure?"

That was probably why he was so driven to put them behind bars.

"Positive. Not sure which one pulled the trigger, but Tom captured her." After Sam got a fire going, they dropped to the rugs, and he told her how Beth had died.

"Tom and his brothers waited until I was gone and broke into our home. I'd been chasing Tom for a year for robbery, playing cat and mouse. By the time I got to the house, him and his brothers had evidently hatched a plan. I sat out there watching. I heard Beth's screams, and then she yelled my name and begged me to come and"—his voice broke—"begged me to save her. Each time I made a move, they unleashed their guns, and I had to retreat."

The fire popped and sizzled in the quiet, putting off steady heat.

"That must've been a nightmare." Cheyenne squeezed his hand.

"Other rangers were supposed to have come, but I waited and waited for nothing. The sun finally set, and suddenly, Tom burst from the barn with a woman on the back of his horse." Sam took a deep breath that seemed to settle him. "I thought it was Beth and gave chase. Never caught him, and when I got back to the house, I found Beth inside, crumbled like a rag doll. The other Doolins had long gone. They'd tricked me and used the time to finish Beth off and get away. It happened on Christmas Day of all times."

"That's why you were so against celebrating Christmas." This explained everything—why he'd come to this desolate part of Texas, away from family and friends. And why he'd became a shaggy recluse. Beth's death shed light on so many questions.

"I couldn't bear the thought of facing such a joyous occasion without her."

"I understand." She curled her fingers inside his large hand. "Thank you for telling me. That she died on Christmas makes it even more heartbreaking. Being with your family could've helped, though."

"Everywhere I looked was a reminder of her: knitting in her basket, the tree we'd picked out together. I had to go to a place she'd never been."

The flames of the fire cast flickering shadows on his strong cheekbones and resolute features. Unshaken determination sat in his dark eyes.

"It makes sense that you wanted to immerse yourself in making knives."

"I needed something different to learn, and I've come to enjoy bladesmithing a great deal." He got to his feet.

"And you never knew who the other woman was on the horse?"

"Nope. One of Tom's women, I'm guessing."

"I don't know what to say except I'm sorry. My heart breaks for all you've lost. I see everything clearer now. Thank you for telling me." She let Sam pull her up.

His wife must've been very young and so in love with him. Tears welled in her throat. Life was so unfair. She prayed he'd make the Doolins pay dearly.

"Cut my hair." He pulled some scissors from his duster pocket.

She remembered Ellen acting mysterious and handing him something. She slid her arms around his neck. "You're a sly fox, Sam Legend."

"I didn't know if I'd go through with it once I got here."

"Then, let's go outside and get started before you change your mind." She took the scissors and led him to his shearing.

They found a barrel for him to sit on, and she went to work. Long strands of hair began to fall as she cut. "How short do you want me to go? I don't know how you looked before."

"Leave some on the neck or I'll freeze to death."

"That would not be good."

Cheyenne bent, twisted, slanted, and snipped as she shaped the wild mass. It was a job, and occasionally she'd stand back to view her work. At times, Sam touched her or lifted a lock of her hair and set her heart fluttering. Slowly, a handsome man began to emerge from the profusion. He only possessed a broken piece of mirror, and when needing direction, she'd hand it to him.

At last, she stood back. "I think I'm done. At least until I do something with your beard, then I may go back for another snip or two."

He felt across his neck. "It's short."

"Did I take off too much?"

"No. I just meant that it feels like I'm bald after having so much for so long."

"It'll feel very strange for a while. Do you want to go on?"

"Yes, there's no stopping now. Aaron and Ellen won't know me."

She laughed. "That's for darn sure. Shadow will think you're an intruder and bite you."

"I reckon so." He stood and let her brush the hair from him.

Using the scissors again, she whacked off his beard to about a fourth of an inch, then laid the scissors on a barrel she was using for a table. "I'll go heat some water for the rest of your beard."

"You'll find shaving soap in the trunk where I put it over a year ago."

"Thanks. I was wondering if you had any." At the door, she paused and looked back. "I like it."

That he trusted her with this meant a lot. Excitement raced along her body to see what had lain under the long, bushy beard. This was like watching a butterfly emerge from a cocoon.

⤫

Cheyenne wrapped Sam's face in a hot towel to soften the bristles, and he closed his eyes, soaking up her tender touch. "I know this is a little late, but have you done this before?"

"No, but I've watched the barber shave my father."

"Now's a fine time to tell me."

"You can only blame yourself for not asking." Her voice got husky.

Was this kind of favor in too close a proximity to him? He knew how her nearness always affected him, so he figured that took the blame for the change in her voice.

"Are you all right?" He opened his eyes and cut them around to her.

"Couldn't be better." Her fingers trembled against his jaw. "Tell me how you want your beard. Or would you rather go for clean shaven?"

"How about trimming it close, and then I'll decide on whether it all has to go?"

"Your wish is my command, fair prince. If we were on the ocean, you would be a pirate." She moved closer and unwrapped his face. "Mmmm, as soft as a baby's bottom."

Sam frowned, not sure if he liked being compared to an infant. But a pirate most certainly. She lathered his face good with shaving soap, bending over to get the other side. Her firm, rounded breast was so close. He squirmed. If she didn't move soon…

Then she reached for the sharp straight razor and moved his head to the side, applying it to his throat. The stroke was slow and firm with nary a nick. Another stroke like that and she moved behind him, tilting his head back to clear more from his throat. He rested his head on the softness of her breasts, inhaling the scent of her.

Stroke after stroke, she cleaned his face and neck, twisting, moving in close, backing up. It seemed a well-choreographed ballet.

With each movement, each brush of her breasts against him, Sam's breathing became raspier and more ragged. He must've been out of his mind to ask this of her.

Although the breeze was cool, a fine sheen of sweat covered his forehead.

"Just about finished," she murmured, her face so near, her fragrant breath fanning his cheek.

He couldn't have said a word if his life depended on it, so he just grunted.

Cheyenne stood behind him again and drew his head back against all her fragrant softness, clearing the last bit of hair from the space where his throat met his chest. His breath hung suspended.

A quiver danced up the length of his body, and a hiss escaped through his teeth.

"Did I nick you?" she asked.

"No. I'm perfectly fine." The lie seemed to appease her, thank God.

"Good." She continued making long, smooth strokes with the razor.

Then everything changed. She kept wetting her lips, and perspiration dotted the area above her upper lip. Her head began to drop very slowly.

Unhurried, she lowered her mouth and pressed her lips to his. The lazy, sensual kiss curled Sam's toes. Kissing upside down put a whole new meaning on it. Their lips melded in a soul-searing scorcher of pure heaven.

Sam couldn't tell if he was up, down, or sideways. This wasn't part of the plan.

But wasn't it?

A rumble escaped from his throat. Oh yeah.

How he hungered to strip her bare, to take everything she was willing to give. But it had to be her choice.

She raised her head, and Sam stood. Breathing hard, he took her hand and led her into the wickiup. He released her hair from the pins holding it and let the silky strands spill over his hands in a glorious mass. Then he pulled her blouse from the skirt and unbuttoned it, kissing the satiny skin of her neck and shoulders. Then her skirt and petticoat were in a heap on the floor.

His mouth bone dry, he slowly tugged the ribbon of her chemise and swallowed hard as the cotton fabric parted and her milky breasts came into view. For a long moment, he forgot how to draw air into his lungs or swallow. The sight was beyond anything he could've imagined.

With trembling hands, he touched each one and watched the nipples pucker.

"Beautiful." The word slipped from him unbidden as he touched his tongue to the hard nubs.

A quiver raced up him as he pulled the chemise over her head. Her russet hair flowing over her shoulders and down her back gave her the appearance of a beautiful, naked goddess. If he lived to be a hundred, he'd never forget the sight, the softness of her skin.

She reached for his gun belt and unfastened it, laying it aside. Then, pulled off his boots. Piece by piece, Sam let her undress him down to his long johns. Those he made quick work of.

Her breath hitched as she got a good look at him. He prayed to relieve her trembling and take her fear. Likely her mother would've shared the basics. They tumbled to the bed, a tangle of arms and legs, their lips sealed in another scorching kiss.

The warmth of the fire filled the small abode and provided a cozy lair.

Breaking the kiss, Sam raised his head from his position on top of her to stare into her bewitching green eyes with shaving soap all over her face. "I want you, Chey."

Her pretty eyes sparkled in reaction to the pet name he'd longed to say.

"I've wanted you since I first laid eyes on you, Sam Legend." Breathless, she moistened her lips. "I've never felt this way about anyone or felt this need. My whole insides have this strange tingle running up and down. Please be gentle. I've never been with a man."

"I'll be easy." It just called for doing things a little slower, but if he did this right, the pain would be minimal. He didn't mind savoring every touch, caress, and kiss. His life and everything else could wait—all except making love to this charming, intelligent woman who captivated his thoughts.

Sitting up astride her, he wiped the shaving soap off him with a shirt lying near, then wiped hers away as well. He felt naked with all the hair gone, but it was nice, because it heightened every particle of feeling on his skin.

She placed a fingertip on his chin and drew it ever so slowly down his chest, down his belly, down… He stilled, not moving a muscle as she moved still lower.

There she stopped, seeming unsure whether to proceed.

The blood pounded in Sam's ears. Aching with hunger, he struggled to speak. "It's okay to touch me. I want to run my hands over your body too."

Inhaling, she curled a palm around his hardness. Pleasure exploded in his head. Her tender touch, and the fact that it had been over a year since he'd been with a woman, aroused him to the point that he'd go off if a breath of wind rustled across him.

"Lady, you must like playing with fire."

"I like playing with you, touching you." Her eyes widened, and she whispered the words as she kissed the hollow of his throat.

A strand of her hair brushed across the newly exposed and very sensitive skin on his face.

"Enough." He shifted to lie beside her and ran his fingers down her throat to her full breasts, over each straining pink tip, and on to her stomach, where he smoothed his palm over the flatness. Everywhere his hand went, he left kisses trailing behind.

"You're so beautiful. So perfectly formed. Your skin is like satin." His voice was hoarse.

Aware of the change in her breathing, he continued to stroke her. He caressed each shapely leg, kissed her toes, then slid his palm along her curves, up to the hot wetness between her thighs.

Each change in her, no matter how small, allowed Sam to learn more about her. A brush here, firmer pressure there, his fingers danced over her body. He closed his eyes and let the shifts in her breathing guide him. He made love as much with his mind as he did with his hands.

Always moving, kissing, flitting over her like a weaver making a vibrant-colored tapestry. Or a bladesmith shaping a knife from a hot piece of steel. They needed each other. The realization of just how much made him tremble.

Cheyenne had brought him back to life, made him feel again when he thought he'd buried all that. Putting the past aside, he turned his full attention to the woman who held his future.

She released a sharp cry and thrust her hands into his hair, winding the strands around her fingers. "Don't stop, Sam. Don't ever stop."

Over and over he drew her to the brink, then backed off until she quivered, calling his name, touching him, caressing, nibbling. He kissed each breast and drew the straining tip into his mouth. He took his time in loving her delicious body, drawing her toward the ultimate pinnacle for which she strained.

Shudders built to a peak, and as she tumbled over the edge and was swept along, he gathered her pulsing body and held her tightly to his chest. Strands of her long, silky hair fell across his arms, and even though he'd dearly loved Beth, he'd never felt this way about anyone before.

This first was all for Chey, to ready her body and to reduce the pain when he took her. He laid next to her, listening to her wild breathing, every uttered word. A light hand on her stomach allowed him to feel every spasming muscle. Sam soaked up the emotion so thick it strangled him. He'd tried to lock his heart behind a wall, but she'd found a way inside.

Now, he couldn't push her out again. He lacked the strength. When she recovered, she opened her eyes and traced his mouth. "I don't know what just happened, but I want more. I've never... My bones are liquid. Thank you."

"Chey, you're amazing. I'm so in awe of your strength, your zest for life. I've never known anyone like you. In a way, you're like a piece of steel that I'm shaping. But it's more than that. We're shaping each other—me as much as you."

She slid her hand between them to touch him. "I want all of you, Sam. Every delicious inch."

He nuzzled behind her ear and down the long column of her throat, held each weighty breast in his hand. She released a cry and tugged at him.

Rolling a nipple between his thumb and forefinger brought moans. She arched her back, pushing herself against him.

When she'd reached a fever pitch once more and moaned his name in that throaty voice he loved, he climbed on top and slid inside her heated wetness. Sam closed his eyes as her muscles clenched around him. For a long moment, he barely breathed. The pleasure that swept through him was the sweetest he'd known.

Like hot steel ripe for molding, shaping, the temperature of Cheyenne's body was exactly right. She was ready. He thrust deeply and she responded by grabbing his back and holding him fast to her.

Every stroke was pure ecstasy. He couldn't breathe, think, or swallow, just feel. Every movement, no matter how tiny, seemed magnified. He wanted to crawl inside her and stay. He poured kisses down her neck and across her shoulders. Her breasts strained against his chest as though aching for more delicious friction that aroused every nerve ending.

Her heated flesh surrounding him was like a forge pushing him toward fulfillment.

At last she shuddered, crying his name, clutching him with a staggering passion and overwhelming need.

Sam took his release in an explosion of light and color. He was traveling across the sky and walking with the stars.

Yes, this was what he'd sought—with Chey.

For what seemed hours but must've been only a few minutes, they lay gasping for air, their bodies entangled in a sheen of sweat, clinging to the last pulsating ripples of pure heaven.

In that moment, Sam couldn't ask for more. He seemed bound to Cheyenne by something beyond the planes of earth.

Thirty-one

"Sam, you have magical hands." Cheyenne brushed the hair from her face so she could see him better. "I don't know how to describe that, but the immense pleasure carried me to a place I've never been in my wildest dreams."

The fire in the wickiup had died down to the glowing embers that still put off heat, just like what was inside her.

He rolled to face her and propped himself on an elbow. "I didn't hurt you?"

"Just a twinge."

"Next time will be different. I promise." He nuzzled behind one ear. "You smell like sunshine after the first big snow. As much as I'd love to stay here all day, we can't. I have some things to do."

"I heard you and Cap talking about town." Worry found a way into her voice. "Please be careful. Now that you're sheared, they'll recognize you."

"I'll think of something. Cap needs his things, and I have to see if my father's telegraphed."

Sam stretched out on his back, his beautiful body open to her. Stirrings knotted in her belly, but like he said, time was up. Maybe she'd invite him into her bed tonight. They could lock the door and speak low. A laugh rose. She was pretty sure they might've heard her the next county over as much racket as she made.

"What's funny?" Sam asked.

She told him, and he confirmed her suspicions. "Well, I can try to do better." She met the twinkle in his eyes and twirled a strand of his hair around a finger. "I won't keep away from you. I can't. Sorry."

"There's always your place." He brushed her cheek with a knuckle. "I have to see you like this again."

Sam rose and pulled her up from the bed. She trembled as he held her to him. Ever so slowly, he sucked her bottom lip into his mouth and ran his hands down her back to cup her derriere. She'd never felt so complete, so cherished.

This and Sam Legend were everything she ever wanted.

But could she keep him? Danger was all around, and bad men wanted him dead.

A foreboding washed over her. She waited for it to pass before she spoke. "Let me put the finishing touches to your beard before we go. It just needs a little more cropping."

"Make it fast."

Dressed and back outside in the sunlight, she clipped and snipped until his dark beard lay just right on his jawline and around his mouth. She'd never seen a more handsome man. He looked nothing like the recluse he'd been. He resembled a profitable business owner or a riverboat captain. He smiled, showing his white teeth, and her knees buckled.

Sam extinguished the fire, and with the scissors tucked into his duster pocket, he helped her onto her little pinto, then swung onto Rio. "Ready?"

"I hate to leave." Her center where all those wonderful sensations ended still put out small quivers, and her swollen breasts retained the feel of his mouth and tongue. The thrill of his body lying skin to skin on hers would last the rest of her life.

"We'll come back," he promised. "This place'll be here."

"I want to come visit Tarak's grave soon. Make his resting place festive." She'd tell her old friend about this day.

"Set a time, and I'll bring you." Sam grinned and pulled his collar up. "Damn, it's cold."

"I know just how to warm you up, cowboy."

"That you do."

Her laughter caught on the wind, and she'd never been so happy or carefree.

❧

Around noon, Cheyenne walked into her kitchen and stood with mouth agape, the smell of burned flapjacks stood in the air. Flour was strewn from one side to the other, and globs of wet batter were on the floor with Shadow lapping it up as fast as she could. Aaron and Ellen were covered in the mess, both licking batter from spoons. Cap sat at the table, beaming as though they'd done something miraculous.

"Miss Cheyenne, I hope you don't mind me teaching the kids how to cook," Cap said. "I know they've made a mess though, and they're gonna…" His sentence trailed off when Sam strode in.

"It's fine, Cap." She watched the children's faces. They didn't recognize Sam and hung back shyly.

The ruff on Shadow's neck rose, and a growl rumbled in her throat.

"Here, girl. It's just me. Come." Sam patted his chest.

She inched toward him, her eyes wary. When she got close, she sniffed him. Finally, recognizing her master, she lowered her hackles and let him rub her ears. The dog had as much flour on her as did the kids.

"It's just Mr. Sam, kids." Cheyenne pushed them toward him.

"I didn't know him," Ellen said, then ran to hug him.

"You look like a regular person now." Aaron followed his sister. "Where's your hair?"

"Cheyenne got mad at me and whacked it off."

"Oh, I did not." Cheyenne felt her face heat. "Don't let him fool you, kids. Of all the things to say."

"Just teasing." He winked at her, then handed Ellen the scissors and asked her to put them back. "I just got tired of looking like a bushy hermit."

Cap finally unstuck his tongue. "Well, kiss my butt on a Saturday night!"

"Is that all you can say?" Sam asked.

"I'm in shock. I ain't seen that face in a coon's age. Damn near forgot what you looked like without all that bush on your head and jaw."

Cheyenne giggled at the stir Sam had caused. "Maybe I should've made introductions."

"For sure, young lady." Cap waved a hand at Sam. "This staggers a man's mind."

"You mean like this kitchen did when we walked in?" Sam asked.

"It's all right, Sam. They were having fun, and this is Christmas." Cheyenne removed a smoking pan from the fire. "It'll clean up."

Hearing the children's laughter was worth the extra work it would take setting things back to rights.

"Someday I'm going to let my hair grow long and never shave," Aaron announced.

"You'd best think about that again, young man." Retta stood in the doorway, looking better than Cheyenne had seen her. "Not while I'm bigger than you are."

"Here let me help you." Cheyenne helped her to the table and put water on to boil for tea. "It's great seeing you up and about."

"It's nice to be able to move around. That bed got tiresome." Retta glanced at Sam. "I like the new look. Very nice."

"I think so too." Cheyenne's gaze tangled in Sam's. "I was surprised when he asked me to cut his hair and beard, and for a while, I stared at it, not knowing where to begin."

"You did a great job." Sam sauntered to the table and pulled out a chair next to Cap, glad to see the two sick ones looking better.

Retta smiled at Sam. "I really do like being able to see your face. I guess that's where you and Cheyenne were."

"It was. I didn't want an audience, so I got Cheyenne to ride with me to my place. It's not that far away. I hope you didn't mind."

Retta laughed. "Good heavens, no. I think I'm able now to look after my kids for a bit."

Deep in thought, Sam propped his elbows on the table. "Ellen, if you could have one thing for Christmas, what would it be?"

"My daddy home," she said without hesitation.

Cheyenne had to turn away to hide sudden tears. That would take a miracle. Their father was in so much danger, yet she could think of no greater surprise than for him to walk in on Christmas morning. But could they beat the odds?

"Besides that. Can you think of one thing?"

A wistful look crossed Ellen's face. "A dolly. One with real eyes that move. I'd rock her and sing songs."

"That sounds real nice, sweetheart." Sam shifted to Aaron and asked the same thing.

The boy put his hand to his head and sighed. "I'd really like a baseball bat and ball in the worst way, but they cost a whole lot of money. Maybe I'd better wish for just a ball or some marbles."

"Son, you can wish for anything," Sam said softly. "Wishes are free."

Yes, they were. She'd made one herself. Cheyenne was very glad he was drawing the boy out. He was much too withdrawn and serious.

Retta drank some tea, then started coughing, and Cheyenne helped her back to bed. When she returned, Cap had gone back to the bunkhouse, and Sam had the kids in a huddle, talking low.

"What's going on?"

"We got a secret," Ellen whispered. "Don't tell Mama."

"Okay, I won't."

Cheyenne and Sam tackled the kitchen mess. After Aaron and Ellen did what they could to help and got themselves cleaned up, they went to the parlor to play.

"Would you like some coffee before you ride into town, Sam?"

"Most certainly, and I'll take some to Cap." He got to his feet and sauntered to her side, lifting a strand of hair. "You smell really nice."

His low voice and memories of the morning sent heat from her stomach. "Thank you. I wish we could sneak away again, but don't see much chance of that."

"Not until tonight. I'll figure something out." He was quiet a moment. "I'm going to need your help with something."

"Sure, if I can."

"I'm going to get the kids to put on a little Christmas play for their mother. Hopefully, their dad too, but I don't know if I can make that happen. If you have some old clothes they can wear, that would help."

"That's a great idea. Of course, I'll find something suitable. What are you going to do for a baby Jesus?"

"Not sure. Any suggestions?"

"The barn cat has had kittens. I saw them this morning, and in another week, they'll be big enough. Maybe use one of those? Or else it'll have to be Ellen's rag doll."

"That can wait until later." He chuckled. "Now, I have to find them some lines to say."

"Best make it simple since Ellen can't read."

When the coffee was ready, Sam filled two cups. "Soon as I drink this, I'll head into town. I probably won't come back in the house until I return."

She held the door. "Please be careful."

"I will, Chey. You've given me plenty of reasons to want to live." His hands full, he leaned to meet her lips.

The kiss swept her away, and for a moment, she fought to keep her knees from buckling. The endearment, the man, her life finally going right and erasing the horror of that night in the desert proved too much. She collapsed into a chair.

Her remaining secret was like a gray specter floating between her and happiness.

To tell Sam would risk losing what she'd found. She just couldn't do that.

~⁊~

Sam whistled all the way to the bunkhouse, trying not to slosh coffee from his and Cap's cups. Shadow ran circles around him, barking excitedly like she'd discovered an old friend. Sam set the coffee on a barrel and opened the door.

Shutting the door with the heel of his boot, Sam handed Cap the coffee. "Thought you could use this."

"Yep. Thanks for thinking of me."

"I noticed you didn't stick around for any of the cleanup after turning the kids loose in there."

Cap rubbed his bristles. "I felt real bad about that, but if you'd have seen those gloomy faces, you'd have done anything to change that. They had fun."

"I know." Sam sat down. "There's not much to do here with them stuck inside and their father missing. It's hard on kids."

They lapsed into silence for several heartbeats. Shadow scratched at the door, and Sam let her in.

"You could've knocked me over with a match stem when you walked in that kitchen earlier." Cap rubbed Shadow's ears. "Did Miss Cheyenne have anything to do with your change of heart?"

"Nope. It was all my idea. I figured it's getting close to arresting the Doolins, and I don't want them to mistake who's putting them behind bars. And I didn't want any google-eyed people standing around watching my shearing, so Cheyenne and I rode to the wickiup."

Sam grew hot recalling the pleasurable way in which they'd killed time.

Cap glared. "So now I'm a google-eyed person?"

"Not in so many words, but I know how you are, and you'd have kept running your mouth. Also, I didn't want the kids watching. It was nerve-wracking enough without all that. I wasn't sure I could go through with it." He took a sip from his cup. "I haven't been into town yet to get your things. Sorry."

"Don't you think you should've waited until after you got back before you decided to join the human race?"

"Thought about it, but since I couldn't show up like I was without giving away that we're in cahoots anyway, I decided to go ahead. As it is, the hotel clerk and maybe Frenchie will be the only ones to see me this way. Should start quite a stir when the clerk tells the Doolins some stranger collected your belongings."

Cap laughed. "I like the way you think, Sammy boy. That's the only way you'll protect Miss Cheyenne and the Mitchell family. Should make the Doolins nervous Nellies having a new stranger in town. As long as they can't follow you, it's perfect."

"I'll make sure. And if I pull my collar up around my ears and have my hat pulled low, no one will see that much of my face, which will add to the confusion."

"Better leave that Appaloosa here, or he'll give you away."

"Thanks. You're right. I might borrow the wagon, and that way I can go by and pick up those tumbleweeds by Heck's place." That would be the only way to get them home. Pulling them behind a horse would break them all to hell.

"Yep." Cap drummed his fingers on the table and sighed. "Sure wish I was going with you. But since I'm dead, I might start to stink."

Sam barked a laugh. "What makes you think you don't now? Cheyenne will bring some water over."

Cap glared. "I might catch my death for real."

"Then I have another suggestion. I talked to Aaron and Ellen about putting on a Christmas play for their mother, and I need someone to write lines for them to say."

"You mean like a playwright?" Cap hooted.

"Nothing complicated since they'll have to memorize them." Sam shook a finger. "And no profanity, liquor, or loose women. These are children."

"You sure are bossy since you cut your hair. Know that?" Cap said sourly.

"But you love me anyway." Instead of his sheepskin coat, Sam slid his arms into a long duster some cowhand had left hanging on a nail and put his hat on as he moved toward the door.

His hand on the knob, he glanced back at his old friend and blinked hard. If a man found one good friend in life, he was rich beyond measure. Sam had hit the jackpot in Cap McFarlan.

Thirty-two

THE WAGON RATTLED DOWN THE EMPTY STREET OF TASCOSA. With half the town having headed for greener pastures, nothing much moved save for a couple of hounds snarling over something dead. The deserted street worked to Sam's advantage. He decided to stop at the telegraph office first, so he parked alongside the front and set the brake. The duster flapped against his trousers as he climbed down.

The bell over the door announced his presence, and Duggan Flannery bustled from a side door. He didn't recognize Sam. "Can I help you, sir?"

Sam removed his hat. "Checking to see if I have a telegram from my father, Sam Legend Sr."

Flannery squinted at him. "And who might you be?"

"Sam Jr." He moved closer. "I got sheared, so I'm not surprised you don't recognize me. I was in here a few nights ago with my father and Texas Ranger Cap McFarlan."

"Well, I have to say you don't look the same." Flannery chuckled nervously, still halfway unsure about Sam. "I guess you gave up the wild look."

"You might say that. I needed to change for the Doolins."

At the mention of the Doolins, Flannery finally relaxed. "Yep, you'll fool anyone. Folks are buzzing about the ranger getting himself shot. That's a shame, but not surprising."

Deciding the less people knowing Cap was still breathing the better, Sam didn't tell Flannery any different.

"Back to my father. Any word?"

Flannery nodded and reached for a piece of paper. "This came about an hour ago."

Sam unfolded the yellow slip and read. *Pigeons have flown.*

Damn, just when everything seemed set to make the arrest.

He glanced up. "Have the Doolins gotten any messages?"

"One. It was rather odd, so I copied it before Tom Doolin picked it up." Flannery thumbed through a stack of paper and pulled one out. "Here it is."

The message read: *Fire's hot. Stop. Put grease in the skillet.*

The first two words made sense, especially after Senior's message. But what the hell did the second part mean? If you put grease in a skillet, you might be getting ready to cook. To Sam, it seemed to warn the Doolins to get ready. But for what, dammit?

Sam handed it back to Flannery, along with his thanks. "Let me send a reply to my father." He scribbled out two words: *CM shot.* "Send this right away." He pulled two dollars from his pocket and laid the bills on top of the message.

"Will do."

Sam started for the door. "Flannery, is there any way I can buy a bottle of whiskey off you? I don't want to show my face at the saloon."

"I reckon so. I'll have to go upstairs, so you'll have to wait."

"I don't mind." Sam stood at the window, watching the street.

Flannery returned with it shortly. Sam paid him and left.

Outside, he climbed into the wagon and turned the team toward the nameless yellow hotel. As he passed the row of saloons, he kept an eye out for any of the Doolins but saw no one.

The town had seemed to turn up its toes and die. Except Sam knew it hadn't. Eyes were watching him. The hair on his neck had risen. If Shadow had been there, she'd have a growl rumbling in her throat.

He stopped in front of the hotel, pulled the collar of the duster higher and his hat lower, and went inside. No one was at the desk, so he dinged the bell.

A man wearing a bobcat fur hat with a tail hanging from one side limped from the back. "What'cha want?"

Laughter started to well up. Who did he think he was? Daniel Boone?

Sam cleared his throat and deepened his voice. "Key to Room 10. The man got shot and died. I'm a friend."

The clerk tilted his head and squinted through one eye. "He owed me money."

"How much?"

"Ten dollars."

"Better think again." Sam pulled out two dollars and slapped it down. "For your trouble. Now the key."

Grudgingly, the man handed it over, snatching the money off the counter.

Upstairs, Sam stuffed what belongings he could find in Cap's saddlebags and hurried out. There was no sign of the clerk, but Sam's gut said he'd gone for the Doolins. If any of them saw him, his goose would be cooked.

Throwing Cap's saddlebags into the buckboard, he flicked the reins and set the team in motion. No one had gotten a clear view of his face, so he counted the trip as a success.

The wind had turned markedly colder, and moisture was in the air. He'd hurry by for the tumbleweeds and get himself home to the fire.

He was rounding the bend going out of town when he spotted a man darting into the brush. Something seemed familiar and made him stop. He peered into the tangled mass of undergrowth that had long lost its leaves. Not a good hiding place unless a man was desperate. Even then, it left him awfully exposed.

"Mister," Sam called. "Need a ride?"

A rustle of breaking limbs reached him.

"Hey, I don't mind taking you wherever you need to go. It might start snowing anytime."

The man stood, shivering. He wasn't wearing a coat. Sam recognized Jared.

"Get in, Mitchell." When the ranch hand hesitated, Sam realized he didn't know him without all the hair. "It's me—Sam Legend."

"Sam, thank God." Jared climbed up. "Pardon me for not recognizing you."

"I got my hair cut. What are you doing?"

"I escaped the Doolins. I saw my chance and took it." His teeth were chattering. "Had no time to get my coat."

"Hold on." Sam pulled off his duster and put it around the man, then he pulled the wagon off the road, down into a wash where they wouldn't be seen. He faced Jared, who'd hunched into the duster. "Did something happen? Did you finish the plate?"

"No. I sabotaged it where it's unusable. The Doolins don't know yet." Jared rubbed his nose with his hand and coughed. "I just wanted free of them so I can see my Retta and the kids."

"Jared, all your leaving will accomplish now is leading them straight to the Ronans. This will put your family at great risk. Did you even think about that?"

"You're right. I just couldn't take any more." Jared coughed again.

"Look, we're just about ready to make our move and arrest this whole ring." Sam squeezed his shoulder. "Give us a few more days. Can you do that? Can you go back and pretend all is normal until we have things in place? You don't want to be looking over your shoulder for the rest of your life, do you? Help us get these rats and end everything."

It killed Sam to talk him into going back because he knew how much Jared wanted to see his wife and kids.

Jared stared straight ahead, resigned to returning. "What do you want me to do?"

"Be our ears and listen. I know the Doolins got a telegram from their boss in Austin. Do you know what 'put grease in the skillet' means?"

"They're coming, and they're telling the Doolins to make ready. All the big bosses are converging here. I heard them talking about it."

Excitement rushed through Sam. "Do you know when?"

"No specific date, but they'll arrive in the next few days."

"This is what we need. Are you game for going back for a little longer?"

Jared gave his head a jerk. "If I can end this, I want to do it."

"I'll come into town each night and meet you behind the telegraph office where we can exchange information. What time can you get away?"

"About eight. They moved me from that shack they were staying in. I'm in town now, and that's when they let me go to bed and get some rest."

"Sounds good. I'll be there. If we can round this ring up while they're all together, it'll go much easier."

"How is my wife?"

"She's very much improved, the baby too. Each day her color gets better, and she's stronger."

"Thank God. And the kids?"

"They worry about you. Retta hasn't told them anything. She thought it best to hold back. At least for now."

"That's best. So much can go wrong."

"It won't. We're going to see to it that you get back with them." Sam turned the wagon around and they headed back to town, turning down the nearest alley and letting Jared out at the church. "Be careful. I'll see you tomorrow night. And, Jared, if anything goes wrong and you have to run, go to the telegraph office. Duggan Flannery is on our side."

With a nod, Jared removed the duster and handed it back to Sam. "Thanks."

The tall ranch hand darted around the buildings and disappeared from view. Satisfied, Sam got out of town as fast as he could, shrugging into the duster as he drove. The wind had become like ice. He almost decided to skip going after the tumbleweeds, only to keep heading that way. He found them exactly where the doc said. He grabbed two of the largest ones and put them in the wagon.

All the way back to Cheyenne's, he kept thinking of Jared Mitchell. Maybe he should've let him keep running. The man missed his family, and if anything happened to Jared and he ended up losing his life, Sam would bear the blame.

Hopefully, by tomorrow night, the situation would be closer to a resolution.

It was late afternoon by the time Sam saw the lights of home. He pulled up to the barn and was unhitching the horses when a sound made him look up. Cheyenne stood in the door of the barn, her russet hair blowing in the freezing wind, cheeks rosy. He stared, transfixed, heat sweeping through his body.

"I'm glad you're back, Sam."

"Me too. It's getting a lot colder, and I'm about frozen solid. Everything all right?"

"It's fine. I was worried about you." She came on inside, hugging the coat to her. "There's so much danger, and when you leave, I don't know if I'll see you alive again." She gave a strangled cry. "I don't think I could bear it if you don't make it back one day."

"Come here." Sam pulled her into the circle of his arms. He held her tightly until she stopped shivering. Then he brushed back her hair and kissed her, anchoring her face with a hand under her jaw.

Deepening the kiss, he cupped the weight of a breast.

Cheyenne put her arms around him and held him, little sounds coming from her throat. The kiss held all the intensity of a sudden summer squall rolling across the prairie, complete with jagged lightning and rumbling thunder.

They broke apart, breathless and wanting more. Sam wasn't sure when she'd come to mean so much. Maybe all those nights when she'd asked him to hold her and put the ghosts to rest.

"Chey, Chey," he mumbled against her temple. "I don't know how all this is going to end, but I'm certain that what we have is more than a flash in the night. You're the first thing I think of each morning and the last thing at night. You give my days meaning."

She glanced up with solemn eyes. "I feel the same way. For me this is very real."

They both seemed to avoid naming whatever it was they'd found. Maybe it was too soon, so they danced around it.

One more kiss, a light one this time, and he turned back to the horses. "If you want to go put some coffee on, I'll be along in a minute."

"I have a pot already done and waiting. I'll help, and the work will go faster." She turned toward the wagon that sat in the shadows. "Oh, you got the tumbleweeds. Aaron and Ellen will be so happy."

Sam undid the last of the traces, and Cheyenne led the horses to their stalls. After giving the team some oats and water, he grabbed Cap's saddlebags and whiskey, leaving the tumbleweeds for later.

Putting an arm around Cheyenne, he stopped by the bunkhouse first to drop off the saddlebags and whiskey. It had been a good day. He was still alive, and so were the ones he cared about.

The night air dancing around them, Cheyenne snuggled against his side. Sam lowered his mouth to her hair and breathed in the Christmas baking scents on her clothes and skin, wondering how Cap would feel about having the place all to himself tonight.

Thirty-three

THE WARMTH OF THE EMPTY KITCHEN ENGULFED CHEYENNE when Sam opened the door, but most of that warmth had to do with him and this newfound happiness buzzing inside her. Oh, the things he did to her calm, orderly world. Laughter bubbled up.

"What's funny?" Sam asked.

"Nothing. Just brimming with so much joy." She met his dark eyes. "A year ago, I was at the government school and miserable. I saw firsthand how they were treating those poor, scared children, stripping them of their dignity, their families, and their homes. Now it's Christmas again, and my life is totally different. There's laughter inside this house." She paused. "And in my heart."

Although Cap's booming voice and high-pitched giggles came from the parlor, it seemed they were alone for the moment. Cheyenne loved this closeness.

"The miracle of the season?" Sam pressed a kiss to her temple.

The tenderness of his lips sent a quiver through her.

"That and much more. Christmas is such a special time. It puts love and hope and forgiveness in our hearts." She laid a palm against his face. "And sometimes it changes people."

"It has for me. A month ago, I was missing Beth and had nothing to look forward to. My life was pretty bleak and miserable." He kissed her fingers. "You've helped me see that I had to turn loose of what was and open up to the possibilities of what is."

Ellen appeared in the doorway, and they broke apart. "Mr. Sam, you're back. Wanna come hear Mr. Cap's stories?"

"Sure, honey. Let me get some coffee first and warm up."

"Okay, but you better hurry, or you'll miss the good part." She giggled and skipped from the room.

Sam chuckled. "It's not like I haven't heard them a million times anyway."

Cheyenne slapped at his arm. "Hey, we haven't, and I'll have you know he's a very interesting man."

"Yeah, well, they get pretty boring after the tenth time. A lot he makes up and could never have happened." He sauntered to the stove, his bootheels sounding on the wood floor, and peered into a pot. "Smells good. What is it?"

"Chicken stew. I knew it would make a lot. I've got to get some cornbread on." She reached for a bowl, flour, and cornmeal.

"You can't go wrong with that." He poured two cups of coffee.

Ellen ran back. "Come on, Mr. Sam. We saved you a seat."

"I'm coming."

Balancing the cups, he shrugged at Cheyenne and went with the sweet girl. Warmth curled inside her. Sam was every girl's dream. His caring for people and animals went bone deep, and it didn't matter if he had long, wild hair or short, well-kept locks. He was who he was, no matter his appearance.

Tarak had been an excellent judge of character, and that he'd taken Sam in, shared his knowledge of bladesmithing, and offered him room in his wickiup told her a lot. Her old friend had never been wrong.

Nor had she in most things.

In the quiet of the kitchen as Cheyenne stirred up the cornbread, she knew she'd fallen in love—and with the man himself, not his appearance. Yes, there was no mistaking. She hugged her secret.

She was in love with Sam Legend.

Worry snuck into her head. There was a slight problem with the woman who'd loved him first. And the secret she herself guarded that could destroy everything.

In the parlor, Cap paused in one of his stories and took the second cup of coffee from Sam. "You're a mind reader, son."

Sam chuckled. "No, it's just that I know you."

He spoke to Retta and noted the sparkle in her eyes. She was losing the sickly pallor in her face. He'd find a quiet moment to tell her about Jared.

"I hope I didn't miss the good part that Ellen promised." He sat next to Aaron, who grinned up at him. Shadow padded over and rested her muzzle on Sam's leg. He rubbed her face.

"I can start over," Cap assured him.

"No. There's no need. I'll catch up, and I'm good at filling in the blanks."

The tall tale was about Cap's experience in tracking a killer through the rugged South Texas desert. He found himself in a den of a hundred rattlers and started slinging them right and left, miraculously only getting bit once. Sam rolled his eyes, recognizing the story. There'd been only one snake, and Sam had shot it before it bit anyone.

The children's eyes bugged out. "Then what did you do?" Aaron asked.

"Well, I cut an X on the wound and sucked that poison right out of there. Yes sireee. When I woke up the next morning, I was cured."

Ellen swallowed hard. "Wow! You were lucky, Mr. Cap."

"That's right, sweetheart. Mighty lucky."

Catching the longwinded ranger between breaths took a lot of doing, but Sam was finally able to jump in. He told the kids about the tumbleweeds he'd hauled in. "Tomorrow, you can start making decorations to hang on them."

"Oh boy!" Ellen jumped up and down. "We'll make some real pretty ones."

"Can we pop popcorn and make those strings?" Aaron asked.

"Yes, you can," Cheyenne said from the doorway. "And paper chains and other pretties."

The kids both hollered and clapped.

Retta held up a hand to quiet them. "You don't have to go to so much trouble, Cheyenne."

"No trouble. I want to. This is as much for me as it is for them."

Sam sucked in a breath, staring at the way her russet hair flamed in the blue-and-orange light from the fireplace. She looked like a Christmas angel. Far prettier than any ornament on a tree. It took little to imagine stripping her clothes off one by one and kissing her senseless.

"What's the matter, Sam? You look like a kid on Christmas morning." Cap's drawl jarred him from his daydream.

Maybe he was. Sam growled, "Isn't a man allowed to think?"

"Let's eat, everyone." Cheyenne held out her hands to Aaron and Ellen. "We don't want to put cold cornbread in our stew."

Cap ambled behind them.

Sam offered his arm to Retta. "Let me help you to the table."

"Thank you. Sometimes my legs don't want to work too well."

"I'm glad for an opportunity to speak privately. I saw Jared while I was in town. He's getting anxious to finish this job so he can be here with you and the kids. Just a little longer."

She gripped Sam's arm. "I wish he could be here now. My heart aches to have him beside me. The children need their father, and I need a husband." She rested her free hand over her swelled stomach. "I really need him."

"I'm sorry. He's doing the best he can to survive."

"As are all of us," Retta whispered softly. "Thank you for letting me know he's still alive. I just hope he stays that way." She wiped away a tear. "Sometimes I lie awake thinking about him, wondering if he's hungry or cold."

Telling her how his teeth were chattering, his body frozen was nothing Sam would share.

"This nightmare will be over soon. Things are coming to a head," he murmured, lending the woman his strength as they moved toward the laughter and gaiety Retta didn't feel.

After supper, he made plans to meet Cheyenne later. "If it's okay, we might use your little house. It's private."

Her eyes shone. "That'll be perfect. I'll put the kids to bed and see to Retta."

"I have to talk to Cap about some things anyway." He gave her a kiss on the cheek, called Shadow, and followed Cap to the bunkhouse. The dog padded to the stove and lay down.

Sam filled Cap in on the developments. "I'm sure Senior is on his way, but I don't know if he'll get here in time."

Cap smoothed his mustache in thought. "I may not be the best, but I've fought battles in worse shape than this. Between the two of us, we'll whip those devils."

"And we have Jared, don't forget." The ranch hand might sway the odds in their favor. With him on the inside and the Doolins none the wiser, Jared would have his pick of targets. "I think the higher-ups will arrive very soon. I'm to meet Jared tomorrow night behind the telegraph office."

"I'll damn sure be there too."

Sam had seen the same determination in Cap's eyes before and wouldn't bet against the ranger. While it may not be pretty, they'd find a way to win somehow. "The weather is going to help us."

"Yep. It'll force them inside, and once they're all together, we'll lock 'em in and pick 'em off one by one as they bust out." Cap picked up his saddlebags and laid them on his bunk. "There's not a man alive that don't struggle against something. Poverty, injustice, right and wrong, hunger, you name it. Any of that sure puts a powerful fight inside a man."

"I agree. We all have something we struggle against." Sam knelt and put more wood on the fire. For him, it was making the Doolins pay for Beth. If he could do that, he'd be satisfied.

"Thanks for getting my stuff. And the whiskey."

"I bought the bottle from Flannery. He's proving to be very helpful." Sam paused for a moment. "Flannery will probably join us in the roundup if we ask him."

"Maybe some of the other townsfolk as well. Hey, that's good thinking, Sammy boy." Cap uncorked the whiskey and took a swig. "Want some?"

"No thanks. I have plans."

Cap jerked around. "What plans?"

"You're awful nosey. I'm meeting Cheyenne."

"Well, you could've told me."

Sam shut the door on the potbelly stove, dusted his hands, and stood. "I just did. By the way, you'll have the bunkhouse to yourself tonight."

"You'd better not go trifling with Miss Cheyenne's feelings." Cap shook his finger. "She's a fine woman, and you hurt her, you'll answer to me as well as her pa."

"I have no intentions of hurting her, so stop."

He did care about her. More than any woman. But enough to marry her? The question jarred him. He blinked hard, unfastening the top button of his shirt. He couldn't imagine a life without her in it. Nope, he couldn't see that at all. When he thought of a future, it was her face he saw, her eyes glimmering with hope.

His nerves settled. Everything was at it should be. He'd be a happy man to spend the rest of his life with his beautiful Chey.

◆

The house was quiet, and the kids were in bed. Cheyenne was unwinding with a hot cup of tea, waiting for Sam. She'd already gone over to her little house and lit a fire. The rest would wait until they got there. Nerves made her bounce a leg. She wanted to do this, that wasn't the problem. Before, they hadn't planned anything. It had just happened, and that seemed to be the problem.

She closed her eyes and tried to pretend that this was any ordinary night. Like the ones when she'd asked him to hold her.

It's funny but the ghosts hadn't bothered her of late. Maybe Sam had put them to rest.

No, not Sam, she realized. She'd been the one to open up and talk. But one secret remained, and she'd tell Sam tonight—tell him the whole rotten truth. Then there'd be nothing between them.

It would be hard, though. He might turn away in disgust. A chance she'd have to take, because she couldn't live like this. She owed herself to speak of the horror.

The knob turned, and Sam entered, rubbing his hands and blowing on them. "I hope I didn't keep you waiting. I went by your house, and you'd already laid a fire."

Her breath hung in her throat as she stood. Not used to this new look yet, she stared as though seeing him for the first time.

His wind-ruffled dark hair fell in disarray, a few tendrils curling on his forehead. Her gaze dropped to the V of his open shirt where wisps of hair curled, then to the close-cropped beard darkening his jaw. There was a firm strength about him that said he never backed down or gave up from a fight. When he'd retreated to the Texas Panhandle, it had been to heal and find his bearings again, not because he was weak.

"Yes, I went over so it would have time to warm up in there." She glanced down at her cup. "I was having a cup of tea. Would you like something?"

This formal back and forth seemed more in line for strangers, not intimate friends, but she didn't know how to change it.

"I don't think so. The kids in bed?"

"They are." She stepped over to him. "They should be fine until morning, and if not, their mother can see about them."

Sam put an arm around her shoulders, and everything returned to normal. She inhaled the manly scent on his clothes and brushed her fingers along his dark jawline.

"Chey, if you don't want to do this, it's fine. I won't push you into anything."

"I know and thank you for giving me a choice. I want to spend one night in your arms and wake up with you beside me." She pressed a kiss to the hollow of his throat. "I want you, Sam Legend. All of you. For a lot more than an hour or two."

He knelt on one knee, taking her hand. "Cheyenne Ronan, I'm not much for words, but I've found in you something I can't let get away. Will you consider taking pity on me and becoming my wife?"

Shock swept through her. This was unexpected. She'd been content to make love with him and not ask for more. In truth, she never thought he'd take this step.

She never thought he could love another after losing his wife so tragically. She swallowed hard, her stomach clenching.

"I hope you understand what I'm about to say." She couldn't bear to see the disappointment on his face, so she lowered her eyes. "I need some time to think about this. Marriage is a lifetime commitment, and I want to make the right decision. There are some things about me that you don't know."

"I see." Sam slowly rose, hurt in his deep voice. "I don't care whatever these things are that stand between us. I love you, and I want to make you my wife. We can work out our problems if you trust me."

"Trust has nothing to do with it." She stuffed her hands in her pocket. "You're the finest man I've ever known. All I'm asking for is some time."

"Take all you need." He squeezed her shoulder. "I won't pressure you."

"I appreciate that." And somehow during the wait, she had to find a way to tell him about the dark stain on her heart that wouldn't go away.

Wordlessly, he stood and lowered the wick in the lamp, then opened the door and went out into the cold night. Alone.

Through scalding tears, she watched his tall figure disappear. What had she done?

Thirty-four

SAM DIDN'T COME IN FOR COFFEE OR BREAKFAST THE NEXT morning, and Cheyenne's heart had never felt so empty and cold. She needed this man. His arms. His kisses. His love.

How could she turn down what he wanted to give?

The answer was, she couldn't and live with herself. She couldn't lose him.

Cheyenne bit her lip. She had to tell him. There was no putting this off. She grabbed her heavy shawl and hurried toward the bunkhouse.

Shadow bounded up, and Cheyenne was so relieved to see him and to know Sam hadn't moved back to his wickiup, she knelt and kissed the dog's head. Continuing on, she knocked on the bunkhouse door.

Cap opened it. "It's awful early in the morning to get such a pretty visitor." His famous grin was missing. "I suppose you're looking for Sam."

"I am." She craned her neck around the ranger's big body.

"Sorry to disappoint you. He's saddling Rio, then leaving for that poor excuse for a house on top of that bluff. I don't know what happened, but he sat up next to the fire all night."

"Thanks, Cap. I don't have time to explain." She kissed his cheek and ran.

Her steps slowed as she neared the barn. Her heart pounded. "Sam?"

He didn't answer. She yanked open the door so fast she scared an owl roosting in the rafters. It swooped down almost on top of her head. Cheyenne yelped and waved her arms. Thankfully, it went back to its spot.

Sam stood watching. "What do you want, Chey?"

Now that she'd found him, she didn't know what to say. She moistened her dry lips. "I missed you at breakfast. You didn't even get coffee. Are you leaving?"

"It's best."

"Please stay." The words were so soft that for a minute she thought she hadn't spoken them.

"Why? Will it change anything?"

"Maybe." She pulled her shawl tighter against the frigid air. "We have something hanging between us. You must've felt it. Can we talk?"

"The only thing that would make a difference in the way I feel about you is if you tell me you're promised to another."

"Nothing like that. It's about my time with the Apaches. Things happened on our trips across the desert. We were caught several times, and I spent two months at Fort Wingate until some of my fellow guides broke me out. It was…hard." Her chin quivered, and she wouldn't look at Sam. "They used starvation tactics, allowed the soldiers to expose themselves at me, but the nights when they released scorpions in my cell were the worst. I would huddle in a corner in a ball, afraid to move or they'd find me."

She finally raised her gaze and found dark anger on Sam's face.

"I can't imagine what you went through," he said softly, squeezing her hand. "I know there's far more than you're telling me. No wonder you were so thin at first. Now I understand why you need arms around you, bracing you."

"But that's not all I have to tell." She dragged air into her shaky lungs. "On the last trek we made across the desert, we had a young Apache woman heavy with child. About two weeks out, she went into labor. We decided that I would stay with her, and the rest of them continued." Her mind returned to that desolate stretch of ground dotted by cactus, sage, and mesquite. The pitch-black sky, no moon, clouds blotting the stars. Kushala's horrible cries that pierced Cheyenne's soul as she tried to help. "About an hour after she gave birth, a man found us. It must've been around midnight. He wore no uniform, and to this day I don't know who he was. He had the evilest mean look on his face and glittering eyes of hate." She put a hand over her eyes. "When he saw Kushala was Apache, curses flew from his mouth, and he went into a rage, stomping around, throwing things. I tried my best to protect her." A cry slipped from Cheyenne's mouth. "He…he shoved me aside, stomped on the woman's stomach, then grabbed the babe."

She stopped. Oh God, she couldn't do this. She made it to the barn door before the contents of her stomach spewed on the ground.

Sam murmured soothing words. He held her hair back, then helped her to a hay bale. "I'll get some water from the well."

He hurried out and came back with a dipper of water, holding it to her mouth. "Rinse."

After several rinses, she spat out the bad taste, then drank. "Thank you, Sam."

"You're freezing." He pulled her into his arms and held her shivering body.

She snuggled into the folds of his coat, borrowing from his warmth. "I'm sorry."

"You have nothing at all to be sorry for." He tenderly smoothed her hair and rubbed her arms. "Not one blessed thing."

When her teeth stopped chattering, she went on. "The man threw the newborn to the ground and raised a foot. I couldn't let him kill the child. I sprang to my feet, reaching for the knife Tarak made for me. I—" Her voice lowered to a whisper. "I plunged that knife into his stomach and twisted it hard. I killed him, Sam. I took the life from him, and I still see his accusing eyes, face. I'm sorry I waited so long to tell you. I didn't know how."

Sam cradled her head. "It's all right. You did what anyone would've done. Did the babe live?"

"Miraculously yes. I got both of them to safety in Mexico with her people." She glanced up at him through her tears. "I think I must be a bad person to kill. Do you think God will forgive me?"

"Without a doubt." He took her face in his hands. "But you have to forgive yourself too. It's important."

"I keep seeing him. He won't let me be. Will it ever fade?"

"In time. Just remember that the blame belongs to him. You took the only option he left open. If you hadn't stopped him, he'd have killed all three of you. And everyone else."

"I'm sure." Cheyenne rested her head against his chest, completely drained, but relieved to have finally told someone. A few minutes passed, then she sat up. "Is your offer of marriage still open?"

"It is."

"Then I'd be happy to be your wife. I couldn't accept your proposal until I bared my soul. I had to leave you a way out."

His dark eyes glowed. "I don't need a way out. I only need you." He tenderly smoothed her hair. "You make me the happiest man on earth."

Excited ripples swept through her as she tilted her head, waiting. His lips met hers in a searing kiss that swept aside every doubt, every fear, every insecurity.

This man with steel in his blood was hers and would be for the rest of her days.

⌘

That night she slipped into the frosty air with Sam, and they crossed to her little home where a single light burned.

A cozy fire greeted them. Sam shrugged out of his coat, then removed hers. Sweeping her long hair to the side, he kissed the back of her neck. Tingles danced up her spine. She'd never known such tenderness, and tears welled in her eyes at his caring attention.

She turned to face him. "You make me feel like a princess, so special and adored."

"Because you are." He took her face between his hands and pressed his lips softly to hers.

The kiss transported her to a familiar paradise, as hunger for more raced through her. Cheyenne gripped his shirt, giving all the love she had inside her.

The future was unclear, and their path uncertain. This could be all they'd have together.

One night. One beautiful man. One glorious, forever love.

Sam reached into the corner for a thick roll of something and pulled it out, releasing the ties. A large, luxurious bearskin unfurled. Cheyenne recognized it as the fur piece Sam had put her on that first night after she'd broken into his wickiup and held a knife to his throat.

She laughed and shook her finger. "You're a sneaky, sneaky man, but I love it."

"Thought you might."

He spread it in front of the fire. They undressed each other and lay on the velvet cushion. The heavenly feel against her naked body was nothing she'd ever experienced before and knew she may not again.

"You're full of surprises, Sam." She lay on her side facing him and stared into his expressive eyes, tracing the lines of his mouth. "You are a most sensual man."

A gust of wind outside banged that shutter that she'd forgotten to fix.

"I'm glad we're safe inside these walls." She dropped kisses across one collarbone, then examined a small protrusion on his shoulder. It was some sort of sinew or bone. She moved to his upper arms. "Your body seems shaped by both of your professions.

Working with steel and wielding a hammer all day has given you these big muscles."

"Yep, I guess," he murmured, cupping a breast.

His hands on her skin made her breath hitch. But when he rolled a nipple, deep, quickening sensations passed through her stomach.

"I'm glad we don't have to hurry." He gently pushed her back and reached for what appeared to be a length of ivory cloth measuring about two feet long that he must've placed under the fur.

"You really prepared for this, didn't you? What is that?"

"An ascot from my more refined days. Actually, it was a prank gift from my brother Hector. I found it stuck in the bottom of my trunk." His dark eyes smoldered. "I hope you like what I'm about to do with this silk."

Anticipation curled around her spine. She'd always loved the feel of silk.

Appearing to barely breathe, he moved the silk slowly across her face, down her throat, then over the sensitive mounds of her breasts and nipples. She cried out, arching her back. Never had every nerve ending felt so exposed to each pass of the cloth over her skin. The mere flutter of his breath brushing her skin aroused her, made her ache with desire for this man.

Sam moved the silk down her body, across her stomach, and around each leg. Delicious shivers raced through her each place the smooth cloth touched.

When he finished with the soles of her feet and toes, he pulled the silk up between her thighs and dragged it very slowly across the raised flesh there.

Cheyenne cried out with sheer, throbbing pleasure. "Please, Sam."

She pulled at him, and he crawled on top. She thought she'd die from the fire raging inside, threatening to consume every part of her. He positioned himself and plunged into her entrance. A powerful force of hot waves began to build inside. Exquisite plea-sure shot through her each time Sam withdrew and plunged again.

A series of pulses gripped her, building higher and higher, then she was tumbling down into an abyss where her ragged cries were met and measured by her wild heartbeat.

Cheyenne lay gasping, dragging air into her tortured lungs. Sam collapsed beside her.

She didn't know how long they lay there and was barely aware when he pulled a blanket over them and held her in his arms. She was safe and filled with deep love for this man of steel and justice.

∞

It was still dark when Cheyenne woke to Sam kissing her. "What time is it?"

"I think around midnight, but that's a guess. I left my watch in the bunkhouse. The fire's gone out, so it's been several hours." He rose and started the fire again, then crawled back under the covers. He stretched out and pulled her close with her head on his shoul-der. His voice was sleep roughened. "Lady, you sure know how to sap a man's energy."

"Me?" She laughed. "You were the one with the magic silk."

"First you say I have magic hands and now magic silk cloth. There's nothing magic about it. Just love."

She became still inside, Sam's heartbeat next to her ear. "What are you saying?"

"I love you, Chey. I love you so much." He kissed her hair. "I think I have since that first time you asked me to hold you and I took you in my arms. You seemed to need a protector, and I was willing to take the job."

She swiveled and raised on an elbow so she could see his eyes. The eyes never lied. His glittered with passion and commitment. "I love you too, and I realized last night in my kitchen just how deep my feelings go. I want to have a life with you, to be more than your 'sometime lady.' I want the bells and fireworks, the sunshine and storms, the quiet days and noisy nights. I want our life to be a love story everyone will talk about—like Frenchie and Mickey McCormick."

"Chey, you shake me to my soul. Get any thought out of your head right now that I only want you sometimes. What I have in mind for us matches your ideas, and God willing, I'm going to make this legal as soon as I can."

They slept for a while, then an hour before dawn, they made love again. Cheyenne took charge of the ivory silk ascot and soon had Sam in the same aroused state he'd had her in. When they took their pleasure, hers was the strongest, most earth-shattering thing she'd ever felt.

Maybe finally shedding her guilt and shame played a big part and set her free.

Her mother once said that there were two kinds of guilt—the kind that kept your soul locked away, and the kind that spurred you to some higher, more selfless action. Cheyenne sighed at that truth. How she missed her mother and hoped she'd come home soon.

She toyed with Sam's hair. She had lots to tell. Unbelievable things.

～

The morning that had begun so early had a head of steam in no time. Sam gathered the eggs and took them to the kitchen, then went back out to feed the cattle and check their water supply. Doc Tyler arrived while he was finishing up. It seemed hard to imagine that it had only been two days since someone shot Cap, and they still had no clue to the identity of the culprits.

Sam opened the bunkhouse door to an argument.

"I don't need no damn laudanum or morphine or any pills, and that's final," Cap yelled. "Take your bag and leave."

Doc Tyler's face turned purple. "I've never seen a more stubborn cuss in all my days. I know you're in pain. That wound is angry and swollen. I'm trying to help you."

"Dammit, I don't need that mess. When I hurt, I take a big swig of whiskey an' that's all I need." Cap pointed at Sam. "Ask him."

Sam raised his hands. "Hey, leave me out of this. I'll just say Doc has medical expertise."

Cap barked a laugh that was anything but happy. "I got experience in living, and that counts where I'm concerned."

Doc sighed. "Of course, it counts. That wasn't what I was saying."

"I'll bet a two-dollar bill you sicced Doc on me, Sam. Wouldn't put it past you."

"Well, I didn't." Sam took Tyler's arm, set his hat on his head, and picked up the black bag. "How about me taking you over to the house?"

"Yes, I need to see Mrs. Mitchell anyway." Doc glared at Cap. "She'll be much more accommodating *and* appreciative of my services."

Cap growled and showed his teeth like a rabid dog.

Smothering a laugh, Sam hustled Doc out the door and over to the house while the getting was good. Things weren't much calmer over there. Aaron and Ellen were already up and running around the kitchen table like wild heathens while Cheyenne was making breakfast.

Was this Christmas morning and he'd forgotten? But no, that was still six days away.

"What's going on in here?" Sam asked.

Ellen pushed her long brown hair out of her eyes. "We get to make pretty things for the tumbleweed tree, an' we're happy."

"Isn't your mother still sleeping?" Although how she could in that noise was beyond him.

"Nope, I am not." Retta laughed from the doorway. "Sleep isn't possible anytime around Christmas." She noticed Tyler. "Good morning, Doctor."

Tyler dragged his hat from his head. "Mrs. Mitchell. I have to say, you're looking very well."

"Thank you. I feel better than I have in a while." She sat down at the table, and Doc Tyler followed suit.

Cheyenne set the coffeepot and some cups on the table so they could serve themselves, then went back to her cooking.

Sam wandered over to Cheyenne and kept his voice low. "Good morning—again. You're like a rose in bloom this fine day."

"Thank you, kind sir. You alone bear the credit."

"Want some help?"

"Sure. I have the biscuits ready to roll out. You can cut them out for me and put them on a pan."

"Yes, ma'am." Sam washed his hands and set to work, thinking how much fun it would be to get into a flour fight with Chey. "The weather's nice if you want to take the children out to do calisthenics with you after breakfast. It might not be a bad idea to get rid of some of their pent-up energy."

"That's a wonderful idea. I will. Would you like to join us?" Her eyes twinkled.

"I just might. Of course, I'll probably be too busy watching the teacher to do any of the exercises. She's a real beauty."

Cheyenne laughed. "You say all the right things to flatter a girl."

"What's so funny?" Aaron asked.

The boy caught Sam by surprise. He'd been too busy flirting to pay attention to the kids. He groped for an answer and finally hit on one. "We're just talking about how funny it would be to put Mr. Cap in the Christmas play."

Aaron giggled. "Yeah, he could be a donkey or a camel."

That wasn't a half-bad idea. It deserved some pondering. The boy wandered away.

"Hey, where is Cap this morning?" Cheyenne turned the sausage patties.

"He and Doc had a fight, and he's sulking in the bunkhouse. Probably glued to the window and will be over as soon as Doc leaves." He told her what the disagreement had been over.

"That's crazy."

"Yep. He's always been one to dig his heels in when someone tries to tell him what to do."

Doc drank one cup of coffee and examined Retta, then left. True to Sam's prediction, Doc had no sooner driven away before Cap blustered into the kitchen and started joking with the kids. With Shadow added to the boisterous mix, the house became a deafening hotbed of noise.

Sam stood watching for a moment, his heart full. He loved each of these people, especially the woman doing the cooking, who made life worth living again.

A sudden thought brought a goofy grin. With everything going on with the Doolins, he couldn't go home for Christmas, which meant he'd get to celebrate with Cheyenne.

And he didn't need a script to know how that would go.

Thirty-five

"I SURE WISH I'D BROUGHT THAT BOTTLE," CAP GROUCHED, beating his chest with his one good arm. "I could sure use a swig about now."

Sam released a long-suffering sigh. "Keep it down. I said you didn't have to come, but oh no, you had to be my shadow."

"You're forgetting that I'm the one in charge here," the ranger snapped.

They'd ridden into town after dark and hid out in the church steeple where they had a good view. There had been no telegrams for either side the last time Sam had checked with Flannery before climbing up here. He wished he knew what was happening. Maybe Jared would have some news when they met in an hour.

"Hey, somebody has to keep watch on your butt," Cap replied in a gravelly voice. "Miss Cheyenne is counting on me doing that."

That was news to Sam but entirely possible. "She is, huh?"

"Yep. I think she might've taken a fancy to you, but why, I don't know. You're not easy to get along with. You got the disposition of a mangy coyote. Certainly no prize."

Movement on the far end of the street caught Sam's attention. He raised the binoculars for a look. A man drove a wagon slowly toward them. A coffin was in the back.

He nudged Cap. "Take a look."

Before he died, Heck Raines had mentioned that a man by the name of Nate Seymour bought a coffin from the undertaker and loaded it in the back of a wagon. Was this the same man? Regardless, why did anyone need to haul around a coffin after dark?

"What the hell?" Cap murmured.

"I'd like to know what's inside there. Come on. Let's go see."

"I'll go, but I ain't opening it. My heart ain't up to seeing no dead body with worms crawling out of its eyes."

They climbed down the ladder, taking two rungs at a time, and emerged from the church as the wagon rumbled by. Keeping to the shadows, they followed the man behind the Hitching Post Saloon. He set the brake and climbed down, then tapped on the back door. Tom Doolin let him in.

Sam swung up into the wagon bed. The coffin lid wasn't nailed, just lying on there.

"Get a leg on," Cap whispered.

Muffled voices reached Sam, and he knew he had to hurry. He lifted one end of the loose lid and peered inside but couldn't see anything but blackness.

The door of the saloon opened. His heart racing, Sam ducked down out of sight.

"It's a pleasure doing business with you, Lem. Both of us are gonna be rich one day."

Sam peeked through a crack in the side boards to see the driver and Lem shake hands.

"Let's get the coffin loaded so you can get warmed up," Lem said.

"I'll park behind the hotel for the night and leave out in the morning." The driver stretched. "I'm beat and half-frozen."

Lem handed him a bottle of whiskey. "This'll warm you up, Seymour."

The driver was, in fact, Nate Seymour. One piece of the puzzle slid in place.

But now, Sam was stuck. He couldn't climb out with them standing right there, and he for sure couldn't stay where he was. He put his arm across his mouth to hide the cloud of foggy breath.

"Hey, wouldya have a match?"

The slurred voice came from a man stumbling toward the two men, clutching an empty whiskey bottle. Who the hell was that?

The drunk's face was hidden in the folds of a coat, and his hat had slid down to his eyebrows.

Then Sam recognized the coat.

Cap.

Yep, the ranger was saving him.

"Get the hell out of here, you two-bit moocher. Beat it!" Lem hollered.

While their attention was on Cap, Sam scooted from the wagon and ducked behind some barrels. He'd no sooner gotten into place than men began filling the coffin with boxes. When they finished, they hammered the lid shut.

The mystery of how the ring transported the money was no longer. No one would think to look inside a coffin.

"You lose this shipment, you best run for the hills," Lem warned. "They'll kill you."

"Have I lost one yet?"

"No, but there's always a first time."

The two men said goodbye, and Seymour climbed into the wagon box and got back on the street. With Sam and Cap right behind, Seymour drove down to the same hotel where Cap had stayed. The crook stopped next to the back stairs and came around to the wagon bed. His feet crunched on the small rocks as he unfolded a tarp and threw it over the coffin. Then he opened the hotel's back door and went inside.

Time crept by. Sam and Cap huddled in the deep shadows, waiting. Surely Seymour would return to unhitch the team and take them to some shelter for the night.

Still more minutes ticked by with no sign of the man.

"I've never been so thankful for no moon. And for you, Cap. You play a good drunk. Could've fooled me."

"I spend enough time with 'em so I oughta. I knew if I didn't do something, they'd find you. I think the coast is clear."

Sam's gaze swept the alley and found no movement. "I'll climb in the back. You get in the front and drive the rig someplace out of sight."

"This is thievery, you know."

"We'll bring it back. How else are we going to nail this lid shut when we're done? We do it here, it'll wake the dead and bring out every gun in town."

"You've got a point, but what if the man comes out and finds all this gone?"

"We won't go far, and we'll work fast. Hurry, we're wasting time."

Cap got up on the seat and moved the wagon down a little, turned onto a pig trail, and parked. Darkness completely engulfed them.

Sam picked up the hammer the men had used and removed the coffin lid. He opened one of the boxes and released a low whistle.

"Well?"

"Counterfeit money. Just as we suspected." He opened the others and found the same. "Here, I'll hand these out. Stack them in some brush until we can come back and get them."

One by one, they removed the boxes and hid them, then began filling the coffin with rocks. Finally, they nailed the lid back on and threw the tarp over it.

In no time, they parked the rig where it had been and made haste to their horses.

"With luck, Seymour won't open this until he reaches his destination." Sam grinned. "His butt will be in a sling when he finds our surprise."

Cap laughed. "I wouldn't want to be in his shoes. I think we just have time to meet Mitchell. I hope he knows something."

They made their way to the back of the telegraph office and settled in.

An hour later, they were getting ready to give up when Jared showed. "Sorry to make you wait. Couldn't get away." The tall, lanky ranch hand cupped his hands, blowing on them.

"I understand." Sam noticed his weary eyes that were filled with worry. He told Jared about Seymour's wagon and the coffin but held back that they'd relieved the counterfeiter of his load. "Do you have anything new?"

"One of the bigwigs will arrive tomorrow around noon. Name's Finley Booth, but everyone calls him Pope. Several more will be with him, but I didn't catch their names."

Sam's ears perked up. He was finally going to see Pope.

Cap leaned closer. "Get ready. Tomorrow night we'll swoop in and round them up."

A look of relief crossed Jared's face. "It'll be good to get this finished and behind me."

"I don't know what time we'll hit, so be ready." Sam squeezed his shoulder. "You still have the gun I gave you?"

"Yep."

"Okay." Sam's gaze followed a rider going slowly past. The man dismounted in front of one of the other saloons. Sam turned back to Jared. "Get a good night's sleep. If things go as planned, you'll be with your family by this time tomorrow."

"Won't come too soon." Jared turned to go when a loud crash sounded and two black cats ran past them, screeching. Jared jumped, his face turning white.

Cap laid a hand on his shoulder. "Relax. It's nothing."

The ranger should talk. Even Sam's nerves were getting to him. Jared was far worse.

The man had barely disappeared before Cap turned to Sam. "Wish we had some way to let Senior know about the new developments."

"Me too, but he's already left Austin with no way to reach him."

"Dammit, we'll have to manage as best we can without him.

Let's go get the wagon, Sammy Boy. I'd sleep easier with those boxes moved."

"I know of a small cave nearby where we can stash them."

The clock read past midnight by the time they crawled into their bunks. Sam was snoring almost before his head hit the pillow. He dreamed of Cheyenne entering a church wearing a satin-and-lace wedding gown.

He hoped it was an omen.

                      ✎

A peddler ringing a bell pulled up in front of the house in a tall wagon the next morning about ten o'clock. Sam had gone into town on some mysterious errand. Something was about to happen, and he didn't want to talk about it. Cheyenne and the children were doing calisthenics. The kids ran to see the colorful wares and spinning apparatuses hanging from the sides.

"Do you have a baseball bat?" Aaron asked.

"I want a doll." Ellen jumped up and down.

Cheyenne laughed. "You must be Felix that Doc Tyler spoke of."

The man climbed down, swept his hat off his head, and curtsied deep. "Yes, I'm Felix."

"Welcome. Pardon these children. They're so anxious for Christmas." She got Aaron down from the wagon. "Tell me what goodies you have. Maybe we can haggle." Her gaze was drawn to a little stuffed monkey on a stick clutching a tambourine that would be perfect for Ellen, but she couldn't do anything while they were watching.

Felix's eyes sparkled. "For such a pretty lady, I will perform. Only for you will I do tricks."

Before she could reply, the spry man that was barely her height began doing a series of flips and somersaults, ending with a bow.

She and the kids clapped excitedly. "You're very good, Felix." She moved closer to the wagon. "What do you have for a man?"

"Does he need a watch chain?" Felix opened a box and pulled out a length of silver.

"That's nice but he has one."

Cap rode up and dismounted. "Shopping, Miss Cheyenne?"

"Just looking for now. I'm trying to find Sam something. Any ideas?"

"Not off the top of my head."

"He has lots of good stuff." Aaron picked up a harmonica and blew on it.

"I can see that. I used to have one of those," Cap answered. "Don't know what happened to it."

Ellen pouted. "He don't got any dolls."

"Honey, it's not the end of the world." Cheyenne laid a hand on her shoulder. "We can look at the mercantile."

The girl brightened. "Oh, goodie."

Felix dug around and came up with a pair of black leather gloves. "These only have a small hole in one thumb, but they're nice otherwise."

"No thank you." Cheyenne stood on her tiptoes and peered over into his pile of wares. The toes of a pair of dark-brown boots barely stuck out. Sam's were in pitiful shape, the right one had a burn, probably by a piece of hot metal.

"May I see those please?" She pointed to them.

"Yes, ma'am." Felix stood on the hub of the wheel and reached over, dusting them off. "I forgot about these. They're hand-tooled leather, but too steep for most of my customers."

Cheyenne held them, loving the buttery-soft feel of the leather. They had stars and swirls on the vamp and shaft. They seemed like something a Texas Ranger would wear. "What size are they?"

"Ten," Felix answered.

She turned to Cap. "Do you know Sam's shoe size?"

"Same as mine—ten. I know because he once had to wear my boots when his got stolen."

Her eyebrows lifted in question.

"It's a long story."

Not surprising. None of his stories were of the short variety.

Felix grinned. "I can give you a good deal, ma'am."

"Actually, I wonder about a trade. I make woven baskets, and they would add a lot to your stock. You'd have no trouble selling them. Would you like to see them?"

"Sure. Doc told me about them, and that's the main reason I came out this way. Normally, I only go out a few miles from town."

"Me and kids will go get them." Cap got Aaron and Ellen and they went into the house.

"While they're gone," Cheyenne said quietly, "can you put that little monkey and harmonica aside, Felix? I know I want them, but I don't want the kids to see."

"I understand." He stuck the two items out of sight.

Cap and the children returned with the baskets. Cheyenne set all twelve of them in a line. "They're various sizes, as you can see, and they're made of willow from the Canadian River here."

Felix looked them over. "My customers will snap these up."

"Before we get down to business, Cap, would you please take Aaron and Ellen back to the house? I hate leaving Retta alone so long."

Cap winked at her and grinned. "I don't mind one bit. You just take your time."

When they were out of earshot, Cheyenne swung around to Felix. "Now, let's see what we can swing so it's fair to both of us."

They haggled back and forth and finally agreed on an even swap plus five more baskets by Saturday and a ham from the smokehouse for Felix's Christmas dinner.

Very pleased with the arrangement, she watched him drive off, then gathered up the boots and the kids' gifts and took them to her little house.

When she opened the door and saw the bearskin rug still on the floor, memories flooded over her, and she went weak. Sam's silk ascot lay on a chair. Lifting it, she drew the smoothness across her face and down her throat. Remembering. Savoring.

A horse sounded outside, and she glanced through the curtain to see Sam riding in. Hurriedly stuffing the boots under the bed, she went to meet him.

The scent of smoke lingering on his clothes, he drew her against him for a kiss. "I missed you."

"The peddler came and took my baskets plus he wants five more on Saturday. I have enough willow left if I can find the time."

"I'll help you, and it won't take long, plus Aaron's pretty good too." He brushed a knuckle across her cheek. "I wish we could hide out in your house for a week. I'd keep you naked, moaning my name and begging for more."

"I like that idea, cowboy." She slid her hands inside his coat and placed a palm over his heart. "Unfortunately, this is Christmas, and we have lots to do."

"More's the pity." His smile faded, and uneasiness darkened his eyes. "Cap and I have to go into town tonight. We're going to arrest the Doolins."

Cheyenne gasped. "By yourself?"

"Can't be helped. The big bosses of the ring will be here, and it's our one chance to get them all. We think we can enlist a few of the townsfolk."

"What about the sheriff?"

"He's working with the Doolins."

"I don't like this, Sam. I don't like it one bit. What if you get wounded?" Or killed. But she wouldn't say those words out loud. She wouldn't even let herself think them. "I could go along. I'm not real good with a rifle far away, but I can hit a close target."

"No. I need to do my job without worrying that something will happen to you."

"But you need help."

Ellen ran from the house. "Mr. Sam!"

They broke apart, and he put on a smile. "How's my girl?"

"The peddler took our baskets an' I think he gave Miss Ann some money."

"That's what I'm hearing. You and Aaron get fifty cents apiece for helping."

"Really?" Aaron asked, hurrying up.

"For true." Sam pulled some coins from his pocket and dropped two quarters into each of their palms.

"We're rich!" Ellen hollered.

"Yes, you are, honey." Cheyenne laid a hand on the sweet girl's back. "You and Aaron are rich."

"Yeah, 'cept we don't have a daddy." Aaron stared hard at the ground, looking determined not to cry.

Sam met Cheyenne's gaze, and she knew how badly he wanted to tell them. But if he did and Jared got killed tonight, he'd never forgive himself. From what she could see, they'd be lucky if any of them emerged in one piece. Her knees shook, and she steadied herself with the Appaloosa's firm neck.

Her whole world would crumble into ruin to lose Sam.

Thirty-six

THE FIRE IN THE POTBELLY STOVE CREATED A WELCOME SOUND when Sam and Cap converged in the bunkhouse after returning from the morning scouting in town. It had to be around noon, and Sam's stomach was letting him know.

"Did you happen to see any movement from where you were, Sam?" Cap massaged his shoulder, then held his hands out to the heat. "I noticed a lot of horses and wagons coming and going at a building behind the Hitching Post."

"I'm glad we split up and went both high and low. The Doolins came from the saloon with two gents in fancy clothes. One had to be Finley Booth, a.k.a. Pope." Sam turned a chair around and straddled it. "I got close enough to hear him say he'd be riding out at first light. He seemed skittish, worried that the rangers were right behind him, closing in. He mentioned Senior's name and seemed to have a healthy respect for him."

Cap chuckled. "He'd better. Senior ain't to be messed with. I don't know why I drew the long straw and got the church steeple. I think you cheated."

"You'd gripe if you were going to be hung with a new rope. Tonight, we'll switch. Does that make you happy?" Sam shook his head. "It doesn't really matter to me one way or the other. I'm just helping out if you recall."

"Stop pretending that you're not a ranger. You're as much as I am." Cap turned around to warm his backside. "It puzzles me why Senior and more rangers haven't shown up. Makes me nervous."

"Wish we could wait a day or two." Sam would like to prepare more.

"Can't lollygag around with them about to ride out. We gotta do this while the big bosses are here, or they'll go underground, and we'll never find 'em. It's gotta be tonight." Cap lapsed into silence for a moment in thought. "I'm bringing some lengths of rope so we'll have something to tie them up with."

"Good idea. I was thinking about asking Flannery to help out." Sam rubbed his face that felt odd without his big beard. "Trouble is, he's not that anxious to get himself shot."

"Well, neither are we, but it's our job if it comes right down to it."

Silence filled the room. Outside, Shadow was running with the kids and barking to beat all. Sam loved the sound of the children's laughter.

"Cheyenne asked to come," he said quietly. "I told her no, but I'm not that sure she listened."

"Hell, you gotta make her listen." Cap sat at the table.

"I know." Sam sighed. "Not sure she'd take well to me tying her up though. I tried that once."

They wound up the discussion and called the kids into the bunkhouse. Sam needed some normal to settle his nerves. The uncertainty of the night hung over him like a heavy blanket.

Cap pulled a sheet of paper off his bed and thrust it into Aaron's hand. "Read these lines and memorize them. You'll be Joseph and Ellen will be Mary."

"Hark! Here come some shepherds and wise men." Aaron stopped. "What does hark mean, Mr. Cap?"

"It means listen up, Mary."

"Oh." The boy rolled his shoulders and started again. "Listen up, Mary. Our baby is real special. He's got a star hanging over his manger here, and I can hear a bunch of people bringing gifts. Jesus has a mighty big job to do when he gets big."

Sam rolled his eyes. This is what he got for letting Cap write the play.

"When do I get to talk?" Ellen pouted.

"Right here, sis." Aaron pointed to the paper. "Our little baby will bring salvation to the whole world."

Sam got his pencil out and tweaked some of the lines, and they worked with the kids until Cheyenne called them in for lunch.

The hours passed, and as the evening shadows grew, his gut began to twist and spin like a man-killing bronc.

So much could go wrong. Life and death seemed to swing like a giant pendulum.

∽

Before Sam was ready, it was time to saddle the horses. He slid his rifle in the scabbard, then stood with Cheyenne. Tears gathered in her beautiful green eyes. "Try not to worry. Have faith that we'll be back none the worse for wear and the counterfeiting gang will be behind bars."

The most uncertainty surrounded Jared Mitchell and surviving this mess. A hundred things could go wrong there.

"I can't help it. There are just the two of you against so many. Can't you wait?"

He held her tight, rubbing her back. "No, it has to be tonight."

"I have a bad feeling."

"It's just nerves, Chey. Nothing more. Never doubt my love for you. When fear tries to take hold, think about the life we'll make for ourselves when all this is over." He poured his heart and soul in his kiss, absorbing all her goodness, her sweetness, her kind spirit.

She wound her arms around his waist with a fierce strength, returning all he was giving. A little moan slipped from her mouth.

Damn, he wished he didn't have to go. But it wouldn't end until they finished the job.

When they broke apart, she inhaled a deep breath and stepped back. The night breeze lifted a tendril of russet hair, laying it across her eyes. She brushed it aside. "I won't feel relief until you come back." Her voice broke. "Be safe, cowboy."

"It's time to mount up, Sammy boy," Cap said quietly, already in the saddle.

With one more longing glance at his pretty lady, Sam silently put a foot in the stirrup and swung onto Rio. Then without a backward look, he started toward his fate. Whether they'd win or lose remained to be seen. It was too late to change anything.

Two against a small army wasn't the best of odds. But he'd been there before.

≈⊱

At the edge of town, Sam and Cap turned into the dark alley that ran behind the telegraph office and tied their horses. They climbed the outside stairs and tapped on the door of the living quarters.

Mrs. Flannery let them in. "Duggan is expecting you."

He rose from a chair. "You got a telegram." He reached for a slip of paper on a nearby table and handed it to Sam.

It was from Sam's father. "Senior says he's riding hard but doesn't know if he'll get here in time. I know if it's at all possible, he'll make it."

Cap turned to Flannery. "I wonder if we could get your help. No close fighting. If we could get you into the church's bell tower with a rifle, you could pick off a few from up there. That's all we're asking. Sam and I will handle the rest."

Flannery exchanged a glance with his wife and nodded. "Let me get my coat."

Red and green streamers hung from a pole, the gay Christmas cheer a bit out of place on this night when lives were on the line. All six of the saloons were in full swing with music and laughter blaring from each. Occasional gunfire punctuated the noise, a reminder that Tascosa was still a wild and dangerous town.

A light burned in Sheriff Jim Winslow's office. A reminder that they'd have one more to bring down before the night was over.

They helped Flannery into the bell tower, then strode to the alley behind the Hitching Post, watching from behind the barrels where Sam had sought cover before. Nothing moved. A while later, a dancehall girl came sashaying out with what looked like a young patron and began kissing and hugging. The more worked up the cowboy got, the more her hands went to searching his pockets.

Cap rolled his eyes and murmured, "Poor guy don't stand a chance."

The lovebirds were interrupted by a wagon rolling toward them and went back inside.

"Who's this?" Sam squinted but couldn't make out the driver.

The wagon stopped, and a man jumped down. A sheriff's tin star caught what light streamed from the door when he opened it.

Jim Winslow.

He went inside and emerged with a handcart loaded with large boxes. While Winslow stacked them in the wagon, the guard that was always in front of the locked door came out with another handcart full of the same.

"I think they're packing up," Sam whispered.

Cap nodded. "Seems you're right. If we don't get 'em before they scurry underground like rats, we never will."

The two finished the loading, left the carts by the door, got in the wagon, and left.

No guard. It seemed an open invitation.

Sam stood. "I'm going inside. You follow the wagon." He hurried across the alley to the door and slipped inside.

He was in what appeared to be a dark storeroom with kegs of beer and boxes of liquor. Another door beckoned. He opened it to find himself inside the room that had once housed the printing press. It was swept clean. Not so much as a scrap of paper or ink stain on the floor.

The Doolins had flown the coop.

More concerning than that was Jared Mitchell. Where was he? Had they killed him?

Guilt sitting heavy, Sam spun around, then went back out. He'd talked Jared into staying. Had he also talked him into his execution?

He had to find him and fast. Out in the deserted alley, he gripped his rifle, glancing first one way, then another. What about one of the hotels? That seemed the logical place for the big bosses to stay. They wouldn't stay in that dump of the Doolins. But then the hotels were pretty much run-down too. Needing to move, he raced through the dark alley on foot to the yellow hotel where Cap's room had been. Two horses were tied in the back.

Sam crept up the back stairs to the room down from Cap's where the mean-looking fellow came out and surprised them a few nights ago, then later almost certainly shot Cap.

Loud voices drifted from inside, and something slammed against the wall.

"I know them rangers are around here someplace and waitin' to grab hold of us," said one man. "I ain't goin' to prison for the Doolins."

"You will if they say," barked another. "They pay us well enough."

"I won't die for them, and that's a pure and simple fact. I shot that one ranger. They say he's dead, but I ain't seen a grave yet. I think he's alive and he's out to get me."

"Get hold of yourself. This ain't helping." A chair scooted on the floor. "Right now, we gotta get moving. You heard Ford Doolin. We'll all be out of here by daylight."

"I'll be glad to be shed of this town."

Footsteps struck the floor, and the knob turned. Sam hurried to the stairs and made it down two steps before the door opened. That was close.

Back in the night air, Sam moved silently to cover where he had a good view of the stairs. He'd stick to these two like prickly pear. He didn't have to wait but a few seconds. They came out and got on their horses. Sam wished for Rio, tied at the telegraph office. If the two outlaws rode out of town, he'd have to get the Appaloosa and probably lose them in the bargain.

The men rode at a slow pace, allowing him to keep up. Knowing they wanted to separate themselves from the Doolins must account for their lack of enthusiasm. Sam chuckled low.

Tascosa was laid out in no particular order with only the one main street. Adobe houses were stuck willy-nilly amid the saloons and whorehouses, and a good many were vacated by owners leaving town for greener pastures.

Not far away, the two pulled up at a house with a lamp burning in the window. The dwelling, half-hidden by mesquite trees and a large cottonwood, would've been difficult to find if he'd not been led here. The wagon the sheriff had driven was parked in front. Cap had to be somewhere close.

The two men stopped to pet a large dog before Tom Doolin opened the door and said something, ushering them inside.

The animal changed things. Although the wind was blowing from the direction Sam faced, the dog would pick up his scent sooner or later and alert the group.

Plus, they wouldn't be able to bar the doors, keeping everyone inside. Shit!

A slight rustle of brush announced a visitor, and Sam turned to see Cap. "We have a dilemma," Sam whispered.

"You ain't whistling Dixie."

The dog perked its ears and ran toward them, barking.

"Cap?" Sam looked around for a stick or someplace to run. He measured the distance to the low branches of the cottonwood a hundred feet away and took off with Cap right behind.

They clutched their rifles as they ran, Sam praying to reach the tree.

Breathing hard, he handed his rifle to Cap then grabbed the rough bark, bending a nail back, and scrambled up to a bare branch.

"Here, Sam, take these rifles." Cap tried to keep his voice down, though it held urgency.

Sam grabbed them then tried to pull the ranger up to his limb.

The dog caught the seat of Cap's trousers, but with Sam's help, he managed to make it up. The dog jumped at the base, barking its fool head off.

The door of the house opened, and Lem Doolin stepped out to holler, "Bruiser! That's enough. Come here!"

Bruiser turned to look, then resumed barking.

Thank goodness for the darkness that hid them perching on the branch like a couple of buzzards. Lem called again, and Bruiser stopped the attack and lay down. Lem closed the door. The dog cocked his head to the side and looked up at them.

The ranger raised a length of rope. "Make friends with the blasted thing. I'll put this rope around his neck and tie him up at a saloon."

Make friends? Sam glanced down at the sharp teeth of the animal. Yeah, sure.

"How's this? Give me the rope and *you* make friends."

"It's my rope, Sammy boy," Cap pointed out. "Just talk to him real gentle. You know, like you talk to Miss Cheyenne."

Sam sighed. Seeing no choice, he began to sweet-talk a dog that wanted to eat them, one bone at a time. "Hey there. We need you be a good dog and let us down. Want to go over to the saloon and let the pretty women pet you and give you treats? They'll bend over and you can look down their dress. Huh? That's a good dog. Nice doggie."

He'd never felt so ridiculous in his life. However, this was very important.

The door opened again, and a woman in a hat and expensive dress emerged with a rifle.

Thirty-seven

SAM MADE HIMSELF AS SMALL AS HE COULD. WHO WAS SHE, AND why was she dressed like a woman of wealth and carrying a rifle? Nothing made sense. Had she spotted them in the cottonwood?

A man joined her, kissing her cheek. He walked with her to the wagon and helped her onto the seat. They were talking too low to hear. Suddenly, the man whistled, and Bruiser bounded over and into the wagon. She turned the wagon around and drove off with the contents from the gang's room at the saloon in the back.

The man glanced up at the sky, and light from inside the house erased the shadows from his face.

Sheriff Winslow.

He turned and went back inside the house.

"Who was that woman, Cap?"

"Your guess is as good as mine. I don't think she's his wife, though. Likely a mistress."

Sam grunted. "Now that the dog's gone, we'd best get on with rounding this gang up before she comes back. We may not be through with Bruiser."

Climbing down was easier than going up, and they were soon on the ground.

Cap patted the seat of his britches where the dog had nabbed him. "I don't think they're torn."

"That's good. Come on."

They ducked low and raced for the house. Each took a window. Sam removed his hat and eased up to peer inside. The men sat around a table, talking and drinking.

Everything seemed calm until one of the two men from the hotel leaped to his feet, gun drawn. "I want my share, and I want it now. Ain't gonna be no waitin' to get caught."

Tom Doolin let out a curse. Calling the man every name in the book, he reached into a pouch and threw some bills in his face, half of which landed on the floor. "Take that, and if I ever see you again, I'll blow your head off."

"Suits me fine!" The disgruntled member slid his gun into the holster, then dropped to the floor, picking up his money.

When he emerged from the house, Cap struck him on the head with the butt of his weapon. Sam helped drag him into the brush and tied his hands with some of the rope Cap had brought.

"That should do him for now." Sam stood. "We'd best get back. Have you seen Jared?"

"Nope. Kinda strange. Maybe they're keeping him in a back room."

Or maybe they had killed him.

Sam shoved the thought away. No sense speculating. Spying two barrels the gang had probably used for seating, he rolled them in front of the door, blocking the escape, then went around back. Cap had already slid a heavy piece of wood through the handle to bar it shut.

Now that the gang was contained, Cap returned to the front. Sam stayed in back.

Cap cupped his hands around his mouth. "You're surrounded by the Texas Rangers and you're all under arrest. If you do not surrender peacefully, you will be shot."

"You'll never take us!" one of them hollered.

Glass broke in the windows and guns erupted, blasting away at them. Cap and Sam returned fire. An occasional yell or curse told them when a bullet or flying glass had struck home.

Then out of the blue, the gang stopped firing, and the silence became deafening.

A voice hollered, "You rangers still out there? Better stay on your toes. We're not near ready to give up!"

Fear raced up Sam's spine. They were planning something. But what?

Minutes crept by. Nothing moved inside the house, and that made him nervous. Even with the doors barred, they could still sneak out the windows. The outlaws were far from bottled up.

Cap's gravelly reply split the air. "We're still here. Got all the time in the world for you boys. I'm whittling a toy for a child's Christmas. Might have a whole slew of 'em before we're through."

"You trying to take Saint Nick's job?"

"Yep. Heard he needs some help."

A bit more back-and-forth jawing and the conversation died out. Sam kept his eyes glued to the door and windows. Waiting. A black cat strolled by and disappeared into the brush. There was no sign of the woman returning with Bruiser. Who the hell was she? It bothered Sam that he didn't know. Something whispered that her identity was important. Could she be the woman who'd ridden out behind Tom Doolin when Beth was killed?

His thoughts whirled, and the wait played on his nerves. He thought of Jared Mitchell. If the husband and father died, his blood would be on Sam's hands. The faces of Retta and the kids swam in his mind. So much stood at stake.

Maybe he should've let Chey come. She'd have been one more than they had.

Dammit, what was going on inside the house? This was crazy.

Before he could do any more thinking, the door facing Sam blew off, and men poured out like rats. A similar explosion in front told him Cap had his hands full as well. Sam raised his sidearm and fired as they ran past. Some he wounded and others escaped.

Men on horseback swarmed over him, and his stomach twisted. It was over. They'd lost.

Everything they'd planned had blown up in their faces.

The best he could do now was try to deflect a kill shot.

He had to fall back. His head was screaming to find a place to hide. But when he whirled, he came face-to-face with a gunman.

Thirty-eight

CHEYENNE PACED THE LENGTH OF THE KITCHEN, HER thoughts on the man she loved.

Somewhere out in the cold darkness, Sam was battling the Doolins with everything he had. They'd killed his wife, and now they wanted him dead as well. Her heart ached for all he'd been through.

Shadow also seemed restless from her spot on an old blanket. She raised her head at each little noise.

A child's cry came from the bedroom. She went to see which one and try to soothe their fears. Shadow padded right behind her.

The low lamp cast a soft glow over the room. Thank goodness Loretta hadn't woken. Cheyenne followed the sobs to Ellen. She touched the child's back. "What's wrong, honey?"

"I'm scared."

"What made you scared?"

"I dreamed a bad man was here, and I tried to run, but I couldn't."

Cheyenne picked her up and carried her to the parlor, taking a seat in the rocker. "There's no bad men here. It was just a nightmare."

Ellen snuggled against her. "Sometimes I think they'll get me."

"Only they can't." Cheyenne set the rocker in motion. "I sometimes have bad dreams too and my heart pounds when they wake me."

"I miss my daddy a whole, whole bunch."

They talked for a little bit about Jared, and Ellen remembered some funny things about him that lightened her mood. Cheyenne sent up a prayer that Jared would survive this night and be here for breakfast. The kids desperately needed him. And so did Retta.

"Would you sing me a song?" Ellen asked.

Outside, the wind picked up and rattled the window. Sam and Cap were out there in it—maybe hurt bad. A song would help Cheyenne's nerves as well.

"Okay. Let me think of one." "Away in a Manger" sprang to mind, and she softly began to sing.

Before long, Ellen had drifted off. Cheyenne carried her back to bed and put her next to Aaron, tucking covers around them.

Everything once again peaceful, she resumed her vigil in the kitchen with the dog that seemed to sense something wasn't right. Putting water for hot tea on to heat, she glanced through the curtains. For a moment, she thought she heard riders, then decided it was only the wind.

She'd faced endless nights before, but this one promised to be the longest of her life.

∞

Survival instincts kicked in, and Sam tightened his finger on the gun's trigger, staring into the muted face of the man blocking him.

"It's me, son. Don't shoot."

The voice sounded like his dad's. Was it possible?

"Dad? Is it really you?"

"Sorry I'm late to the party. I brought some men with me, and it looks like just in time."

"I'll say. I thought we were done for."

"Time to get busy."

Chaos and the deafening noise of horses and men around him, Sam threw himself in front of a fleeing outlaw, relieving him of his weapon. Working in tandem, another ranger grabbed the man's arms, binding his wrists.

Sam charged into the house. Tom Doolin was his. He'd waited an entire year.

But the smoking ruins yielded no one. Coughing, he strode out into the clear air, and that's when he saw him. Tom jerked a ranger from a horse and threw himself into the saddle.

"Stop!" Sam raised his gun, but just as he fired, someone grabbed his arm.

"Legend, I can't let you shoot my brother!" Ford bellowed, hanging on.

"Turn loose or you die!" Sam gasped for air, the blood pumping through his veins. He couldn't let Tom get away. He jerked free, but when he looked again, he saw no trace of Tom Doolin.

Sam held his gun to Ford's temple. "Where is he going?"

"You'll be too late to do anything." Ford's gloating smile made Sam's blood boil.

"This is the last time I'll ask. Where is he going? I promise you'll hang if you don't tell me."

"You were followed today, Legend. He's after your woman, and it's too late for you."

Oh God! Sam's stomach turned to lead. Tom was riding hard for the Ronans and Cheyenne. He had to stop him. This couldn't end like it had for Beth. If he did nothing else, he had to make sure Cheyenne lived.

Sam leaped onto the first horse and spurred it into a gallop. His pounding heart was about to fly out of his chest, and he gasped for air, his lungs starved.

Freezing bits of sleet stung his face, feeling like the sharp tip of a knife poking his skin.

Leaning over the long mane, he urged the horse full-out, watching the ground fly past. Only to Sam, they were moving so slow. He prayed that Tom would get lost in the dark and couldn't find the way. Or that his horse would pull up. Something. Anything to slow him.

He could not lose her. She was his sun and moon. His guiding star. His last love.

It was crazy, but the horse seemed to sense his urgency and kept going faster and faster.

Cheyenne had no part in this. She shouldn't have to pay for his mistake. Tears clouded his vision, and he knew if he lost her, he'd stop living.

❧

The kitchen door suddenly rattled and Cheyenne froze, her teacup at her mouth.

Before she could rise from the chair, a great force shattered the door and frozen air rushed in. Her heart pounding, she stared at a stranger. "Who are you? What do you want?"

"You Sam Legend's woman?"

"I am, but that's none—"

He grabbed her up. "You're coming with me."

The hardness of his eyes and the grate of his voice told her that arguing, reasoning, or fighting would be useless. She tried to jerk free to no avail and raised her chin. "I'll come, but hurting me will gain you nothing." She reached for her coat that she'd lain on the chair so it'd be handy when Sam returned.

"No time for that."

"I will take my coat." She slid her arms into the sleeves. "Let me guess. You're one of the Doolins."

He was young, so it wasn't the father. Probably Tom. He was the one with the grudge.

"You're nosy." He pulled her out the door, then paused. The faint sound of thundering hooves striking the ground reached them.

Sam. It had to be. How could she help him? How could she help herself? Sound traveled a ways in the countryside and he could still be a mile away.

Buy time.

A glance showed nothing to use to hit her abductor with. But she had her knife in her pocket. That would work, but to feel the blade sliding into muscle and tissue again, to take another life, would send her backward. Still... She tightened her jaw. If it came to that, she would.

Whichever Doolin it was stopped. "Back in the house."

She slipped a hand into her pocket and pulled the knife from its sheath. "Rot in hell!"

In one swift move, she yanked out the weapon and plunged it into him. She'd aimed for his chest or belly, but he turned, and it slid into his side. Not deep enough though, since it had to penetrate his thick coat.

With a guttural growl, Doolin released a curse, snatching the knife away. He drew back a hand. The force of the blow drove her face to the side. "You should not have done that."

He shoved her into the kitchen and into a chair. Ripping off her coat, he tore a length from her petticoat and bound her tight. A dish towel served as a gag. In one flourish, he whipped the tablecloth off the table. Then he drew matches from his pocket and made a pile, then spied a candle on the windowsill. He whacked the candle low and set it in the middle of the matches. Cold fear rushed up her spine. She could do nothing as he struck a match and lit it.

Cheyenne froze. He meant to burn the house down. Retta and the kids!

Doolin was barely out of the door before she desperately started to work at her bindings. She thought it odd that he took her coat with him.

Why?

Then it hit her. Tom Doolin had tricked Sam before by making him think Beth rode on the horse behind him. Except she hadn't seen a woman. Had she kept out of sight?

Chills raced through her.

The ruse had given them time to kill poor Beth. Only this time, it was to let the short candle burn down.

And kill her in addition to Loretta and the kids.

Thirty-nine

SAM PULLED INTO THE RONANS', BREATHING HARD, HIS HEART thudding against his ribs, as if he'd been running a footrace. Tom Doolin burst past with what appeared to be a woman on the back of the horse, wearing Cheyenne's coat.

Dear God, he had her. He'd kill her just like he'd done Beth. He had to catch Tom.

Yanking the reins to the left, Sam took out after him. But ten lengths in pursuit, he stopped, realizing what Doolin was doing. He'd not make the same mistake again. Let the man go for now.

He pulled up and turned around, praying to find Chey alive. His stomach did a sickening twist with the possibility that his efforts would be in vain.

The horse hadn't even come to a stop yet before Sam leaped off and burst into the kitchen. Cheyenne gave an excited jerk, trying to talk. He quickly took the gag from her mouth and blew the candle out. It had burned down to a fraction of an inch from the matches.

After he made quick work of untying her, Cheyenne threw her arms around his neck, crying.

Trembling, he held her tight. "I almost fell for his trick again. I could've lost you too."

"But you didn't." Tear droplets poised on the tips of her long lashes. "Go after him, Sam. Don't let him get away. He can't have gone far."

"I will." He kissed her and turned for the door.

"Sam, I stabbed him. I don't know how bad, but he should be losing blood."

"You did good, Chey." He raced out into the cold, thankful he'd listened to his gut.

The horse was young, and he was grateful for those strong legs carrying him across the frozen ground. It appeared that Tom was heading south toward Tascosa, and farther still was the new town of Lubbock, even though that was a far piece. There were trading posts scattered all over. The one at Yellow House Canyon was still operating. Tom might have that in his sights.

But a few miles from the Ronan house, Sam spied him just ahead, limping along, the fake woman still on the back. His horse had either a thrown a shoe, picked up a rock, or turned up lame. As Sam approached, Tom leaped off and took cover.

A gunshot rang out from the blackness, the bullet missing.

A muttered curse left Sam's lips. He quickly dismounted and hid in a gully that ran alongside the road. Best he could judge, the outlaw was about fifty feet away—unless he was on the move, which was entirely possible. Sam had no choice but try to flush him out before Tom decided to make a run.

As silently as he could manage, Sam crept through the tangled thorns and dead sage. A circle should take him pretty close.

A night creature scurried out in front, startling him. His nerves were stretched thin. Each movement, each breath could be his last, and he'd never see Chey again. Extra caution cost time though.

Another shot rang out, which told him two things. Tom hadn't moved. And he was jumpier than frog legs in a hot skillet.

Slow and steady, Sam gripped his sidearm and made his circle. Finally, he saw his nemesis a few yards ahead. His breathing shallow, he took in the scene. Tom was hunched over, his coat clutched around him. Whether from nerves or from the cold, he was shivering.

Sam's eyes narrowed. Judgment day had arrived. Closing the gap a little more, he barked, "Toss your weapon. Now!"

Tom whirled, shooting. The bullet would've struck Sam if he hadn't ducked.

"It's over, Doolin. I'm taking you to jail."

The man tried to fire again but his gun jammed. Throwing it down, he ran at Sam, tackling him. Sam's Colt flew into the blackness. They traded blows, then Sam flipped Tom over his head. Tom landed with a thud on the frozen ground. He quickly got to his feet and came again, ramming Sam with his head, then jerked a knife from his boot and slashed the air.

"All this time I didn't know you were Fletcher. You pulled the wool over my eyes," Tom said, wincing. "You must've gotten a good laugh."

"Nothing in regard to you is the least bit funny." Sam leaped back to avoid the sharp blade. "You killed my wife. I'm glad for a chance to get her justice."

When Tom danced a fraction too close, Sam grabbed his knife hand and relieved him of the weapon, tossing it away. Seizing advantage of the turn in the situation, Sam sent a fist into Tom's stomach. Spit flew, and the outlaw doubled over.

An uppercut finished him off.

His breath coming in gasps, Sam wiped blood from his mouth. "Had enough?"

Tom lay there, winded. "You might have me, but you don't have Pope. She's the brains of this outfit, you know."

Pope was a woman?

Sam's head reeled. All this time they were looking for a man. But Heck Rains had sensed something off with Pope. He'd said the man had a funny voice. If that was her, she'd worn men's clothing several different times. Still…

"Finley Booth doesn't much sound like a woman to me. I think you're up to your old tricks. Get up, Doolin." Sam grabbed his Colt from the ground and held it on Tom as he slowly got to his feet, laughing.

"Pope liked dressing as a man. Too bad she's beyond your reach." Hoots of laughter filled the air.

"You might want to think again. The Texas Rangers' reach is mighty long." And now that they knew who they were looking for, finding her would be easier. Sam didn't know why outlaws always thought they were so much smarter. "Let's go."

"I think my horse threw a shoe."

"Then I reckon you'll walk."

"It's probably eight miles or so, Legend."

"Sit down and don't move, or I'll shoot you." Sam put Tom where he could he see him and lifted the horse's leg that it was favoring. Sure enough, the shoe was missing.

"Told you so, Mr. Big Shot," Tom sneered.

"Get in the saddle. We'll walk it to town."

Once Tom was seated, Sam tied his hands tight to the pommel, then keeping a firm hand on the reins, he climbed onto his horse. "Keep quiet or I'll gag you."

The trip was slow and silent for the most part. About halfway there, Tom felt the need to explain. "I never would've bothered your wife if you hadn't dogged me so hard. Every time I turned around, you were right there."

"I was doing my job. Beth had no part in any of that."

"Yeah, but you loved her, and I had to hurt you bad. It was the only way to stop you."

Sam wasn't about to let him know losing Beth had destroyed his life. And Tom wasn't happy to stop there. He'd tried to take Cheyenne tonight. "It'd be best to shut up while you can," Sam warned. He didn't know if he could stop himself if he lit into Tom Doolin.

The wind seemed to drop another ten degrees, and Sam was near frozen by the time they reached Tascosa.

His father rode toward them. "I didn't know where you went. Looks like it turned out well."

"Tom went after Cheyenne and would've killed her if I hadn't seen him riding away." Sam leaned on the pommel. "Where are you putting the gang?"

"We built a cage in the Painted Pony. We arrested the sheriff too."

"Good, he was crooked." Sam leaned from the saddle. "Dad, the ringleader—"

Just then Tom spurred the horse but didn't get far seeing as how Sam had wrapped the reins around his hand. "Try that again, and I'll chain you up outside," he growled.

Tom Doolin shrugged. "Worth chancing."

Senior waved another ranger over and asked him to take charge of Tom. Sam gladly relinquished the horse's reins. He thought Tom had lost his swagger when the ranger led him off to the cage. At least some of it.

"Dad, the ringleader that we want so bad is a woman named Finley Booth but uses the alias of Pope. She's been posing as a man, which is why she's so hard to catch."

"Well, I'll be damned!" Senior rubbed his jaw. "I never would've guessed."

"I saw her earlier tonight in a fancy dress at the Doolin house. She rode off with the printing press and a dog." Sam's horse side-stepped and snorted. "We've got to find her. Tom tried to say she'd left town, but I'm not buying that." He cast a glance down the street. "Either in pants or a dress, I'm sure she's around here someplace."

"I'll get the men busy canvassing the hotels."

"Dad, I've been thinking. A woman like her would probably choose a rooming house. Just a hunch."

Senior called one of the rangers over and told him to start a search, then moved his horse close enough to squeeze Sam's shoulder. "You did real good, Son."

"Thanks, Dad. Just doing my job." Sam paused. "Any sign of Jared Mitchell?"

"Nope. I've been looking for him."

"The Doolins and their henchmen might've killed him." God help them if they had. Sam would make sure they paid. Hopefully at the end of a rope.

"We haven't found his body. Is there any other place they might've hidden out?"

"Jared mentioned a house outside of town, but they always blindfolded him, so he didn't even know what direction it was." Sam stared toward the Painted Pony. "Maybe we can get one of the gang to talk. I have to find him, Dad."

"We will. But first is locating that woman." Loud voices drew Senior's sharp eyes. Someone seemed to be objecting to being arrested.

Sheriff Winslow was trying to jerk away from a ranger. "I'm the sheriff of this town, and you have no right to ride in here and arrest me."

"Sir, you're going to jail," the ranger said calmly. "Easy or hard. Take your pick."

"I'll have your job!" Winslow yelled.

"Yes, sir, I believe you might try. But for now, you'd best get through that door," the ranger answered. "If not, I'll call for help."

Winslow stared at a large man with a badge walking toward him. The ranger had to stand around six eight or so. Evidently seeing he was no match, the former sheriff lost his bravado. Sam chuckled. The bigger ego they had, the harder they fell. But they all did fall at some point.

Senior swung back. "Your friend Mitchell might have to wait until we get the woman."

Even Sam had to admit that Jared was probably dead. But telling Retta would kill him. Right here at Christmas. "I have a little more to do here before I ride home. The bunkhouse is open if you need it, Dad."

Senior scrubbed his weary face. "A bed sounds good. I've been on the move since yesterday, but I doubt I can get any rest for a while yet. We've got to find Finley Booth."

"Well, if you can, you know where to come."

The senior Legend started to turn away and stopped. "That telegraph man Flannery was a big help tonight. Glad you recruited him."

"He didn't much want to get involved, but he came through for us."

"That he did."

A fog had set in, dropping visibility and enshrouding the buildings in a misty-white veil that looked downright spooky.

"I'm going to question Tom Doolin and see if we get some information from him." Sam gave a two-fingered salute, and they parted ways.

He took his borrowed horse to the livery and turned toward the Painted Pony. His boots resounded on a short piece of boardwalk in time with the rhythm of his heartbeat. Right now was probably the quietest the town had ever been, and it gave him the willies. But when he entered the saloon, the like of cussing that greeted him blistered his ears.

Sam approached the ranger guarding the outlaws. "I need a word with Tom Doolin. Got a place where I can question him?"

"A storeroom in back should work." The ranger pulled out a key and turned.

In moments, Sam again stood face-to-face with a sullen Doolin. "Handcuff him."

"I got nothing to say," Tom spat. "Put me back."

"Scared of me?" Sam eyed him narrowly. "Afraid of what I'll do?"

Doolin spat on the floor. "Wouldn't put it past you to kill me."

"Aw, not before the first dance," Sam answered smoothly, pushing Tom toward the storeroom.

Inside, Sam lit the lamp and motioned to the only chair. "Sit."

The sullen man sank into the chair in a slouch, his glare boring a hole in the ranger. Sam was silent for at least a full minute and made Tom fidget.

"Whatcha waitin' for? I'm missing my beauty sleep."

Sam leaned against a wall and stuck a match stem in the corner of his mouth. "I'm trying to figure out why you turned rotten. Maybe it was your daddy's influence. Or maybe you just have the devil inside you."

"You always thought you was better than everybody else, with all your money and that big ranch," Tom sneered. "It was easy to hate you. I wanted to take everything you had."

If he only knew how close he'd come. Good thing he didn't. Knowing how much Sam had suffered would give Tom fuel.

Pushing away from the wall with lightning speed, Sam grabbed Tom's throat, knocking the chair over. "Where's Jared Mitchell? What did you do with him?"

Tom's strangled laugh filled the room. "So, that's what this is about?"

"I made a promise to his two kids. Did you kill him?"

More laughter, then Tom spat in Sam's face. "Figure it out for yourself, *lawman*."

Before Sam could stop himself, he slammed a fist into Tom's face. Blood flew. But the jackass only wiped his bloodied mouth, grinning. Nothing was going to make him talk. Finally, Sam took him back to the make-do jail.

Leaving the saloon, he went after poor Rio, left in the cold for so long.

Sam ran a hand down his neck. "Hey, boy. Let's see about warming you up a little."

The horse shook his head and snorted.

McCormick's Livery had room for one more, so Sam left him while he did some scouting. He wouldn't leave town without meeting up with Cap and joining the other group of rangers looking for Pope. They'd only begun to search the two hotels and various rooming houses stuck in here and there.

Cap caught him as he was about to enter the first building. The older man looked him up and down. "I don't see any blood, so I guess you did all right, Sammy boy."

"Yep, but Tom Doolin tried to kill Cheyenne. I'll tell you about it when I have more time. No one's seen Mitchell, and I'm worried."

"Yep, doesn't look favorable."

They rousted people from bed and searched each room, but there was no sign of Pope.

Or Jared Mitchell.

Nothing but soggy red and green streamers fluttered in the foggy December air.

Forty

Daylight neared before Sam, Cap, and Senior rode back to the Ronans'. Cheyenne heard the horses, then saw them making their way to the barn and put the coffee on. She drew in an easy breath for the first time in very long hours. Thank God they were all right.

She didn't see Jared Mitchell though, she noted with a frown.

Throwing a heavy shawl around her, she ran out to the barn. The men turned. "I couldn't wait to see how everything went. Why isn't Jared with you?"

Each, to a man, looked dead on their feet. Especially Sam.

Sam's grim face said it all. "We haven't found him. We turned the town upside down. Nothing."

"Oh no! Do you think they killed him?"

"Too soon to say." Sam gave her a one-sided smile. "I'll search more in a few hours."

What would Retta do without her husband and a new baby on the way?

"How are you, Miss Cheyenne?" Senior asked, removing the saddle from his horse. "I hear you were lucky."

"If Sam hadn't come when he did, I'd probably be dead. Not only me, but Loretta and the kids too. Tom Doolin didn't intend for me to live. Sam, did you find out why he took my coat?"

"Yep." He hung his tack on the wall. "He'd made a crude person out of hay, threw one of your tablecloths over it to look like a dress then stuck a stick through it all to mimic a person's spine. Your coat was the last touch. He'd had to do it so fast, grabbing what he could, so it didn't look very good. Although in the pitch-black at fifteen yards away, it looked pretty convincing."

She slipped a halter on his horse and led him to a stall. "I'm just so thankful you came back in time. Did you catch Doolin?"

"Yes." Sam put an arm around her. "We rounded up all the Doolins and their gang."

"Wonderful."

Cap rubbed his face. "We got all except the ringleader. She got away somehow."

"A woman was head of that counterfeiting ring?" She'd never heard of anything like that.

"That's right," Senior answered. "She wore several different disguises. One was men's apparel down to the hat. Hard as hell to catch."

"I can imagine. Pretty ingenious," Cheyenne admitted. "By the way, I put coffee on before I came out."

"You're quite a woman, Miss Cheyenne." Cap squeezed in between her and Sam. "If Sam doesn't marry you, I certainly will."

Sam snorted. "Not on your life. Get your own woman. This one's taken."

"Am I hearing right?" Senior asked. "What's this about marriage?"

"I asked Chey to marry me and she said yes." Sam's arm tightened around her. "I still can't believe it."

Happiness wove around her heart. "I hope you'll be happy for us, Mr. Legend."

"Miss Cheyenne, if you only knew how long I've waited for this moment," Senior said from behind. "I don't have a dog in this fight, but I like how you think. And you make some awful good coffee."

The men cut up all the way to the kitchen, Senior as much as the younger guys. They were beat and needed an outlet to unwind and forget the terrible events of the night. As Cheyenne walked along with them, she was never so grateful to be alive.

They discussed the woman ringleader and the fact that she'd fooled them all. Such a devious, cunning woman posed more danger than a wounded lioness and would kill anyone who stood in her way. What felt like shards of ice pierced Cheyenne's back.

A dark storm was brewing, drawing ever closer. A bitter taste sat on her tongue. Only this wasn't skyborne. This was a storm of evil, and she didn't know if they'd survive it. A shiver of foreboding rushed through her like a raging river crashing against the rocks. God help them.

The last ones in, Sam caught her at the door. "I missed you, lady. After a few years' sleep, I'll show you how much."

"Deal, but I can wait." She tilted her face for his kiss that settled all the jumpiness inside her.

Close voices from inside broke them apart.

"Sam, take the bed in my little house and let your dad have the one in the bunkhouse."

"I'd planned to. But I can't sleep long. I have Jared and Pope to find."

"You will. I know it."

"I love you, Chey. If you didn't know it before, you'd best know it now."

"I see it in your eyes and know it's real." Cheyenne buried her face in the hollow of his neck. "Sam, storms never last, do they? You will catch that woman and find Jared?"

"No, storms don't last, darlin'. They come and pass. I'll do my best to set things right."

A few minutes later, they were sitting at the table, talking and drinking coffee when Aaron and Ellen burst into the kitchen.

"The Texas Rangers are back!" Aaron hollered.

Ellen frowned. "They're fun, Aaron, but I wish it was Daddy."

"Me too."

Hot tears stung Cheyenne's eyes. Jared might not ever get to see his kids again or kiss his wife or see the new baby.

Her heart ached for the little broken family. Hope of putting them back together seemed lost.

Loretta appeared in the doorway, and Sam went to her. "Miss Retta, we need to talk."

"Jared." She gasped, her face turning white.

Oh dear! Cheyenne started toward her but stopped. Sam needed to do this.

He caught Retta when she crumbled. "Let's go to the parlor." His voice was soft as he picked her up and carried her.

Cheyenne's heart ached for this wife and mother. And also for Sam, who blamed himself for everything.

∽

Sam seated himself next to Retta and took her hand. "Jared was not with the counterfeiters when we arrested them, but I want you to know that we're still looking. We'll move heaven and earth to find him."

"Will he be alive though?"

He glanced away and struggled to keep his voice from cracking. "Ma'am, I can't answer that. I just know that we're on the good side of bad and so is your husband. That has to count for something in the good Lord's eyes."

Retta wiped her eyes and raised her quivering chin. "He's alive. You'll see."

"Yes, ma'am." Sam glanced up to see Cheyenne in the doorway.

She smiled at him and came on into the room. "Retta, let's get you and the children some breakfast. Maybe you feel like stirring the gravy."

"I certainly do."

And just like that, Loretta Mitchell gathered strength, got to her feet, and went to help. The human spirit was so resilient and always amazed Sam. Most folks would give out long before they gave up.

He ate a quick bite with the men, then sought rest in Chey's little house. In three hours, the men would get up and ride back to town to resume the search.

With his boots off and the scent of Cheyenne on the pillows, he drifted off.

She awoke him with a kiss at the appointed time, lying next to him. Her eyes reminded him of a spring meadow awash with lush green grass.

"I wish you could get more sleep." She laid a soft palm on his jaw. "That wasn't near enough."

"It'll have to do." He sighed. "I wish I knew where the heck to look for Jared."

"Someone has to know, Sam. What about Flannery at the telegraph office? Wouldn't he have delivered messages out at the other place? You said they'd gotten some."

He sat straight up and kissed her. Of course. The man should have directions to the house outside of town. Sam sat on the side of the bed and pulled on his boots. "I have to get to town."

She hurried to her feet. "I'll get you something quick to eat."

"No time." He grabbed her and kissed her again. "Thank you."

"You're welcome."

"Can you tell my dad and Cap I've already left? And can you work with the children on their lines for the play? I'd appreciate that." Without waiting for a reply, he scooped up his coat and headed to the barn.

Despite the previous long frigid night, Rio appeared ready to run. He snorted, pawing the ground when Sam led him into the weak sunlight.

"All right, let's do this." Sam swung into the saddle and waved to Cheyenne, who stood watching from the kitchen door, then galloped toward Tascosa.

He didn't slow until he reached Duggan Flannery's. The telegraph office was open, and a bell over the door announced his presence. It was empty except for the proprietor.

Flannery glanced up from his desk. "Sam, how can I help you?"

"I need some information. When you received messages for the Doolins, did you ever deliver anywhere but to the saloon?"

The man scratched his head. "Most of them went to the Hitching Post, but once I took one outside of town."

Sam tamped down his excitement. He didn't have anything yet. "Do you remember how to get there or what the house looked like?"

"I only went there once, and it was quite some time ago, after they first arrived. I recall how surprised I was that Sheriff Winslow answered the door like he owned the place."

"Just think a minute. No hurry."

Except there was. Still, Sam wouldn't get results any faster by pressuring. He went to the window and took in the view of the street. Some of the rangers were sitting in front of the Painted Pony, their rifles across their laps. The prisoners weren't going anywhere.

At the Hitching Post, someone had boarded up the door. It appeared the arrival of so many lawmen had scared many of the good people of Tascosa, most of whom probably had things to hide.

Sam suppressed a chuckle. This part of Texas had been overlooked far too long. Hell, there were a lot of folks across the state who thought this area belonged to Mexico. Of course, they were the ones unable to read or write and messed up pretty bad when they even talked.

"I remember!" Flannery exclaimed. "It's south of town. Before you reach the train tracks, you'll see a bent tree that has rocks stacked up about three feet tall at the base. Turn east, and it's a short distance to the house. It's made of stucco and has a red-tile roof. Used to be pretty fancy back in the day, but it's beginning to fall into ruin. You can't miss it."

"Much obliged. And for last night also. I hear you were a big help to my father."

"Glad to do it, but I fear it's a little late for saving this town. More folks pulled out this morning. They've had enough. Me and missus will probably join them."

"That's too bad. Well, thanks once more for all you've done."

"Wish I could've made a difference a lot sooner. Take care, Legend."

Sam hurried out and rode south toward the train tracks. The day was a little warmer than the last several. In Texas, you never knew what you'd get. One day it could be drifting snow and the next bright sunshine and fifty degrees. Only a crazy person would try to predict the weather.

He didn't let himself think about the woman or Jared. To think about them would set himself up for disappointment. Instead, he filled his thoughts with Chey and the kids. It was good that they had a distraction with the Christmas decorations and play. He imagined Chey would have them out doing calisthenics today, and exercise was good for them.

Cheyenne's parents had been gone for what seemed ages, and even though she didn't talk about it, Sam knew she missed them. Maybe they'd return for a Christmas surprise.

The bent tree with rocks at the base came into sight, and his heartbeat quickened. It wasn't far now. The road was as narrow and bad as Flannery had said.

A hawk circled overhead, its sharp eyes looking for prey, and rabbits scattered, leaping through the thorny brush.

Sam rounded a stand of mesquites and got his first view of the stucco dwelling with its red-tile roof. "Whoa," he murmured to Rio, reining the horse to a stop out of view.

Nothing moved outside, and there was no sign of the wagon or team of horses. Probably in the barn. But what if Pope had caught the train? The tracks were less than a mile away. His breath hung in his throat. He swallowed hard.

What if he was too late, and Jared was dead?

He went back to the night that Jared had escaped and Sam had talked him into returning. Was he destined to regret that mistake the rest of his life?

Well, he wouldn't know anything if he didn't go on up to the house, but it would be best done on foot. He dismounted, slid the rifle from the scabbard, and looped Rio's reins around a mesquite branch. One foot in front of the other, he proceeded carefully, every nerve stretched taut. Birds flitted overhead and called from the brush. Prairie dogs and gophers scurried into their holes. Rabbits leaped this way and that.

Each sound registered, was identified, and set aside.

Sam finally pressed against the side of the house, then ducked beneath a window to peer inside. A woman, dressed about the same as the previous night, sat at a table, sipping from a cup as though she were in some castle.

Good. She was still here.

He went from window to window, looking inside. In the last one in a far corner of the house, he spied Jared, sitting chained on the floor, his head on his chest. Sam couldn't tell if he was alive or dead. His clothes were bloody. He wasn't moving.

Okay, now to get inside. He went to the front and tried the knob. Locked. He'd have to bust the door down. Shouldn't be too hard. The hinges appeared to be rusty.

Gripping his Colt, Sam backed up to the edge of the wide porch, lowered his shoulder, and ran. It shuddered but didn't give. The noise would surely have attracted the woman outlaw. A quick second try met with success, and he stood in the entryway. A hall must lead to the kitchen, and that's where he hurried. He paused at the door, listening. Nothing.

Gun drawn, Sam burst around the corner only to find the room empty.

Disappointed, he continued carefully through each room of the house and ended where Jared had been. He pressed against the side of the open doorway. Chains rattled.

Taking a deep breath, Sam peeked around the corner. The woman sat on the floor, using Jared as a shield, her petticoats billowing around them. She squeezed off a round from the weapon she held, and the bullet embedded in the doorframe next to Sam's head.

In the quick look he'd gotten, Jared had his eyes open and held his head up. He was alive. Thank God.

"It's all over, Finley or Pope or whoever the hell you are! Let Mitchell go."

"Not on your life, Sam Legend. He's my ticket out of here," she snarled.

"You got no place to run. He has a wife in the family way. Kids. Let him celebrate Christmas with them."

"I die. He dies. Got that?"

Desperation colored her voice—and fear.

"Yes, ma'am. But you don't want to die."

Silence filled the space.

"I'm curious. Were you there with Tom Doolin when my wife was killed?"

For a moment, he didn't think she'd answer. Then she said, "Yes. I took her life when Tom chickened out." Her voice was as hard as granite. "I always have to clean up people's messes when they don't have the guts."

Sam sagged against the wall, his knees giving out. He'd chased the wrong man. Wanted to kill Tom Doolin.

To Finley Booth, Beth was nothing but a mess to clean up. He fought back a rising sob, blinking hard.

Finally, he straightened and cleared his throat. "She never hurt you. She loved everyone."

"I had to prove that I'm strong enough to be a leader. I lusted after power. And I took it. I showed them all." Her voice was brittle. "Your wife was the means to an end. She just happened to be there."

Just happened to be there with her beautiful smile and kind ways. The means to an end.

Three more shots came in rapid succession and embedded in the wall behind him.

"It's over, Miss Booth. Done." Breathing hard, Sam slipped around the door. "You're under arrest, ma'am."

"You'll never take me." Finley tried to fire again but Jared swung his body, knocking her arm. The bullet blasted into the ceiling.

Sam snatched the gun from her lifeless fingers and pulled her to her feet just as horses galloped up outside.

"Let me go!" Finley pulled and jerked. "I demand you release me!"

"Not on your life. You're going to jail for a long, long time."

"I'll get you one way or another! I have people to do my bidding. They'll kill you!" Her face had lost its pretty features and was tight and drawn now, ruthlessness glittering in her eyes.

Although he didn't know her age, she'd advanced in years over the last few minutes, looking old and worn now.

"They might try," he answered, then turned his attention to Jared. "You all right?"

The ranch hand nodded. "I've been worse." He chuckled. "I've also been a whole lot better."

"Glad you still have a sense of humor." Sam turned toward the shouts. "In here!"

"I'll kill you!" Finley screamed. "I'll kill you all. You won't get away with this. I have connections."

Cap and Senior led a group of lawmen into the room.

"It looks like we're a little late." The senior Sam took hold of Finley and handcuffed her.

"You could've waited a minute for us!" Cap barked.

Sam shot Jared's chains. "I know, but then it would've beaten me out of the chance to hear you gripe." He helped Jared to his feet. "I'm sure you're anxious to go see your family."

"You said a mouthful." Jared rubbed his wrists. "You know your friend Heck Rains?"

"What about him?"

"I overheard something that might interest you. Lem and Tom were talking about Heck taking some of the counterfeit money and had gone out there to confront and possibly kill him. Rains told them he was going to turn it over to the Texas Rangers, but before they could find out where he'd hidden it, Rains keeled over with his heart and died. The Doolins never knew if he'd gotten the money to Ranger McFarlan. But they thought he had."

At last, his friend was vindicated of all suspicion. It felt damn good.

"Thanks for telling me. Cap found the jar of money, but we didn't know why Rains had it or what he meant to do with it."

Behind them, Finley continued to rant and rave her head off, spewing vile threats.

Jared stared at the woman who'd tried to kill him. "I think Rains was as decent a man as ever lived."

"Yep, me too. We'll get you cleaned up before taking you home. You'll scare the kids."

Jared rubbed his bristly jaw. "I'd appreciate that."

This was going to be a Christmas like none other. Sam couldn't wait to see the children's faces.

Forty-one

THE CHILDREN WERE PLAYING OUTSIDE THE BUNKHOUSE WITH the barn kittens when Sam rode up alone. The men had hung back so he could find out where Aaron and Ellen were first before coming in. Jared wanted to surprise them.

"Hey, what you doing?" Sam propped his foot on a barrel beside Ellen.

She looked up with a glum expression. "Playing. These kittens have a mommy but no daddy. Just like us."

Sam sat on the step. "It sounds like a sad state of affairs. How about we go into the kitchen and find some hot cocoa?"

"I want some." Aaron's eyes livened with interest. It was a proven fact that he loved cocoa.

"Okay." Ellen sighed. "I guess I will too."

"That's the spirit." He helped put the kittens back in the barn and herded the children into the kitchen.

Cheyenne glanced up from her mixing bowl. "What's going on?"

"These kids want some cocoa." Sam whispered his news in her ear.

Her eyes widened. "That's wonderful. Yes, cocoa. Coming right up."

Sam went out and waved to the men, then returned to the kitchen. "Have any coffee?"

"No, I'll put some on in a minute. A trip to the mercantile will be in order soon. We're getting low."

"I'll go tomorrow." Sam listened for the men but didn't hear them yet. "Have you heard anything from your folks lately, Chey?"

"No, and I'm getting worried. I guess they have a lot to take care of with Aunt Betty's death and seeing to the farm, but I hate for them to be gone on Christmas." While the milk heated, Cheyenne reached for the cocoa, pulling the fabric tight across her breasts.

Sam's mouth went dry. He was becoming a lecherous old man. But now that all the trouble had been resolved, he meant to devote full attention to the woman he loved.

Footsteps sounded outside the door, and the knob turned.

"Say, does anyone know where Saint Nick lives?" Jared stepped inside.

"Daddy!" Ellen screamed and ran to him.

Tears ran down Aaron's face, and he stumbled over his own feet in his haste to get to his father.

"Come here." Jared scooped them both into his arms, hugging them.

"What's all the commotion?" Loretta asked from the doorway.

Jared stared, set the kids on their feet, and went to her. Tears of joy created a path down their faces as he took his wife in his arms.

Sam blinked hard and pulled Cheyenne close. "We did it."

"Yes, you certainly did." She reached for a dish towel and wiped her eyes.

Cap and Senior quietly slipped in the door and sat at the table, grinning.

For once, Cap had nothing to say. He met Sam's gaze and winked. They'd done good.

For some time afterward, they all sat at the table, drinking coffee and cocoa and reliving the last two days.

Then the senior Sam rose. "I need to ride to Amarillo and catch the train home. I haven't seen my wife in what seems a coon's age and have a great desire to rectify that. I've enjoyed meeting you all and cleaning up Tascosa—again."

"Won't you stay 'til morning?" Cheyenne asked. "It'll be dark by the time you get there if you leave now."

Senior's smile showed white teeth in his tanned face. "No, I really want to get home."

"I'll see you out." Sam put on his hat and they went into the sunshine. He hated to see his dad go but knew they'd see each other again soon. Either at Christmas or after. He wanted to introduce Cheyenne and her to the family to the Lone Star.

After his father collected his things from the bunkhouse, they stood by his horse.

"Tell Mama I'll come to visit before she can blink, and I'll send her and Marisol's gifts as soon as I can. My little sister will not be happy it's late." Sam studied the ground for a moment, then looked up. "Dad, Cheyenne really is the one for me. I can't wait to marry her."

"I know. I'd have to be blind not to see that." Senior gave him a hug, clapping his back. "Miss Cheyenne is a keeper, that's for sure. I'm very happy for you both." He stuck a foot in the stirrup and swung up. "Think about having the wedding at the Lone Star."

"Yeah, I will."

His dad trotted toward the road, waving.

Sam was a little lost and sad for a minute. Then Chey stole to his side and put an arm around him, and his world was suddenly full of love and kindness. A beautiful future beckoned like a green oasis in a parched desert.

❧

That night, they let the Mitchell family have the house to themselves. They needed space where they could talk privately and become a family again. Cap had the bunkhouse to himself again, except for Shadow. Surprisingly, the dog had chosen the ranger. Cheyenne and Sam curled up in the bed in her house.

They lay in each other's arms, a blissful state of contentment winding around them. With only three hours' sleep in the last twenty-four, he wanted some rest.

That was okay with her. She understood, but it didn't stop her from touching him.

Her head on Sam's chest, Cheyenne ran her fingers across his arm, tracing the raised veins that spoke of strength. Hammering steel day after day had sculpted the muscles in his chest and arms.

A question had niggled in her brain all afternoon, and she wondered if he'd leave now.

"Sam, will you return to the Texas Rangers full-time?"

A male sound rumbled in his chest like it sometimes did before he spoke. "Cap asked me the same thing. How would you feel if I did go back?"

She'd hate being halfway across the state from her parents. Yet she would support Sam's decision, no matter what. That's what a loving wife did.

"I want whatever you do, Sam. I can make a home anywhere, but this is your life."

He smoothed her hair with a large hand. "I won't go back to the rangers. I've found what I want here. Few people seem to understand how much I love forging knives. It brings a peace that's hard to explain. This isn't a hobby or something I do in my spare time. This is who I am." He lifted a tendril of her hair and worked it between his fingers. "I want to sleep beside you every night and look at you anytime I want. That's something money can't buy."

"Have you thought about where we'll live?" She raised her head to meet his look. "As much as I love the earthiness of the wickiup, I don't want to raise kids there." She chuckled, glancing up at him. "It's a bit too rustic for my taste."

"Aww, come now." He wore a look of utter shock, but the twinkle in his eyes said he was teasing. "It has a bed and a fire and sometimes keeps the rain out. What more could you want? I hope you're not going to be a hard wife to please."

"I'll try my darndest to be pleasant."

"You don't have to try. You're perfect." Sam pulled her closer.

"When spring comes, I'll build us a house there. You can design it to your satisfaction. I love standing on the bluff and watching the sunrise, listening to the sounds of nature, and knowing I'm where I'm supposed to be."

"I want that too. I'll be there right by your side."

He ran his tongue across the seam of her lips. "I won't stand in your way if you want to continue helping the Apache. That's important to you."

"It is, but so are you. If I go back, you're coming too, my cowboy." She gave a contented sigh. "About us…I like a simple life, a house that meets our needs but isn't extravagant. My only stipulation is having a large bed where your feet don't stick off the end."

"A bed it is. Although, my toes won't know what to do without the extra ventilation."

They were silent a moment, then the sheets rustled as Cheyenne propped herself on an elbow. "How about us going to Amarillo for an overnight trip? You never sold your knives or delivered the ones that were special ordered. We could do some shopping and eat at a restaurant. Jared can take care of Retta and the kids." She paused, then added, "That is, if you have the money."

"Yes, I have more than enough." He kissed her fingers. "I think it's a great idea. We'll have to leave in the morning though to get back by Christmas Eve."

"Oh good. It will be so nice seeing real stores and picking out a few items for the kids. Sam, we need to buy a few things that Jared can give his family, since he can't shop for himself."

"I was thinking the same thing. We'll do that."

Cheyenne snuggled back beside him only to remember the peddler. She popped up again. "Sam, in all the excitement, I forgot to make those five baskets for the peddler! He'll be here tomorrow. What'll I do?"

"We'll get up an hour earlier and start in on them. It won't take that long."

"You always have a plan."

He growled. "Now, lay down and let me sleep. You're like a jack-in-the-box tonight."

"You should've warned me that you're grouchy before asking me to marry you. I may have to reconsider." Smiling wide, she lay on her side, her naked body loving the feel of his and the warm palm curling around the edge of a breast.

She'd take him just as he was, irritable loner and all.

∾

The next morning, Cheyenne scurried around to make the extra baskets. Cap offered to make one. Sam rolled his eyes. But after several false starts the ranger got the hang of it and, to their surprise, completed the best of the five.

"Thank you both for your help. I couldn't have done it by myself." She took the baskets from them and set them on the front porch.

Cap grinned. "Who knows? Weaving might come in handy sometime, and I'll know how."

"My pleasure, sweetheart." Sam kissed her cheek. "I'll see to the cattle and gather eggs if you'll make us some breakfast."

"Deal." She patted his chest. "I can't wait to leave for Amarillo."

An hour later, the peddler came for the baskets. "Folks snapped up all you made, and I have customers waiting for these."

"I'm happy they liked them." They'd made a great trade, and she itched to give those fine boots to Sam.

Finally, they saddled the horses, and Cheyenne tied her small carpetbag to the saddle horn. She felt a little scandalous, especially for not packing a nightgown. She giggled. Why take something she would have no need of?

"Exactly," she murmured.

"Did you say something?" Sam asked.

"Who me? No. Must be the wind." Excitement swept through her. She turned to Jared. "Make yourself at home, and don't let Cap boss you around."

"Yes, ma'am. I'll take care of the place, and Retta's feeling well enough to do the cooking. We'll be fine." He looked at the ground, moving closer so as not to be heard. "Ma'am, if you'll get some things for Retta and the children for me, I'd sure be obliged. You can take it out of my wages."

"That's between you and my father." Cheyenne laid a hand on his arm. "I'll be happy to pick out what I can."

Ellen came running and waved. "Bye, Miss Ann."

"Don't worry about you know what," Aaron said with a grin. "Mr. Cap will help."

Cap stepped close to Cheyenne, keeping his voice low. "We'll work on the play. You just enjoy yourselves." He pulled out a couple of dollars. "Will you buy something pretty for me?"

"Anyone in particular this will be for? A niece? A sister?"

A red flush rose up his neck. "A lady friend."

"Of course." She put the money in her pocket and accepted a boost into the saddle. "I'll find her a lovely gift."

She and Sam rode out to waves and shouts. You'd think they were never coming back. But it was nice to know they'd be missed.

"Are you warm enough?" Sam asked.

"Perfectly." Although the day was cold, her heavy coat kept her comfortable. "I'm as excited as a kid in a candy store."

"I think we'll have a good time." His eyes seemed filled with the same hunger that was smoldering inside her.

The day was perfect, and she enjoyed the sunshine on her face. They talked as they rode along, but there was also plenty of time for thinking. Her thoughts went to her parents, and she wondered if they'd decided to extend their visit. It didn't seem right for them to be gone so long.

After stopping for lunch at a little stream, they rode down the dirt streets of the bustling town of Amarillo. She'd been once or twice, but not since it'd grown so big. They left their horses at a livery and checked into the Amarillo Hotel.

Signs of Christmas were everywhere she turned, and people hummed carols as they went about the town. Such a stark difference from Tascosa that was shriveling and dying.

A band played at the train depot, and she strained to see.

Sam took her arm. "Must be a dignitary of some kind or another coming in on the train. I need to deliver the knives to my clients and take the rest to the shop that will buy the others. There are some ladies' dress shops, milliners, and other type stores up and down this street."

"You go on. I'll be fine. We can meet up at the hotel in a few hours."

"Wait." He took some money from his pocket and handed it to her. "Buy something you want for no reason at all, not anything you need. But I want to shop for the kids with you."

"I'd like that." She glanced down at the money. "This is too much."

"I want my soon-to-be-wife to have something special, and since I don't know any sizes, buy whatever you want."

She kissed his cheek. "You're spoiling me already."

His chuckle filled her with warmth.

"You've discovered my plan."

They parted, and she wandered down the busy street with its colorful displays. Pulling her coat tighter around her, she spied a ready-made dress of green velvet in a window. She pushed inside the shop for a closer look. After trying it on, she discovered it fit her perfectly. She felt like a kept woman buying it, but she did anyway. It would be very lovely on Christmas Day with Sam, Cap, and the Mitchells, who had become like family.

She eyed the hats and even tried one on, but shook her head at the disappointed clerk. Anything fancy like that would be wasted on a bladesmith's wife. The candy store caught her notice, and she bought a piece of dark French chocolate, the cost outrageous. At home, she could make enough candy for a dozen people for that amount of money.

A horseless carriage came whizzing down the street, honking and motioning for people to get out of the way. She decided then and there she'd stick with riding horses.

Her feet beginning to hurt, she went back to the hotel, put the box holding her dress in their room, then got a cup of hot tea in the dining area. A group of women sat at an adjacent table, talking about various and sundry subjects. When Sam entered, heads turned, and Cheyenne couldn't blame the women. Her breath caught as well at his dark good looks and lean form.

Smiling, he bent to kiss her cheek before sitting. "I thought I might find you here."

"I looked my fill and decided to wait for you here."

One of the women at the adjacent table leaned over. "You're a very lucky woman."

"Thank you, ma'am. I do think I am. We're to be married."

"I should've known," said another very attractive woman.

Sam turned five shades of red and shifted as the group left.

"They're certainly right." Cheyenne took his hand. "You're every woman's dream."

"Don't want to be anyone's but yours." He kissed her fingertips and ordered coffee when the waitress came. "I noticed the dress box in our room. I'm glad you bought something. Maybe you'll try it on for me."

"You won't even have to beg." She took a sip of tea. "Were you successful?"

"Very. The ones who gave me special orders seemed happy, and the gunsmith purveyors next to the general store bought every one of the others, so I'm more than satisfied."

"I had no doubts. I knew everyone would snap them up. You're very talented." She added low, "In all areas."

"Maybe I'll prove it tonight."

"You already have."

After they finished their refreshment, Sam led the way to a very nice mercantile where they bought a pretty doll with movable eyes for Ellen and a baseball and bat for Aaron. Those would be for Jared to give them. Cheyenne and Sam's gift to the children would be the monkey on a stick and the harmonica.

The jewelry beckoned, and Cheyenne looked at it for Jared to give Retta but didn't really see anything she liked. Then she spied the music boxes. Perfect. She got one for both Retta and Cap's lady friend. You couldn't go wrong with these. For Retta, she added a pretty comb and brush set.

Then she looked around for something for her parents. Even though they might not be home yet, she'd save the gifts for when they were.

Sam told her he'd made a knife for her father. Their mothers would get a long necklace with a lady's watch on the end. His little sister was the hardest, but Sam bought her a pair of riding gloves and a leather-tooled breastplate for her favorite horse.

"I think that does it." Cheyenne put her arm through his. "Let's go."

Minutes later, they strolled arm in arm into the hotel dining room and were seated in a secluded, intimate corner. The lamp on the table seemed to bring out Sam's handsome features even more. She had a hard time concentrating on the menu but finally made a selection.

While they ate, they discussed their wedding.

"I want my parents to be there." She wouldn't consider marrying without them.

"Of course. They will be no matter how long we have to wait." Sam agreed. "Can we talk about a location? Would you consider having the ceremony on the Lone Star? My grandfather is up in years and not able to travel much. He's been such a huge part of my life, and I'd like to have him there if possible. And there's no question of putting your parents up."

"Then it's settled. The Lone Star Ranch is where we'll begin our wonderful journey together as husband and wife."

The thought raised goose bumps. She was really going to become Mrs. Sam Legend, the wife of an extraordinary blade-smith and fighter for justice.

Forty-two

"Wait just a moment." Sam left Cheyenne standing in the hotel hallway outside their room and squeezed through the door. He hastily shoved her Christmas present under the bed and went back. "Okay, you can come in."

She stepped inside, glancing around. "What on earth was that about?"

"Secrets are not to be shared until the time is right, darlin.'" He shut the door and worked at the buttons on her dress.

"A couple about to be married should not have secrets, dear."

"They're allowed at Christmas, sweetheart. Didn't you learn that rule?" He pulled the fabric from her arms and nibbled the long column of her throat as the dress pooled to the floor. "Besides, I know you're keeping one. A little birdie by the name of Ellen told me."

"Oh, Sam, that was supposed to be a surprise." She pouted and unbuckled his gun belt, laying it aside. "What am I going to do now?"

"Not. One. Blessed. Thing." With each word, he moved lower, trailing kisses across her shoulders. Brushing her chemise aside, he buried his face in her luscious breasts. She smelled of summer wildflowers wafting on a fresh breeze. *Wholesome* and *natural* came to mind. Expensive perfume stirred up in a laboratory didn't come close.

Her breath hitching like it did when she got aroused, she finished undressing him, running her smooth palms over his body. Caressing. Flicking her tongue here and there. Loving.

In a frenzy, they fell onto the bed, a heap of arms and legs. The climax swift and shuddering.

Afterward, Sam held her next to him, stroking her beautiful russet hair. Outside in the lamplight, a group of carolers began to sing Christmas carols. Although they were on the second floor, the pretty melodies still reached them. He put on his trousers and opened the window.

Wrapped in a blanket, Cheyenne joined him, and they listened for a while.

"Their voices blend together so nicely," she murmured, his arms around her, his chest to her back. "The songs are what I love best about the holidays, I think."

"I love you best, lady," he whispered in her ear.

She turned to face him. "I'm glad we could take this little private trip. You're all I dream of, Sam. To have you, I won't ask for anything more."

Aching with love for her, Sam slipped a hand inside the blanket and pressed a palm to her flat stomach. "Let's go back to bed."

At her nod, he shut the window, swept her into his arms, and carried her to the soft down. Pulling the blanket over her, he removed his pants.

Cheyenne sighed and snuggled into the folds. Sam burrowed beneath the cover, found her center, and took her into his mouth.

Folks probably complained of the racket, but Sam didn't hear any coming from his beautiful Chey, who was the only one who counted.

❧

They took a slight detour on the way home and went by the wickiup. Cheyenne laid yaupon branches bursting with red berries on Tarak's grave. Grateful that Sam piddled around his forge, giving her some private time, she told her old Apache friend about her love for Sam and the upcoming wedding.

"I wish you were here to be a part of it." The words choked her. "I miss you so much."

It meant a lot to her that Sam sensed her need to come here. He truly cared for her happiness and showed it in countless ways.

They rode into the homestead a short while later. Between the dog and the kids, they received a boisterous welcome.

Cheyenne hugged them all and some twice. "I'm so glad to be back."

"Today is Christmas Eve," Aaron said with a wink. "And we're ready."

"That's wonderful. Would you and your sister like to help carry some of our purchases?"

Ellen jerked to attention. "I'll help, Miss Ann."

Cheyenne handed them a couple of wrapped packages. "No peeking."

Aaron shrugged. "How can we? They're tied up."

"Just don't accidentally untie them," Retta admonished. "I know how these things happen. And I know the strength of your curiosity."

"Aw, Mama. I won't peek."

The kids took off for the house. Cheyenne handed Cap his music box and Jared his bundle, but her eyes kept straying to the mysterious gift Sam had strapped to the side of Rio. If she could just see it better, she could guess what it was. She knew she could, but he kept her from getting a full view. It was wrapped in a large blanket and tied with thick twine.

If she could just get a peek...

"How was everything here?" she asked Loretta and Jared.

Odd that it was Cap who shrugged and blushed. "I might've had a guest while you were gone."

"Might've?" Sam jostled him. "Don't tell me we have a maid now."

"Nope. No maid, and now that you're back, I'm moving into town."

Cheyenne put her hands on her hips. "I won't hear of it, Cap

McFarland. Not here at Christmas. You're family. You bled on our bunkhouse floor, entertained the kids with your stories, and helped all of us."

The old ranger stepped in front of her and placed his hands on her shoulders. "You tolerated me, and I'm grateful. But I have a life to get back to. A lady friend I enjoy spending time with."

"One more night won't hurt a blessed thing," Sam said quietly and moved closer so that only Cap heard. "You have to watch the kids' play. Even if you leave afterward."

Cap nodded. "Reckon I do have to be here for that." He hurried off to the bunkhouse with his lady friend's gift.

With his eyes on Aaron and Ellen heading back, Jared thanked her and Sam for buying something he could give his kids. "It means a lot."

Sam put an arm around Cheyenne, chuckling. "We had fun."

"Now, I need to see to supper if we're going to eat." Cheyenne headed for the house with Retta at her side.

Bright spots colored Loretta's cheeks where pale had been. "I took the liberty of putting a roast on this morning. I hope that was all right. It sure smells good and will save you the work of preparing a meal after traveling."

Cheyenne stopped. "You're amazing. Of course it's all right. Thank you."

"Miss Ann, we decorated the tumbleweed tree. Come see." Ellen took her hand, pulling her.

They'd put it into a corner of the parlor and mashed a lot of the tumbleweeds together in the shape of a tree. It was very pretty with popcorn strands, cranberries, tinsel, and paper chains. But at the top was a large metal star that shone in the firelight.

"How did you make the star?" she asked.

"Daddy did it." Ellen twirled around the room like a ballerina, resembling nothing of the shy, sad little girl she'd first been.

Jared grinned with Loretta at his side. "I cut up cans and put the star together with pitch, then covered it with shiny cigar bands. Like it?"

"I love it." She turned to Sam. "Jared is quite talented."

"I agree." He held out a piece of paper. "Merry Christmas, Jared and Loretta."

"What is it, sweetheart?" Cheyenne asked.

"A voucher for a hundred dollars for help in rounding up the counterfeiting ring." Sam stuck out his hand and the men shook. "If it hadn't been for you, we'd have had a harder time, and the governor recognizes that."

Jared shook his head. "I can't accept this. I didn't do near enough."

"I say different."

Cheyenne hugged Retta. "How did it get here, Sam?"

"My father left it with Cap, only he forgot to give it to Jared."

They laughed. Those lady friends could sure mess with a man's mind. Cheyenne laced her fingers through Sam's, soaking up the warmth of giving that filled her heart. "That money will help you start over, settle you in a good place where you can raise these two kids and the new one on the way."

"Amen." Tears stood in Jared's eyes. "Thank you."

Wiping her own, Cheyenne went to the kitchen to get out the plates. The creak of a wagon reached her. Curious, she opened the door and stepped out. Her mother and father climbed from the wagon bench and thanked the driver for delivering them.

"Well, I'll be." Sam hurried around her to help Bert unload the bags from the back. "You made it."

"By the skin of our teeth." Bert stared as the driver pulled away and crept closer. "Sam?"

"Yep, it's me."

"Well, land's sake!" Cora's mouth hung open. "You're sure a handsome man."

"Thank you, ma'am."

Cheyenne slid an arm around him. "I think so too, Mama."

"I didn't recognize you at all, Sam." Bert put an arm around Cora. "Thought you were someone new. What made you cut your hair and beard?"

Cheyenne listened for Sam's answer, admiring his proud bearing. One who came from the best stock.

"I got tired of living in the past, and when I arrested the Doolins for making counterfeit money, I wanted them to know who I was and that I wasn't about to let them get away with killing my wife."

Bert nodded. "Glad you settled an old score." He glanced around. "Man, it's good to be home."

Crying happy tears, Cheyenne hugged her parents. "I'd given up hope on you making it."

"We had to be here, honey." Her mother kissed her cheek. "We had to."

"I missed you both so much." Cheyenne wound her arm around Sam's. "We have news, and I can't wait to share."

"What is it, honey?"

"Sam asked me to marry him—and I said yes."

"That's wonderful!" Cora gave Sam a hug.

Bert shook his hand. "You're the one I picked out for her long ago."

"I always thought of you as my son, and now it's come true." Cora patted his arm.

"Thanks, Mama Cora." Sam kissed her cheek. "Let's go in the house. You're tired."

Jared, Loretta, and the kids crowded in the doorway.

"Oh, we have company." Cora clapped her hands. "We have children again."

Sam ushered everyone inside. Cheyenne stood in the door, staring out at the big, fat snowflakes falling. They'd be a white sparkling wonderland by morning.

Christmas miracles were everywhere.

Sam pulled Bert aside. "I should've waited and asked you for her hand. Sorry. Things happened pretty fast, and we didn't know when you'd be home."

"I understand and would've done the same thing." Bert fixed him with a look. "I just need to hear you say it...do you love my daughter?"

A month ago, Sam would've had to think about it. Not now. "With all my heart and soul. Chey is one of the most kind, caring women I've ever known. She loves giving of herself, but I want to see that she gets back half of what she doles out to others if it takes me a lifetime. I pray to never disappoint her."

Or make her cry. Sam had seen married women try to hide tears when their menfolk were hurtful and angry. God willing, Sam would never be the cause of Chey's tears.

"Before we left, I saw the beginning of something and had hoped it would lead to more." Bert got a far-off gaze in his eyes. "When Cora and I fell in love, her parents threw a real hissy and disowned her. Thought I wasn't good enough. I promised myself I'd never do that to my daughter. Her mother and I are happy to welcome you to the family."

"Thank you, sir. I appreciate that."

"Like Cora said, you're a son to us already. A wedding just makes it legal."

"I've always been fond of you both." Sam put a hand on Bert's back. "Let's go in."

Excitement tingled inside him at the thought of the evening ahead with Chey.

The dinner table was awash with laughter, and Cap entertained as always with outrageous stories. Cheyenne often thought that for a man to have done so much he would've had to live many, many lifetimes. But maybe he had. The ranger's eyes had that old-soul look and lots of wisdom. If not for his prodding, Sam would be stuck in the past and living a mountain of regret, unable to move forward.

She reached for Sam's large hand, loving the immense strength she found there.

Sam Legend was her protector. Her partner. Her first and last love for all time.

For a moment, she listened to her heartbeat keeping time with the pulse in his hand, steady and strong, knowing they were made for each other. She would never try to change him as some women did their spouses and carve away the flaws they didn't like as a whittler did with a piece of wood.

The whole man was much more interesting, and she wanted every piece of him to stay just as it was. Sure, he was as stubborn as the day was long. A bit too driven at times, letting his creative passion absorb him to the point of all else. And he scowled. A lot.

But he was hers—or at least would be soon.

He leaned over to whisper, "I can't wait to get you in bed, lady. The things I'll do to you."

"Is that so?" Her heart raced, and anticipation sizzled along her body like a lightning strike.

"Every bit of it and more."

"What about my parents? For me, I can tell them I'm sleeping in my own house."

"I'm not above sneaking. I'll do whatever I must in order to see you."

"You're a scoundrel of the highest order, my cowboy."

"Why are you grinning, beautiful Chey?"

She ran a fingertip down his throat. "Because I love tall, dark scoundrels with a discerning eye."

"My, my." The smoldering heat in his eyes promised a night of passion.

Her heart fluttered madly. Aware they were drawing attention, she talked quietly with her mother for a few minutes, then turned back to Sam. "Let's exchange gifts after the play."

A sparkle filled his dark, smoldering eyes. "I do love your ideas."

Aaron prodded Cheyenne. "When can we do the play?"

It was time to get to that.

"Very soon. You and Ellen go change into your costumes while I clear the table and wash dishes."

"Okay." The boy nodded to Ellen, and they went out.

Cheyenne stood. "We have a surprise that the children have been working on, so let us clear the table and get ready. I think you'll love this."

Her mother began reaching for plates.

"No, Mama. Go sit down and rest. You've had a long day. Sam and I will do these." Cheyenne took the dishes from her. "You're tired. Go."

"I'll go help the young'uns," Cap announced, leaving.

With Sam's help, she had the kitchen spic-and-span in no time. Alone in the room, he untied her apron and hung it up, then pulled her against him. "You light up a room with your kindness and love. How did I manage to get so lucky?"

"I don't know. I think we had help."

He nuzzled the sensitive flesh behind her ear, then settled his lips on hers. The slow kiss weakened her knees, and she clutched him for support.

This big man who loved working with steel made her feel like the rarest, most expensive china.

Breathless, she took a half step back. "Happy Christmas Eve, my love."

Forty-three

EVERYONE MOVED TO ONE END OF THE BUNKHOUSE AND SAT IN chairs that Sam and Cap brought in. At the other end was a curtain behind which was a chair, a box, and hay scattered on the floor. Everything was simple.

Cheyenne got the children into place, then stood out front. "As I mentioned earlier, Aaron and Ellen have been working on a Christmas play. But up until two days ago, they thought this would only be for their mother. God and the angels were busy behind the scenes and delivered their father to them. They missed him so badly and worried they'd never see him again. His return was nothing short of a miracle. So, in celebration of that and their mother's recovery to health, I present Aaron and Ellen Mitchell."

The curtain pulled back along the rope that held it. Ellen was seated on a milking stool with a wooden box in front. Aaron stood behind her. The headdresses both wore were made from a sheet.

"Mary, this is a blessed night indeed," Aaron said stiffly. "The world is celebrating the birth of our son. He'll grow strong, and I'll teach him to be a carpenter. He'll make chairs and coffins and stuff."

When the laughter died, a meow filled the room, and a gray tail waved above the rim of the box.

Cheyenne put a hand over her mouth to smother the giggle.

"Jesus is the perfect name." Ellen glanced into the box and stroked the furry baby. "Be still," she whispered loudly. "We will love Jesus very much, and he'll grow strong."

The door opened, and Sam and Cap entered in black Stetsons,

boots, and denim. Sam had a hand on Shadow's head. A white sheet covered the dog, and she had cotton on her face. They stood next to the box.

"I'm a shepherd, tending my flock." Sam patted Shadow's head. "I come with frankincense, whatever that is, and tallow for you to make candles to honor your little baby Jesus."

Cap cleared his throat, but his voice still came out gravelly. "I am a wise Texas Ranger who comes from afar. Been chasing outlaws and vermin but followed the star here to Bethlehem to see this little baby. I bring gifts." He patted his pockets and glanced around. "Seems I forgot to bring 'em." He pulled out a piece of paper. "I do have a warrant though."

Retta laughed, and Jared had trouble keeping a straight face. Cheyenne's parents were leaning forward in their seats, eyes aglow. Everyone seemed to enjoy the simple play with a Texas twist.

Suddenly, the mama cat leaped from the box. "Jesus, get back in there!" Ellen scolded, jumping to her feet and putting her hands on her little hips. "Come back here at once! Jesus!"

But the cat appeared to have other ideas, racing around the room with Shadow chasing it.

"Jesus, you're a bad, bad kitty!" Ellen hollered, near tears.

"I'll get him." Aaron took a diving leap, barely missing the barn cat.

Soon everyone was reaching and grabbing. Finally, Cap caught the animal and put it outside, then wrapped the blanket around a pillow and put it in the box. "Here you go, honey."

The children finished the rest, then stood in front of the gathering, holding hands.

"Thank you for coming," Aaron said. "We're a family again and it couldn't have happened without Mr. Sam, Mr. Cap, and Miss Ann. We was broke down and Mama sick, an' Miss Ann took us in and healed Mama. We ain't never gonna forget you, Miss Ann."

They ran and put their arms around her waist.

Tears sprang into Cheyenne's eyes and she swallowed the lump in her throat. She cradled their heads. "I won't forget you either. I love you both so much."

As the Mitchells hugged their children and her parents congratulated them on their play, Sam slid an arm around Cheyenne. "We did it. I think it turned out pretty good, don't you?"

"Yes, I agree, Mr. Shepherd. You looked mighty handsome up there."

"It took all of us." Cap tucked a wrapped gift under his arm. "I got someplace to be. I'll be back in a few days."

Cheyenne shook a finger at him. "You'd better not leave the Panhandle without a proper goodbye, Mr. Wise Texas Ranger. I hope your lady friend and you have a nice time."

Nodding, Cap whispered, "I think she's the one."

"Then she must be very special." Sam clapped him on the shoulder. "Maybe you'll stick around for our wedding. I want you for my best man."

Cap grinned. "You old dog! Wild horses and mangy outlaws won't keep me away. How soon?"

"We haven't decided on a date yet, we still have some discussing to do, but it'll be soon," Cheyenne assured him.

"I'm of the notion never to put things off." Cap held up the gift and winked. "Which is why I must be on my way."

Thinking how nice it was for everyone to have someone, Cheyenne kissed his cheek. "Christmas dinner is tomorrow. Bring your lady. I won't take no for an answer."

"I don't plan to be awake." Waggling his eyebrows, his droopy mustache draping his mouth like a curtain, he went out into the night.

Cheyenne laid her head on Sam's shoulder. "I'm so glad he won't be alone."

"Me too. Over the years, he joked about women so much, I never paid him a lot of mind. And I never saw any, so I was beginning to wonder if he wasn't blowing hot air." Sam pulled his attention back to Cheyenne. "Ready?"

"Absolutely."

Before they could escape, Cora appeared at her elbow. "Can I have a minute, Cheyenne?"

Her gaze met Sam's. "Go ahead, I can wait."

Cheyenne and her mother went to the house.

"Before she passed, Betty asked me to give this to you." Cora pulled a little box from her pocket. "Maybe you'd like to wear this on your wedding day."

Opening the box, Cheyenne gasped. Nestled on tissue was a square diamond pendant on a gold chain. "This is gorgeous! Was it Aunt Betty's?"

"It belonged to our grandmother. Betty kept it for you since she had no children." Tears glittered in her mother's eyes. "She loved you so much."

"And I loved her." Cheyenne kissed her mother's cheek, remembering a conversation they'd had a year ago. Her mother asked that if and when she married, she'd wear her wedding dress. "This will look perfect."

❧

Sam waited until the coast was clear, then hurried to Cheyenne's house. He opened the door and walked into the warmth, his attention riveted on the beauty in front of the fireplace. Light from the flames flickered around her russet hair, creating a fiery halo.

Air whistled through his teeth. He'd remember this moment for the rest of his life.

"I'm glad you thought of lighting the fire earlier. This is heaven." Cheyenne let him help with her coat, eyed the bearskin on the floor, and grinned.

"I wouldn't want you to catch a chill."

"Not a chance. Thank you for leaving the rug."

For her, he'd do anything, even walk over glowing coals.

"I had to. Some of my happiest moments were on that fur." He shrugged out of his coat. "But before we get to any of that, I want to give you my Christmas gift."

"You don't think we should wait until after?"

"Nope. Close your eyes. Are they closed?"

"Yes, I am not peeking."

"Good." He reached behind the sofa for the canvas. "Okay, open your eyes and sit."

When they were seated, he handed her the wrapped gift topped with a large red bow.

"I can't imagine what this is. I think it's a painting but of what or who I have no clue."

"Then open it and find out, sweetheart." He sat silently, watching her face.

It was fun seeing how she removed the bow and began to tear off small strips of paper. Most people seemed to have no restraint with such things and ripped into gifts. Not Chey.

Finally, he could no longer stand the wait. "Let me help or we'll be here all night."

They both removed the wrapping, and Cheyenne gasped. "Oh, Sam. It's beautiful, but I don't recognize it."

"It's our house, darlin'. The one I mean to start building."

She stared, open-mouthed, tears filling her eyes. "Ours? Really?"

He nodded. "What do you think? The design isn't set in stone, so I can change it to suit you."

"This is more than I ever dared dream." Her gaze searched his face. "Do we have the money? This looks very costly."

"I've lived very frugally over the past year, so I saved a lot plus sold my knives." Sam pointed to the house. "Read what's over the front door."

"Mr. and Mrs. Sam Legend. I love that. The sign makes it real. My own house. Our house. Where we'll raise our children and grow old." She slid her fingers into his dark hair. "I thought my time was past, that I'd never marry or have a family." She made a face. "Spinsterhood seemed to be in my future." A bright smile lit up her face. "But now, this."

"Nope. You'll soon be a married lady." He gazed into her eyes and gently tucked a strand of hair behind her ear. "One that is very loved."

Placing a hand behind her neck, Sam tugged her to him and pressed his hungry lips to hers. This kiss held heat and the promise of a night of lovemaking.

When they broke apart, Chey jumped up. "My turn to get your gift, although I can't possibly top a house."

He followed her with his gaze, admiring the way her hips moved. If he didn't marry her soon, he'd go flat crazy. She was everything he wanted. And more. Oh what a life they'd have.

Chey came back with a box and handed it to him. "Merry Christmas, my cowboy."

Curious, Sam unwrapped and opened the lid. The boots were some of the nicest he'd ever seen. "I sure needed these. How did you know?"

"I have eyes."

"All this time I thought you were looking at my face, now I find out it was only my boots," he kidded.

"I notice all of you, sweetheart. Every. Single. Thing."

"As I do you." Eyes smoldering with blue flame, he clutched the boots to his chest, his gaze never wavering from hers. "Looks like a perfect fit."

"A little birdie told me your size."

"Cap at work again." Sam laughed, then sobered. "I love 'em. I'll show my thanks before this night is through."

"I don't doubt that." She snuggled into the circle of his arm.

"Let's talk for a little while. Tell me more about our house. And will we live in your wickiup while we build?"

"No, the wickiup is good enough for me, but my lady needs firm walls around her." He kissed the top of her head, inhaling the fresh scent. "I think we'll live right here in yours."

"How many rooms will we have?"

"Three downstairs. A parlor, a large kitchen, a nice sunroom for you where you can sit and read, sew, or nap. Upstairs, we'll have three bedrooms and a water closet."

She sat up, excited. "I've only seen a couple of water closets. We'll have our very own?"

"Absolutely. With hot and cold running water and a porcelain tub."

"No outhouse?"

"Nope. We'll use the water closet."

"Oh my!" Her grin grew wide.

"I want my wife to have the very best. It's how the Legend men treat their ladies. Your needs will come before my own."

"Stop. Your needs are as important as mine."

"Not to me. And when we have children, they also will get the best I can manage." He grinned. "Are we having our first fight?"

Cheyenne's pout was fetching. "Do you have to ask?"

"Hey, I just wanted to make sure. Oh, the fun we'll have making up. I'm ready now."

In absence of a real answer, she began unbuttoning his shirt.

Soon, all thoughts of disagreements had vanished. Sam's breathing quickened as he laid her on the furry rug and plied her body with kisses.

"Sam, you know what I like," she purred in that deep-throated tone. "Let's go to paradise together and find heaven amongst all the stars."

"I've already found heaven here in your arms, my bewitching Chey."

"None like this."

Outside, the snow fell, putting them in a deep freeze. But inside, her heated touch moved lower, and that old familiar tightening pooled in his belly, spreading upward.

They were in no hurry. They'd have a lifetime of loving together.

Her soft hands and flitting tongue were driving him out of his mind as she took a meandering path across his straining body. The struggle to hold back took every bit of willpower.

At last, when she was as hot as steel needed to be for shaping into a knife, he crawled on top, and when the release came, they strolled among the stars again—together, as it would always be with them.

Sam collapsed on top of her, caressing her hair and face. "You're my world, my life, my every dream. Never doubt that for a second."

She nibbled along his throat. "Mmm, you say the sweetest things and make my heart flutter like a nest of butterflies."

"Let's set a date for our wedding. What do you think?" He lazily drew a heart on her palm with his tongue. "How about New Year's?"

"I kinda like that. And I already have a dress. My mother wants me to wear hers of champagne satin with lots of stunning old lace. And I have my great-grandmother's diamond necklace to wear. It's a family heirloom."

"Then I think we're set. Cap's standing by as my best man. Are you sure about the location?"

"Positive. Your Lone Star Ranch is perfect," she said without hesitation.

"With both our families looking on," he added.

"Merry Christmas, my Legend," she whispered against his ear. "Put your feet in the stirrups, cowboy, and hold on tight. We're going to make memories that will curl our kids' hair."

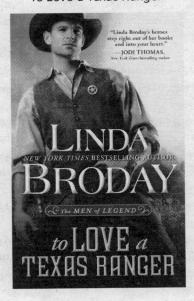

One

DEEP IN THE TEXAS HILL COUNTRY, WIND SIGHING THROUGH the draw whispered against his face, sharpening his senses to a fine edge. A warning skittered along his spine before it settled in his chest.

Texas Ranger Sam Legend had learned to listen to his gut. Right now it said the suffocating sense of danger that crowded him had killing in mind. He brought the spyglass up to his eye and focused on the rustlers below. All fifteen had covered their faces, leaving only their eyes showing.

Every crisp sound swept up the steep incline where he crouched in a stand of cedar to the right of an old gnarled oak. He'd hidden his horse a short distance away and prayed the animal stayed put.

"Hurry up with those beeves! We've gotta get the hell out of here. Rangers are so close I can smell 'em!" a rustler yelled.

Where were the other rangers? They hadn't been separated long and should've caught up by now.

Letting the outlaws escape took everything he had. But there were too many for one man, and this bunch was far more ruthless than most.

He peered closer as they tried to drive the bawling cattle up the draw. But the ornery bovines seemed to be smarter. They broke away from the group, scattering this way and that. Sam allowed a grin. These rustlers were definitely no cattlemen.

A lawman learned to adjust quickly. His mind whirled as he searched for some kind of plan. One shot fired in the air would alert the other rangers to his position if they were near. But would they arrive before the outlaws got to him?

Or…no one would fault Sam for sitting quietly until the lawless group cleared out.

Except Sam. A Legend never ran from a fight. It wasn't in his blood. He would ride straight through hell and come out the other side whenever a situation warranted. As a Texas Ranger, he'd made that ride many times over.

From his hiding place, he could start picking off the rustlers. With luck, Sam might get a handful before they surrounded him. Still, a few beat none. Maybe the rest would bolt. Slowly, he drew his Colt and prepared for the fight.

Though winter had just given way to spring, the hot sun bore down. Sweat trickled into his eyes, making them sting. He wiped away the sweat with an impatient hand.

"Make this count," he whispered. He had only one chance. It was all or nothing.

The first shot ripped into a man's shoulder. As the outlaw screamed, Sam quickly swung to the next target and caught the rider's thigh. A third shot grazed another's head.

Damn! The next man leaned from the saddle just as he'd squeezed the trigger.

Before he could discharge again, cold steel jabbed into his back, and a hand reached for his rifle and Colt. "Turn around real slow, mister."

The order grated along Sam's nerve endings and settled in his clenched stomach. He listened for any sounds to indicate his fellow rangers were nearby. If not, he was dead. He heard nothing except bawling steers and men yelling.

Sam slowly turned his head. Cold, dead eyes glared over the top of the rustler's bandana.

"Well, whaddya know. Got me a bona-fide ranger."

Though Sam couldn't see the outlaw's mouth, the words told him he wore a smile. "I'm not here alone. You won't get away with this."

"I call your bluff. No one's firing at us but you." The gun barrel poked harder into Sam's back. "Down the hill."

Sam could've managed without the shove. The soles of his worn boots provided no traction. Slipping and sliding down the steep embankment, he glanced for anything to suggest help had arrived, but saw nothing.

At the bottom, riders on horseback immediately surrounded him.

"Good job, Smith." The outlaw pushing to the front had to be the ringleader. He was dressed all in black, from his hat to his boots. "Let's teach this Texas Ranger not to mess with us. I've got a special treat in mind. One of you, find his horse and get me a rope. Smith, march him back up the hill. The rest of you drive those damn cattle to the makeshift corral."

The spit dried in Sam's mouth as the man holding him bound his hands and pushed him up the steep incline, back toward the gnarled oak high on the ridge.

Any minute, the rangers would swoop in. Just a matter of time. Sam refused to believe that his life was going to end this way. Somehow, he had to stall until help arrived.

"Smith, do you know the punishment for killing a lawman?" Sam asked.

"Stop talkin' and get movin'."

"Are you willing to throw your life away for a man who doesn't give two cents about you?"

"You don't know nothin' about nothin', so shut up. One more word, an' I'll shoot you in the damn knee and drag you the rest of the way."

Sam lapsed into silence. He could see Smith had closed his mind against anything he said. If he ran, he'd be lucky to make two strides before hot lead slammed into him. Even if he made it to the cover of a cedar, what then? He had no gun. No horse.

His best chance was to spin around and take Smith's weapon.

But just as he started to make a move, the ringleader rode up beside on his horse and shouted, "Hurry up. Don't have all day."

Sharp disappointment flared, trapping Sam's breath in his chest. His fate lay at the mercy of these outlaws.

They grew closer and closer to the twisted, bent oak branches that resembled witch's fingers. Those limbs would reach for a man's soul and snatch it at the moment of death.

Thick bitter gall climbed into his throat, choking him. The devil would soon find Sam had lost his soul a long time ago.

The steep angle of the hill made his breathing harsh. The climb hurt as much as his looming fate. He'd always thought a bullet would get him one day, but to die swinging from a tree had never crossed his mind.

As they reached the top, an outlaw appeared with Sam's horse. The buckskin nickered softly, nuzzling Sam as though offering sympathy or maybe a last good-bye. He stroked the face of his faithful friend, murmuring a few quiet words of comfort. He'd raised Trooper from a foal and turned him into a lawman's mount. Would it be too much to pray these rustlers treated Trooper well? The horse deserved kindness.

"Enough," rasped the ringleader with an impatient motion of his .45. "Put him on the horse."

Sam noticed a crude drawing between the man's thumb and wrist—a black widow spider. Not that he could do anything with the information where he was going.

One last time, he scanned the landscape anxiously, hoping to glimpse riders, but saw only the branches of cedar, oak, and cottonwood trees swaying gently in the breeze. He strained against the ropes binding him, but they wouldn't budge.

Panic so thick he could taste it lodged in his throat as they jerked him into the saddle. His heart pounded against his ribs. He sat straight and tall, not allowing so much as an eye twitch. These outlaws who thrived on violence would never earn the right to see the turmoil and fear twisting behind his stone face.

Advice his father had once given him sounded in his ears: *When trouble comes, stand proud. You are a Legend. Inside you beats the heart of a survivor.*

Sam Legend stared into the distance, a muscle working in his jaw.

The ringleader threw the rope up and over one of the gnarled branches.

Bitter regret rose. Sam had never told his father he loved him. The times they'd butted heads seemed trivial now. So did the fights with big brother Houston over things that didn't make a hill of beans.

Yes, he was going to die with a heart full of regret, broken dreams, and empty promises.

The rope scratched, digging into his tender flesh as the outlaw settled the noose around Sam's neck.

"You better find a hole and climb into it, mister," Sam said. "Every ranger and lawman in the state of Texas will be after you."

A chuckle filled the air. "They won't find us."

"That wager's going to cost you." Sam steeled himself, wondering how long it took a man to die this way. He prayed it would be quick. He wondered if his mother would be waiting in heaven to soothe the pain.

"Say hello to the devil, Ranger."

With those words, he slapped the horse's flank. Trooper bolted, leaving Sam dangling in the air. The rope violently yanked his neck back and to the side as his body jerked.

Choking and fighting to breathe, Sam Legend counted his heartbeats until blackness claimed him. As he whirled away into nothingness, only one thing filled his mind—the vivid tattoo of a black widow spider on his killer's hand.

Two

A MONTH AFTER TEXAS RANGER SAM LEGEND ALMOST DIED, AN ear-splitting crash of thunder rattled the windows and each unpainted board of the J. R. Simmons Mercantile. The ominous skies burst open, and rain pelted the ground in great sheets. A handful of people scattered like buckshot along the Waco boardwalk in an effort to escape the thorough drenching of a spring gully washer.

Sam paid the rain no mind. The storm barely registered—few things did, these days. The feeling of the rope around his neck was still overpowering. He reached to see if it was there, thankful not to find it.

The nightmare had him in its grip, refusing to let go. More dead than alive, he moved toward his destination. When he reached the alley separating the two sections of boardwalk, he collided with a woman covered in a hooded cloak.

"Apologies, ma'am." He glanced down by rote, then blinked. All at once, the world and its color came rushing back as Sam stared into blue eyes so vivid they stole his breath.

A pocket of fog drifted between them. Was she just a dream? He could barely see her.

She nodded and gave him a smile for only a brief second. He reached out to touch her, to see if she was real, but only cold damp air met his fingertips.

The man beside her took her arm and jerked her into the alleyway.

"Hey there!" Sam called, startled. He'd been so focused on

those blue eyes he hadn't realized anyone else was there. "Ma'am, do you need help?"

He received no answer. Through the dense fog, he watched her companion force her toward a horse at the other end of the alley where a group of mounted riders waited. The hair on the back of his neck rose.

Intent on stopping whatever was happening, Sam lengthened his strides. Before he could reach them, the man threw her onto a horse, then swung up behind her. Within seconds, they disappeared, ghostly riders in the mist.

Sam stood in the driving rain, staring at the empty alley. It had all happened so fast he could hardly believe it.

Hell, maybe he'd imagined the whole thing. Maybe she'd never existed. Maybe the heavy downpour and gray gloom had messed with his mind...again. Ever since the hanging, he'd been seeing things that weren't there. Twice now he'd yanked men around and grabbed for their hands, thinking he saw a black widow spider between their thumbs and forefingers. The last time almost got Sam shot. Folks claimed he was missing the top rung of his ladder and now, his captain was sending him home to find it.

Crippled. The word clanked around in his head, refusing to settle. But even though he had full use of his legs, that's what he was at present. The cold fear washing over him had nothing to do with the air temperature or rain. What if he never recovered? Some never did.

His hand clenched. He'd fight like hell to be the whole man he once was. He had things to do—an outlaw to hunt down, a wrong to right—a promise to keep.

Sam squared his jaw and drew his coat tight against the wet chill, forcing himself to move on down the street toward the face-to-face with Captain O'Reilly. Again. It stuck in his craw that they thought him too crazy to do his job. The captain thought him a liability, a danger to the other rangers. Wanted him to take a break.

His heart couldn't hurt any worse than if someone had stomped on it with a pair of hobnail boots. Maybe the captain was right. If he'd imagined that woman just now—and he really couldn't be certain he hadn't—then maybe he *needed* the break. Sam Legend, who had brought in notorious killers, bank robbers, prison escapees, and the like, had become a liability.

But one thing he knew he hadn't imagined, and that was the blurred figure of Luke Weston standing over him when he'd regained consciousness that fateful day. There had been no mistaking those pale green eyes above the mask. They belonged to the outlaw he'd chased for over a year—he'd have staked his life on it.

When his fellow rangers had ridden up, Weston disappeared into the brush, leaving Sam with questions. Had Weston cut him down from the tree? Was he with the rustlers? And why had the outlaws left Trooper behind? Awful considerate of them.

So what the hell had happened, dammit?

Rangers who'd ridden up told Sam they'd seen no one. He'd lain on the ground with the rope loosened around his neck, drifting in and out of consciousness.

Those questions and others haunted him, and he wouldn't rest until he got answers. Somehow he knew Weston was the key.

At ranger headquarters, he took a deep breath before opening the door. He pushed a mite too hard, banging the knob against the wall. Captain O'Reilly jerked up from his desk. "What the hell, Legend? Trying to wake the dead?"

"Sorry, Cap'n. It got away from me." It seemed a good many things had, recently.

The tall, slender captain waved him to a chair. "I haven't heard this much racket since the shoot-out inside that silo with the Arnie brothers down in Sweetwater."

Sam removed his drenched hat, lowered into the chair, and stretched his long legs out in front of him. "I hope I can talk you out of your decision."

O'Reilly sauntered to the potbellied stove in the corner and lifted the coffeepot. "What's it been? A month?"

"An eternity," Sam said quietly.

"Want a snort of coffee? Might improve your outlook."

"I'll take you up on your offer but doubt it'll improve anything. I need this job, sir. I need to work." Revenge burned hot. He'd not rest until he found the men who'd try to hang him, and when he did, they'd pay with their blood.

"What you *need* is some time off to get your head on straight. I can't have you seeing things that aren't there." O'Reilly sighed. "You're gonna get yourself or someone else killed. I'm ordering you to go home. Rest up, then come back ready to catch outlaws."

"Finding the rustlers and catching Luke Weston is my first priority."

"That wily outlaw has been taunting you for the last year." O'Reilly's eyes hardened as he handed Sam a tin cup. "It seems personal."

"Hell yeah, it's personal!"

Weston had been there. That much he knew for damn certain. The outlaw could have strung him up himself. Why else would Sam remember those green eyes, so pale they appeared silver?

In addition to that, and though it sounded rather trivial when compared to a hanging, Weston had taken Sam's pocket watch during a stagecoach holdup a year ago. Sam tried to protect a payroll shipment, but Weston did the oddest thing. The outlaw took exactly fifty dollars, a paltry sum compared to what remained in the strongbox, and left the passengers' belongings untouched. He did, however, seem to take particular delight in pocketing Sam's prized timepiece. The way the wily outlaw singled Sam out was downright eerie. Weston knew exactly where to find the treasured keepsake. No rifling his pockets. No fumbling. No uncertainty. Memories of how Weston had flipped it open and stared intently at the inscription for almost a full minute before tucking it away drifted through Sam's mind.

"Makes me mad enough to chew nails." The thought filled Sam's head with so many cuss words he feared it would burst open.

The captain leaned back in his chair and propped his boots on the scarred desk that Noah must've brought over on the ark. To make up for a missing leg, someone had cut a crutch and stuck it under there. "Sometimes we all get cases that sink their teeth into us and won't let go."

"I just about had him the last time." And now the captain was forcing him to take time off. Sam would lose every bit of ground he'd gained.

Luke Weston had led him on a chase this past year from one end of Texas to the other. To this day, other than a vague outline of his figure, Sam had yet to glimpse anything solid except a pair of cold, pale green eyes glaring over the top of a bandana. Eyes that only held contempt and anger. Except for this last time, when they'd seemed to hold concern. But maybe he'd imagined that.

Damn! He really didn't know what was real and what wasn't anymore.

Maybe the captain was right.

Reaching for a poster that lay atop a pile on his desk, Captain O'Reilly passed it to Sam. "Got this yesterday." Bold lettering at the top of the page screamed: *WANTED! $1,000 reward for capture and conviction of notorious outlaw Luke Weston. Sought for robbery and murder. Armed and considered extremely dangerous.*

The murder charge was new since the last poster Sam had seen. The reward had been only two hundred dollars then. He stared at the thick paper and narrowed his eyes, wondering whose fate had intersected with Luke Weston's.

"Who did he kill?"

O'Reilly's face darkened. "Federal judge. Edgar Percival."

"Stands to reason Weston would turn to outright murder

eventually. Seems every month he's involved in a gunfight with someone, though folks say they were all men who needed killing."

And yet the new charge did shock Sam. He'd come to know Weston pretty well. A period of four months separated each of the outlaw's robberies, with only fifty dollars taken each time. And in every single instance, Weston had never shot anyone. Maybe he robbed out of boredom…or to taunt Sam.

"A bad seed." The ranger captain's chair squeaked when he leaned forward. "Some men are born killers."

This poster, as with all the others, didn't bear a likeness, not even a crude drawing. There were no physical features to go on. Frustration boiled. The lawman in him itched to be out there tracking Weston. The need to bring him to justice rose so strong that it choked Sam. Weston was *his* outlaw to catch, and instead, he'd been ordered home.

Hell! Spending one week on the huge Lone Star Ranch was barely tolerable. A month would either kill him, or he'd kill big brother Houston. The thought had no more than formed before guilt pricked his conscience. In the final moments before the outlaw had hit his horse and left Sam dangling by his neck, regrets had filled his thoughts. He'd begged God for a second chance so he could make things right.

Now, it looked like he'd get it. He'd make the time count. He'd mend bridges with his father, the tough Stoker Legend.

Family was there in good times and bad.

Despite his better qualities, Stoker had caused problems for him. Sam had driven himself to work harder, be quicker and tougher, to prove to everyone his father hadn't bought his job. Overcoming the big ranch, the money, and the power the Legend name evoked had been a continuing struggle.

Captain O'Reilly opened his desk drawer, uncorked a bottle of whiskey, and gave his coffee a generous dousing. "Want to doctor your coffee, Sam?"

"Don't think it'll help," he replied with a tight smile.

"Suit yourself." The hardened ranger put the bottle away. The white scar on his cheek had never faded, left from a skirmish with the Comanche.

Sam studied that scar, thinking. Although Sam had intended to keep quiet about the woman he may or may not have bumped into on the way over, out of fear of being labeled a lunatic for sure, he felt a duty to say something. He wouldn't voice doubts that he'd imagined it. "Cap'n, I saw something that keeps nagging at me. I collided with a young woman a few minutes ago. All I said was sorry, but a man grabbed her arm and shoved her into the alley between the mercantile and telegraph office. I saw fear in her eyes. When I followed, they got on a waiting horse and rode off. Can you send someone to check it out?"

Sam winced at how quickly doubts filled O'Reilly's eyes. The captain was wondering if this was one more example of Sam breaking with reality. Hell! If he'd conjured this up, he'd commit himself into one of those places where they locked up crazy people.

O'Reilly twirled his empty cup. "After the bank robbery a few weeks ago, we don't need more trouble. I'll look into it."

"Thanks. I hope it was nothing, but you never know." Relieved, Sam took a sip of coffee, wishing it would warm the cold deep in his bones.

"When's the train due to arrive, Legend?"

"Within the hour." Sam would obey his orders, but the second his forced sabbatical was over, he'd hit the ground running. He'd dog Luke Weston's trail until there wasn't a safe place in all of Texas to even get a slug of whiskey. He'd heard the gunslinging outlaw spent time down around Galveston and San Antone. That, Sam reckoned, would be a good starting point.

O'Reilly removed his boots from the desk and sat up. "I seem to recall your family ranch being northwest of here on the Red River."

"That's right."

"Ever hear of Lost Point?"

Sam nodded. "The town is west of us. Pretty lawless place, by all accounts."

"It's become a no-man's-land. Outlaws moved in, lock, stock, and barrel. Nothing north of it but Indian Territory. Jonathan Doan is requesting a ranger to the area. Seems he's struggling to get a trading post going on the Red River just west of Lost Point, and outlaws are threatening."

"I'll take a ride over there while I'm home. Weston would fit right in."

"No hurry. Give yourself time to relax. Go fishing. Reacquaint yourself with the family, for God's sake. They haven't seen you in a coon's age."

"Sure thing, Cap'n." The clock on the town square chimed the half hour, reminding him he'd best get moving. Relieved that O'Reilly had softened and allowed him to still work a little, Sam set down his cup. "Appears I've got a train to catch."

O'Reilly shook his hand. "Get well, Sam. You're a good lawman. Come back stronger than ever."

"I will, sir."

At the livery, Sam hired a boy to fetch his bags from the hotel and take them to the station. After settling with the owner and collecting his buckskin gelding, Sam rode to meet the train. He shivered in the cold, steady downpour. The gloomy day reflected his mood as he moved toward an uncertain future. He was on his way home.

To bind up his wounds. To heal. To become the ranger he needed to be.

And he would—come hell or high water, mad as a March hare or not.

Right on time, amid plumes of hissing white steam, the Houston and Texas Central Railway train pulled up next to the loading platform.

Sam quickly loaded Trooper into the livestock car and paid the boy for bringing his bags. After making sure the kerchief around his neck hid his scar, he swung aboard. He had his pick of seats since the passengers had just started to file on. He chose one two strides from the door.

Shrugging from his coat, he sat down and got comfortable.

A movement across the narrow aisle a few minutes later drew his attention, as a tall passenger wearing a low-slung gun belt slid into the seat. Sam studied the black leather vest and frock coat. Gunslinger, bounty hunter, or maybe a gambler? Bounty hunter seemed far-fetched—he'd never seen one dressed in anything as fine. Such men wasted no time with fancy clothing. A gunslinger, then. Few others tied their holster down to their leg. No one else required speed when drawing. Likely a gambler too. Usually the two went hand in hand.

His coloring spoke of Mexican descent. Lines around the traveler's mouth and a gray hair or two in his dark hair put him somewhere around the near side of thirty. Though he wore his black Stetson low on his forehead, he tugged it even lower as he settled back against the cushion.

The fine hairs on Sam's arm twitched. He knew this man. But from where? For the life of him, he couldn't recall. He leaned over. "Pardon me, but have we met?"

Without meeting Sam's gaze, the man allowed a tight smile. "Nope."

Darn the hat that bathed his eyes in dusky shadows. "I'm Sam Legend. Name's not familiar?"

"Nope."

He'd been so certain the man looked familiar. "Guess I made a mistake." Maybe his madness had taken over again. Odd that the man hadn't introduced himself, though.

"Appears so, Ranger."

How did he know Sam was a ranger? He wore no badge. "My apologies," Sam mumbled.

The train engineer blew the whistle and the mighty iron wheels began to slowly turn.

Sam swung his attention back to the gunslinger. A few more words, and he'd be able to place him, surely. "Would you have the time, Mr....?" Sam asked.

"Andrew. Andrew Evan." The man flipped open his timepiece. "It's ten forty-five."

"Obliged." Finally, a name. Not that it proved helpful. Sam was sure he'd left his real one at the Texas border, as men with something to hide tended to do. By working extra hard trying to make himself invisible, Evan had as much as declared that he had things to conceal.

Worse, the longer Sam sat near Andrew, the stronger the feeling of familiarity grew. And that was something Sam's brain had not conjured up. He glanced out the window at the passing scenery, trying to make sense of the thoughts clunking around in his head. When he next looked over at Andrew Evan, Sam wasn't surprised to find the slouching gunslinger's head against the seat with his hat tilted over his eyes.

The hair on his neck rose. Sam felt Andrew's eyes watching from beneath the brim of the Stetson. Then he saw a muscle twitch in Andrew's jaw and watched his Adam's apple slide slowly up and down.

Tension electrified the air.

As Sam stared at Evan's hands, searching for the tattoo, a woman rushed down the aisle. She came even with them just as the train took a curve and tumbled headlong into his lap. He found himself holding soft, warm curves encased in dark wool.

Stark fear darkened the blue eyes staring up at him, and her bottom lip quivered.

A jolt went through him. Lucinda? But no—it couldn't be her. Yet this girl had Lucinda Howard's black hair and blue eyes framed by thick sooty lashes.

His body responded against his will as he struggled with the memory. Hell! At last, he realized this girl was not the faithless lover he'd once known.

But she *was* the woman he'd collided with on his way to Ranger headquarters.

"Are you all right, miss?"

"I—I'm so sorry," she murmured.

He felt her icy hand splayed against his chest through the fabric of his shirt, where it had landed when she tried to break her fall.

"Are you in trouble? I can help."

"They're—I've got to—" The mystery woman pushed away, extricating herself from his lap. With a strangled sob, she ran toward the door leading into the next car.

Sam looked down. Prickles rose on the back of his neck.

A bloody handprint stained his shirt.

About the Author

Linda Broday resides in the Panhandle of Texas on the Llano Estacado. At a young age, she discovered a love for storytelling, history, and anything pertaining to the Old West. Cowboys fascinate her. There's something about Stetsons, boots, and tall, rugged cowboys that gets her fired up! A *New York Times* and *USA Today* bestselling author, Linda has won many awards, including the prestigious National Readers' Choice Award and the Texas Gold Award. Visit her at lindabroday.com.

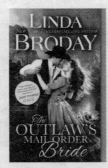
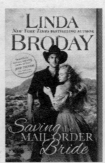
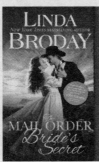

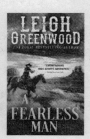
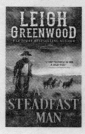
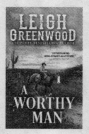